DEREK B. MILLER

RADIO LIFE

Jo Fletcher
BOOKS

First published in Great Britain in 2021 by

Jo Fletcher Books
an imprint of
Quercus Editions Ltd
Carmelite House
50 Victoria Embankment
London EC4Y 0DZ

An Hachette UK company

A CIP catalogue record for this book is available
from the British Library

HB ISBN 978 1 52940 858 4
TPB ISBN 978 1 52940 859 1
EBOOK ISBN 978 1 52940 860 7

10 9 8 7 6 5 4 3 2 1

Typeset by CC Book Production
Printed and bound in Great Britain by Clays Ltd, Elcograf S.p.A.

MIX
Paper from
responsible sources
FSC
www.fsc.org   FSC® C104740

Papers used by Quercus Editions Ltd are from well-managed forests
and other responsible sources.

RADIO LIFE

For my daughter

seaglass lake

gone world

the crossing

EMPTY QUARTER

keepers colony

N

yellow ridge

The Ancients decided that the earth was no longer safe for their Knowledge and so they put it all in the sky and hid it away in the clouds. But the sun considered the sky her own domain and so she scorched the clouds and burned them off. After that, no Knowledge could rain down on the people of the earth. Their memories grew weak, the land grew dry and in the cold they had to start again learning to make fire from sticks.

Children's Fable. Central Archive,
Arts & Literature, Oral History,
Class 3 Knowledge, The Commonwealth.

CONTENTS

I

PARADISO

TRACOLLO

Two riders trace the ridge of the sand sea, miles from the Commonwealth and the protecting walls of the Stadium. They are unhurried. It is the *oscuridad*, when the sun falls below the horizon and the line separating the land from heaven vanishes. The dry season has begun and the temperature drops with the sun. Later, crystals of ice will form into fields of broken glass at night, their edges cutting the bitter Chinook winds.

Night comes. The riders and their mounts are silhouetted: blackened against a sky that is alive with colour. They cover their faces with scarves as the winds pick up and the shimmering green streaks of the night appear above the remaining line of day. No one living remembers darkness to the nights here. Black skies of white stars are only known by stories and songs.

To their right, below and far into the Empty Quarter, a sand pillar forms in the wind. And another. They dance together, and the riders stop to look. The fine golden grains capture the night: greens and violets and blues that reach upwards as if to offer a gift to the gods. Beyond the shimmering dance, far off and familiar, six Gone World towers rise, all straight lines and crisp angles. From here, their surfaces blot out the stars; they are conspicuous by what they hide.

The horses are relaxed, experienced. They know this route and have not been ridden hard today. The habits of nightfall are familiar: they will be fed soon and afterwards, silence will envelope them. Stillness is bred into their line.

The shorter of the two riders takes the lead when the sand pillars settle and the moment has passed. She turns them off the road and towards a depression where they will hide them for the night. The horses descend slowly, stepping cautiously. They are laden, but the burden is fair and balanced for speed. The woman's horse carries more because she weighs less. On the side of her mount is a long rifle with scope and bipod. On his, a long lance with small levers built into the grip and a short carbine. In his boot there is a knife.

It is flat at the bottom of the ravine where the woman halts to look back. She cannot see the Gone World or the High Road from here, which means neither can see her. Away to the south is a long stretch of land, but there are no roads there and few reasons for travellers to cross it. She clicks her tongue once and the man scans the horizon. In agreement, he nods.

Together they dismount. The man ties his horse to a dried-out bush and scratches the animal behind the ear. From the back of the woman's horse he removes a canvas sack from which he pulls out a black triangular object made of a matte fabric that absorbs light and reflects none. Releasing a small catch at one corner, he flicks the triangle forward and – with a cough – a dome appears that is large enough for two adults to rest in.

The woman ties her horse beside his before unstrapping her rifle and a small backpack and disappearing into the tent. The man takes one last look at the undulating green lights of the night sky. Away from the fires of the Stadium, their colours are more vibrant and pleasing. A moment later he follows her inside.

The woman has already set up a small stove no larger than a palm that creates heat but no light, and is warming spiced beans and stalks of green onion with slices of carrot. She cuts two modest portions of dried beef and places them over the plant-food to soften. The two riders sit cross-legged over the stove warming their hands. The fabric of the tent allows them to see out, though it mutes the colours. The food, the tent and their bodies quickly warm. She turns down the heat, which will linger.

The man uses his boot knife to divide and distribute the portions onto two small steel plates. He hands her the better share, for she has not been eating enough lately. She pushes it back but he ignores her and eats his own portion.

They share a litre of water and drink it all.

Soon, he sleeps, while she leaves the tent and keeps watch outside. There is little to see but the sky – there are few animals this far from the wadi running beneath The Crossing, and those that scurry through the Gone World sleep at night too. Only big-eyed birds and flying mice hunt in the dark.

There was a time, when the woman was young, when the bandit trade was heavy. Now the Big Road is secured by the Dragoons and the Commonwealth controls outwards from the Flats beyond the AIRBUS to the edge of The Crossing. But tonight they both feel an unease in the air and so they take greater precautions, because tonight is unique: the man's lance is full with all six flags. It is the first time a Raider had returned with this much bounty in almost twenty years.

*

5

The deep night arrives while she is on guard. The horses have stopped stirring and the moon has sunk below the ridge that shields them from the road, creating a thin line of pearl-white along the edge of the dunes under the autumnal sky.

Into the quiet, but heard clearly by the woman, there is a sharp but distant explosion. Experienced and careful, she edges up the ridge to bring the Gone World towers into view. A light – maybe a fire? – burns through a glittering window. Two more small explosions follow: she sees them before they reach her ears.

The horses stir.

After a pause there is a low, heavy rumble that grows.

She brings the rifle into position, but does not look through the scope; instead, she looks over it for the wider view. She digs her right hand into the dirt, looking for a hard surface that might carry the vibrations. There is a heavy rock and she feels how it shakes as though from the Earth's core. The sound is so low and deep it is more like a feeling: a heartache or nostalgia. It is nothing she has heard before but the longer it lasts, the more confident she becomes of her supposition.

She knows what it is.

When she is certain it is over and she has stopped counting the length of the rumble, she returns to the dome where he is already awake and sitting.

The man cannot see his wife's expression but he understands her body movements and the nuance of her breath. They have almost thirty years together, and one daughter. They are the most decorated Raiders of the Commonwealth. Much passes unspoken between them.

'What was it?' he asks; his voice barely a sigh.

'A Tracollo.'

The man shifts onto his elbow. He rubs his eyes and allows

himself an understanding smile: he slept. She did not. Their days have been very long. The desert can provide dreams either way.

'It must have been something else,' he says gently.

She allows him a moment to invent what else it could have been. She is patient and watches him fail as he tests each possible explanation against his wife's experience and intelligence.

When they both sense his failure and his smile vanishes, she speaks again. 'It made the ground shake – even at this distance. I counted thirty-five seconds. I think a whole tower went down.'

The man sits, his legs crossed. 'The last Tracollo was Lilly's and that was fifty-four years ago. The chances of one actually falling after all this time are . . .'

'The same as they were then,' she says. 'No one knows why that one fell,' she adds, adjusting her rifle, 'but this time, it was helped. There were three smaller detonations before the collapse.'

The woman places her hand on the earth. The vibrations in the rock and sand are gone but it makes her feel closer to the proof. 'I think someone knocked it down.'

He considers the implications. 'You think someone else has figured out how to make explosives?' he asks. His grogginess shaken off, having forced himself back into the moment, he is alert now.

'It would change the balance,' she admits. 'Unless they found some. Which would be better, though still not good.'

'What time is it?' he asks.

'The moon is down.' The woman dons her wool cap again and twists the scarf around her face and neck. She opens the door to the dome and the tent fills with cold.

7

'I'll be glad to get back home,' the man says before she is gone.

'We may need to stay,' she replies. She grips her rifle and steps out.

The horses are awake now. She places a hand on her own mount's muzzle to calm him as she passes to climb the ridge.

At the top, as the Gone World comes into view, she opens the bipod, switches on her scope and resumes her prone firing position. The wind is low but constant and moving towards her. The scope measures it at 4.2 knots. She switches on the night vision and magnifies.

Tower three – the one people used to call Aladdin – is gone. In its place is a massive cone of debris that blots out the colours in the sky behind it.

She crawls forward a careful metre, which places her slightly higher on the ridge, giving her a better sight-line to the land where the towers emerge.

The towers are to their northeast. On her right, in the direction of The Crossing, fires are being lit. They are green through her scope, their centres burning white. Shadows are already on the move as the valley comes alive and she feels the energy of choices being made. Though her hand is steady, the images are out of range and so is the meaning of their movements.

She can only guess.

'Roamers,' she concludes flatly, knowing her voice will carry to her husband and no further. 'Too far away to see who they are. We might know them, we might not.'

Behind her she feels his hand gently squeeze her ankle. She turns.

His meaning is clear: *he is asking her to consider the wisdom of her action.* He will trust her judgement. But they are partners, and it is his job to force the question.

She does not crawl back down the hill and instead watches the fires approach the Gone World.

'The plume is enormous,' she says, describing what she sees. 'It's not like anything I've ever seen before. I can see four teams on their way over but my view is flat. I can only see left and right. Everything is too dark.' She pauses before adding, 'It's so dangerous these days with that tribe encamped on the Ridge.'

They are called the Keepers.

He does not know what they are keeping.

'Henry,' he says, 'come back. There's nothing we can do now.'

'They'll be pulling finds from the Trove, Graham. The last time there was a Tracollo, Lilly came back with the Harrington Box and changed everything. We need to know what's coming out of the depths.'

'We're carrying Full Flags, Henrietta – precisely because of the Harrington Box. We have no idea what value this already has. We can't risk what we have for the unknown.'

Henry tips her head towards the missing tower. 'That's the largest unknown we've ever seen.'

Graham nods. This is true.

They are talking too much, they know it, but the attention of the world is fixed elsewhere. Chatter in the night is now expected. The world adapts.

And this needs to be discussed.

Graham appeals to Henry's sense of history: 'When Lilly and Saavni and General Winters were kids, things were tougher and the Stadium unruly. We have systems now.'

'They didn't have a military force building up on Yellow Ridge back then either.'

He runs a hand over his face and does not answer her. His thin riding scarf is slack around his neck. After a moment, he nods again. This is also true.

Two Runners have gone missing since the Keepers arrived two moons ago. It is rumoured they were killed, but there are no bodies and no way to Attest. But the concern is mounting.

Henry waits for his answer. She knows what he knows; neither claims wisdom over the other. She does, however, tend to be the more convincing.

'Fine. We wait for now,' Graham says, a small concession. 'We'll visit the Tracollo in the morning, then The Crossing. Now, though, we wait,' he insists. 'And it's your turn to sleep.'

Henry watches the Roamers approach the plume of debris and imagines the shinies and Knowledge they will soon be pulling from the hidden depths of the Gone World.

It will be very hard to sleep.

BEAUTIFUL

Earlier that night and before the collapse, across the valley and on the flats above Yellow Ridge, a tent community is resting, cold under the green streaks of night. However vivid and inspiring, still the colours have turned grey for their leader since the Sickness arrived and his wife fell ill.

Don't sleep beside her, the sages advised. *You will become ill too, in the way that rot spreads through touching fruit.*

No, he said. *It doesn't work like that. And what would it matter if it did? The warmth of our bodies together is what life is for. Why forego what is good in the world only to have less of it for longer?*

Yes, they agreed. *That is why you are our leader.*

This was not why. He knew he had no wisdom, only conviction: one born from the momentum of an earlier decision that he cannot question because doing so would be a great undoing. But he does not correct them. Correcting them would turn their minds most unnaturally – the way that night birds turn their heads to look back. People are not meant to look back this way.

Their desert encampment has more than a hundred tents, grouped by extended family. There is room for many more, and

11

many more are coming. They are close to a cliff wall facing the Empty Quarter where water is most scarce but they have a well and purify what they draw using the sun's light in plastic bottles.

They can see The Crossing to their west; the Gone World is beyond, though everyone knows it lies beneath them too. There is a cliff and a drop to their west before the rolling sands begin. It is close, but not so close that the children risk falling. It is not far enough away, though, to sooth the fears of the mothers.

'You don't have children,' they say to him. 'You don't understand.'

No, he agrees. Not any more.

He has been awake beside his wife for hours. He often wakes this way now, his soul torn between wanting to watch her sleep and his body needing sleep itself. Being torn disrupts his peace and prevents him from existing fully in the moment, as is the way of their people. The Chinook winds warm what should be the icy desert floor, keeping the night dew on the sand from freezing. It arrives at his tent as a rippling breeze over the roof and threatens the sealed walls, turning the shaking home into a frightening song. Still, it is the permanent sound of change and there is a warmth – a certainty – to be gleaned in recognising how permanence and change are part of the same truth. His people do not see a contradiction in this but instead a poetry.

The Chinook. The wind carried its own name after the world was destroyed and whispered it into the ears of the people it found. How else would such an ancient word survive with no lips remaining to speak it?

*

Awake in the dark beside her, the Leader traces his wife's sleeping face with his fingers. He is gentle enough not to wake her. Later, he rests his hand on her chest and feels it rise and fall with each breath and the magic of living: the human heat that is warm but never burns. There on their bed he listens to her stir and like a child he plays the game of matching his own breathing with hers so he might feel what she feels. They are no match, though. He is so much larger, stronger, a model of health, with lungs that could hold a storm. His breath is too deep, too slow. The balance is forced: it cannot last, because all unnatural things are buried eventually. As the synchronicity is lost, the feeling of union passes and this stirs an emotion from a part of himself beyond his control.

In this way and that quickly – a grain of sand on a night wind – he is whisked away from serenity.

He knows this genie that is disrupting him; this curse. They call him *Time*. Time the Titan who is the enemy of Now. They battle, these two, in the legends of his tribe, a poetic battle that explains much to children and informs the talk of the people. Time's face, they explain, is never the same. He never stops moving. Wanting. Needing. Feeding. He circles as he hunts.

Now, Time's nemesis, does not move, but crouches on the earth, always present, always ready, prepared to be any and all things as circumstance demands. And the more Time prepares his attack, the more he circles his prey and clangs his armour and threatens and taunts, the calmer Now becomes. Now is steadfast in the only truth we can know for certain: I am here and here I am.

Poor Time, the lesser of the two Titans. Time cannot exist

in a single moment. Time can never be in one place. There is no rest for Time and so he is restless. Agitated, he lashes out where he can.

Tonight, Time is pressing on the Leader's mind, instilling an instant and complete understanding that the happiness he feels and the love he has for his wife is going to end. *Because life*, Time says, *is not the wind. It is not permanent.* 'It is mine,' he says.

Soon his wife's warmth will end and her breathing will stop. Knowing this splits him in two – here with her and also there after the end. It is in that glance back at himself from that other place that he becomes unmoored, because one part of himself leaves the here and now and becomes planted in the future. It is beyond painful because he knows that every moment they have left is precious. Most precious. This fills his chest with a terrible pressure that builds behind his eyes that distracts him and robs him of what is most dear – their final moments.

He is two men now, one looking back to the instruct the other:

Take it all in before it is too late, he tells himself. *Give all this a name. Place everything here in your mind. The texture of her skin. The curve where her nose meets her cheek, the exact shape of her eyebrow, because it will soon be gone like the billions of Ancients who are now dust and died in the Gone World at the height of a permanence they thought was theirs, only to be rent from his earth in a flash and their future obliterated. Will you choose to forget love?*

You know you won't. Because you remember her too.

Veronique.

The Rise. The land filling up and covering everything. Only the tops of the highest towers are left poking through. All those people who once breathed this same air – did Time not talk to them too?

Take it in, the voice says to him.

His wife stirs and he is back. He rolls her onto him so nothing is wasted. His beard becomes one with her hair. She inhales, and the pull freezes his chest. She exhales, and it burns. He cups her cheek in his palm where it was made to fit by Destiny. Her right hand finds his belly and rests there, fingers open. If only he could pour his own life into hers so they could share it evenly, divide it between them as rainwater drawn from a cistern.

'I don't want to go yet,' she whispers to him.

He did not realise she was awake.

'I don't want you to go at all,' he answers her.

'What if we're wrong? What if there is a cure but we've been headstrong by ignoring it? The Prophet arrived fifty years ago in the east and spoke of a world beneath the world. What if there are answers there we've ignored? What if there was a cure . . . before?'

'Your death saves us all,' he says by rote.

'How?' she asks, though she knows the answer. She likes his voice. She will listen to him saying anything.

'Trying to make the world better is what killed the Ancients. We accept the world as it is so that it will not die again, appreciate what we have so we don't lose more.'

He feels the crease of her smile on his breast.

'That's what we tell everyone,' she says.

'Because it's right,' he answers.

She does not reply but instead, she runs her hand around his chest, down his belly, running her fingernails along his soft penis.

15

'You're still beautiful,' she says. This may be her answer. It may not.

'I would take your place,' he says.

A puff of air through his chest hair. Her last laugh.

'Our brave leader.'

'I fear life without you more than death. Taking your place would be the coward's way, and I would take it.'

'There is no future,' she whispers, repeating their marriage vows. 'There is no past. Our words vanish as we say them. There is only now, and it is now we have each other, until that moment when we do not.'

Now it is his turn to smile.

'That is what we tell everyone,' he says.

He scratches her bare back until her breathing slows. It is laboured and heavy. The Sickness is a rapid and fading death. A few days. A week. They say it comes from deep beneath the towers of the Gone World where the bodies remain, the bones piled up. The Roamers and Explorers and bandits who would venture downwards either add to their number or bring it out fresh.

No one knows for sure.

Their blanket is made of sheep's wool, separate squares sewed together, given by a neighbouring clan. Each square is a picture or shape from everyday life. It is a worthy gift.

He folds the ragged edge so it does not disturb his wife's neck.

Twenty years of marriage. They are not meant to count them but they do.

For a time he looks at the ceiling of the tent and tries to feel, with every part of his body, the experience of her being there with him. It is a lie, he knows; this pretence of there being no past. And yet it works. Collective forgetting is possible because memory lives in talk, and talk lasts only as long as the wind. It is the personal forgetting that is harder, because that is written for ever on the soul. Silence erases one, but sometimes that only sharpens the other.

This life, this love, has left its mark on him, deeper than any wound, and what is theirs will become his alone once she is gone and he dons the white robe and red sash for his time of mourning. He will be expected to step forward into a new day and wordlessly carry the entirety of his wife's life inside him: her memories, her words, her face, her body, her ideas. Alone. Who else will know? Who else will remember?

There are others – more comforted spirits – who work to forget. They heal by unclenching their fists and allowing the sand to run through their fingers. But he is not such a man. Though he pretends, his faith in the teachings is not sure enough.

And so he tries to remember everything he can: is her breast warmer than her arm or are they the same? This is the heat of her.

When her head is below his chin and her leg curls over him, where does her bent knee touch his leg? This is the size of her.

When she relaxes her sleeping hand on his shoulder, how far apart are her fingers? Because this is the touch of her.

He feels the flutters of her eyelids on his chest. They blink, and blink again, faster now. He saw this before with their daughter. He breathes very deeply. He is not sure whether it is for both of them or simply out of fear.

'I can't see,' she says.

'I'm here.'

'Don't look,' she says. 'Don't look. I don't want you to remember this.'

Her eyes will be pale: a film of pearl across them that separates the world from her. Their daughter flailed when this happened. Five years old; she could not understand it. If she couldn't see her parents, she didn't believe they were there. Sound was not enough. Touch was not enough.

It is the light. We need the light.

Veronique was her name.

That was ten years ago.

She is here with them right now. His family is together. He knows this because he can smell her hair.

'Picture her,' he says to his wife. 'It is all you need to see now.'

'It is not our way.'

'Do it.'

Together they lie there, listening to the tent singing to them. She begins, slowly at first, and then faster and harder, to bang her head against his stomach as though she is trying to work her way into him so that he can absorb everything that she is and merge their lives together completely.

He accepts the pain until the line of her dignity is crossed. He clenches her head between his palms and stops her. But he does not look down.

'Don't let those people destroy the world again,' she pleads. 'They are going to make the same mistakes. You promised me when Veronique died – you promised that her death would save us all. Promise me now that you will protect what we still have, because it is too beautiful to lose. This life – it is all so beautiful.'

This is why he brought his people here. This was when their journey began; when their daughter died and they heard soon after a story about a people following the ways of the Ancients: a people committed to relearning all that was lost, all that led from peace to war, from life to death. That is when he knew what they had to do, what they needed to keep.

Her hand reaches up to find his face. She presses her palm against it, her fingertips closing his eyes so that, for a moment, all three of them can be as one.

'Too beautiful,' she says.

There is a deep tremor through the ground.

'It has already begun,' he promises. 'We are not strong enough yet to take their fortress and stop the madness, but we will be and soon. Tonight we committed – we announced ourselves. It was for you.'

With this, as much a gift as a curse, they fall asleep. Their remaining time together is both perfect and wasted.

He emerges in the morning naked and bathed in the orange light of dawn. A woman wraps a white robe around his shoulders and ties a red sash around his waist.

Barefoot, he walks the full distance through the camp to the edge of the cliff and seats himself on a rock. A silent crowd gathers around him and they join him facing east.

The painted greens of the Aurora lights have retreated and vanished behind the majesty of the dawn, each colour more vibrant than the spice at the southern markets or the blood that lingers on the butchers' blades.

His Deputy, expressionless, takes his hand in his own and washes it with water from an ancient bottle made of real glass. The water is cold and for a moment he resents it: the wet seems to be washing his wife's scent and touch from him – but this is the purpose. The cold is to shock him back to the world around, to stimulate an awareness of what is still here, including himself.

He takes the bottle from the Deputy's hand and drinks heavily. He is parched.

Together, the men and women and children of the encampment sit around him and watch the sun rise and the new day begin.

It is, as his wife said, beautiful.

THE HARD ROOM

Elimisha, daughter-of-Cara, wakes on a cold, polished floor in what might be morning. The act of drawing breath means she survived the chase, the explosions and even the collapse. It is too soon to even wonder how.

This cave smells of fine chalk and unwashed hair. Dust, older than memory, has settled on her brown skin the way ash from the night fires at the stadium falls on the arms and curly hair of her younger brother, to his endless delight.

She wrote his name on his forearm, and he looked up at his older sister – Elimisha! A Runner! – and walked away, proud and staring.

The written word: on their own flesh!

The floor tiles feel good against her cheek but are no distraction from the pain in her leg and hip, which does not throb from a single spot like a puncture wound but *pulses*. It feels like her heart is beating from her leg.

She reaches down. The blood is tacky and cool around her hip. This is better than wet and hot. There is no haemorrhage. She is not dying. Not yet, anyway. But she is damaged.

21

To calm her heart and slow the blood she tries to remember *how*, if not exactly *why*.

She had been slinking her way across the rooftops last night, moving through shadows, beneath downed girders and along troughs in the ruins to stay out of sight and ensure her Route remained secret. Thoughts running through her mind repeated: *I am an Archive Runner. I am the youngest Runner in twenty years. I am sixteen years old and proving what is possible.*

I am going to get this right.

True to Protocol, her black leather jacket had been zipped to the neck, her gloves fastened tightly, her sling-bag cinched over her left shoulder. She had already made her Knowledge drop at an Archive called Prydain and was on her way back via the Orange Route when she saw one of the tribesmen.

The Orange Route is a high run across the rooftops of the urbanscape. Her return was to be a night journey during a half-moon and she set out after a small meal of soft bread, dried meat and a full litre of water. Her mother had given her an apple too.

An apple: a loud, crunchy, shiny apple. If there was one thing she couldn't eat on an urban run it was an apple.

Mothers.

The Archive Chief had ordered her to drink the entire litre and watched her as she did. Now, lying on the floor, Elimisha understands the rule – in fact, she wishes she'd had even more to drink. She is thirsty.

Last night, the blues in the sky were deeper than she had seen in months, the fiery tips of purple more pronounced than she remembered. She would have stopped and taken in the beauty if she'd been allowed.

The Ghost Talkers like to read the sky as though it's a tome with stories of its own to tell. No one believes them, but everyone likes the tales. Strange that people whose minds are tilted off the True have the most amazing stories.

The view from the tops of the remaining buildings in the Gone World is the best. Much better than at home, where the fires that burn in the Stadium every night always block out the stars, hiding their light – other than that one spot behind the Stadium where the underground waters fall to the river below and roll out into the Western distance beyond the farming fields that feed the Commonwealth. And there is that time in spring, when the sun sets perfectly over the river as if falling into it: that moment when the great orange ball is cut in half by the horizon but is made whole by the waters below it.

It's always so crowded, though. It's not like anyone can enjoy it alone, not like on an urban run in the dead of night.

This was her tenth run: a milestone. It was a chance to prove to the High Command that their reluctance to trust younger Runners was ill-founded.

There was going to be cake.

Elimisha had been ordered by Lian, Chief Librarian of the Central Archive, to make the drop at Prydain and then work her way back as quietly as a shadow to make the Signal Mirror at dawn. There, she'd bounce the rising sun off the reflector and twist the blinders in the code that would announce her return. The Spotters would confirm her message and signal back her orders, then, after the shade fell over the entrance and everything in them disappeared into a shadow of black so intense that even the hunting birds above wouldn't see her go in, she'd make her way to one of the hidden tunnels.

She had made the Knowledge drop (as usual, with no idea

what was in the box she handed over) just as planned and was coming back, on her way to the Signal Mirror.

Elimisha heard the Tribesmen before she saw them.

Many tribes have passed through the region over the years. The old people, like Chief Lilly in Weapons and Communications, say they started coming when the Stadium began growing. They had talked about this when Elimisha did her apprenticeship there last month.

'When I was your age,' Lilly said, 'no one would to trek across the wastelands or the Empty Quarter just for water. People knew the Stadium was here. Some did come for trade, but there was little else in this region, because the Gone World had already been picked clean by previous generations and naturally, no one ventured inside the remaining towers because of the Sickness. Even now we're not really located conveniently between any two places. So if they come here at all, it's for us and The Crossing.

'As I assumed you learned in school,' she continued, while unwrapping a new package of ammunition, 'The Few arrived about a hundred years before I was born. They found the Stadium deserted but not gutted. It had power systems, high walls and fresh water, all encouraging them to stay. From them, a very small community grew. There was nothing else around the Stadium at the time. There was the Gone World and its towers, but there was no reason to go and visit other than to gawk and wonder at everything that had been before. Not much grew in the sands and there were few Finds of any value. The High Road didn't exist then.'

'So why did others start coming?' Elimisha asked. Traders had arrived that day with the ammunition that – fortuitously – had been set into plastic and the air sucked out by the Ancients.

24

Lilly had told her they did this to avoid corrosion, and that chemicals in the plastic preserved the bullets even across these hundreds of years. It was her theory that they'd done this deliberately during the final moments of their lives, knowing that ammunition rotted, and if they survived they were going to need it. But then they died so fast they couldn't use them. With so few people in the region, there is still ammunition to find; the problem has always been matching it to the weapons. Most of the numbers printed on them made no sense to them and even those that seemed to fit the gun barrels occasionally blew up or fired out wildly. Lilly used a carved-out stone box for a testing chamber, pulling a string tied to the trigger to avoid getting hands, fingers and faces blown off. Elimisha's job was to open the packages, load the weapons and – after Lilly had fired them – measure the clustering of the holes to see if the match and quality were both viable. Lilly insisted they always use three test shots. 'It's never unwise to measure well,' she explained.

They were firing .38 special ammunition from a Colt .357 Python and found that it worked. They had no idea what made the ammunition special and they didn't know what a Python was. Or a Colt, for that matter.

'We're still not entirely sure how The Few arrived in the first place,' Lilly said. 'We know there were thirty-eight of them, and they came from the north. According to the stories we've heard, they succeeded by marshalling the resources of the Stadium successfully and somehow avoiding the in-fighting and politics that ruined most small communities during the chaos after The Rise. When I was your age there were fewer than a hundred and eighty people in the Stadium. The next year, when I opened the Harrington Box, things really changed and now there are more than a thousand of us. Beyond the walls, tribes and Roamers and Ghost Talkers and traders and Explorers and adventurers and . . . oh . . . all sorts – they pass through now, partly because of The Crossing. But these people?' Lilly had said, 'who just arrived a few months ago? They're different.'

'How are they different?' Elimisha had asked.

'They won't talk. General Winters sent people there to open relations, but they didn't respond, and still don't. And they won't accept our offer to come and visit. So we watch each other and so far, we aren't learning much. But the tensions are growing. They appear to be hostile to Knowledge, but that's all we know.'

At seventy-one years old, Lilly's hair is still long and blonde and her eyes still the colour of heavy ice.

The reason Elimisha had heard the tribesmen before she saw them was because they were a clumsy people. The Runners had spread word of this when they met and this rather proved it. Stopping on a slab of concrete behind one of the steel fan-boxes on the roof, Elimisha closed her eyes to listen to the shuffle of the fools' feet in the fine-grain sand that settles up here on every flat surface; the fine-grain sand that shouts out the location of every foot-fall and records every step across its surface so that the experienced can know the size and weight and number and direction of all the fools who crossed there and didn't have the foresight or systems to mark their routes in advance – to give them names, to train their people, to maintain them unseen, keep their locations safe – so that no Runner of the Commonwealth would ever be a fool.

Imagine, she thought, *to just wander around with no training, no preparation, no Order of Silence to build and maintain their routes and set traps to protect them, no schools and sessions to train their people.*

'If you are not careful,' she had wanted to shout to her pursuer, 'you might find a soft patch on the roof, worn by centuries of sun and water and rot. If so, you'll have a nice drop into the world of Yesterday. You won't like it much, but there will be plenty of bones to keep yours company.'

In nine runs she had never been seen or followed. Now, though, she had. Why does bad luck align most closely with consequential moments?

When she stopped, he had stopped too. When she started moving again he gave chase and his footfalls were hard and long – a sprint. She did the same. And she was faster and better prepared.

Elimisha leaped onto stones and bricks and pipes that all absorbed her weight and didn't shift or speak or sing out below her feet. She sprang the way rabbits do, dodging to the sides, looking behind them, staying out of sight. This was her training, her strength, her speed, her cunning – and the reason she'd been entrusted as a Runner so young.

She was moving quickly and the breeze was hot. Breath control was part of her training too: in through the nose and out the mouth, keeping the rhythm like a song in her head. Watch the feet, hit the marks, pace it out, remember the route.

Around a square hunk of steel she glimpsed another of them – to the south, blocking another Route she was *not* on. That was when she'd become nervous. How did they know how to flank her from both sides unless they knew the Route she was running? But no one knew the Routes, not even the people at the Commonwealth – unless they were Runners, former Runners, Archive Chiefs or members of the Order. And the penalty for loose talk was severe. And if spies were caught? Death, and the bodies returned to their masters in pieces. That was how General Winters wanted it, especially these days. It was grisly but it appeared to be working.

If not spies, she wondered as she ran, was it possible that these beasts had been watching them and actually learning? These people who are said to hate Knowledge itself?

Did they see no contradiction in that?

Or did contradictions not even matter to them?

Two Runners had gone missing since this tribe had arrived. Elimisha wasn't supposed to know this but she did.

She sprinted across the surface of the rooftop towards the edge. Across from her was a taller building rising up eight storeys. There was a gap between the edge of this roof and the flat face of the building ahead: a two-metre jump. For them it would be a Black Jump – a jump into the unknown with no way to return; a full-on gamble with death.

Not for her, though. This was Marker Eighteen on the Orange Route. She had trained for this on the Green and had now run it nine previous times:

You plant your foot to the left of the orange marker and you hurl yourself towards the opposite wall. You meet the wall with your hands and your feet at the same time. There is nothing there: no foothold, no window. The surface is sheer. The force of your jump will plaster you against the wall for a brief moment. And then you will drop.

'Drop?' one of the other students had asked. He shouldn't have asked. He should have shut up and waited until the instructor was done. If he'd done that, he wouldn't have had to clean the horse stalls.

You will drop straight down if you meet the wall correctly. Trust the world's pull. It never fails.

She practised it on the Green of the Stadium a hundred times by leaping from a raised wooden platform and smashing herself against a wooden wall across from it. And then she dropped and learned to trust the Order.

Elimisha sprinted for it as the tribesmen closed in around her, close now, but behind her, the way trailing birds flock after a leader.

There it was, as promised: the marker, a pipe sticking out of the wall and painted orange. The Tribesmen would not be able to follow her even if they had the courage. This is what she was taught.

The one on her left had a gun. She could see he was pointing it as he ran, but he was too slow, she was too fast, and bullets are rare so no one practises. No one can hit a mark on the move.

Twenty metres.

Ten.

Why were they chasing her? What did they want? Her bag? Her body? Her death? The Knowledge in her mind? *Why?*

Elimisha adjusted her final strides so she could meet the edge of the roof to the left of the marker with her right leg, which was the stronger. Closer, closer, closer still . . . hop with the left, plant the right, and then *pop*.

Up and out.

She flew over the alley below and slapped the wall with hands and feet. The force – promised, predicted and practised – suspended her there as the tribesmen took aim and before they could shoot . . . she fell.

Exhausted and injured and thirsty, Elimisha pauses her recollection and raises her head from the tiled floor. She looks down, past her feet, to the massive door, now sealed shut and locking her in here: in this Hard Room; the kind that the Adamists insisted was real even if no one had seen one since Chief Lilly pulled her finds from one so long ago.

The door has a massive wheel in the centre. The seal around the door is black and as thick as a snake. There is a light on above it glowing red – a colour she has never seen from a bulb before. She tries to remember, through the pain, whether the room was red when she entered.

No. It was definitely black when she came in. When she had rushed down the stairs and thrown herself in here it had been as black as a grave. The door, then, had been open. Maybe the light came on when the blast sealed it shut behind her.

'The light,' she says through the pain. The words come back to her in an echo – not as an exclamation but as a question.

The light?

How can there be a light here?

If nothing had caught her, she would have dropped twenty metres to her death on the broken metal spikes and debris below. But this was no Black Jump.

'When you drop, you twist,' her instructor had said.

So drop and twist is what she did.

Down, down two metres until . . . *contact*. She landed with both feet on an extension bridge. *Clang, clang*, two steps and three, into the open window of the building she came from and out of the night air. She was suddenly into the forbidden world of the inner walls.

Once inside she found the promised white rope dangling from the ceiling. With two hands she grabbed it and pulled with all her might. The rope spun across a pulley and untied a knot that released the extension bridge so that it plummeted to the alley below.

Try what I did, she challenges her pursuers.

Elimisha paused to catch her breath. She had never been inside one of the buildings before. The other times she had stayed above. This part of the route was for emergencies. She was standing now where the Ancients used to live and work doing . . . what? The massive room around her held nothing – nothing on the walls, nothing to sit on. Not even a plastic bag. It had been scraped clean by time, like almost everything else.

She breathed in, tentative; worried for a moment about the Sickness in the lower chambers. Another breath, more deeply this time. It struck her that this room was mapped: The Commonwealth wouldn't have sent her here if it was dangerous to breathe.

She slowed her heart, regained her balance and confidence, and assessed.

From this angle there was nothing the Tribesmen above could do; there was no way to swing in after her.

What had followed her in, dangling down on a string, was some kind of white metal egg. It was much larger than a chicken's egg and had a pattern on its surface of cross-hatching. At its top was a silver tube of some kind. The tube displayed pulsing blue light that was speeding up.

They were swinging it.

When it was inside the room with her, they released it.

The first lesson she was taught as a cadet in the Agoge – when she was a little girl, only five years old – was this: *If you see something from the Gone World that is very very beautiful or very very ugly . . . DON'T TOUCH IT.*

Elimisha was five storeys above the sand of The Rise. In line with the Route, she was now supposed to go back up the stairs across from her on the left wall below the EXIT sign and return to the roof, completing a loop and coming out behind her pursuers in a spot invisible to them.

Going *down* the stairway itself was forbidden because there was no exit downwards. There was also no light. There was less air and what air there was, was bad. *Buildings are tall coffins,* she'd been taught.

The egg blinked and it was extraordinarily beautiful, almost hypnotic.

Recovering her mind and remembering her training, she broke from its spell and ran for the stairwell and as soon as she did she heard another metallic thump-thump-thump coming down at her from above.

During her apprenticeship in Weapons and Communications, Elimisha had seen Ancient Tech, most of it grouped into a broad category of 'shinies' because no one knew what they were or what they did. Unlike the inanimate shinies in Lilly's workshop, these eggs had their own sources of electricity and had been thrown after her with malice.

Away was where she needed to be.

Down was the only real choice.

So against all Protocol, down into the stairwell she went; into the Hollows where no one went, not since Death himself took residence there, people said. He waited there with his long arms and strong claws to pull down the curious and foolhardy and the brave alike.

She flung herself over the bannister to a landing and then she did it again. Three steps and she was in the middle of the third flight of stairs downwards when an explosion detonated above her.

This was no small charge like she'd seen troops use as they

practised formation drills and defensive lines. This was no ammunition detonation from a gun. This was not a small blast from a pulse rifle. This was a fireball. Above her the air turned orange like the morning light and a heat pressed down as though the air itself were on fire. A cascade of flares and smouldering debris rained onto her shoulders and the heat poured over her.

She rolled down the stairs.

On her feet again, head hurting, and glad – *so glad* – she was encased in protective leather and a back-guard, per Protocol, she followed the stairs downwards by feel, downwards to where nothing yet burned, nothing was illuminated by the orange cloud rolling above.

Another explosion – and far above her came the sharp cadence of falling plaster and concrete that was joined by a tremor of deeper crashes as the primary structures of the building – for so many centuries tortured by the elements after whatever they had endured in the wars that once felled everything else – finally surrendered their integrity.

She jumped and jumped down again and again with one thought only: they want me dead.

Her run was vertical and off-route and unprepared. She was exploring now, not running. Throwing herself into the Black.

Elimisha put all her faith in the presumed symmetry of the building's architectural design, flinging herself from bannister to step to bannister to step, hoping with each irrevocable leap that the minds of the Ancients were consistent and logical and reasonable like the minds of her own people.

Her feet slapped the steps as she landed but she could barely hear them as her tumbling progress gained force and certainty.

From a pocket on her right leg Elimisha pulled a glowstick.

33

She cracked it open and the tunnel became greener than the night. There, at her foot on the landing between the two stairwells, was the corpse of a man, skin shrivelled, one clawed hand still at his own throat, boots on his feet.

A smell was pouring down the staircase now; it rather than fire was making her cough. She was sure it was a kind of poison.

Down. Down further, past more bodies.

Was she breathing death itself?

The Urban Explorers and the Adamists would have known. They invited her to run the Off-Routes. The nut-jobs actually went *inside* sometimes. They were drawing new maps of the upper levels and the first ones below the ground of The Rise – eight floors deep. Teenagers were pretending they were Adam from half a century ago: the exiled Prophet who claimed to have drawn the Underworld and went crazy with what he saw.

No thank you.

And yet, there she was, with the bottom arriving up at her as she ran. The air was so thick and stale it was almost unbreathable; she had to pull it into her lungs as an act of will.

Ahead, in the glimmering light from her glowstick, was the basement level. It was a generator room with antique machinery encased in sheet metal, thick pipes running over her head, back and forth through gaps in the walls.

The ceiling shook. A door ahead had the word STAFF on it. Elimisha slammed her shoulder into it and fell in past the carcase of an old rolling chair. The closet-like enclosure had an open door and nothing inside except more bones – not a complete skeleton, though. Something had dragged much of a person here, then eaten the pieces. There was nothing else left, though, both predator and prey long gone.

At first she thought she had reached a dead end. Spinning around, she checked to see if there was another way out, but there wasn't. The STAFF door was the only one. Brushing falling plaster from her face, Elimisha spun around again, trying to find somewhere to go, and saw how the shaking had started to change the shape of the flat wall in front of her.

The green glow from her stick had been showing her a smooth, flat surface. As the shaking became more violent and the walls themselves trembled under the shifting weight of a million tonnes of stone and steel, the outline of a perfect black circle formed on the wall – a line at first, until, in an instant, the top-most edge crumbled, chipping a wedge from the green-glowing wall and giving away a blackness behind it that screamed out to her an invitation to *go*.

Elimisha dashed at the wall and curled her upper body into a tight ball as she whacked into it, sending plaster and grit exploding inwards, into a tunnel that was now the barrel of a gun shooting her as she ran as fast as she could, the cloud of debris building behind her as she ran.

After that she wasn't sure. The tunnel split at some point. At the end was a perfectly flat wall that was either the edge of her coffin or another paper-thin board. What she does remember is deciding that it didn't much matter how hard she hit it.

Elimisha rammed through that wall the way the Dragoons burst from the battle tunnels below the Stadium and out into the wastelands before the Gone World.

Free of the tunnel there was a room, but she had only a second to take it in and make a choice. One way was up: heavy industrial stairs of solid concrete invited her to run eighteen flights to the surface, which was impossible. The other way was *in*.

Smack in her way was the thickest door she had ever seen: much thicker than the primary doors to the Stadium leading into the Commonwealth, thicker than the secondary doors beyond the holding pit. Even in the Archives she had never seen pictures of anything like this, thicker than her forearm was long. It was also open – just wide enough for a girl to slip inside.

It sounded like the Hard Room Lilly had described to her once, but this one had no water, no dead, no bones.

She was barely inside when a blast of air from the collapsing building hurled her body into space. The Tracollo behind her had sounded like the world in its entirety was being cracked open and the demons of the dark had all screamed outwards from that hollow centre, shrieking in their collective fury as they celebrated their freedom in her deafened ears. Had the door not slammed shut behind her from the blasting wind, she is convinced she would now be dead.

The light above the closed and sealed door is red, which makes the blood in her leg harder to see. Easier is the pipe or rod or spike jabbed into her thigh. Reaching down, she can feel the tacky blood. There's no blood-spurt, though. When there's blood-spurt, people can bleed out and run dry like a pierced bag of water. That could still happen if she pulled on it, though. Maybe it will and maybe it won't. She's no doctor. She's just a Runner.

Tenth run and now this. It takes a coincidence to spoil a party, that's what the Raiders like to say.

This is not what Elimisha promised her mother. This is not what she expected from becoming a Runner.

She will not cry, though. She will remember her vows and the sequence of survival: Water – Food – Escape. Signal – Return – Rest. All of this, in that order. That is her training.

Now, though, all of that can wait. She's had water and she's not hungry so what she needs is rest. Now she needs to sleep and hope that, while dreaming, the air and the Sickness do not kill her while her eyes are closed.

THE CROSSING

Henry sleeps fitfully as Graham watches over them both for as long as he dares, knowing that if he lets her sleep too much he will have to endure a full day's ride with her eyes narrowed and her mood sullen. With the Tracollo pulling them one direction and the weight of their finds pulling them another, he knows it is already going to be a tough day.

'Henry?' he whispers to her from his perch on a rock, her rifle across his lap, the sun's reveal of the land still to come.

'I'm up,' she says, her voice muffled inside the dome. 'Are the Roamers still working?' she asks.

Graham powers the scope and takes aim at the activity around the Tracollo.

'Busy as bees,' he says quietly.

Henry rolls onto her back inside the tent and rubs her face.

With the arrival of dawn and good visibility over land – and the attention of the world elsewhere – they can risk more talk.

'What's a bee?' she asks, sitting up.

'The most industrious of all ancient creatures.'

'You're just saying the phrase backwards,' she says, calling his bluff and ready now to rise.

He smiles beyond the scope and says nothing.

With her right hand she grips the puller and slides it silently upwards, allowing fresh air into the dome. She is tired, but after motherhood, nothing feels truly tiring any more. Alessandra was a terrible sleeper as a baby. It wasn't until four months into it – child screaming, black circles for eyes, a far-away stare fixed to her face – that she chose to ignore all parenting advice and simply lock Alessandra's lips to her own nipple at night, which permitted them both to pass out. The girl grew strong and healthy and powerful and Henry pulled through it.

The pain of childbirth she barely remembers. The fatigue, though: that walked hard on the mind; it left tracks.

Henry shuffles out of the dome to a shrub to relieve herself before joining Graham at his perch. She takes her own rifle from his hands and peers at the activity.

'They're digging?'

'They seem to be hauling,' he tells her, 'and excavating. They've started sifting too. I figure the small Finds will go first to The Crossing – probably the least valuable, at least as far as anyone can tell. They'll make rumours about the better ones, let those stir, see what kind of interest develops and what else comes out of the hole before they share the good stuff.'

'No one knows what anything is,' Henry mutters. 'My parents used to do this – that's what brought us out to these parts in the first place.'

'I know,' he says, although Henry doesn't speak often of her parents. Their deaths were the reason she remained here, though – the reason the two of them met. The reason they have a daughter.

'You know more than me,' he says. 'I'm just piecing it together with words. Helps me, anyway.'

'I didn't mean to bark,' she says.

'You didn't.'

'It's going to take weeks for word to spread beyond the region. Unless,' Graham adds, 'it doesn't get out at all because of these Keepers.'

Henry lowers the rifle and looks with her naked eyes, but she can see nothing from here. 'Maybe there's something coming out that Lilly can use,' she says.

'Like what?'

'You should check her list. The things she wants are useless to everyone else.'

Hours later the white sun is a fist above the horizon, pale enough to stare at. They ride towards it as though it was singing to them. They try to look uninterested, riding slow, watching for people on the road, trying to take in the mood. In silence they share the same wonder that a sun so big doesn't warm the land even more.

In an hour they are on the High Road. It will be three more to The Crossing if they let the horses walk easy. Henry is curious about the Tracollo itself but Graham shakes off the idea like rainwater. One delay is enough, he says, and she knows he is right.

Henry is first to see the travellers moving towards them. With her right hand she detaches the scope from the rifle and puts the cup to her eye. Her crosshairs align to the chest of a child sitting between her parents, all riding atop a wagon pulled by two mules. Behind them are three other families on similar contraptions cobbled from Gone World kit. The last wagon is hauling a cistern. The vehicle shimmies to a rhythm Henry knows: those tyres are thicker; the mules are pulling harder.

'They're hauling water,' Henry says.

'Children?' Graham asks.

'Unfortunately.'

'Dream Walkers, all of them,' Graham said. 'Never going to learn.'

'Maybe we can turn their minds,' she says.

'How often does that happen?'

'Often enough to give worth to the trying.'

In the time it takes to walk once around the Stadium, they cross paths. Henry and a female driver raise their hands in greeting and the men raise palms in peace. The first family pulls the mules to stop and the caravan halts. The horses snort out a morning mist.

Beside the woman is a girl. She is well dressed and her big brown eyes are healthy. She does not smile, but her gaze on Henry and Graham is deep and curious.

'You've rolled in at a strange time,' Henry says. 'You've heard about the Tracollo.'

'Strange times,' says the woman, 'but that's no interest to us. We have what we need and we have little to trade.'

Graham indicates west where there is still a moon. 'You look to be going west. Out to the Commonwealth? Those are our people. You're welcome to visit. We trade in Knowledge, not only objects.'

'Have no interest in the Commonwealth,' says the man beside the woman. He is unarmed. He strikes Graham as too chipper to be wise.

'We have a daughter,' says Henry to the parents. 'We wouldn't be taking her out into the Empty Quarter, though.'

'We have seen the vision,' says the man, smiling, confirming Graham's hunch. 'We know about the city that survived The Rise. It is like a Crossing for the entire world. We're going

41

there. It's only thirty days past the Stadium and along your river.'

'There's no city,' says Graham. 'That's a bad story. We're from the Stadium and we know the land. There's nothing out there. Water's good for six days out: our turbines clean it and everyone's welcome to it beyond the walls. After that, it's undrinkable again because it picks up the poisons in the ground. The greenery dies off quickly and the animals stop coming. It's the hard end, an easy line to see. Our Raiders have crossed fourteen days past that into the wasteland, that's twenty days out. You need to carry a fortnight's worth of water to visit the nothing that's out there and a fortnight's water to get yourself back to the sweet stuff. That's a lot of hauling for an ugly journey.'

'You didn't hear me, brother,' says the man. His shirt is bright red. Graham thinks Henry could shoot him from a mile away. 'I said *thirty* days. Add a bit to those two fortnights and there you are.'

'On the way,' adds Graham, as though the man hadn't spoken, 'our people found nothing. No footprints, nothing dropped, no campsites, no old fires. There's nothing but hardpan and sand.'

'They must have come another way,' says the man who will not learn. 'We've got enough for thirty-five days.'

'You'll die. First the mules will drop dead, because the pulling gets tough once the road ends, and then the little ones, old ones, the men, and finally, the women. Women last longest because they need less food and water to travel. But they'll die alone and saddest.'

Some of this was untrue. The Commonwealth had set up depots with fresh water at five-day intervals along the river. Raiders – and members of the Order of Silence – stocked it for thirty days west to where the mountains began and water ran cleaner from the high peaks. Officially, it was for the benefit of the Explorers and some Runners bringing Knowledge to far-off Archives, but whatever the real reasons, it was an order straight from High Command and had been for some forty years. These provisions were only needed, though, because the land was truly as Graham had described.

He was sure because he and Henry had both looked themselves.

'You haven't seen what we've seen,' said the soon-to-be-dead man, no longer smiling.

'Why not leave the kids at the Commonwealth?' said Henry, knowing where this was going. 'You're going to pass by the Stadium anyway. Find the city and then come back for the children later with your good news. We're more than eight hundred strong behind those walls – the most powerful city on Earth, as far as we know. Your kids will be happy as clams.'

'What's a clam?' asks the man.

'The happiest of all creatures,' says Graham.

'No, no. We need to find the Shining City together.'

'You should go north,' Graham says, as a last effort to redirect them. 'Long ago, when there were waters running past the forest, tens of thousands of bottles broke apart, maybe more. We don't know how it happened exactly but we think the bottles broke out of hundreds of those rectangular containers you see here and there. Time broke them up and the waters wore them down. Later, those water receded and now there is a lake of sea glass like nothing you've ever seen. As long as the Stadium, maybe even as wide. I like to imagine it goes down for ever. It shines in the day and glints like a dream at night: all reds and blues, purples and yellows, greens of every kind, and cloudy whites as soft as a morning kiss. Just up north, a mere nine days' ride from here. The children will never forget it. See it instead. Let it refresh you.'

The child looks to her father but he is shaking his head. 'Next time, Bee,' he says to her. 'Next time – on the way back.'

'If you change your mind,' says Henry, 'you go to the Stadium – unarmed – and tell them that you're the guests of Commander Wayworth. Our people will let you in and the girl can stay as long as she wants.'

'Your graciousness will be rewarded by the birds in the sky and the fish in the sea,' says the woman.

Raising their hands once again, the caravan makes its departure to the west following their own black shadows cast by the rising sun.

Three hours later, the sun is a copper orb that dries the land without warming it. The shrubs are thicker here on the path and the first greens supported by the under-earth water present as small, dark leaves on spindly plants in the lower valleys. Small birds of mottled browns zip through the canyons faster than arrows, collecting bugs in their bellies and beaks for return to their young. The people leave them in peace. They are too small to eat and killing for sport leads to vultures and things that bite.

Henry reads the movements and faces of travellers and Roamers the way that Scribes and Evaluators read the contents of the Harrington Box. She measures their numbers, the cadence of their horses, the levity of their talk, the expressions on their faces. The inexperienced show their moods in a constant waxing and waning of emotion but the weathered and rode-out tend to hold it all back. It's when those people crack that a sense of the day is revealed.

The news of the Tracollo has spread as they expected and as Henry and Graham approach The Crossing, they converge with others doing the same. Not as many as she would have thought, though. There is a heaviness marring the anticipation, and more here than a hunger for early pickings and new finds. It is something she cannot yet name, but her suspicions run to the Keepers.

Graham trots on ahead of her, joining a line of weary travellers who are in no mood for talk. They slump low on their mounts, eyes focused on the tails of the horses ahead. Henry, coming up slowly, examines the make of their cloth and the quality of their weapons to gauge the distance of their journey. They are from a colony to the southwest, before the Empty Quarter begins, a five-day ride off. They are smelters, known for metal work. They must have set off long before the Tracollo, but they do not appear elevated by the news, which is an oddity, because if nothing else, the finds can be turned into Raw.

She matches her speed with a man looking more alert than others.

'How's the journey?' she asks him.

Their metal stirrups are polished, but the leather on which they hang is cracked. His lips are cut. She hands him a bottle of water and he drinks heavily and hands it back.

'Long,' says the man, not looking at her.

'You're from the south. Did you bring seed for the trade?' she asks.

'The old breeds are failing,' says the man. 'The new breeds are failing. The ancient ones from the Troves bear fruit but no seed. We can't figure it out.'

'About fourteen days' ride to your south there's a gathering at—'

The man scratches at his beard and shakes his head low. White bits of skin emerge like a cloud of snow. 'Yeah, we know. Nothing new there either,' he says. 'They won't flower.

We've tried everything. No way to know if they're *Semilla solos* until it's too late.'

'What about the New World crops?'

'Nothing wrong with new seed. Problem is the soil. The two don't like each other any more. We've pulled too much of the same out of the ground and now it's all barren. We need something new or all of this' – he did not look around, did not wave a hand. His meaning was already clear – 'won't be here much longer.'

Henry is about to nudge her horse forward to reach Graham when the man lifts his head to her. 'You're Commonwealth folk.'

'Yes.'

'Collecting all those books, learning what the ancients knew. Following their footsteps, right to the grave.'

'Is that what people are saying?' Henry asks.

The man spits something to the ground. He looks forward again. 'Things are getting worse. May be it's not your fault,' he says, 'but you don't look like no solution neither.'

Graham has stopped where The Crossing appears through the mist that often rises from the wetland below it.

Henry pulls up beside him. It is always a sight, changing with the light of day and the seasons of the year.

Before it became known as The Crossing it used to be called the Bridge to Nowhere. A plush green river of trees and brush pass beneath a glimmering, pristine arching bridge that rises from the dirt and sand on one side, ascends seventy metres above the tallest trees below, runs more than fifteen hundred paces from start to finish and descends with perfect symmetry into a scrabble of rock on the far end. The bridge rises from nothing and arrives at nothing. The Rise buried the roads that must once have approached it, and it buried the river it once crossed too. Some ground water remains, though, flowing unseen and unheard, but close enough to the surface for the most stubborn of plants to drink what the people could not.

Outside the Gone World towers and the towering tail of the AIRBUS, the bridge is the only structure that survived whatever had made everything else fall.

The surface of the bridge is glass, rising as one sheet to the apex where it splits into two – each lane passing around a Pavilion at the top – and rejoins on the other side for the descent.

Most beasts are shy to make the climb until they grow used to the idea. Henry's own horse was brought here as a foal. The distance and the dry it hadn't minded so much. Not even the cold. Flying over a forest, though: that was something new.

Since Lilly, though, the Bridge has been called The Crossing: up one side, down the other. There's no turning back. You miss something, you go around again. Other rules include no loitering beyond the last light; no bedding down on The Crossing, even for the shopkeepers, and there's no violence in the Pavilion at the top which commands the most excellent view of the Territory. The penalties for breaking these rules are severe.

There is a queue to get onto The Crossing. Henry and Graham can see the Militia standing with sword, spear and rifle. When they reach the front, the man who greets them is as spindly as starving wheat; it exaggerates his height. His mouth is as thin as wire and his eyes and voice are lifeless from boredom. His skin is unusually pale for these parts. There's word of some fair people in the far north – more pink than brown, like Lilly – but few around here. Maybe he is from up there.

47

'You're new,' Graham says to him from atop his horse.

The man assesses Graham and Henry. He checks their raiments for evidence of origin and intention. New he may be, but he is clearly trained for the job.

'You're from the Commonwealth,' he concludes.

'Yes,' says Henry.

'Royalty,' he mutters.

'What's coming in from the Tracollo?' Graham asks.

'Raw and shinies. A few Indies.' A line is forming behind the Raiders but the toll-taker is unhurried. 'Nothing an adult hasn't seen before. Those giant glass windows, though: those are going to be serious for building materials. A new village is going to rise out of those. What are you trading?'

'Knowledge,' answers Henry. 'Any books come in?'

The man snorts at the word 'books'. He's heard the word, but has no use for it. Literacy for his line died when there was nothing left to read, it never having occurred to his people to write something new.

Graham moves on. 'It should be busier. It should look like black birds on kill, but it doesn't.'

'May be too soon,' he says. 'Takes time for word to travel.'

'So be it,' Graham says, 'but this is thin. This is like any other day.'

'They say the Tracollo has released the Sickness into the air,' the man says.

'Well, you look fit as a fiddle, so . . . that can't be right.'

'What's a fiddle?'

Henry gives Graham a look.

'Who knows?' Graham tries to make Henry smile with some sleight of hand. 'Something at the peak of health.'

'I'm not that healthy.'

'At least you haven't lost your sense of humour.'

'If not the Sickness,' he added, not understanding Graham, 'it might be the new tribe. There are tents in the eastern cliffs before the Sands begin, a lot of them now. Largest colony I've ever seen outside your walls – four hundred and growing, they say. Those people don't smile. That might have something to do with it. But *quién sabe por qué sucede algo*,' he says.

'We don't speak that,' Henry says.

'It means . . . who knows why anything happens.'

'I took you for the north,' Graham says, 'not south.'

The man doesn't reply to that. He has one more question. He speaks low. 'Is it true that you have Big Electricity at the Commonwealth?'

At this Graham laughs. 'Oh yes,' he says, becoming serious again. He leans forward on his horse and whispers, 'We grab the lightning from the clouds when it rains. And we capture it in barrels.'

'Okay,' says the tall man.

'And later, we fill all the Gone World shinies with power and they talk to each other and come to life and reveal their secrets to us.'

'You can go on up.' He signals the Militia to let them pass, and preferably soon.

'And a cure for the Sickness.' Graham chuckles. 'We think it involves fruit.'

Henry spurs her horse onto the glass surface of The Crossing. The horse has been here before and understands it can walk across. Other animals, not so well trained or experienced, have been known to buck or refuse. There are stables for their use – the price for ignorance, as always, is high.

Their horses fall into step. A man with a wide broom cleans the bridge beside them. Children to their left are standing around a large pot where a man stirs smoking red nuts that

49

release an aroma that helps mask the horse manure and travel smells.

Henry shakes her head at him in judgement for his performance.

'You kill a rumour with sarcasm,' Graham says, 'not denial.'

'You killed it,' Henry says.

They don't ride far. Graham dismounts by a cluttered hut on his left, on the northern side of the bridge. The southeasterly sun lights it, making its drab colours more welcoming.

Three strong men are moving both Finds and Raw to a container beside the hut. They are sorting them, but their criteria is confusing. Outside the canvas door to the tent is a table, behind which sits a woman with a face lined like an old plum. She is short, with glassy eyes that are too pale for her dark skin. She is expressionless as Graham approaches.

'Good morning,' he says.

'Same to you,' she answers.

'You're new too.'

'I'm old,' she says.

'What have they pulled?'

'It's early. It's going to be weeks or more before they get to the bottom of it, assuming they don't come up with green skin and breath like death.' Her voice has gravel in it. Her teeth are bad but her skin is clear. 'So far there's a lot of Raw, usual stuff. Some shinies. Nothing that does anything, though; it's all a bunch of useless Deps. Go on in. First sale of the day is good luck.'

'The machines – they're inside?'

'Same price as the Raw now. They don't do nothing, like I said.'

'Why bother separating them out?'

'Habit.' She nods towards the three strong men. 'If I tell

50

them to stop separating I'll never get them to start again. You manage your affairs and I'll manage mine, handsome.'

Graham glances at Henry and steps into the dark of the storage shed.

THE FIND

Graham has been inside the room of corrugated steel metal before. Every few months, on a whim, he passes by the stalls that stockpile junk so that he can check through for possible spare parts. There is seldom much to find, even though there is plenty stacked into piles. Raw, even out here in the desert, is easy enough to come by. The challenge is finding what you're looking for.

The odds today are higher because there's more of it. The men have been hauling loads, leaving behind their scent. The room holds the heat and Graham quickly removes his jacket, scarf and hat before cracking his neck and stretching. There is a pile in front of him larger than he is tall. The light inside is poor, the bright glare from the doorway behind him putting the machines in his own shadow.

Graham wipes his face in preparation for the pain yet to come. The left side of the room is only too familiar. Unbeknownst to the shopkeeper, over the months and years he's been scratching small hatch-marks on the units he's already examined. So that's about fifty units he doesn't need to eviscerate.

Leaving, perhaps, another hundred still to go.

What might have been order when the men started to stack the new Finds is now a system of consolidated chaos. Shelves along the walls hold a variety of machines with buttons and knobs and keys, thin sheets of glass and tiny switches. There are sometimes words or letters beside, on top or underneath them. ON and OFF are common. Words of no discernible meaning like TREMBLE or BASS are painted white above controls. There are combinations of letters that have meant nothing to people for generations – EKG, or Highland HME109, QUINTON Q-STRESS, and AUX – COUPLING – FINE.

The rapid accumulation of new material has been hostile to the order of the shed. In only the one night and morning, the shelves have already been filled up and a large stack – a pyramid, really – has taken form in the middle of the tent.

Graham removes a small hand mirror from his jacket and reflects the light of the doorway onto the surfaces of the machines.

For more than ten minutes he searches for the words that Lilly once asked him to look for: BAND, MODE, TRANSCEIVER.

Nothing.

What he does come across is one that reads MOTOROLA.

He knew a girl named Motorola, from a smithing village. Nice name. A better week. He flips it over.

From his pouch he removes a folding tool that contains a series of heads which often match the bolts and screws on shinies. His tool says 'Leatherman' and it's one of his prize possessions. By keeping it well-lubricated with flower and herb oils and resisting the urge to sharpen it too often, he's found its head-shapes can open the vast majority of Gone World devices. Failing that, a rock usually does the trick.

This box has six screws that Alessandra – when she was five – called 'plus screws' on account of the shape. Graham used to tease her and insist they were X screws by rotating them, but Alessandra was insistent and would rotate them back, still arguing. One day, Alessandra removed one of her father's tools from the Leatherman and showed him how the shape was indeed arranged like a plus and not an X by virtue of its alignment to the hilt. By rotating the screw to match the tool she proved her point and Graham conceded his.

He then tickled her until she was blue.

Most screws are brittle and break when he rotates the heads, or else the screws are held fast in place by a red crust. In this case, the screws are strong and silver and do not break. With some insistence Graham is able to make them surrender their grip, allowing the tops to twist out into gleaming spiral spikes that he briefly admires before tossing them to the ground.

After wiping his nose, he eases off the plate and a cloud of fine dust floats into his face, which he blows away. The innards are beyond comprehension and the letters and numbers inside – although easy enough for the literate to read – do not otherwise convey any meaning.

In Weapons and Communications, Lilly has entire teams trying simply to find patterns in old tech in the hopes that an understanding will naturally evolve.

'Differentiate among things that are different,' she would often say. 'Before the Harrington Box, we never considered how much Knowledge might exist, how much we might be missing by not thinking widely, or how much we could still lose if we didn't pay attention to every category of importance. Once we found that children's game and considered the implications, everything changed. If nothing else, it's why we have our agenda now. We have things we want to learn and missions to learn them.'

To some extent this has worked. From as far back as he can remember, Lilly has been classifying shinies as *Indies* or *Deps* based on the first, global distinction: Indies – or *Independents* – are Gone World artefacts that do something independently: a knife that cuts; an axe that hacks; a glowstick that illuminates; the massive water-spun turbines below the Stadium that generate power. Lilly includes objects or machines that use electricity.

When he heard this thirty years ago, during his own apprenticeship with her, he asked the obvious question: *Independent of what?*

'Yes,' Lilly had said, liking his mind immediately, 'that's the question. Independent of what, or Dependent on what? Because I'm certain that most objects are dependent on something we can't see, hear, feel, or perhaps even imagine. But whatever it was, it was real and it permeated everything, and most Indies were eventually upgraded and replaced by Deps that – I have to suppose – worked better, when they worked at all.'

'I'm not really getting this,' Graham had said. They were at her work desk. They were always at her wide stainless steel and very cluttered work desk.

'Here's an example of a Dep.' She showed it to him: a beautiful hand-held object of opaque glass that gently curved to fit the hand. There was a sleek silver button on the side and nothing else.

'The Stadium, as you know, runs partly on Human Kinetic Power. So the more we bounce around on the Green and in the corridors, the more power we generate, which goes to the batteries, and when they are sufficiently charged, we get Big Electricity that we can use for any number of things: lighting, powering the pulse rifles, refrigeration, et cetera. This little

55

thing seems to have a similar system inside it, so when we shake it for a few seconds it comes to life. But it doesn't *do* anything.'

She shook it and after a moment the shape of an apple appeared against the black. It was a lovely thing, and completely useless.

'It never moves beyond here. Almost every object we find has a related problem. Even ninety per cent of the refrigerators won't operate without completing that mysterious connection; they all remain dormant things. Whatever once gave them purpose or instruction isn't here anymore.'

Lilly's theory – which she maintains today – is that the world shared a kind of 'spiderweb' which once connected all Deps together in an elaborate system, and the reason they do nothing now is because that system either can't be reached or no longer exists. Most of the things that people used to do with Indies, Lilly believes, they eventually started doing with Deps. 'Books were once on paper, but after 2046 we can't find any more new books. Pictures were once on paper and those stopped too, but we can't find out which year. Music must be out there someplace,' she reasons, 'because it would be odd for a civilisation to evolve to the point where it could fly to the stars but then rejected all music. Even Moishe's electronic piano in the music room can record itself.'

So far, the search for books, photographs and music has been a failure, with not a single large trove found since the Harrington Box, only a few scraps here and there.

The object in front of Graham in the shed looks like an Indie, and once he blows off the dust, everything inside looks rather fresh.

He removes a small leather-bound notebook from his inside pocket and checks Lilly's wish-list.

It's always something with her. All the Raiders and Traders are slaves to her shopping lists in some ways.

From his backpack Graham removes a grey cloth bundle held together with a purple ribbon and unwraps it. At its centre are nine small objects Lilly has told him to find. One is a tiny glass tube with steel tips on either end. With one hand he holds up the mirror to reflect the sunlight from a roof hole into the device he's molesting and with his other he runs his fingers over the illuminated surfaces looking for a match.

He finds one – or something akin – between two U-shaped clamps on the green board. With his folding blade snapped into position he gently eases the tube from its fasteners and releases it. With his dirty fingertips he holds the two pieces up to the light and compares them. The new one has a tiny filament inside, like a thread. The one Lilly gave him, however, is different; its thread has snapped and curled.

Electricity, Graham knows, travels on roads – usually roads of metal, but water works too, as do some other substances. The broken thread in the old tube must be like a fallen bridge, not allowing the electricity to complete its journey. As they will be unable to fix the bridge, the tube itself needs to be replaced.

Graham rewraps the broken piece and walks out with the new one in his palm.

Henry is standing beside her horse. The sun is stronger now and the heat is coming, shining down through the dirty glass road to the green valley below her feet. The tallest trees do not reach this far up. It is the only place on Earth where people can see the top of a living tree. One could marvel at such a sight for a lifetime.

In an effort to look busy as she scans the crowd for danger,

Henry holds up a dress recovered from the Tracollo. It is blue with purple and yellow flowers. It has no arms and falls to her knees. It is in excellent shape – it even smells good. Clothing Troves are rare in this region, but they are very common else-where and there is a robust trade. Finding something that's nice, that fits, that's clean and that flatters the figure is never easy, and it seems to be harder for women.

'For me or Alessandra?' she asks Graham when he emerges, sweaty and dusty from the shed.

'You're the same size,' says the husband and father with the same lack of interest as every other husband and father.

'That's not the point.'

Graham leaves the argument to her and approaches the shopkeeper again.

'Find anything?' she asks, uninterested.

Graham holds up the tube.

The woman looks from the object to Graham.

'We charge by weight, handsome.'

Graham places the tube in his satchel and removes a small desert flower that he hands to the woman. Despite herself, she smiles.

Henry pays for the dress by teaching the woman how to make a knot for joining two ropes of different diameters together. The woman is instructed to perform it three times, which she does diligently. Once the Knowledge is transferred they agree the debt is settled and their trade-bond strong.

Together, she and Graham collect their mounts and continue their ascent of The Crossing towards the Pavilion. They walk slowly, leading the horses.

'What's your Find?' she asks.

'Something Lilly's been after.'

'Important?'

'Small,' he says.

The surface of the road is undulating, and it is not as slick as glass. There is a grip to it even when slippery and the horses, once accustomed to the walk, are surefooted.

Above them are wisps of white clouds in a soft blue sky.

At the top, they cross the Pavilion on the southern fork and pass it without entering. Henry mounts her horse again to gain vantage, to try to better understand the sullen mood of those assembled, all of whom should be more full of wonder and curiosity and attention than they are.

Graham watches her surveying the crowd in fine detail. Occasionally she smiles and waves to make it look as though her viewing has another purpose.

Her face is a smile but her eyes are not. Graham knows she does not like what she sees.

He mounts too, and keeping the reins at the withers, he presses the horse with his right foot, bringing the horses together for a more intimate talk.

'What?' he asks.

'The shopkeeper you charmed back there,' Henry says.

'What of her?'

'There's a tribesman talking to her.'

'So what?'

'So she's not smiling any more.'

'My charm doesn't work this far out.'

'I've spotted four others like him here. They're asking about us.'

'Everyone's interested in us. We're Commonwealth.'

'You're not seeing,' she says to him. 'Two explosions and then the Tracollo – and now they've sent their people here to learn from the movement on The Crossing. The people here sense it – a shift is happening. A new wind,' she concludes. 'We need to get back.'

Graham looks now with fresh eyes and sees that she is right.

This is why she carries the long rifle and he fights with a knife.

They alight from The Crossing on its eastern side and turn for the narrow northern road that circles back through the forest beneath the bridge. Meeting the High Road, they leave the activity behind them and head west in the direction of the Stadium. It is well past high noon and for a time they press the horses to a trot to cover ground, not sure if they are being pursued.

Henry gestures towards one of the break-off paths, a protected route to the tunnels, and Graham nods consent.

The land drops here and the rocks are brittle and larger and scattered about for no obvious reason, as if left behind by duelling giants. At a familiar boulder they turn off the path and direct the horses down a dried rill to a plain, where they slow their pace and let the beasts breathe out their hurry.

Graham is fussing with his lance again and Henry looks at him to examine the progress he hasn't made.

'You're working yourself up,' she observes.

'I told Lilly three times these new harnesses weren't working.'

'She'll sort them.'

'When?'

'Next time.'

Graham tries to fix what the entire Weapons and Communications Division has been unable to fix and fails. He's annoyed. 'I don't understand it,' he mutters. 'She's our greatest engineer and this is a stick on a hook.'

'She likes you. That's why she talks your ear off whenever you're there. When her team adjusts it you won't come back to fight with her as often or listen to her stories about the old days.'

Graham eyes his wife. 'Lilly is seventy-one years old.'

'She looks good, though.'

They stop in the shadow of the AIRBUS tail when Graham's horse grows twitchy. He and Henry check the ground for snakes or other causes, but they find nothing.

'It's something,' Graham concludes on instinct alone.

They share a litre of water before continuing. They are an hour out from the Stadium's first defences.

A shiver runs through the horses.

The sun is on its western arc. The road to The Crossing in the Gone World is far behind them. The horses know this route, although it is unmarked. By night, the Order will cover the trail and leave false markings to hide the Stadium's concealed entrances.

For now, remaining watchful, they keep moving. Silence is Protocol but Henry is thinking about Alessandra and wants to discuss their daughter before the return. She knows Alessandra is readying herself for a Choosing Walk. Graham took his when he was seventeen and returned to the Commonwealth within a year. Alessandra is still expecting to go, but for Henry, the Tracollo changes the calculation. Stadium-born Graham is wedded to the tradition. Henry, however, is Roamer-born and is not. She knows she must approach the topic gently:

'Benedicta,' Henrietta says, 'told me she brought in a Trove of three books two weeks ago. It's been keeping the Scribes busy. Lian actually smiled, I'm told.'

'Where had she been?'

'With the traders on the Golden Sea up north. Word coming down is that there are still Finds on the big waters to the northwest. They've been having luck with floaters and coastal drifters. The thinking is that containers get dislodged from the northern ice and they take long rides on the currents – that's when some come ashore.'

'Hmm,' says Graham, scanning the land for unwanted company. 'And there were books?'

'Picture books with hard covers. One of the books was about wine. Have you heard of that?'

He shakes his head.

'It's a dizzy drink made from grapes.'

'Oh,' Graham says, 'you mean *vin*.' He smiles at the memory. 'Thirty years ago there was a colony to the north. They spoke a language called *Français*. They called it *vin*. The kids would sneak into the storage rooms and steal the grape juice before the adults ruined it. They were nice people,' he says, 'but they hated speaking our language.'

'They didn't make it?'

'No. There's still an Abbey in the forest, though, past Sea Glass Lake, maybe another four days in. Almost no one knows about it and I haven't told many people back home. They're quiet folk with good humour. I knew a guy named Francis – I haven't seen him since those days. But no, that colony is gone.'

'This was during your Choosing Walk?'

'Yes.'

Henry knows this. She remembers his stories better than he does.

'I don't like the idea of Alessandra on a Choosing Walk, not these days,' she starts, arriving at the topic. 'We're not supposed to know this, but two Runners have gone missing.'

Graham says nothing.

'It's not a time for a Choosing Walk. This made sense back in the days when the Stadium was small and the world out here was empty, back when people needed to make a real choice to stay or go. It's a dated ritual now – especially for the young.'

'I don't think it is,' Graham says. 'The Commonwealth means more once you've chosen it. Just being born into something doesn't make it a choice. You were born a Roamer and you chose the Commonwealth. Now you're the best shooter and a decorated Raider. That matters.'

'Alessandra shouldn't be wandering the hardpan wondering where she belongs. She belongs at home. Exploring is a youthful conceit and I understand it, but she's ridden with us since she was five. She's seen more of this world than General Winters.'

'Alessandra may have something else in mind instead of a Choosing Walk. I'm not supposed to tell you.'

'You're not supposed to tell me what?'

There is a very distant bark of a dog. Henry's horse shakes its head.

Henry unhooks the leather stay holding her rifle in place.

Graham places the carbine around his shoulder and chambers a round. It is beyond instinct now.

'Definitely something,' he says.

ALAN FARMER

A lone figure on horseback charges across the untamed desert with the speed of a peregrine in stoop. He leans forward in the stirrups, whipping his horse's flanks with the reins. His lance is fastened tight to the left of his saddle and he carries no rifle, only an energy pistol in an ill-fitting holster across his chest that slaps against him to the beat of the stride. A hundred metres behind him and closing the gap are a dozen war dogs, their right sides painted blood-red, their left sides as yellow as an autumn leaf.

The man has seen this before. They belong to the Keepers; he once saw three bandits devoured by them. The dogs are fearless and experienced in downing a rider, and their trainers – Hunters – cannot be far behind. There is no fighting the dogs on account of their speed, their numbers and their indifference to deaths in their pack. They do not retreat if the battle is lost. Those who try, he believes, are killed to keep the line strong.

He whips the horse again and it keeps its speed up.

The man is tall. His skin has a pinkish tint that turns red when it burns from the sun. His hair is the colour of dry sand. His dark eyes squint into the wind as they tear.

When the dogs close to fifty metres he draws the pistol. He is a Raider for the Commonwealth, but he is no marksman. He twists, bouncing in his saddle, for the proper angle. He has no sure platform, no certainty in his shot – he is an archer on the sea taking aim at a bird. He will miss and he knows it.

With his thumb he presses the selector, then a second time for a scattering shot. When the dogs are clustered together enough, he fires.

An explosion of blue light draws out to a cone as quick as Ancient bullets. Three of them disappear in one animal, which tumbles to the earth, dead, and skids to a stop as the remaining pack grows even more ravenous in pursuit. The rider shoots twice more and misses both times. The pistol is spent.

He returns it to his holster, reaches down to the right side of the horse and removes a cloth bag. It is filled and folded like a parachute. The dogs are closer now. They are trained to bring a horse to a stop, to pull a rider to the ground, to rip that rider apart. He will not die by these beasts, whatever happens. There is another way.

Two dogs have broken off and are running beside him now on the path, while those in pursuit are forming a tight pack. He hurls the small sack behind him and faithful to Lilly's design, it opens in the wind, dropping dozens of sharpened jacks onto the ground.

One dog takes a wrong step, its paw immediately punctured, and falls back, but it is not enough.

The rider pulls his scarf across his mouth, reaches down and removes a canister from his bag. He pulls the pin and lowers his arm, trailing a poisonous green dust.

Two more dogs drop their chase and, falling to the ground, lie there writhing and scratching at their eyes and snouts,

65

trying to get out whatever is already inside them. He throws the empty can at one of the dogs because he wants to.

The route becomes more complex as he twists and turns through large rocks and around brush and trees. He is not yet following a prescribed route maintained by the Order but is fighting to reach one, which will have snares and supports.

The dogs are more agile than his laden horse. Seeing they are gaining ground, he cuts loose his sleeping dome, his bedding and food – anything that might gain them a little extra speed. He has been a Raider for many years and knows this land. He is charging towards the boundary line of the Commonwealth's immediate domain. If he can make it, there will be support and defence. If not, he is on his own.

Behind him, beyond this first wave of dogs, he can hear the barking of a second pack, and behind them, as sure as the moon chases the sun, are the Hunters.

Ground and distance and time are his only allies and they are fast abandoning him.

Henrietta can finally see the mêlée through her scope. She has taken a prone position in the shadow of a rock and has magnified her sight to its greatest power. The rider is darting through the scree, hustling along off-route and trailing Lilly's countermeasures, but the second wave of dogs is in view from her angle. His efforts will not be enough to save him.

'That's Alan Farmer,' she says.

'It can't be him. He went south – he's been gone for months.'

'I'm looking right at him.'

Alan had Attested to their marriage vows. He was to care for Alessandra if both Henry and Graham fell.

'He's not going to make it,' Graham says. 'Not to the boundary.'

66

He is two kilometres away, if he were a bird, but weaving through the boulders, with the dogs at his heels, it is longer.

'We can help him,' she says, extending her bipod from the rifle stock. 'Set position. Light a flare. He'll see it and draw them towards us. I can clear the road. The closer they get, the easier the shots.'

'And once you do that and he passes us, the second wave will be on us and then the Hunters. You have five bullets in the gun. It won't be enough for both waves,' Graham says. 'We will not survive that. And we're carrying.'

Henry lowers her eyes from the scope. She knows her husband is right. She has one breath remaining before she has to say it aloud and she holds it as long as she can.

'He deserves to know why,' Henry says.

She swings into the saddle and, pulling taut the reins, yanks the horse into position. She spurs forward and together with Graham they ride for the higher ground on Yellow Ridge. The ascent is steep but with the sound of the dogs in their ears, the horses are eager for action and they rally for the climb.

Yellow Ridge forms a natural high wall half a mile long at the far end of the Stadium's patrolled domain. From there, the view is commanding in all directions: the Gone World's towers, The Crossing, the cliffs to the east, the Empty Quarter, the Stadium – Alan Farmer.

When she is certain that Alan can see them, she says to Graham, 'Fly the colours. Let him know.'

Graham removes the lance and with a gesture made fluid by repetition he flicks six small knobs on the pole and from it emerge, one below the next, six coloured triangles of blue, brown, green, pink, orange and yellow. From a pocket on the saddle he removes a small black stick that he strikes against his rifle; it bursts into light, glowing like a fallen star. He affixes it to the top of his lance and hoists it tall into the air with purpose and clarity: a sign to the valley below.

For Alan Farmer it becomes an understanding of why he is about to die.

Through his frozen tears, Alan Farmer sees his two oldest friends in the distance. Their poise and their proximity to one another reminds him that they are the only married couple in the history of the Commonwealth to both be Raiders. She is holding a rifle and he a glowing lance with six flags extended. It doesn't need the flare atop to draw his attention; the full flags do that. They are too far away to help and he knows it. And displaying the flags like that means that they know it too.

They look to him like the ancient gods everyone learned about from the Edward Gibbon book Lilly daughter-of-Rachael recovered against all odds from the Harrington Box half a century ago: gods who would stand on Mount Olympus and watch the fate of mortals from high above, with pity, but also with purpose.

Alan Farmer, awake to the truth, resigns himself to his fate and chooses to die fighting. He pulls up his horse, draws a short sword and hacks at the dogs. His last act will be to make time for Henrietta and Graham Wayworth to cross back into the Commonwealth's domain and protect the Knowledge they carry.

Henry watches Alan Farmer kill four dogs with his blade before a Hunter's bullet strikes him in the head. Every muscle falls and limp he slips from the saddle, sword still in hand as the dogs set to, tearing him apart.

'We have to go *now*, Henrietta!' yells Graham, not wanting to waste the time Alan has bought them.

Henry pulls her horse around and spurs it forward into a full gallop. Together they pound along the path in the direction of the Stadium, the second wave of dogs now over the far ridge and coming towards them as Graham had forewarned.

'Take point,' Henry calls out. 'We're close to the switch. You flip it and that'll give us the time we need.'

'To do what?' he asks, but she is gone.

Graham kicks his own ride into a hard gallop, riding upright, his head as level as a still lake. He angles his lance forward now, the flags slapping the stick in the heavy wind, and rotates the pole so that its small jutte arm faces outwards, ready to make the catch.

'Don't miss,' his wife yells to him from behind and so as not to lose focus, he tries to pretend he didn't hear her.

In his decades as a Raider Graham has thrown the switch twice. In practise, on the Green, he has made the catch a thousand times or more. His fellow Raiders would set up gauntlets on stadium grounds and the spectators would pour sand and dust, hurl old food and bang drums in odd rhythms to confound and unbalance the challengers, who had to fight the distractions and ensure speed and precision if they were to successfully trip the levers to activate the mechanisms that would let Lilly's deadly device halt their pursuing enemy.

But sport and combat are not the same. They train hard so war will be easy, but there is no pretending that the fake can ever replace the real.

Ahead on his left is the single ashen pole he has been looking for. It's hardened by tricks of fire and lacquered against the elements with pitch and tar. The pounding of the hooves is rhythmic. He finds the melody and levels the lance.

'Stay close,' he yells to her, knowing it is the only thing on her mind.

The dogs are close too. He hears the crack of Henry's rifle, followed by the squeals of a dying hound. His heart is pounding and it shouldn't be. He should be experienced enough now to stay calm in such moments. His family really is too emotional.

Graham flashes a look to check Henry's distance.

Two lengths.

One beat.

Close enough.

He knows the character of this horse across flat earth, knows how to measure distance as time.

He counts down from five.

At the mark he slams his lance into the weathered switch and feels the jolt through his arm and shoulder and back. The stick is cast forward and cracks to the earth in front of him, releasing a spring below ground and causing the earth behind them to release a hundred spikes in the direction of the dogs, each a metre long and – in a moment – a metre deep.

Six dogs are impaled on the weapon of Lilly's own ruthless design. The next are going too fast to stop and they leap over the front spikes to spear their soft underbellies on the next. Those of the second wave approaching the spikes are leaderless. They remain at the barrier, whimpering and barking.

Graham slows to a canter, waiting for Henry to catch up, but instead she dismounts quickly, landing on the ground in a crouch.

'What are you doing?'

Not answering him she scampers up a low rise on this side of the spikes and flicks open the bipod built into the stock of her rifle.

'They're out of range, Henry. The rifle's a hundred years older than the scope. Just because you can see—'

'I know what it can do,' she says quietly enough to silence her husband.

She sites them through the scope at nine hundred metres: the Hunters. These *Keepers*. Four of them – side by side – their robes not moving and hanging low.

There is no wind.

Henry Wayworth selects the figure second from the right for no particular reason, aims for the centre of mass, waits for the weaker of her two heartbeats to finish and squeezes the trigger.

There is a crack, a pause and a report from the answering rocks. The figure falls from his horse.

Graham watches. He cannot see the men from here, but he can see the shape slither off the horse and become dust. He looks to his wife. On her brow there is a twitch, a tiny crinkle along her scope-eye. He knows she is satisfied.

As Henry takes aim again, the three riders fall back, leaving the body. There is a distant whistle and the remaining dogs now retreat, returning to their masters.

Henrietta looks at Graham and sees herself in his gaze. 'What?' she asks.

'I don't know,' he says. 'Something.'

THE COMMONWEALTH

Alessandra is no stranger to the long absences of her parents. Her earliest Attested memory (by her father) is a moment when she was two years old and was brought to the top of the Stadium walls to sit with a Spotter and watch the arrival of her parents on horseback across the Flats. In one way it was an unremarkable image: two riders, side by side, crossing open terrain under an iron sky. But the meaning of that image changed for her over the years. It was only later that she learned that no one else's parents were both Raiders. No one else's parents formed a scouting team. No other scouting teams had two Raiders of such equal and high rank at the Commonwealth. Her parents, she learned, were special: not only because each was special, but because they were special *together*.

This, for Alessandra, was no surprise at all. *Obviously* her parents were special.

The hunger to be like them grew in her belly like a seed under the warm sun of admiration she saw from all the people. Her parents were smart and strong and brave and – she would also come to learn – rather attractive. Her mother's beauty emerged from her like a light. It wasn't the shape of her so much as the way she moved: a grace, a poise, a confidence. People watched her because they had to.

Her father had a charm, an easy way with people, a strong ear for listening and a soft way with words and humour. He was not strong in the way of the biggest soldiers or the blacksmiths or the heavy traders, but he was dexterous and surefooted and a brilliant rider; not the very best in the Stadium for speed and fighting, but one of the most experienced. Like her mother, Alessandra's father had seen every kind of terrain, weather, obstacle or danger. Being fast, he liked to say, means nothing for a man riding in the wrong direction.

Until she was five, the Stadium was her entire world, and it was enough. More than enough. At the centre of the Stadium was the Green, which for her was a world in itself. Soldiers practised there. The Ekklesia voted there. The Runners learned their routes; the Phalanx their formations; the Archers their instructions. At every full moon there was a party and a fire blazed in an enormous metal basin raised on a tripod. There was music and dancing and from the time she was ten, Moishe son-of-Tikvah played the electric piano from the centre of a half-shell stage made from the fuselage of a Gone World aircraft. The sound projected outwards and filled the night with melodies that parents had passed down to children through the ages and that Moishe turned into music.

Around the Green were the stands. There were once seats there, her mother once told her, but aside from those at the highest levels used by Spotters, they had been removed ages ago and their parts used for Raw, restitched or smelted, banged into new shapes or repurposed into something useful. They were long gone by the time she was five. Graham said that when his own parents were young almost everyone was forced to wear the fabrics from the seat cushions. 'They were awful and itchy,' her mother said, 'but they lasted for ever because the fabrics were cursed. When the trade routes intensified after Lilly found the Harrington Box, the arriving clothes were much, much better. The Gone World had vanished so quickly, and so few people remained, that there has always been enough clothing. The trick was finding it and trading it. They didn't have robust trade routes back then, so . . . it was seat fabrics.'

The Stadium's structure was filled with hundreds of rooms. Many on the second and third levels were now homes, while those above were for work. The ones underground were off-limits to those without business there but Alessandra knew what was down there because her parents told her things that other parents did not. The hydroponic farm with the constant electric lights was beneath them; the Weapons and Communications centres for research, testing and development; the storage rooms and stockpiles; the last of the Gone World fertilisers and seeds; the stables for the horses and some of the animal farming along or beneath the northern sections.

Above it all was the Snake Tower: wide at the bottom, it tapered towards the top where it met the glass viewing stand where the High Command kept watch over the flats in front of the main gates and the hard-scrabble land flanking it to the north and south. Only the cliffs and the waterfall and the river were out of sight from the tower.

Alessandra did not stay five. As she grew in stature she grew in ambition too. 'One day,' she thought to herself, 'I'll be elected to the High Command, or else I'll rise through the ranks of the military to General and sit there without needing a vote.' Other times – before she grew impatient and adventurous – she would imagine herself Chief of the Archive with Scribes and Evaluators working for her; Runners under her command and the secrets of the off-site Archives tucked away deep into her mind. Yes, there was also the third pillar of the community, the Ekklesia, with its Mayor and the daily runnings of the harvests and the waters, the turbines and the solar cells, the traders and market, the non-military education of the youth and the Attestation of all births and marriages and deaths and so on. But that was a bore. When Alessandra had turned sixteen the previous year and come of age to take a position supporting the Commonwealth, it became clear to her what she really wanted: to someday become Master of the Order of Silence.

No, the Order could cast no votes or tell any secrets, but they were the ones who knew *everything*. The Master of the Order was the spider at the centre of the web; the one who whispered in every ear and knew the secrets of all three pillars: the only one who saw it all.

That's what she really wanted. And being the only child in the Commonwealth whose parents were *both* senior Raiders? Whose mother had been born a Roamer and had only come to the Commonwealth as a teenager with her rifle slung over her shoulder? Whose father was both a ranking Soldier *and* a former Scribe who specialised in nature and science and was a close personal friend of Chief Lilly, daughter-of-Rachael?

Alessandra drew a picture in the sand with a stick once to imagine how the Order was the seeing-eye at the secret centre of the Commonwealth; there in the middle of the triangle made of the Ekklesia, the Archive and the Military.

Yeah. My chances are good.

According to a Spotter named Calvin, both Henry and Graham Wayworth have been seen approaching The Stadium with a full Dragoon escort.

Running across the Green now, Alessandra dodges Archers starting to take formation for some reason and ducks into the shadows of the East Gate, through the doors to the Ring Road inside the structure – now illuminated by a nearly full moon through the glass ceiling – and to the brass plaque by the Inner Walls, which is as close as she can get to the entrance.

'How close are they?' she asks one of the engineers standing by the receiving table.

The girl is only a few years older than Alessandra. She vaguely recalls her name is Clover. She might be wrong, though.

'Close,' said Clover.

Alessandra taps her right foot.

The giant portal here does not open to the outside world but instead leads to an ante-chamber with a locking system designed by Lilly years ago. The inner doors can't open until the outer door is closed. There is room for exactly one Phalanx of ten-by-ten men and women at a time to leave or re-enter. Rumour was that Lilly had also designed an override mechanism because 'she doesn't like to box herself in' and that General Winters could order it, but no one knew for certain. Rumours were popular with Alessandra's crowd.

'Close' feels very far away.

The first time she left the Stadium was when she was five. She still remembers that feeling now: of entering a world without walls.

At seventeen now and looking back, she might have viewed it the other way around: as having *left* a world *with* walls, but that wasn't how it had felt. It hadn't felt like an escape because the Stadium was never a prison. For that reason, the doors were not an exit but an entrance – and outside was the *everything*.

In the midst of it, on her own horse – her legs spread wide just to stay on top of it – the world was vast and expansive and unbounded. When she was little, her father would toss her into the air and she would feel the tickle in her stomach as she soared upwards. That wasn't what she loved most, though.

It was the moment of suspension: the moment when she was free of all weight and all constraints, taller than the tallest man, lighter than the smallest bird.

A breath of pure existence.

This was her favourite feeling. Her friends – especially her girl-friends – talked all the time about falling in love. Alessandra had never been in love (not really – she'd kissed a few boys, but that was only the hunger mixed with curiosity and a salty dash of boredom). If love was really something special, it was going to have to be better than flying. It would have to be better than looking back at the perfect whites and glass surfaces and steel struts of the Stadium as the horse took to a trot, leaving it all behind.

Love would have to be better than sneaking out of the Stadium on dark nights to explore the Gone World with her friends in the Urban Explorers.

Love was going to have to be pretty damn great.

Until it proved itself? No interest.

'When you say "close",' Alessandra says to Clover, 'do you mean close enough that I should be standing here like an idiot waiting for them, or close as in . . . probably sometime today?'

'I really don't know, Alessandra. I'm not in the Snake Tower. I'm standing here next to you.'

When she was five and she finally did go out to see the tail of the AIRBUS extending into the sky and visit the perfect arch of The Crossing over the river of trees below, she did return to the Stadium later. She must have done – she's here now. But it's funny that she can't remember that. It's almost as though she left a piece of herself behind out there and ever since, has been trying to re-unite with it.

Henry and Graham are close.

They trot their horses to the edge of the Flats where six members of the Dragoons have joined them and are now accompanying them to the gate: an honour escort, one for each flag they fly.

From the outside, the Stadium is still. There are no guards, no traders, no movement. General Winters has locked it down. Though the glass of the Snake Tower is tinted and dark, both Henry and Graham know they are being watched on entry. No one under twenty-five years old has any memory of Raiders returning with six flags unfurled. It is a sight and an accomplishment – and one that holds absolutely no interest or joy for either of them; not after watching Alan's death.

Henry and Graham dismount and lead the horses between the widening gap between the massive portals that open outwards and soon close, enveloping them in the safety of the Stadium's defences.

When the ante-chamber portals open, Alessandra jogs to her mother first. They touch each other's faces as Henry's mount shakes off the battle. It is clear to Alessandra from the sheen of their coats and the quivering of their muscles that the horses have seen action in the last few hours. That means her parents have as well.

'What happened?' Alessandra asks her father, who hands the reins to a stable hand but doesn't send him off quite yet.

'A lot,' he says, dusting off the Gone World from his clothes as though it were possible.

Without her noticing, Alessandra runs her thumb across the muzzle of her mother's rifle and finds the black powder of a recent shot.

*

Around them, the Stadium is whirling with activity and talk. The Tracollo was seen by everyone and Henry and Graham are the first to return to the Stadium since it happened. The excitement is palpable.

Graham unhooks his carbine from his saddle and puts it on the engineer's table where Henry is now placing her Remington, then waves off the stable hand.

The Engineers are staring at Graham's lance.

'Snap out of it, kids. We've had a day already,' he says, removing his gloves and tossing them into his sack.

The older of the two – a young man named Sorel – speaks as though to the lance: 'You are requested in the Central Archive,' he says.

'We know the drill,' Graham says.

'No, Commander, immediately.'

Immediately?

'Says who?'

'Chief Archivist Lian,' says the Engineer.

'Well. That puts the flame out, doesn't it?' Graham says quietly to Henry.

Henry isn't listening; she has matters of her own to address. 'You're new to this, right?' she says to Clover, who is now receiving her weapon. 'I remember you from hydroponics.'

'Yes, Commander. I'm with the Quartermaster now.'

'Let me answer your unspoken questions. This is a Remington 700 M24 SWS. It could be two hundred, three hundred, maybe even four hundred years old – we have no idea. No, we don't know what those words or numbers mean, and no, there are no others like it, although surely, at some point, there were many. It was discovered by my grandfather seventy years ago in a heavy sealed black box in a mountain cave under a pile of bones. It was used by him, then by my father. When he died, it became mine. It is the most precise long-distance shooter anyone alive has ever seen, by far. That includes the pulse weapons, which have no meaningful range. The Quartermaster knows this gun and has the cleaning kit. I fired it today. I want him to clean it,' she says, holding it up, 'thoroughly and gently. I want it treated like it's the last rifle of its kind on Earth.'

Clover looks timid before the challenge and therefore nothing like Alessandra, who from the youngest age feared nothing. It was not a trait either Henry or Graham encouraged, but it was nothing they were able to break.

'It *is* the last rifle of its kind on Earth,' said Clover.

'Now you're getting it,' Henry says. 'Off you go.'

Graham had wanted to bring Henry home right after the Tracollo. It had been a sight, to be sure, watching that plume blot out the night sky. Returning, though, had looked to be the wiser course, whereas following Henry's thoughts had seemed – in that moment, at least – the better one. Had they come back then, however, it was possible that the Tribesmen would never have followed them to The Crossing, and perhaps they would not have stumbled on Alan. Perhaps he would still be alive.

And what did they accomplish?

He slips his hands into his pockets and feels the cloth with the tiny tube wrapped in it.

Our one and only prize.

'Dad?' Alessandra says, shaking him back to the present.

'What?'

'Are you going to tell me what happened?'

Graham is honestly not sure.

Three Youth Platoons are in training around them. The youngest – the *tirones*, or basic trainees, aged nine to twelve – are standing in formation and taking instruction on core skills.

Three of them are wearing a red cross, the ancient symbol of health. Their tunics are painted in horse blood. If they are allowed to wear the cross it means they have already been tested for fear and been found steadfast and level.

His daughter used to wear that tunic when she was smaller.

'There was a Tracollo,' he says, hands on his hips, not sure what he has the energy to explain. He wants to bath and shave and put on clean clothes; to remove the road and the rough from his body and hair, ears and eyes. Once he is sorted and centred, he will gratefully spend as much time with his daughter as she needs to understand what has just happened out there. For now, though, his mind is still beyond the walls and he is being summoned to a Sharing that he is in neither the mood nor the spirit to attend.

'Is that all?' Alessandra asks. 'Shouldn't that be exciting?'

'There's more.'

'You were gone for two weeks. The Aladdin Tower has . . . vanished into the earth . . . and you came back with full flags and a foul mood. Mum also fired her rifle.'

'Yes.'

'At what?'

There is a second Platoon training now: the *paidiskoi*. The twelve- to fifteen-year-olds are grappling today. Most are bloodied. They think they are being taught to fight, but in fact the lesson is in the silent suffering of pain. For the Raider, for the Scout, for the Messenger, for the Soldier, endurance and countenance are paramount. The weak or timid are not sorted out from the strong; instead, they are teamed with them so they can become influenced. In war, no one can sit anything out. Alessandra had been near the top of her class. He'd hated seeing her bloodied when she came home at night, but the training only encouraged her.

This was different, though. She'd known Alan since she was born.

The Time Keepers were bringing out oils for the fires. Soon they would be lit and the crier would announce the hour.

Big Electricity? Graham had wanted to answer the toll-taker at The Crossing. *We have more electricity than you could possibly imagine: enough to light a Gone World tower. Enough to turn night into day and make the Stadium glow like a fallen moon. But we light fires with citrus oils and alcohols to pretend we are weak. And so the influence of The Few remains and we choose secrecy and silence and lies over power and truth.*

It is no wonder to Graham that Lilly was removed from the High Command and censured to be merely a station Chief. She was too outspoken, too certain. Too influential.

'Where are you supposed to be?' he asks her. 'Aren't you supposed to be over there?' he asked, pointing at the oldest training group, the would-be Runners, Spotters and Messengers.

'I'm with Lilly this session, Dad. I'm an apprentice now – I have been since the spot opened two months ago. You know this.'

'Right,' he says, his mind a cloud. 'Lilly.'

He reaches into his jacket and withdraws the cloth with the new glass tube and the old one. He hands it to Alessandra. 'Bring this to her. It's something she asked for.'

'What is it?'

'I don't know, something from her list. It might have come from the Tracollo – it came from The Crossing, anyway.'

'Dad,' she tried again, sliding the cloth package into her pocket and trying to get her father to focus. 'What *happened*?'

'The tower was knocked down from the inside using some kind of explosives. We don't know why, but we suspect it was the Keepers. We visited The Crossing in the morning to listen and learn. We were followed after we descended, and somehow or other the Keepers caught up to Alan Farmer rather than us. He was coming back this way at the same time. He didn't make it.'

'He . . . *what?*'

'Alan's dead. We'll send a team out to recover his body in the morning. I'm sorry I can't be more kind about this now. I've been summoned and my mind isn't clear. Go to Lilly. Perform your duties – and don't forget to give her the shiny. We'll meet in the evening, all of us, your mother too. We'll talk more after a rest, after I'm clean and I've had food and water.'

Graham made three strides before turning back and said, almost as an afterthought, 'It's good to see you.'

Alessandra stood on the Green, shocked by the news that a man who was effectively her uncle is now dead, killed by the new tribe in the hills. Another part of her, however, is angry, and has no intention of meeting her absent parents for dinner. If they can be gone for two weeks and ignore her like this on her return, they can wait a little longer for her company.

That is when she sees Naomi.

Naomi is the driving force behind the Urban Explorers these days. The group has been around since the first days of the Adam Map, when Lilly's own Tracollo went down. The High Command have been trying to stop the teenagers from sneaking out at night and exploring the Gone World, but there have always been too many tunnels, too many tiny breaks in the structures to keep people from slipping away. As magnificent as it is, the Stadium is hundreds of years old, not the flawless jewel it pretends to be.

'I heard,' said Naomi.

She was dressed in her Runner's gear: tight leather trousers with padding in the hips and protection in the knees, with a close-fitting black leather jacket to help her become one with the shadows as well as protecting her on slides and falls.

'Are we going?' Alessandra asks.

'No,' said Naomi.

'No. The most interesting thing to happen in half a century and . . . *no*?'

'Winters is going to lock everything down.'

'So what?' We can get out—'

'The problem has never been getting out, Alessandra. The problem is getting back in again without being shot. We've got Spotters, snipers, patrols, sealed tunnels. We can't do it.'

'For how long?'

Naomi shook her head.

Henry and Graham Wayworth enter the Central Archive. The enormous room is three levels down on the western wall, with natural lighting from tall, narrow windows. Absent any proof, it is the held opinion that awards were once presented here. The room provokes a sense of occasion.

Now, its walls are covered in books and boxes, artefacts and art. There are tables for study and for the Scribes and Evaluators. In the middle of the room is the largest table; the Raiders seat themselves here to await the Chief Evaluators.

'Do you think they know about Alan?' Henry asks.

'If they do, I plan on behaving very badly,' Graham says.

'They'll look to me to stop you,' Henry retorts.

'They don't know you as well as I do.'

'No. They don't.'

At the centre of the table is the symbol of the Commonwealth, fashioned from Lilly's first pull from the box: a circle divided into six symmetrical triangles, each one representing a division of Knowledge. Graham's pole flags have been placed on the Evaluators' side of the table in front of their respective chairs, waiting for their occupants.

In the four corners of the room are the customary Guards from the Order of Silence, draped in ornamental cloth. They are as still as statues, witnesses to the exchange. They have taken vows of secrecy and the penalty is ostracism or death.

Graham ignores them, which is easy to do as they don't move or speak, and places his feet on the stone table.

'There's a start,' says his wife.

'I haven't bathed, I haven't eaten, Alan's dead. You killed somebody. I handled things badly with Alessandra. And I really need to—'

The six Evaluators walk into the room from their ante-chamber.

Graham removes his feet from the table and stands with Henry.

Chief Lian is short. She may be over sixty but her thick hair is still black. Her eyes taper at the sides more than most. She pronounces words too well. She wears the green robes of the Chief Evaluator for Science and Nature and she is also wearing the iron seal of the Commonwealth around her neck, denoting her role as Chief Archivist – the position Lilly invented and held until she was ousted for deciding, after five years of playing with the library's structure, that the system found in the game was all wrong and they needed to re-build everything from the ground up.

'One hundred and twelve years ago to our counting,' Lian recites, 'the Stadium was discovered by the wandering Few. Finding fresh water and power, high walls and no people, they entered the Stadium without resistance. With wisdom and hard work, they reinforced the walls, organised themselves and managed their relationships, forming the foundation for—'

'Alan Farmer is dead,' Graham blurts out.

Lian turns to him. 'We know.'

'Why are we here?'

'We'll be brief,' Lian says. 'The High Command insisted you join a Sharing immediately.'

Henry raised a finger. 'The High Command asked us to come here, not to go there?'

'Yes,' says Lian.

'Why?'

'I didn't ask.'

'You're the Archive's representative on the High Command—'

'And so the judgement was mine to make. May we continue, Commander?'

'This speech is falling on the informed,' Graham says.

'It is our way, Commander. We recite to remember, not to learn. Afterwards . . . we'll be brief.'

'Let me help,' says Graham, more weary than defiant. 'I remember the destruction of the Gone World as though I was there. I remember the warring times that followed and the songs that warn us of the choices that led to it. I remember the first Tracollo, and how Lilly rescued the box from Cardo at the Pavilion and outsmarted everyone by opening it. I remember finding the books and photographs and a child's board game that Colonel Harrington, knowing that the end of the world was coming, packed away. I remember that it was Lilly's idea – as a teenager – to use the categories of *Trivial Pursuit* to structure our libraries and research agendas that we've continued to support by Spade, Raid or Trade.

'I remember too,' Graham went on, 'that Lilly was removed from her role as Archive Chief when she suggested that the categories and tokens weren't good enough and we needed to think of Knowledge in a new way – that maybe a children's game was a nice place to start but a bad place to end. And I can't help but think – on this day of days – that if we had listened to her, Alan might still be alive because Henry and I would have made a number of different decisions, given that the flags we flew all overlap and, frankly, don't matter. So forgive me for not wanting to hear the story again as it makes me extremely angry.'

'No,' Lian says with controlled voice, 'the world is not only these categories. All systems are imperfect. But the Game and its colours did something more important than give us boxes for new finds. They served – and continue to serve – to remind us of how much there is to know and that we must seek it rather than merely stumble upon it. Do you think it's a fluke, Commander, that we're the only colony which is fully literate? The only one with an Archive? The only one with a thriving and secure population, excellent health, a powerful military and a busy trade? The fact is, Commander, if we weren't using these categories we would be using others. Your job would have been the same, whatever flags you were flying. You should know that.'

Graham does not reply.

'General Winters is locking down the Stadium,' Lian announces, 'and putting the Archers on alert. She is sealing off the tunnels until we have better assessed the threats from the Keepers. While we are here, let's take inventory on what you collected out there. We'll begin with my own field of Science and Nature.' She reaches forward, places three fingers on the green flag and slides it onto the seal in the table covering the space. 'Share.'

Graham reaches down into his brown canvas pouch and

removes a bundle of cloth that he rests gently into the table. The evaluators all crane forward to see better.

Undramatically – because Graham is no master at the stone face – he whips off the layers of cloth to reveal . . . a device.

From the perspective of the evaluators and the Chief, it is round and red, set on tiny black pegs, and has two yellow bells on top with an arching steel handle connecting them.

'Before I turn it around, I remind you to see it for what it can do, not for what it is.'

Graham rotated it to face the evaluators.

It was Chief Lian who read out loud the words printed on the clock's face: 'Mickey Mouse?' she said, incredulously.

'Yes,' said Graham, 'and if you look closely at the bottom it also reads, "Walt Disney Production" – we don't know what that means, though it does sound like a workshop and the first is perhaps a name. Below it says, "U.S.A." which is the United States of America, which is where we think we are. Or what this place used to be, at any rate. If so, it's come quite far through time, if not distance.'

'I see,' said Lian, sitting back.

'It's a working clock, Chief, and while I don't know how accurate it is, I'm sure Lilly can find out by testing against the water-drop method, the sun dial and perhaps her star charts. We have a full moon – or almost – and she has excellent records of when the moon passes in front of various stars at this time of year.'

Lian hands the floor over to a kindly man a little older than Graham with naturally dark skin, eyes of hazel-green and a very short grey beard. He cuts an authoritative stance in his purple sash. He smiles at Henry as he uses three fingers to slide the brown flag of Art and Literature onto the seal. 'Share, Commander.'

Henry reaches into her satchel and removes a document on actual paper. 'This is also a material acquisition.'

All the Evaluators strain forward again, this time to read the unfamiliar words: *BWV 988 Aria.*

'That's music,' says Chief Koro.

'Yes,' says Henry.

'So it's for Moishe, then. We'll have him Attest, see if there's anything to it. We'll have the Scribes copy it in the—'

The doors to the Archive open with a rattling of armour and a barrage of footsteps. Henry and Graham turn to see General Winters, Javier son-of-Carmen, Chief of the Dragoons, and Birch. Along with Lian, that made four of the five members of the High Command.

Unlike everyone else at the Stadium, Birch has no matronymic that names her mother, nor has she earned or adopted a Trade Name for continuing a line of work into a third generation. Instead, she assumed a new name with her new position and in doing so shed her old identity.

Birch is the Master of the Order of Silence.

Birch is slender, and strong. She sits herself beside Graham at the table and crosses her legs. Her long hair the burnt red of cooling embers is braided back. Her complexion is unusually smooth for someone her age who has lived so much of her life on the road. Like most at the Stadium – Lilly being the most obvious exception – her skin browns rather than reddens in the sun. She wears a sleek black suit of leather, like a Runner's, but finer. Like Henry, Birch is in her late forties. Her green eyes are very observant. She nods to the two Raiders, who nod back.

Neither Winters nor Javier are so polite.

As Winters waves her hand, five of the Evaluators stand and take their leave of the meeting: this is no longer a Sharing but a Counsel. The guards leave too, closing the doors behind them.

Together the Wayworths sit and wait for Winters to begin, but she is not the one to speak first.

'When do we attack?' Henry asks.

'We don't,' says Winters, leaning back in the elegant chair of twisted steel.

'Why on earth not?' Henry says.

'There are more coming.'

Graham places his hand on Henry's thigh under the table. Winters has a tendency to talk too much; the trick is letting her, and that requires restraint.

Henry, responding, is motionless and as they'd hoped, Winters fills the space.

'Some of our Explorers go further than we admit. One has come back from the far east – I won't say how far, but far enough to witness a gathering of these Keepers. They are coming here. What we see on Yellow Ridge is only a wave. We could attack now and kill them off, but then we'll have to contend with both the numbers and the wrath of the coming thousand.'

'*A thousand?*' It is Graham this time. 'I've never seen a tribe with a thousand people – we're eight hundred and we're the largest I've ever encountered in thirty years in the wilderness.'

'We're sure of the numbers.'

'How do they feed a thousand moving people?'

'There's plentiful hunting a month out to the east and there's the forest to the north. They salt the meat. You know this,' says Winters.

'Yes, but—'

'They spread out, and they move food and water forward via a system of relays that travel faster than the advancing groups, back and forth, like blood cells through the body. The Keepers slow their march to align with the flow of resources. It is very slow progress, but it's also stable and it works. They also trade.'

'They'd have to be spread out over a hundred miles or more like a line of insects.'

'I don't understand,' Henry interrupts. 'So what are we waiting for?'

'For them to gather and, if we're lucky, attack us *en masse* so we can end them all at once. We'd be too thin to attack their line. We don't have the numbers to fight in the field like that.'

Henry turns to Birch, who has not so much as blinked her eyes.

'Do you agree with this?'

'It is not the place of the Order to—'

'Oh, spare me. Do you agree with this or not? Because I'll share a better idea.'

'Commander,' says Winters, 'it's not your place to lecture the High—'

'We attack the group on Yellow Ridge. We set up a fortress using those unbreakable windows from the felled tower and we launch a series of Dragoon attacks into the on-coming line of Keepers. They'll never have the numbers to counter us because we won't give them time to assemble. We'll be dug in like Romans and they'll exhaust themselves: a thin line of ants crashing against a mighty wall. And if we need to, we'll set up two more positions – maybe take over The Crossing and use the Pavilion at the top as a staging ground. We can pull them into a death triangle and winnow down their numbers until they give up or they don't exist any more.'

Two oil lamps burn out simultaneously, turning the chamber as sombre as the mood. Graham watches the remaining torches flicker in Henry's soft brown eyes. They are warm and kind and therefore seductive. He learned long ago not to read faces but actions because of how easily faces can deceive.

There are children on Yellow Ridge. She and Graham have both seen them.

'Birch,' Graham says very softly, breaking the darkness, 'The Order may be prevented from providing answers and solutions, but it is encouraged to ask questions. What question is on your mind?'

Birch looks at Graham. It is strange to him that her face has remained so youthful and untroubled, given the secrets she carries and the power she commands. Lilly doesn't like Birch's firm adherence to the rules; she feels that she's owed a personal loyalty, having founded the Order itself. But Graham has always been impressed with Birch. Everything seems to work when she's in charge and she can, with a few words, change the direction of the High Command in a moment. Silence does have a power of its own.

'What I would like to know,' Birch says, turning from Graham to General Winters, 'is what they want.'

RADIO

Alessandra makes her way to Lilly's workshop through the U-Ring below the main concourse. Natural light reflects down through the mirrors illuminating the curved walls and the glistening floor. On her left is the famous *Joy Is Power* indicator, showing the Stadium's reserves of electricity generated by walking back and forth on the Green and in the stands and along the Rings at all levels. How the floors turn their own movements into energy is one of Lilly's research projects. Alessandra has never seen the levels exceed fifteen per cent; right now they're registering eight per cent. Lilly says it's because the Stadium was designed for more people and more activity.

'We pulled more than 60,000 seats during the Great Conversion,' she once explained. Our permanent population is less than eight hundred and even with the Green full on Trade Day, we are seldom more than fifteen hundred. To me, it's a wonder we get to fifteen per cent at all. Maybe the Ancients combined the measures with the Turbines and solar, and obviously we use far less electricity than they did but I don't know. The place didn't come with a manual like your mother's rifle, unfortunately.'

Two guards, a man and a woman, are standing on either side of the Weapons and Communications Research Centre. Alessandra knows them both by name, but chit-chat is frowned upon while they are working.

'Can I come in?' she asks the man.

'You left. Are you expected back?'

'I have a delivery from my father and yes.'

Without turning, the man raps four times on the door to announce it is about to be officially opened. He then pauses, waits for two knocks in return and then swings it wide.

Lilly is facing away from the door. Her long pale yellow hair is tied back in a tail this evening to keep it out of the way. She sits on a tall stool over an elevated work bench of thick wood, a rare material here. She prefers it because it's a poor conductor of electricity compared to the metal desk and because – in her words – it has 'character'.

She never needs to turn around to know who's entered the room and Alessandra has never managed to figure out her trick. A mirror or reflection, she once figured, but that isn't it. Without turning, Lilly raises her right hand into the air and with two fingers, draws Alessandra into the room as though on a string.

Across the room to the right are two other apprentices, Simone and Bruno. Simone is a few years older than Alessandra, with black hair, like her own, and soft brown eyes. She is a little buxom and would make a terrible Runner; it is probably a good choice for her to remain here in a job where she'll be seated.

Bruno is more of a mystery. Like a dozen or more children, he was left here by his parents, who never returned for him. He was a teenager then – fifteen, best as Alessandra can remember, and too old for the Agoge, but in the past five years he has worked his way through the lower coursework. The Stadium is the only colony that demands literacy, and those who join late find learning the hardest, but Bruno learned quickly, and demonstrated an uncanny skill for solving problems with his hands. Lilly has some hope for his development as an engineer if he can learn the maths.

'Come in, Alessandra. I figured you'd come.'

Lilly is leaning over a massive hand-drawn map of the world, or at least as best anyone can imagine it. The full list of country names learned from Trivial Pursuit is on a piece of paper, along with names pulled from books and other found scraps. Lilly is convinced that the names and borders of countries changed over time and because the names – Russia, China, United States, India, Namibia, Czechoslovakia, Mesopotamia – don't have dates attached, she has been trying to figure out which of these names and locations existed last, immediately before The Rise. She says it is mostly a hobby because it has no practical importance, seeing as most of these places are too inaccessible ever to get to.

'I thought I'd be seeing you. I heard your parents are back and carrying.'

'They're in a Sharing now,' Alessandra says, plopping down on a cushion in a plastic chair beside Lilly's desk. 'Alan Farmer was killed.'

'I heard about that too. I'm sorry. I know he was very close to your family.'

'My dad's oldest friend, I think.'

'Yes, he was. They were very disruptive in the Agoge when they were young. Alan was studious – and he was also a brilliant Runner. I took him for a future Evaluator in Arts and Literature. It was his idea that different styles and designs come from different periods of time. His theory was that people are influenced and inspired by what they see; that they try to emulate it and improvise. Once he came up with that idea, I started looking at things a bit differently, examining the idea that classification systems don't only vary according to inherent differences, but also change through time based on new needs and new questions. Anyway, he had a real gift. His death is a loss. How's your father?'

'We barely spoke. He's unsettled,' Alessandra says.

She removes the small bundle from her pocket and places it on Lilly's map over a place she calls *Africa*.

'That is an ugly bit of cloth. I don't want it.'

'There's something inside it from Dad. He said it was on your list.'

Lilly peels it apart to reveal the broken tube and after that, the perfect and matching one.'

'Well, now. That is a surprise. Where did he get this?'

'He said they went to The Crossing after the Tracollo. I'm guessing it was from there but they were out for weeks, so I don't know for certain.'

Lilly holds the tube up to the light and examines the filament. 'This might work.'

'What is it?' Alessandra asks, not terribly interested.

'It's called a fuse. All electrical devices,' she explains, turning around to face Alessandra and crossing her legs as she does, 'have to run at a very specific level of power appropriate to their needs. This clever solution right here burns out first if the power is too high. A fuse is like a little soldier who sacrifices himself to save the rest. That's a lot of nobility in something so modest. This one is from my HAM radio. It burned out a while back – actually, must be close to fifteen years now. I used to show it to all the schoolchildren when they visited the different units. They loved it when a voice came through. I used to rush the classes down here whenever we came across something.'

Alessandra glances up at Bruno. He's rather handsome, although he's too calm and his mood is always quiet. There is little about him that invites conversation or engagement. He has the long, lean body of a male Runner – maybe even a Raider, if he stays with it and can learn to talk to people. She's seen him running laps on the Green and practising with the soldiers; if he's worked his way into Weapons and Communications he must have a brain too.

He looks up at her and she turns back to Lilly.

'Well, let's plug it in and see if anything interesting happens,' Lilly says.

Alessandra stands and follows her to a closet door. When Lilly opens it, she studies it as if it were a Trove – which it is, basically. Inside are dozens of devices, each squatting in its own organised space. The smaller objects are stacked on high, the heavy ones are lower. Rectangular and drab, sometimes curved and reflective, each item looks distinct and important here, which Alessandra always finds somewhat odd because they are also the kinds of machines that are thrown into piles on The Crossing and sold as Raw so crafters and blacksmiths can strip them and turn their pieces into something new and useful.

Lilly points to one at knee-level on the right. 'Get that for me – mind, it's heavy. There's a microphone at the end of the coiled rope. It doesn't work but I don't want to make it worse.'

Alessandra hoists the machine over to the work table, then Lilly redirects her to a low writer's desk in the corner of the room. Lilly pushes it back a few centimetres into a usable position before attaching the long black cord to a socket in the wall. She flicks a switch on the radio – and nothing happens.

97

'Open it. The tools are over there,' she says, pointing to a wall where every tool has a place. 'I take it your father showed you how to do it.'

Simone has stopped working. Unlike Bruno's lean physique, Simone is full-figured and curvaceous, her eyes bright and her silence always ready to be interrupted. Alessandra can't see exactly what she was doing but it looked like some advanced maths in relation to the tunnels that ran outwards from the Stadium to various points in the Territory. The tunnel map was among the most guarded secrets at the Commonwealth. If Simone had clearance from the High Command to work on that, she must be higher up than Alessandra had always assumed. She might even be part of the Urban Explorers. But Alessandra was part of that group herself; she'd made more than thirty sorties into the Gone World so she figured she would have heard if Simone was too.

'Are you almost done?' Lilly asks.

'Almost.' Alessandra looks around inside the box with the thousand wires, searching for some kind of slot or sleeve where it might go, like a sheath for a blade, but there was nothing but a manic tangle of shinies and snakes.

'I probably am, but I don't know where it goes,' she admits.

Lilly leans over her shoulder and points to two U-shaped clips on the hard plastic board. Alessandra places the new fuse into position and gently pushes until the machine pulls it into place with a *snap*.

'Turn it on, Wayworth.'

Alessandra presses the little black square button and the radio comes to life. The glass panels glow opaque white and night-sky green. The machine itself makes a terrible squealing sound.

*

Lilly is lithe. Despite her years, she is both dexterous and strong, although with her hips she doesn't like bending much. She began as a blacksmith and there is a memory of that power remaining in her body. She pulls her stool over to the table with the radio, sits and crosses her legs, then begins to adjust the dials.

Alessandra watches Lilly's thick black boots bounce at the end of her jeans. She's over seventy but she's fit. Her mum's jokes about her flirtation with her father don't look so harmless from this angle.

'It's okay, you two. I know you can't focus. Come on over,' she tells Simone and Bruno, who make no pretence of hesitation.

They stare at the device, which is an extraordinary thing. It is a black box, but on one face it has a screen that is illuminated in colours, lines and numbers with words and letters like ATT, HOLD, LEVEL, TIME, EXDP/SET. Other parts light up TUNE, TX, LSB, FIL2, VFO A 1 and more. Outside the colourful window are buttons and knobs that are equally mystical: Power, Transmit, Tuner, Vox/BK-IN, P-AMP/ATT, Notch, NB and NR, Menu, Function, M. Scope and still more.

'What is this and why is it interesting?' Lilly asks with a smile, knowing that – for these youngsters – the answer is *nothing*. 'It's called a HAM Radio. We don't know what HAM means so I simply call it a radio. It can send our voices out into the world using radio waves, and it can receive the radio waves – and therefore voices – of other people using their own radios. What that means is that we could, in theory, actually talk to people who are far away.'

'How . . . ?' Simone starts, but Lilly raises a hand to stop her.

'Hold off for a moment. Already, of course, we have a technique for talking to people far away. We use Signal Mirrors to bounce the light of the sun using codes. We use drums. We use smoke signals. We leave message drops – we have a lot of ways to keep in touch. What I'm talking about here is actual *conversation* with people who are hundreds, even thousands of kilometres away.'

'That's miraculous,' says Bruno.

'I don't know why you say that. The Ancients built those towers in the Gone World. This is hardly more impressive. And we know from the Trivial Pursuit answers that people have been to the moon several times; that an international space station circles the Earth – or at least it once did – and that we even tried to get to Mars. Pity about the outcome.

'The radio has six primary parts,' she continues, 'the power supply, which is why I have it plugged into the wall. The transceiver, which selects the frequencies we use to send and receive. The antenna tuner – which I don't entirely understand – the microphone – which lets us talk, and the speaker,' she says, tapping the black grille, 'which lets us listen. As it happens, our microphone is broken because it was submerged in water for three hundred years, which explains the colour and shape, but I like to leave it there because it completes the look.'

Lilly manually advanced through several bands, letting the apprentices listen for themselves.

'It worked for thirty-nine years and then it blew its fuse. It took me a solid decade to get my head around the basics. As we've discussed during your Induction Lecture, we have two main sections in Weapons and Communications – and don't say weapons and communications. We have – Simone?'

'Engineering and Reverse Engineering.'

'Right. And what's the difference?'

'In Engineering, we're trying to solve problems. In Reverse Engineering, we're trying to solve mysteries. The main one being, how did other people solve *their* problems and what can we learn from that.'

'Good,' says Lilly, 'and now explain it in your own words. You need to understand the intuition behind it.'

'Well,' said Simone, happy to be talking and not working alone with a taciturn Bruno, 'in Engineering, we talk to High Command or the Archive or the Order and find out what problems they're having. Like, how to grow food using less soil, or how to predict weather patterns, or how to build armour into the jackets that the Runners wear so they can come back uninjured after leaping around on rooftops. In Reverse Engineering . . .' she began, but Lilly interrupted her.

'And what's the first thing we do when we face a new problem?'

'Talk to Reverse Engineering.'

'Why?'

'Because maybe they've already learned things that could solve the problem and we can use those.'

'Exactly. Because we don't innovate and create for fun: we do it because we need to, and we've learned some humility over the years. The Ancients had space ships and global communications and weapons we can't imagine, so if we can find out how they solved problems, we do that first. Failing that, we put our heads together and do it ourselves. Reverse Engineering is trying to learn the mysteries of the Ancients by taking things apart, coming up with new ideas, new explanations, new possibilities. The more the Archive grows, the greater the chances of solving those mysteries faster, and the greater the likelihood of solving our problems sooner. That's why Knowledge is power: because the more you know, the more you can do. Now, Alessandra,' Lilly said, turning to her youngest apprentice, 'how else does this section learn beyond engineering new solutions or learning old ones from Reverse Engineering or the Archive?'

'From the outside. By building the Archive itself. Raid, Trade, and Spade.'

'That's our catchy phrase for the children to memorise, but what does it actually mean?'

'Raiders learn from engagement with other people – peacefully if possible, forcefully if necessary. Traders exchange our Knowledge for new Knowledge to create Trade Bonds. And Spaders dig it out of the Gone World with, you know, spades.'

'If this radio were able to talk to other radios,' Lilly says, turning back to the matter at hand, 'we'd be able to find other people – far-off people – and trade without risk. We could learn without effort. We could create trade bonds with people all over, wherever they were. Like tightening a weave in fabric, the world would draw close and rise again with the Commonwealth and the Archive at the centre. That little fuse your dad found,' Lilly said, 'makes it all possible.'

'But we can't talk to anyone,' Bruno says, 'can we? I mean, can the Knowledge from the Archive get out?'

'No, we can only listen. We'll never fix this one. It's dead. But it's not impossible we might find a new microphone somewhere. Unfortunately, we haven't yet.'

'And,' asks Bruno, 'in those thirty-nine years, how many times have you heard other people?'

Yes. That was always the crux of it.

'Seven times.'

'That's . . . not many . . .'

'No,' Lilly admits. 'And those times I did hear people, they spoke in languages I didn't know and we'll never be able to learn. They also didn't last long because the signals were very weak and eventually I lost them. For another radio to work, the person would have to be in a place with the right kind and enough electricity. They'd need a perfectly working radio – preserved, somehow, for hundreds of years without rot – and they would need to know how to operate it, which is not obvious. It took me ages, for example, to learn that I needed to cut and adjust an antenna and mount it on the Stadium roof and then receive signals appropriate to that antenna. That took me seven years – and I'm very smart. It was even longer before I started to understand the basic theory of how radio signals bounce off the atmosphere to reach other radios. They might even bounce off the moon, but that's just an idea I have. There's a relationship between radio signals and how they travel during the day versus the night. Reception was always better at night. Since the main difference between day and night is the sun – and therefore light and temperature – I think that the sun plays a role in radio transmission too. This has been a Reverse Engineering agenda for decades. But I simply don't have enough information to build a good understanding. Radio aren't like guns: they weren't built to be used by just anyone. There was a lot of learning needed, and now that learning is gone. So it's an Indie that's dependent on Knowledge itself. It's quite a thing.'

Alessandra doesn't take her eyes off the strange numbers and words. She listens to the squelching tones that sound like animals approaching one another – shoulders up, eyes low, danger in every step.

'So this radio. It could help the Commonwealth grow and learn more and make us more like the Ancients,' Bruno concluded, 'but probably won't?'

This is what Lilly brought back from the first Tracollo, thought Alessandra, a device that could possibly unify and connect the entire world and find people thousands of miles away – connecting them like one family, one Commonwealth.

And the Box with its books and games and children's entertainment. Lilly did all that.

And the mysterious White Board that in half a century did nothing and guarded all its secrets. Something Lilly took on impulse.

Lilly did all of this when she was Alessandra's own age: seventeen. She did all this without ever having had a father and only a year after her mother was murdered on the High Road. Lilly herself barely made it back alive after a gun battle.

And what was Alessandra doing? *Nothing.* Not making a name for herself. Not standing out meaningfully in any way. She was the daughter of the Wayworths, but she had yet to earn the name on her own.

'You brought all of this back from The Crossing,' she said.

'It wasn't The Crossing back then. It was called the Bridge to Nowhere. But yes,' Lilly said, 'this and the Box and the White Board were recovered from the first Tracollo. Not the one that fell straight down, of course. That buried everything beneath it. This was from Tower Two when it fell over and cracked open. That's how people started exploring below.'

'Why didn't they die from the Sickness?' Bruno asks.

'They did,' Lilly said, 'but not immediately. They made pulls first.'

For fifty years she's been telling this story.

Yes, the Roamers made Pulls that I found at the bridge.

No, I don't know where they came from. Inside, I suppose.

Yes, I did manage to open the Box. I can't tell you how. It's a guarded secret, I'm sorry.

Yes, Cardo and two thugs did try to rape me in the Pavilion when I came for the Box. I blasted my way out with my mother's Python.

The Sickness? Yes, thousands of bodies inside the Tower. You go in, you die.

But these were lies.

All lies.

Lies she told at the beginning – lies she continues to tell now. Lies that needed to be protected and repeated so that the Truth would never be learned and the Commonwealth would always be safe.

Lies that led Lilly to found the Order of Silence; that placed Saavni in charge.

Lies which only Birch knows to be untrue now – Birch, and whomever she has chosen to tell.

BWV 988

Graham and Henry sit together outside at the edge of the Green looking at the two bonfires and the rows of kneeling archers awaiting orders that will likely not come tonight. Henry has been on sniper duty for extended periods before; she knows how tiring the experience can be. It's the concentration and immobility that slow time – that, and the isolation. With no one to talk to it can be taxing. For the archers, though, it's even worse: you stare at your own foot until Anoushka tells you otherwise.

But none of that is her problem now.

Technically, Graham's mood isn't her problem either, but that she can do something about.

'At least you peed,' she says.

He smiles only a little and doesn't look away from the bonfire.

'Go on, complain. I want you to.'

'I'm not entirely sure what we're doing here,' he admits.

'Surviving.'

'That's a pat answer for the feeble.'

'We live long and we live well compared to everyone else in the known world. That's not enough?'

106

Graham looks up at the night sky. The colours are not as intense from inside the Stadium. There is too much light thrown up by the oil lamps and the bonfires, and the presence of all the people gathered there distracts from his pleasure in the natural beauty.

'I think I became a Raider to get outside the walls,' he says. 'Sometimes I find it ironic that you started life there and then decided to come in.'

'You need a new *Seeing*,' Henry says.

'Is that a Roamer word?'

'Yes. Well, no – it's the same word, but it has a different meaning to us. You don't know this?'

'Maybe? I forget.'

'The Roamers believe that everything is in motion: people, places, ideas, time . . . everything. Change is therefore constant and a fact and any effort to resist it is unnatural. We didn't roam simply because we couldn't settle down, we roamed to be at one with the natural movement of life. I was brought up that way. We did talk about this.'

'Not for twenty years. Tell me again.'

Henry rubs her hands in the cold. 'As one moves – through space, time, ideas – there are Crossings.'

Graham removes his scarf and wraps it around Henry's hands. The warmth from his neck is still in the cloth.

'Crossings happen in their own way. They might be planned but we usually refer to them as something unexpected. Like you finding that glass tube. Each Crossing creates an opportunity for a Union. A Union is when some kind of bond – a connection – occurs during The Crossing. Usually it's with another person or an object. If it's with another person, you both have to want the Union. If it's a thing . . . obviously it's just you.'

'So they can be rejected?'

'Oh yes. We have Crossings that don't result in Unions all the time. People and things pass by each other constantly. Those aren't Crossings. Crossings are when a bond is suggested. A face across the room who could become a lover or new friend. Maybe an object that seems to speak to you. In those cases, a Union is either agreed or rejected. A Seeing is when we Cross another way of understanding and embrace it. We don't always agree with it or make it our own, but we take it in. To Cross something that results in a new Seeing is a rare and special thing. It often requires courage and wisdom and an open heart to allow ourselves to be moved into that other place. A Union gives us more than we had before. A Seeing makes us more than we were before. One of the reasons I was attracted to the Commonwealth when my parents died is because Lilly's idea of building the Archive promised new Unions and new Seeings. And she was going to seek them out – not rely on fate or luck, but create an agenda to bring them to us.'

'And you think,' concludes Graham, 'that I need a new Seeing?'

'I think your understanding of our life needs to be refreshed.'

'You make me happy,' he said.

'I know,' she replied.

Inside the Stadium of the Commonwealth, behind a wooden door as polished and refined as a rifle stock, there is a music room. The room is draped with rugs to absorb sound and moisture. Hanging on the walls and touched by only a few are instruments: some are made of wood and string, others are brass and ornate and they all have voices, even though few have names because they have long since been lost. Many are warped or damaged beyond repair and though their shapes look simple enough, no crafter has ever come close to recreating them.

In the centre of the room stands the electric piano. It has eighty-eight keys – fifty-two white and thirty-six black. It has no strings to break or wood to warp, so its tone and action remain perfect. And the Stadium has electricity enough to power it.

Moishe son-of-Tikvah plays the piano. He is thirty-four years old and works by day as a foreman on construction projects. For military service he is part of a Phalanx, but the Evaluators have spoken to Winters because they do not want his unique hands to see war.

When he was six years old he was tested for aptitude like all children entering the Agoge. He was found to have a rare and native understanding of the patterns that create harmonies. He was initially taught to play by the two pianists of the Commonwealth and was then allowed to learn on his own.

He was both dexterous and studious and by the age of twelve there was no new music to teach him, the library having been exhausted. Instead, he was left to create his own, so he took it upon himself to gather the oldest people together and ask them to share any songs they knew – from their travels, from their parents, from their grandparents, from their dreams.

He transcribed them into music that the Scribes copied and had the Runners hide.

At formal events and rare informal evenings he entertains in the Great Hall. He also teaches students. To support the Central Archive, he responds to requests from the Chief Evaluator for Art and Literature. It's not often that he is called to this task, but he welcomes it every time.

He was called tonight.

In his chamber, where he lives alone but pines for Anoushka – who said last month they were finished, but he is not so sure – Moishe bathes and scrubs his hands red in preparation for visiting the Music Room. When he arrives he removes his shoes at the entrance and dons his waiting slippers. He arrives at the piano rested and clean and pristine.

He sits himself on the bench.

The piano is white. He has been told it draws power from the walls and possibly his own movements. How it works matters less to him than what it does.

To the far left of the piano, above the keys, there is a button as clear as glass. He presses it and it glows blue, signalling the instrument's readiness to obey.

The new documents retrieved from the Trove have already been positioned on the piano. He studies them, touching nothing. The paper is old but not the oldest he has seen; it's unfaded, not yellowed or rimmed with crust.

He can read the language at the top of the page. He recognises the name of the composer, a strange name that no one else has.

The letters and numbers *BWV 988 Aria* mean nothing to him.

For a moment he sits with the notes.

The room has one hundred and fifty seats, arranged like an amphitheatre, a semi-circle around the piano, which sits on the stage. The sound in here is excellent, but it changes when the room is filled.

For no reason he looks up and notices two figures seated at the back.

He squints and after a moment, recognises their faces. The Commanders.

He waves once and Graham lifts his hand.

Moishe looks down at the sheet music again and forgets the audience. He has a job to do and they, of all people, will not interrupt.

Beyond English, Français and Español, music is the only

other language he knows to have survived. Moishe does not find this surprising because, to him, it is the language of the angels and if only one language was going to survive The Rise and the emptying of the world, surely it would be music. It will be the language spoken by the dead so that no one will ever be alone in heaven.

There is a logic to every piece of music, however modest or complex. This one has no time signature, so he has to reach out with his heart beyond four hundred, even six hundred years, to understand the feeling that this person – this *Bach* – might have wanted him to feel.

BWV 988. The Goldberg Variations.

Reading before he plays, he sees that the notes are very simple at first. After several measures they grow sophisticated. It suggests the need for an emotional maturity from the very first note, otherwise the integrity will be compromised.

He starts to play and quickly stops. *Too fast.* He slows down, much slower: slow, the way a drop of water falls from an icicle after a thaw. He needs to reach across the boundary separating this moment from centuries before the entire destruction of the Gone World to find the emotion that this composer was feeling when he penned the notes.

Once Moishe finds a balance between melody and moment and mood, he plays again.

These two notes, with rests; a pause, three more, like pebbles dropping into water together, and then six that are given space to breath, separate from one another, but reaching – calling out; carrying the sensation forward.

Moishe plays the aria for three minutes. After three minutes he lifts his shaking hands from the piano and weeps.

II

PURGATORIO

HELLO

Time is hard to judge underground. Three weeks? A month? More?

When she first woke on the floor and opened her eyes, there was a warm red light in a sea of chalky air. She exhaled and her breath formed in front of her: a cone of white against the smooth surface of the floor, blowing off the dust of centuries. The pain in her leg did not radiate outwards from the stick that was jutting into it, instead, it caused her entire body to throb. She could feel the blood pulsing in her neck – in fact, every inch of her was pulsing.

Slowly, she reached for the black strap of the sling-bag, intent on pulling it over her resting head and gently – very, very gently, so as not to alert her own pain – sliding the strap out from beneath her to get access to the material within.

The effort didn't go unpunished. The pain was horrible. Alone, under a million pounds of rubble, she screamed.

Inside the bag was a triangular bandage in a small pouch marked with a red cross on a white background. She opened it, rolled it from the end until it became long and tight, and then she bent it into a circle and weaved it around itself to become a *doughnut* – a term everyone used and no one could define, but it had come to mean this. She placed the doughnut around the stick embedded in her leg. She'd been taught never to pull out something that was impaling the flesh as it might be what's keeping the rest of the blood in. Comforted by the knowledge that if she were going to bleed out it would have happened while she slept, she pressed another bandage to her leg, applying pressure to the wound.

Her trainer on the Green had told her that many of these kits with red crosses had been found in Troves, not just all over the Territory but beyond, in almost every ancient vehicle, in every tower, on every boat or building. The Ancients, Elimisha had decided long ago, were accident-prone and eventually they succumbed. The end.

That was her theory, anyway.

The air smelled bad but it didn't make her cough. Lying there on her back, in the quiet, she wondered whether the Sickness might already be inside her.

This room – this tomb – was unlike any place she had ever been. There was a silence here that was deeper and more perfect than any she had ever imagined. Growing up with two brothers and her mother in their small apartment, noise was constant. Inside the Stadium's rooms and halls, there were always foot-steps and shouting voices and the racket of objects being pushed or pulled around. Out in the Gone World, when she was on a Run and alone, the sounds were smaller but intensified: her footsteps on the sand, or the soles of her shoes grinding over a rock; bugs and lizards speaking in the night, the distant cries of Traders or Roamers – sometimes even singing and music.

And the wind: always the wind.

Here there was nothing. No sound. No movement. She was the only living thing.

116

Elimisha pushed away the fear and the memory of last night's events and visualised sitting up, then standing. She pictured this with the same attention to detail that she used to perform her visualisation of Routes. Eventually – for reasons as mysterious as life itself – the repetitions passed from her mind to her body, and once in her body they became actions she couldn't refuse. In this way, Elimisha rose to her feet.

On her left was the massive door that had slammed shut behind her with the blast. Between here and there, hanging on the wall, was a red and glass box and inside the box was a long, useful-looking axe. Elimisha removed it from under the glass. It was far too short to use as a crutch, so she propped it against the wall before dragging herself to the door. On it was a central wheel she understood to be the lock. She turned it and to her delight, found that it spun easily.

Lefty loosey, righty tighty.

It spun left until it clanked to a halt. She'd seen no hinges, but knowing the door opened outwards, she pushed with all her weight and what little strength she had, leaning into it as though it were an argument, holding the pressure until the pain made her stop. Nothing had even *suggested* movement. This was no more a door now than a painting of a door on the side of a mountain of solid rock. It was going nowhere. Something bigger than her was blocking her exit and unless the world shifted again of its own volition, she needed to find another way out.

Turning to explore her own coffin, Elimisha began to walk.

Step after laborious step, she hobbled her way through the ancient bomb shelter, every part of it as perfect and unravaged by time as the best parts of the Stadium. It was not a familiar place, though: the Stadium had curves and lifts, and unbreakable windows which captured the best of the light. The minds

117

who designed it were obviously trying to create something of majesty, of souring inspiration and technological acumen. This place was all angles and straight lines, a temporary shelter from the forces of death: a hard place.

At the end of the hall was a T-junction and a door that read STORAGE.

To her left was a long corridor. Though far away, she could make out the word on that door too: COMMUNICATIONS. This gave her a destination.

As she trudged towards it, she passed another door on her right inscribed with the words CONTROL ROOM. She tried the handle and found it unlocked, but it was heavy and set on two sizable hinges. Pressing the handle downwards, she pushed it open and it yielded.

Inside was another red bulb inside a cage above the door. The room was filled with machinery and unlike in the hall, she heard a very subtle but clear *hum*. Elimisha poked her head in. The ground was dry, there were no footprints and the smell was the same musty scent as the rest of the dungeon. Not seeing any reason not to, she stepped inside to take a look around.

To her right was a cabinet made of sheet metal. The door had a small metal handle but no lock; pressing a silver button with her thumb opened it. Swinging the doors wide revealed three large machines with knobs, lights and gauges, all dimly illuminated. She had never seen machines quite like this before, although the style was reminiscent of others she'd seen in Lilly's closet in Weapons and Communications. They also looked like the piles of Raw she'd seen at The Crossing.

There were labels reading PRIMARY. RESERVE. FILTERS.

The gauge on the PRIMARY machine was measuring available power of eight per cent, and it was holding steady. Beside it, someone has written graffiti like at the Stadium:

118

Without power . . . it is just a cave.

There was a series of switches directing power to each room, all set to the OFF position. She had seen switches like this before; Lilly called them circuit breakers. It was possible that they had been in the ON position before a surge of some kind knocked them out.

Elimisha pressed all of them upwards. She heard a number of *clicks* . . . there was a flicker of light, another, a pause, and a burst of continuous white light shone from three long bulbs mounted along the top of the wall as the entire shelter came to life. Elimisha closed her eyes for a moment of respite from the pain and to celebrate a moment of good news.

The RESERVE unit's white needle was pressed flat to zero and the FILTERS light was off. Beside them were two buttons, one red, the other green.

She pressed the green button and immediately a whirling sound began, accompanied by a puff of air from a large vent on the wall. A second unit kicked into action, pulling the dust from the air.

Light. Heat. Air.

For twenty minutes Elimisha sat watching her situation improve. She had learned from Lilly how filters were used to clean water back at the Stadium so she surmised these filters were making the air fresher by removing particulates. What she didn't know was whether the machine was pulling out the bad air and pushing in fresh air from the outside or if it was simply recirculating the air that was there already. Was she breathing clean air, or simply fresher versions of the Sickness?

Whatever the truth, it hardly mattered at the moment: she was locked inside and had to breathe.

Looking down at herself in the bright light, she also accepted that she needed to clean herself off and change out of these clothes.

Eat. Drink. Heal.

Elimisha leaned over and pressed her hands to her knees, feeling the cool breeze from the wind-machine against her thick curls. If she could know for a fact that it wasn't poison she could enjoy it. In that moment, though, her ambivalence would have to do.

Strange there would be still be power here.

Her sciences classes at the Agoge had taught her the rudiments of how batteries work. Power goes in, it is stored ('by magic', everyone would joke) and is released to power systems later. How much later? No one knows because the engineers refuse to run down the batteries at the Stadium. What if they never charged again?

It was Lilly, though, who had stared at the brass plaque at the Stadium entrance and wondered what it had meant by 'kinetic power'.

Along with Edward Gibbon's abridged *Rise and Fall of the Roman Empire*, and – of course – *The Complete Calvin and Hobbes*, the Harrington Box that Lilly had recovered contained mostly books written by the Greeks. One book – *The History of the Peloponnesian War* by Thucydides – was written with their own language on the left page and the original Greek on the right. Gibbon, in talking about Latin, had explained how languages evolved and borrowed terms and built new words on others. Lilly had considered this important and she set a team to work on it. Elimisha had found the whole idea quite boring until Lilly explained that the word *kinetic* on the brass plaque might come from the Greek word *kinetikos*, which meant 'movement or putting in motion'. 'Could it be,' Lilly had asked, 'that the

Stadium is partly powered by motion inside it, and that motion is somehow captured and stored in batteries – like rainwater in cisterns – so that it can be re-directed later? When I was about your age, I invented a way to move water from the waterfalls into the well inside the Stadium walls using a kind of screw and a road for the water. Turns out the Romans did too – they called it an aqueduct – so I might not have been the first but I was in good company. What you need to understand,' Lilly said to her, 'is that the world of the Ancients – not the Classicists, like the Greeks and Romans, but *our* Ancients – needed tremendous amounts of power. They had Big Electricity. The biggest. The plaque gives us three sources: the sun, the flow of the water through the turbines and human kinetic power. I think that movement itself can create power. Why not?'

Elimisha looked down at her feet. If the world here caught no sun and no water flowed and no people walked, the bunker probably couldn't produce power. But . . . the earth had shaken. Could the fall of a building have been enough to wake the lights and charge the batteries?

She couldn't know. It was, as her science teacher called it, 'a hypothesis'. But if it was true, it meant that the eight per cent was only going to go down because there was no way to charge the batteries again, and at that point the lights would go out, the air would stop circulating and the heaters would cool. The deeper you go, she knew, the colder it gets – maybe not to freezing, but cold enough, in the dark, to feel like it.

It was going to be a terrible way to die.

What Elimisha thought of, in those early days, was how she could have been with her mother and brothers in their home instead of here in this bunker. Kuende, fourteen always studious; Jabiri – the jokester – seventeen, smart, though undisciplined.

121

He's a year older and is supposed to be the big brother, but Elimisha has been his guide since their father died and their mother fell into a sea of tears and wasn't able to reach the shore for two years.

On her feet again, her leg still burning, Elimisha flicked on the lighting for the remaining rooms and set herself to the task of taking inventory while searching for another exit.

The storage room had the kinds of cans she'd seen in the Archive Museum.

'*Don't open, don't eat,*' the Curator had warned them.

She was not going to touch those.

There was also rice.

She has been told that dry rice can last a thousand years and stay safe to eat. Traders bring the Stadium occasional shipments, so she knows how to prepare it if the stoves are willing to heat and there's any water to use. If she doesn't die down here from the Sickness – or some other illness – she'll have enough food to last months at least. Although what she would be waiting for, she has no idea.

And how long will that eight per cent last? She'd need to measure the drop and calculate it, and for that she'd need a way to tell time.

Maybe something would come up.

In the mess hall she found a jar filled with a viscous brown liquid that moved slowly when she tilted it, much like the tree sap that can be boiled down into a sweet soup that everyone loves – a rare delicacy from the forests between the Commonwealth and the small colony of Anchorpoint. She unscrewed the top and risked a sniff. It smelled wonderful. She dipped in a finger and tasted it. A surge of contentment started at the sides of her tongue, rushed down her neck and seeped into the core of her body – all the way down to her leg, where the happiness was defeated.

She tasted it again and the decided that if the goo *did* eventually kill her it would be better than freezing to death in the dark.

Beyond the control room, towards the communications room, was an empty sleeping chamber with three sets of bunk beds and two sheet-metal closets on the back wall, one between each set of beds. A thin vent on the ceiling continued to blow cool fresh air. Elimisha walked to the closet, running a hand across the woollen blanket on a lower bunk. A small cloud of dust rose from it as her fingers left grooves in the fabric.

The closets there had no locks. Inside were six full-body suits of a material she has never seen before, thick like Runners' leather but lighter and more supple, and cobalt-blue like the tips of the sky fires at night before they reached the green swirls. Each suit was edged in silver. Under the lights from above, they shimmered the way algae does in the moonlight by the edge of the river at the Frontier Command – the spot where the water becomes undrinkable, at the western-most edge of the Domain. She had been there once with her father. He ran his fingers through the algae, making dark rivers, and smiled.

The suits were hanging neatly on hooks. They all looked immaculate – and clean, which was enticing, particularly given her bloodied and filthy condition.

She removed one from a hanger and held it up in front of her to check for size. Unlike most ancient clothing, this one had no labels inside. The only marking was a vertical stripe on the right arm running down from the shoulder. It read 'Haptic Command Gear – HCG®' in red lettering.

Three of the suits were too big and three were huge. Elimisha flung one of the smaller ones over her shoulder and left the room to finish her tour.

The toilets were clean, if covered in the same layer of dust as everything else.

There was toilet paper rather than water and cloths.

All the bulbs worked in the halls and rooms.

As she mapped her surroundings and acclimatised herself, she ran her hands along the walls. She had been taught in the Agoge that Knowledge enters the body through all the senses: the Runner must be keenly aware of the wind on her cheek, the slickness of surfaces, the smell of animals or fires, the changing of the light, all of this at all times. The world is talking, she was told. It is your *duty* to listen.

The paint – the colour of nothing – chipped off into tiny flakes as she drew a line waist-high with barely a touch. The walls were drier than the bones of the dead. She rubbed her fingers together and the flakes fell to the floor as gently as a dusting of snow during an autumn flurry. She wondered whether they might also be soft. Whether, for example, an axe could make a hole in them to the outside.

A question for later.

Leaving the mess hall at the far end behind her, she proceeded at her own pace to the communications room. The shower was calling to her and she was hoping there was water. But for now, the beckoning promise of a human voice was more profound.

What she found instead were human eyes.

In Elimisha's mind, any *communications* room was really a *Weapons and Communications Research and Development Section*: a place run by a Chief, staffed by up to a dozen engineers and hosting ten or even a dozen apprentices. It was a place with thousands of tiny shinies lying around, rifle barrels being matched (or not) to ammunition, orders for repairs or creations being listed for the blacksmiths and messengers running back and forth to the Central Archive with questions for the Librarians or answers from them (usually: *No Idea*).

It wasn't like that in Lilly's private office, of course: that was hers only, with a workbench, a few chairs and a second table for a few invited others to join her. But the main room was all movement and metal.

This room was nothing like that.

After the door finished creaking open it revealed a small, austere work space: a place a Scribe might work, one who needed to be alone to copy a complex diagram from a paper no one understood. The U-Ring had some rooms like that, mostly cleared-out former closets, rooms without windows – rooms no one was ever meant to remain inside for very long. The kind of places the Urban Explorers would occasionally use for meetings in the middle of the night because they were unguarded and unwatched.

The only furniture was a wide table of sheet metal no better in quality than the best smelters could make today. In front of that was a chair with a woven fabric on the backrest and five wheels down below. It reminded her of the fancy chairs she had seen once in the Snake Tower when her class toured it. On the far wall, across the desk, was a calendar that said *Pirelli*. On the bottom portion was a grid for the days of the month for the year 2097. Above it was the most captivating – but also the most confusing – photograph of a woman Elimisha had ever seen.

This photograph was black and white, unlike most of the photographs in the Museum. The woman, who looked to be in her late teens or early twenties, was quite like her friend

Gina, with strangely pale skin and straight black hair. She was standing in a room with white walls and a window behind her and all she wore were thin black panties and a Runner's leather jacket. But it was the strangest jacket imaginable. There were steel studs sticking out everywhere. There was no armour on the shoulders or elbows and if she raised the collar and zipped it to the top to protect her against extreme conditions, the studs would have pressed against her chest!

It was madness.

Elimisha couldn't see her breasts, but she could glimpse enough of her neck and torso and thighs to know that she was beautiful and sexy but she was also very weak. It was a strange combination, like nothing she had seen before. Though her skin was lovely and her eyes deep and tender, she looked like someone recovering from a long illness. There was no muscle to her; no sense of power; no promise of speed or endurance. Her beauty, such as it was, came from her poise and grace and the way the light and shadows played on her skin. How, though, she wondered, could someone so thin and weak have such wonderful skin and be wearing a Runner's jacket? It made no sense. You're either healthy or you're not. And when you're not, your skin doesn't look like that! Or your eyes. And who'd be feeling sexy during such an intense recovery?

Elimisha couldn't imagine what kind of life would have led that woman to a moment where she'd have chosen to be photographed for eternity in a condition like that.

And yet, there she was: an actual *Ancient*. A real person. A young and pretty woman in a stupid jacket, dead now hundreds of years: Elimisha's only company in the cave.

Or maybe there are eleven more girls in the calendar? Yet another question for later.

Elimisha saw the girl first because of her eyes; because of

126

their warmth and soul. What she should have noticed – as an Archive Runner for the Commonwealth with a hole in her leg and a job to do and vows to keep – was the radio.

Elimisha hadn't even been born yet when Lilly's radio had stopped working, but her mother had heard it in Lilly's work-shop. She'd been touring the Commonwealth with her class, learning about the work of the different sections and meeting all the Chiefs. They even got to try their hands at the tasks that animated the Commonwealth into a community.

That day, her mother had told her, they'd been extremely lucky because one of Lilly's engineers had discovered a voice, which was very, very rare. It was even rarer for the signal to be strong. Unfortunately, they couldn't understand whoever was speaking. Many languages existed across the world long ago, Lilly had explained; we knew about Greek and Latin, and Français and Español, but there used to be many more, maybe dozens – maybe thousands! – she had joked.

The fact that they had been able to listen to one of them that day on the radio was proof that people still existed far away and that was enough to stretch the mind beyond the edges of the known world and hint that it was bigger than they had thought.

They listened for almost an hour as the man talked and talked, all by himself, telling a story in a language no one there could identify, let alone understand. More and more people packed themselves into the workshop so they could hear the voice. Before that day, no one there had ever heard a person who was not in the same room. It was a lifetime of inspiration.

Elimisha's mother had asked if they could talk back to him, but all they could do was listen for now.

'Someday we'll find another,' Lilly had said.

Another what? Person? Microphone? Source of inspiration? She didn't know.

They listened to the same voice at the same time of night for the next three days. At the end the man said a final word – *sayonara* – and never spoke again. The word became used at the Stadium, wistfully, for final goodbyes. Maybe that was even what the man had meant.

This box in the bunker was clearly a radio. It was a similar size, with a large glass display illuminating numbers and words. More telling, of course, was the black cable that ran from a port on its face to a free-standing microphone covered in the same black steel mesh as Lilly's broken one.

What intrigued Elimisha wasn't the details of the radio itself (Lilly's was far too complicated to understand at all, let alone to use as a basis for differentiation) but how it was placed on the desk. It looked as if it had purposefully been pushed over to the side of the table and angled towards the operator to make room for a White Board – the same device that Lilly had brought back from her Tracollo.

That's what everyone called it, anyway, although it wasn't really a board. It was actually an elegant, lightweight angled wedge set on a curvaceous steel trellis that was polished more finely than the Stadium's main kitchen. On the taller part, at the back, was a curious bulge in the centre, like the top of an egg. Other than that – nothing. No buttons, no lights, no writing.

When Elimisha had asked Lilly about it during her apprenticeship, the Chief had said, 'I don't know. It seemed important at the time and it wasn't heavy so I put it in my backpack and brought it home. Since then I have learned nothing. I have no idea what it does and I never will.'

Surrender was so uncharacteristic of the Chief that Elimisha never mentioned it again.

She did, in secret, go back and look at it from time to time – furtively, as if it were a crime – she would run her hands over its perfect and inviting surface, wondering about it.

It was, after all, the only thing in the known world to have ever defeated Lilly daughter-of-Rachael.

This one looked almost identical to Lilly's except for the letters *HCG®* and the phrases *ISO Compliant* and *Made in Brazil* perfectly etched into the side.

All of which were meaningless to her.

She touched it and it did nothing.

What Elimisha wanted to do was finish her tour of the facility, clean herself up and change into the new clothes she had found that would be so much better than her own blood-soaked, filthy rags, and to drink three litres of water to replenish the blood she'd lost.

Before leaving the room, though, she pressed the long grey transmission bar and said . . . nothing.

She didn't know what she should say. Lilly's radio hadn't worked in twenty years and they'd never heard a voice in English. No one would be listening.

And yet . . . Her mother had listened to that man – her whole class, everyone crammed into the big workshop – had heard his last stories and thoughts and feelings. They might not have understood a word he said but they had been witnesses to his life – so far away, 'so lonely,' said her mother. Without a word coming back to him, with no proof that anyone could hear him, he spoke all the same. And because of that subtle act of faith – that gentle gesture – he had filled the hearts of hundreds of people with warmth and the promise of limitless possibility.

Buried beneath the earth with a calendar girl and a radio, could Elimisha do any less?

First, however, a shower.

There were still a few rooms Elimisha had not explored but the physical desire to be *well* exceeded curiosity. Leaving the comms room, she returned to the mess hall and kitchen and dragged herself down it, leaving more tracks and stirring up more dust. Hopefully, the filters would remove it.

Before the kitchen were the toilets and adjacent to them, the shower room, and next to that, first on her left after a storage closet, was the infirmary, marked with the ubiquitous red cross.

The lights were on in there too and aside from some broken glass from jars that had fallen during the rumble, everything inside was pristine. The kit contained the usual bandages, some medication she'd been warned – like every child – to *never, ever, ever put inside you*, as well as several bottles of liquid she decided to treat like medication. There was also – there it was – a needle and thread.

This was not for sewing clothing. This was for sewing humans.

Next to the needle and thread, in the same plastic wrap, were scissors, tweezers and various antiseptic liquids, almost everything she needed to remove the spike from her leg and stitch it up. The only thing missing was courage.

Sitting on the operating table, Elimisha cut the leather down to the puncture wound and then laid herself down and, as gently as she could, wiggled out of the trousers. The process took minutes, the anticipation of pain almost as bad as the pain itself.

She cut off her underwear too, then threw her jacket and shirt into the corner. The heaters had brought the room to a comfortable temperature but she was still shivering.

The mirror over the sink was clouded and for a moment she preferred it that way, but soon she became angry at herself for her gloomy mood and weakness. She rolled herself off the table, managed the three steps to the mirror and then swiped away the layer to reveal the truth of herself. Her skin was darker than late autumn leaves and her eyes were the colour of healthy earth. She was thin, but she was strong and had the same 'charmingly round face' and big brown eyes that everyone called 'friendly'.

Her hair, however, was a total nightmare and she was of a mind to take the scissors and teach it a lesson.

'Traitor,' she scolded, and in doing so, heard her own voice for the first time in days.

She tried the faucet below the mirror. A strange sound from deep in the wall answered her call for water: a *tha-thump, tha-thump, tha-thump* that soon brought out a splatter of brownish goo, then brown ooze, followed by brown water and then actual clear water.

The cool stream felt wonderful on her hands and wrists. If it was drinkable she'd be able to eat the rice by soaking it. If the stove worked, she'd even have hot food.

There was an argument for pulling out the metal rod now and stitching herself up before the shower, but another – and better one, to her mind – was being as clean as possible before messing around with an open wound.

Like the faucet, the shower worked. She found soap, or a gelatinous lump that used to be soap, in a box under the sink. It still smelled better than she did, so she spread it all over her body and through her hair. Though she tried to keep her leg away from the water, her wound still burned. Washing around it, Elimisha pictured every kind of result from pulling it out. Maybe the end was as smooth and rounded as this end was – but what if it was more like a Sagittari's arrow? What if it was buried deep in the meat of her thigh and pulling it out would mean ripping through her muscles?

The thought of it almost made her throw up.

Her training had insisted that she learn pain. Forced marches, sleep deprivation and hand-fighting until brutal defeat were all considered necessary to know the extent of what the body can endure so the mind doesn't flinch before reaching it – but this was something else. What if the wound was infected and the whole leg was growing infected because it was covered in some kind of sickness? And right that very minute, while she deliberated and prevaricated and talked herself out of action because she was afraid and feeling weak and alone and scared and naked under a billion barrels of stone and rock, with the front door sealed tighter than a Ghost Talker's mind, it was festering and seething in there, growing black and—

She pulled it out and screamed, falling to the floor in agony.

With her good leg, Elimisha pushed herself back against the wall and watched the blood ooze out and mix with the water and run down the drain to a spot even deeper into the world than she was now.

She reached up, smacked the button and stopped the water. Reaching over, she grabbed a four-hundred-year-old fluffy white towel and pressed it into the wound. The blood soaked in, but it wasn't pulsing, which meant the metal rod hadn't hit the artery, and in this way Elimisha learned that she wasn't going to bleed out naked and wet on the cold tiles of the shower in that place Adam had called (so long ago) 'the world beneath the world beneath the world'.

Over the next hour she suffered one pain after another.

Rising to her feet.

Stitching the wound closed with the sewing kit from the infirmary.

Dressing it.

Dressing herself.

Elimisha slowly pulled on the smaller of the HCG suits. As she gently squeezed the zip and pulled it up over her chest to form a V under her neck, the entire suit – as though it had a mind of its own – shrank to fit around her, as though the air had been sucked out and the cloth constricted.

As a test, she unzipped it – and it expanded again.

She zipped it up and it constricted.

She unzipped it and the suit expanded.

She did this five more times because it was *fantastic*.

After a final adjustment of the steel zip, Elimisha padded down the fabric on her hips as a habit and felt pockets, which turned out to have a very lightweight pair of eyeglasses in one side and a thin pair of gloves in the other.

Elimisha had seen glasses before; they were readily available in the Territory, but most of the time they were broken or too scratched to use. Those which bent images to make them closer were beloved and collected. The ones which bent images to make them further away were often traded. The glasses with darkened lenses were coveted by the Dragoons, Spotters, Archers, Runners, Raiders and anyone who fought in the bright light that reflected off the sands or winter snow. The last type, like these, were the most common, but did nothing at all. However, they were thin, lightweight and almost impossible to break and so they were often worn by horse riders because they kept their eyes safe from debris and wind at speed. Smelters and blacksmiths and builders also liked them as eye protection – and girls with long hair liked them to hold back their tresses.

Elimisha slipped them on to see what kind these were and

was unsurprised to find that they did nothing; no change to the colour, no distortion to the shape of the world.

Why they would be in a pocket for use of people wearing this fabulous suit, she couldn't guess.

Elimisha placed them on top of her head to keep her fully-frizzed hair out of her eyes as she hobbled her way to the communications room.

Settling herself down in the chair opposite the White Board and radio, she could feel that this chair had been a throne of power: a place where someone had sat (or had planned to sit) and talk to people all over the world.

Now, Elimisha was the Queen.

With the glasses on her head for a crown, she donned her gloves too, and like the suit, when she pulled the small zip at the base of her thumb back to the wrist, each one shrank around her hands until it was a second skin. They were so comfortable that she decided to leave them.

The radio, helpfully, had a toggle switch marked ON above and OFF beneath. Without a word or some histrionic gesture she flicked it upwards.

She was queen of a kingdom that might only be discovered, someday, by spade.

Her mother had said Lilly's radio hissed and made noises, 'like a snake strangling another snake.' Elimisha – lowering her eyebrows – had said that if one snake did that to another it would surely be a silent affair, but her mother had raised her hands up beside her face, opened her eyes wide and started chasing Elimisha out the apartment and down the hallway as Elimisha – a little pedantically, in retrospect – called out, 'Snakes don't have hands either.'

Her mother did, though, and they could tickle you until the air was gone.

This one didn't make any noises.

It didn't have any hands, either, so maybe it was working; it just wasn't receiving any signals.

Reaching over with her left hand, she depressed the long grey bar and said, 'Um . . . hello?'

The left side of the screen flickered when she spoke, creating small green hills that receded into the line like a horizon.

'Can anyone hear me?' she said, and watched the hills rise up again.

'Ahhhh!' she yelled this time, and the green bars filled the screen briefly.

Huh.

It wasn't an obvious conclusion, but it looked as though the machine was drawing the sound of her voice. Why it would do this, she wasn't sure, but it suggested that the microphone was working. Otherwise, how else would it know what to draw?

There was no sound, though, no reply. No response. No man in a foreign language to keep her company.

Elimisha placed her right hand on the White Board in front of her and ran her fingers back and forth, the way she often did at Weapons and Communications.

'Hello, hello?' she said after the pressing the button. 'I'm very interesting to talk to. If you're not sure and feeling shy, you really ought to reach out and give it a try.'

Did that rhyme?

Was she rhyming?

She did that to put the boys to bed when they were feeling rambunctious, but this was a sign of mental exhaustion. Her trainers had said this sort of thing would happen – not the rhyming, per se; that was her own madness. But starting to get punchy; to get giggly; to lose perspective; to fail to prioritise and follow one's fancies rather than needs. Fatigue does this and so does dehydration or hunger. The body needs, so you must provide. That's why every Runner, on arriving at a hidden Archive, is immediately interviewed by the Chief and asked the same Protocol questions: Are you injured? Are you in need of water or food? Nothing else matters until these problems are sorted.

Maybe her mind was trying to tell her to sleep as she'd had plenty to drink and the sweet amber was still coursing through her brain – that and a bit of dried meat from her backpack.

Nodding her head, agreeing with herself, the glasses slipped from her hair onto her nose.

A charged sensation pulsed through her entire body, starting simultaneously at the tips of her gloved fingers and the collar around her neck and then shooting up her arms and down her torso, meeting at her chest and flowing all the way down to her ankles where the HCG suit stopped.

It felt like sliding into a pool of water. Her entire body came to life. The sensation was so unexpected, so novel – so titillating – her attention would have been swept away, had something even more startling not happened in the same moment: through the lenses and floating above the White Board was a perfect sphere of what she later learned to be Planet Earth.

As the sphere spun, a gentle breeze seemed to come off it, registering on every nerve of her body.

Beneath the image, the White Board changed shape and a keyboard rose out of the material. Each key was embossed with a letter and some had words like DELETE, CLEAR and END. Above the keyboard, on the remaining surface, were instruments: a clock (15:12), a thermometer (19 degrees C) and a calendar with a year and a date that her mind was unable to register.

Through tiny speakers in her glasses came the soothing voice of a disembodied man.

'Hello,' it began.

LOCKDOWN

In Lilly's view, the Stadium really should have had a party. Over the years she has neglected too many opportunities to celebrate the small accomplishments and so they slipped by unnoticed. Other Chiefs from other sections often make efforts, and the High Command itself occasionally calls for an event when Raiders return with notable Finds. There are festivities when babies are born and named; weddings announced and performed; new Learnings shared by the Evaluators; new stories performed by returning Explorers. Even the turning seasons have their moments. Life is made joyful when effort is applied. Lilly, however, has never quite developed the knack, even when finding a matching fuse for the radio and making it work again should have been ample cause for celebration.

The Commonwealth is two weeks into General Winter's Level One Lockdown and Lilly is alone in her office. It is close to moon-high and Mickey Mouse – looking rather excited about it – insists it is 11:16 p.m. Which it might be. Lilly hasn't bothered testing the clock yet. For the moment she's happy with the company. Mickey is smiling at her and she rather likes it.

'Fancy a drink?' she says to him.

Last autumn Lilly had scored ten bottles of bourbon that were no less than three hundred years old. Traders had brought them in. She'd told them it was lizard poison.

'Do you plan on poisoning many lizards?' she'd asked.

They admitted to having no such plans.

'I'll trade you for a bag of apples, then? With the seeds.'

Too often the Ancient drinks are spoiled, but from time to time – like this time – the bottles had been found in the ideal conditions: dark and cool and underground. Anything called wine or *vin* or *vino* was best left untouched after so much time, but the same could not be said for Kentucky bourbon.

Very smooth.

'*L'Chaim*,' she says to Mickey, using a toast she learned from her mother from a language no one can even identify, let alone speak: *To Life.*

Lilly listens to the radio and it crackles, a static that makes no sense to her.

If the radio signals were plentiful and crashing into one another, perhaps they would sound like paper tearing, but that isn't happening. So what is it, then?

She imagines it as the sound of the universe itself.

Breathing.

According to news from High Command, several Runners have now been listed as missing. The Keepers are building forces on the Yellow Ridge to the east and trade has radically slowed at The Crossing. Food convoys from the forests continue to come in and the Commonwealth continues to send fresh water to wells in the territory as part of the peace strategy for the region (keep them calm, make them dependent on us). But it is a painfully dull time too. During Lockdown, no new traders may enter, no new faces can come in. No unnecessary Runs are made and Explorers requesting entry from signal mirrors or smoke or drums are denied or else told to wait for a critical mass, when they'll be allowed in all at once under heavy guard. Soldiers are placed among the out-wall farms along the river, while the Archers remain at the ready – and bored.

She turns the large black dial very, very, very slowly.

The radio says nothing.

She sips her bourbon.

Lilly should have hosted a party down here. Well, not in her personal office, but perhaps in one of the main work-rooms, after moving out anything that might accidentally kill someone. That was the challenge with hosting parties here. She could have made a speech, told a few more lies about the good old days, made a toast (not with the bourbon, obviously, that's another secret of hers) and then struck up the band for some dancing and frivolity while she ostentatiously flipped the switch on the radio and brought it to life.

A new era! A chance to listen to the voices of the world yet again!

Of course it would all be theatre. Seven voices in fifty-four years – counting the down-time when the radio didn't work at all – is hardly cause for real celebration, but that's rather the point, isn't it? We *create* causes for celebration. They don't exist by themselves.

Why do we need to say goodbye to the last falling leaf from the one tree that stands by the Southern Pass? Or light up the darkest night or dance on the evening of the longest day? We don't, really, except for the need to demarcate time, to foster goodwill in the community, to raise people's spirits and rejoice in the continued success of our existence.

So, put another way: every reason.

Mickey Mouse ticks away. What had been a satisfying sound at first has started to become relentless, like time is pursuing her rather than accompanying her.

Mickey has survived wars, famines and floods, but Lilly might be his last stop.

The radio has a scale of bands. Lilly has never understood them, not by a long shot, but having always found the voices at night-time rather than during the day, and always below 'twenty metres' on the dial, she has never bothered to poke around the higher frequencies.

Now, filled with Kentucky-distilled enthusiasm and for want of anything better to do, Lilly presses the button which makes the radio seek through the higher frequencies, all the way past forty metres – and that is when she hears a voice.

The radio locks onto the transmission and the entire screen lights up with new words, new numbers, new colours, none of which interests her right now because beyond the lights *there is a voice.*

A woman's voice, soft but strong, clear and close, is speaking in their shared language. Although Lilly's speaker is poor, choosing to crackle and distort the words, the voice sounds youthful and full of urgency.

. . . wish I could tell you where I am and what's around. But I can't. I also wish I could see the sun. Or feel the wind or even the rain. Though in a weird way I can see them whenever I want even though they aren't real.

There is a long pause and Lilly reaches for the radio, wondering if she's lost the signal but she hasn't:

I've never talked so much in my whole life without someone speaking back. It's like . . . talking to an Otis Shaft. Dropping words into the Black and – well, I know you can't drop words but – it feels like you can. Like you can toss them in and watch them fall and try and fill up the whole of the world from the bottom up but the words are insubstantial so they can't fill. They aren't dirt and rock. They never help the world rise.

The thing is, I don't know if I'm even reaching anyone. Are you there? I don't know. I may only be talking to myself. I have so much to tell you – so many things, if you only knew . . . Well, I can't talk about that. I can't even talk about what I can't talk about. Those are the rules! Those are the vows!

There is another silence and this time Lilly closes her eyes, still listening:

If you're out there and you have a radio too, please talk to me. Please? I haven't talked to someone real in so long. It's so strange having a con-versation with something that . . . well . . . I can't explain it. Something that talks back but isn't there. It's not really something you can imagine. I'm going to work on the hole now, trying to make it bigger. I'll be back tonight at eight o'clock with my evening programme where I'll read you a poem that used to be very popular. Poems – let me touch this, here – right, so, poems are 'compositions in verse'. I think that means songs without music. I'm not sure yet. But they used to be popular and they're short, so let the Scribes know they won't be here all night.

Okay. Enough for now. Talk to you at eight o'clock, everyone.

The talking ends. Lilly stands and straightens her jacket. Placing her reading glasses in her pocket she walks out the office room and into the main workshop. Bruno and Simone are disassem-bling a Dep and trying to find patterns in the maker's use of the small black chips mounted to the green boards. Letters, numbers, dimensions, anything. It is a fruitless task and Lilly knows it but that is part of the apprenticeship: learning to dive into deep water and manage the frustration, fear and failure.

She examines their faces for any emotion at all.

They are hard to read.

'What did you hear?' she blurts out.

The two look at each other. Four senior engineers at the far end of the room turn. They had barely heard her question, let alone the radio, but now they are interested. There is a chance – however remote – that Lilly is going to kill someone. It has happened before and they like to be on their toes.

'What do you mean?' asks Simone.

'For the last period of time. Hear anything unusual?'

'No.'

Lilly could see that Bruno hadn't either, but unlike Simone – who looks baffled by the question – Bruno is curious.

'What could we have heard?' he asks.

'A lot of angry language,' Lilly lied. 'I dropped something I've been working on for a while and I think I embarrassed myself. You're saying I didn't?'

'What did you say?' shouts Chaudhary from across the room, which makes two other men laugh and one woman smile.

'Come here and I'll act it out for you,' Lilly replies.

Chaudhary raised his hands in self-defence and everyone laughs again.

'Clear the room, everyone,' Lilly orders.

There is confusion for the moment and Lilly repeats her words. She isn't joking. 'No one comes back until I send for you. Consider it a vacation.'

It is Bruno who asks, 'What's a vacation?'

Everyone waits for the answer.

'Go,' Lilly says. 'Learn the answer elsewhere. Out you go.'

When the room is clear, Lilly walks to the front door too and – on checking that the hall is clear – says (very quietly, to one of the two guards), 'No one – not General Winters, not a commanding officer, not a child who forgot something – goes inside. Only me and whoever is standing next to me. Double the guard and keep this silent. Go.'

Leaving the two burly men behind her, Lilly walks off towards the Snake Tower in search of Birch.

At a distance, Bruno follows.

Lilly has forgotten it's day-time. Back when the radio last worked, she always used to listen at night. As she struts down the U-Ring towards the central staircase to the Green above, the sun's presentation is a harsh reminder of the years that have passed, apparently overnight.

The stairs don't help either. When she was young she would take them two at a time, running up them as smoothly as a young horse prancing up a hill. Now she has to hold the bannister. There is still strength in her legs but she is prone to spells of dizziness. She despises them because they make her feel weak, although her mind is stronger than ever.

And her will.

Time is an unjust thing. She concedes that she's probably not the first to notice this.

A senior Runner named Calliope bounds down the stairs and is about to pass Lilly when she is stopped by an outstretched hand. Calliope had been poached by the Order two years ago; her job as a Runner, Lilly knows, is only a cover. When she was younger, it was Attested that the girl had snuck into a bandit camp four kilometres to the northeast, off the High Road, and – singlehandedly – cut free three children who had been abducted and were going to be sold for the usual purposes. Following a path known to the Urban Explorers through one of the Commonwealth's tunnels, she had led the pursuing bandits into a trap, impaling them all on Riser Sticks. Those children are all members of the Commonwealth now. Calliope is on her way up. She was nineteen then. What is she now? Twenty-six? Lilly can't remember. What's getting lost for her as she ages is chronology. She remembers everything, but she can't always place the events in time. Maybe it's because the order of events was never what was important about them.

Calliope is very tall and has the biggest head of pitch-black curly hair in the Commonwealth. It sits on her head like a helmet and while she complains about it being unruly and regularly threatens to cut it off, there is no one who isn't mesmerised by it. Most women with her colouring have soft brown eyes. Hers are green. If she doesn't become General one day it will only be because she is so distractingly attractive.

'Chief?' she says, looking at Lilly's hand on her arm. 'Are you okay?'

'Of course I'm okay. Where's Master Birch?'

'I wouldn't know that, Chief.'

'Of course not. You're a Runner. How could you possibly know where the Master of the Order of Silence is right now?'

Lilly waits until the stairway is momentarily clear. 'It's pressing.'

Calliope checks the surroundings for eyes and ears and seeing none, she whispers, 'The Map Room.'

Lilly has one more question: 'Is anyone . . . unaccounted for? Outside the walls?'

'Chief, please don't ask me to break my vows.'

'Is it a worthwhile question I should ask someone else?'

Calliope hesitates and then says, 'Yes.'

Lilly releases her arm.

Out in the burning light of the day, Lilly walks through the archers on her way to the Thunder Room. It was renamed the Map Room years ago when the Order took it over, but Lilly's mind and memory started long before both and she has never made the adjustment to the new name. After all, it was only forty years ago the change was made.

On her way, she considers her theory: someone from the Commonwealth is trapped nearby with a radio. She has been for weeks, maybe months.

This is both near-impossible and also entirely plausible. To know which is correct, Lilly will need to tell the truth about events from fifty-four years ago, and Birch will have to break her silence. One way or another, it is going to be an interesting conversation.

The Thunder Room is reached down a staircase carved into the rock from a passage that descends from the main foyer by the West Gate. It is unlike any other room in the Stadium and no one knows its original function. The most commonly accepted suggestions are 'pleasure' and 'art' because the design is brilliant, fascinating and mad.

The two guards with pulse rifles standing at the top of passage make it one of the most secure positions inside the Commonwealth. There is a sniper on the roof with a clear shot as well.

'Tell her I'm here, it's important, I need to come down and everyone else needs to go away.'

The High Command can issue such orders to the guards.

Lilly cannot. Not any more.

The guard follows her instruction anyway.

Lilly waits, turning her face to the sun as she hears the guard descend the three hundred narrow steps – steps she will eventually have to climb again.

The tunnel is a little wider than the shoulders of a large man and has only just enough headroom to accommodate the same. There are no lights or torches in the stairway, only a glow from the bottom.

The man is gone long enough for the sun to leave its burn on her cheeks.

Hearing his footsteps close, she turns and he nods once.

At the bottom Lilly passes through an ante-chamber lined with benches on either side. Beyond this is a heavy cast-iron door that is open but can be closed and sealed. Around the edges of the door are mystical creatures – women with the tails of fish, men with the bodies of horses, lizards with wings, dogs with multiple heads, all in stories learned from the Harrington Box.

The chamber beyond the door is round and enormous. The ceiling, carved from the rock itself, is a dome as smooth as glass. The walls, however, are rough and unfinished. The circular wooden table that goes around the entire room has a gap for the doorway itself. Facing due west is the only window, which extends from floor to the edge of the ceiling and curves with the room, offering a shimmering view of the inside of the waterfall, capturing the undulating lights of the setting sun and, at night, the greens and blues of the sky. The mornings here are dark.

The colours dance across the polished surfaces of the room and across the large round table in the middle where Birch is standing with her arms crossed. Whoever had been here before is gone and whatever she had been doing before has been put away.

A guard closes the iron portals, sealing them in.

The faintest whispers cross the curved ceiling and fall like winter snow into the ears of a listener on the other side. There is a science to the movement of the waves that Lilly can observe but not understand. What matters is that the room demands subtlety and welcomes secrets. Speak too loud and the result is thunder.

'Chief Lilly,' says Birch.

'Master Birch.'

'Apparently we have to talk? Urgently?'

'Yes. I'm going to sit,' Lilly says, not waiting for an invitation.

The curved bench that circles the table is fixed in place. It is not especially comfortable, but it will have to do. Leaning forward, Lilly realises she hasn't been here in decades. Despite it now being called the Map Room, it looks exactly the same. She figures the maps must be hidden.

Birch sits across from her. Though the distance is unusually wide, the sound travels across the ceiling. Their conversation is hushed.

'You know I got the radio working again,' Lilly says. 'Graham came back with a fuse. He decided to check an old Indie that reminded him of a girl from . . . well, it doesn't matter. Anyway, I've been playing it since he and Henrietta got back, but heard nothing, as expected. Less than an hour ago I decided to swing over to the most fruitless part of the frequency spectrum. I've never heard a thing over there. This time I heard a voice.'

Birch has woven her fingers together on the table as she listens. Now she opens them slightly to demonstrate dramatic enthusiasm as best she understands it.

'That's nice,' she says. 'It'll inspire the youth. I don't see,' she adds, 'how that's urgent.'

'No. You're not following. I heard a voice in *our* language. It was strong and clear, which suggests it is close – maybe very close. It also sounded . . . youthful.'

'That's certainly much more interesting,' says Birch, 'but I still don't—'

'I think she's one of ours. I think she's trapped in a room

148

with a radio, a room that somehow or other has electricity and has had it for at least a few weeks. And if it has been weeks, it means she has food and water to keep her strong enough to be coherent and focused. What I think . . . Master Birch . . . is that one of your people – or maybe one of the missing Runners – is at the bottom of a tower in a bomb shelter. I also think I know who it is. If you don't confirm it, I can always ask her mother.'

Birch does not stare at Lilly but instead looks at the centre of the table itself. She sits silently for a long time before saying, 'Tell me more.'

Lilly is not a huge fan of Birch's and hasn't been for years. Lilly helped found the Order with her friend Saavni, who was the first Master. Lilly served afterwards until she became a member of the High Command, at which time Birch took over. Nine years ago, however, Winters had Lilly step down for being too 'forthcoming' with her own opinions on military matters. Lilly had never found military affairs especially complicated and had been rather quick to say so. As best she could tell, almost all military actions came down to erecting barriers or overcoming them through superior positioning, movement, manoeuvre, intelligence, command and communications. At least, that was the framework she'd built over the years and it appeared to work better than the Trivial Pursuit categories did for the Archive. The fact that Winters refused to learn from Lilly and found her to be a threat rather than a support came down to temperament and, in Lilly's view, Birch ought to know that. As personal differences amounted to nothing, in essence, Birch should have had the wit to continue to keep Lilly fully abreast of circumstances, thus ensuring that Weapons and Communications could be better prepared to deal with Winter's inevitable blunders – because, in Lilly's mind, these *were* inevitable, and on the way, and all for the same reason:

she was arrogant and refused to listen carefully. If she did that with Lilly, Lilly was certain she would do that with an enemy. And then what?

And yet, Birch did listen. Whatever her flaws in loyalty to Lilly, they were not flaws in reasoning or loyalty to the Commonwealth, and for this, Lilly was prepared to talk to her. Also, she couldn't do what needed to be done without Birch.

'I caught the last few minutes of her talk. She was speaking outwardly, not to another person but into the world, hoping to be heard. The girl said she was trapped. She longed for the sun and wind. She said, 'I can see them whenever I want, but they aren't real.'

'What does that mean?' Birch asks. 'A picture?'

'I have a theory. Let me go on. She also mentioned an Otis Shaft. That was the term she used. Now . . . I know these exist in places other than the nearby Gone World and our towers. They probably exist in whichever towers remain all across the world. But I don't think everyone calls them that. Henrietta Wayworth told us that the Roamers call them "elevators", which makes sense because it has the same root as "elevate" or "to go up". What matters is that within the small space of our territory, different groups use different words for the same object. This girl used ours.'

'Do you have notes?' Birch asks.

'Of course not. You think I would risk writing all this down?'

Birches blinks very slowly, waiting for Lilly to finish her explanation.

'The girl also used the phrase "into the Black". Our Runners talk about Black Jumps, so the Black is usually the unknown or else the darkness into which we don't go because of the Sickness or whatever. She also mentioned The Rise, which is especially telling, I think, because you and I both know that

The Rise is an entirely local matter. In other places – far-off but charted – the land has dropped or the waters have come in or else receded, making the land today unlike the land of the Ancients. So if this girl talks about The Rise, she is probably talking about here. Have I made my case?'

'Almost,' Birch admits.

'She said she can't tell us where she is. And I got to thinking . . . *why not?* Why not tell us where she is so we can rescue her? If she's trapped, doesn't she want to get out? When she mentioned "vows", however, it became obvious. She can't give away her position without breaking her vow.'

'Why not?' Birch queried. 'I can see the risk in being captured by someone else, but that's a danger, not a breaking of a vow.'

'She's sitting on a Trove,' Lilly says, pointing a finger for emphasis. 'If she's a Runner, she has taken a vow to protect information in motion. If she's a Chief, she has a vow to protect information at rest. If she's a Runner sitting on a massive Trove of new Knowledge she will not surrender it to save her own life. That's a vow.'

For the first time, Birch's face shows an expression. If Lilly is reading it correctly – across a twenty-foot-wide table in a room lit only with natural light cast through a waterfall – it is incredulity.

'Have you been drinking the lizard poison?'

'It isn't lizard poison, it's Kentucky bourbon.'

'I don't know what that is.'

'No you don't and you won't find out until I start liking you better. And the answer, incidentally, is "yes" and "probably not enough".'

'Runners,' Birch says, ignoring the bourbon discussion, 'only carry Knowledge which is already safe within the Central Archive. We don't ask them to surrender their lives for simple

151

copies, even if the copy is important; a weapon design, a map or a medical procedure. Almost all Knowledge, as you very well know – because you designed it this way, Chief – is stored at more than one site. Runners don't surrender their lives for copies. Members of the Order might, conceivably, make a sacrifice to defend a Route or a Commonwealth secret or an entire Archive, but the circumstances would have to be . . . extreme. I don't see why a trapped girl would risk a slow death in a Hard Room simply to protect a new Trove.'

'What if it's not only a new Trove? What if it's *the Trove*?'

'I don't know what that means either,' Birch says.

'She was looking up the meaning of the word "poem". That's neither here nor there, but as she did, she said, "Let me touch this here". Does that mean anything to you?'

'No.'

'What about the cloud?'

'In the sky?'

'The information cloud.'

'Chief,' says Birch, her defences now breaking down, 'I have no idea what you're talking about. It isn't completely impossible that a member of the Commonwealth is trapped with a radio and a Trove of books. It's fantastical, but not impossible. I'm not ready to Attest to any of your claims yet. If it were true I'd be prepared to say, yes, rescuing her and having a second radio and a new microphone certainly would be valuable and we can take that to Winters to plan an operation, assuming we know where to look. Any Trove is important. But . . . *clouds*, Chief?'

'We cannot take this to Winters because she won't believe us and she'll shut us down before we start. Listen carefully, Birch. There's a children's story – a fable – my mother told me. I was maybe eight. She learned it from her grandmother, making the story almost a hundred years old, at least. It goes like this: way back when, the Ancients decided that the earth was no longer safe for their Knowledge and so they put everything they knew in the sky and hid it away in clouds. But the sun considered the sky her own domain and so she scorched the clouds and burned them off. After that, no Knowledge could rain down on the people of the earth. Their memories grew weak, the land grew dry and cold and the people had to start from the beginning. "Making fire from sticks" was the phrase she used.'

'We are ignorant and the land is dry,' Birch said, not accepting Lilly's analysis. 'So the storyteller created a fable filled with Knowledge and water and a nice metaphor about rain and clouds to link them together. It's a perfectly serviceable fable, Chief. Beyond that . . .'

'You're a fine thinker, Penelope, and you always have been. But ever since you were a little girl you have refused to make the creative leaps that are necessary for greatness. The problem isn't your mind; it's your personality. You just don't like being wrong, so you plan everything out and play it safe. Of course you became the Master of the Order of Silence! But take it from me: solutions are often on the far side of prolific failure. If we don't risk making a creative leap in the face of this radio transmission now – if we don't consider the massive implications of what it could mean – it will seal our fate because every risk we take in the future will be the product of our cowardice and lack of imagination now. I believe – although I might be wrong, Master Birch – that sixteen-year-old Elimisha daughter-of-Cara is trapped in a nearby but undiscovered room where she has found a portal to the greatest repository of Knowledge in the history of human civilisation. I think Elimisha has discovered the internet.'

From her bag Lilly removes three objects: the White Board

and two devices that look like pulse pistols without barrels. 'And to help you understand my conviction, I'm going to tell you a story that you have never heard before because no one has ever heard it. This is the story of how the first Tracollo really happened, where the Harrington Box was really found, and how I got it open. And perhaps most importantly,' Lilly says, tapping the White Board, 'where I found this and what I think it is.'

FIFTY-FOUR YEARS AGO

Lilly's mother, Rachael, once told her that she'd been named for a flower that used to grow in this part of the world, long before The Rise, 'Long before the deserts rolled in,' Rachael said, 'and the forests died and the sand piled at the base of the towers in the Gone World – a place where the urbanscape glowed so brightly with Big Electricity that the lights would reflect from the clouds at night. The people there,' said Rachael, her hand on Lilly's chest at bedtime, Lilly smiling at the dreamy possibility of it all, 'numbered in millions and when they wanted to leave they travelled in flying ships that zipped through the air faster than birds. And oh, the food there!' Rachael would roll her eyes in ecstasy, which always made Lilly giggle. 'It was so plentiful they would only eat half of what they were given and then just . . . throw it away! And then they'd take a nap on the table and snore.'

And they would laugh and laugh and laugh.

'Was I really named for a flower?' Lilly asked her when she was seven and getting serious. It had always been only the two of them. Her father wasn't a factor.

'Yes. They say it was pretty, but no one knows. We only have the word now, not the memory. But I knew you would be pretty

155

and I liked the sound of it. We take what we know and use it to make what we can. For example,' she told Lilly, 'I knew all about love, so I took all the love I had and I made you. What I didn't know when I made you,' said Lilly's mother, 'was that you would be so smart.'

Ten years later and motherless after the ambush, Lilly stood at the blacksmith's forge where she'd been all morning. She did not feel like a flower and she wasn't feeling so smart either. Her rare and strange yellow hair was matted with black soot from the smith's furnace and her muscular arms were browned and glistening from two hot months under the summer sun. Lunch-break was coming soon, though not soon enough, but the restlessness inside her was not caused by the heat or hunger.

Today was the one-year anniversary of her mother's murder by bandits on the High Road outside the Stadium walls. She chose this apprenticeship with the blacksmith so she could learn to make weapons: the swords and shields and arrows and pikes that already armed the community – but not only those. She wanted to make the ones she had created in her head.

Lilly's imagination was alive with the possibilities of defending the Stadium, but the adults around her were too sunk into habit and complacency to see either the need or possibility. The anger was building inside her like filling a well that had no overflow. Today of all days it was too much. She needed someone to take it out on and there was only one person around.

'I'm not making another damn bucket. I know how to make buckets. I have mastered the bucket. This is an apprenticeship, not a punishment. I want to move on.'

Luther Blacksmith, the Forge Master and Weapons Chief, was a giant brown-skinned man who towered above Lilly. His blue eyes were weary from contending with Lilly's constant disappointment. He knew, however, what day it was and understood the cause of her impatience. He knew the shape of the story: a trading mission to a northern colony that was attacked. Lilly was the only one who made it back to the Stadium, and only after shooting her way out with her mother's own gun.

Lilly had always been a brilliant student but now, with her mother gone, she was sharp and dangerous like the end of a spear; all of her weight – all of her mind and emotion – was pressing down on that one point. Luther accepted her grief and pain, but it was her hunger that worried him. He didn't know what she wasn't willing to do in light of what she'd suffered.

Or not do.

Making buckets had felt like a good idea at the time. It wasn't any more.

Still, it's what the Council had ordered.

'It's what the Council ordered,' he said to her. 'They want forty buckets. We make the buckets.'

Lilly couldn't remember how long it had been since the Crier had announced the hour. The sun's heat was a hammer, making the surface of the courtyard an anvil. She looked up at the sun and considered its distance to the Stadium wall. Once it passed over, the shade would fall here and she would feel a little better.

'We need a better way of measuring time,' she said.

Here we go again, thought the Master Blacksmith. He said nothing. He was in no mood to antagonise her.

'We know the ancients had ways to do it,' Lilly said. 'We know what they measured too. Seconds, minutes, hours, days, weeks, months, years. What we don't know is how they did it. Now we use a stick and a shadow or else watch sand fall through a glass.'

'Stick and shadow work fine,' Luther attempted.

'Not when it's cloudy,' Lilly said.

'Not when it's cloudy,' he conceded.

'Or at night.'

'No. Not at night either.'

'Or when you're away from the stick and the markers that actually tell the time.'

'I suppose not.'

'Hard to argue that it works fine if it works less than half the time.'

'And yet we carry on.'

Luther turned back to work. He struck his hammer on the thin metal in his tongs and then tapped the edge of the anvil in a constant rhythm that was so fluid it became musical. Not all the raw metal from the finds was equally good for casting or re-shaping, but this one was curving nicely. He took pleasure in watching the ends gently turn towards one another like new friends.

'I'm guessing this is why the Ancients built time machines that ran on electricity,' said Lilly.

'I suppose that's true,' he said, only half paying attention.

'Hundreds of years later we can't make new ones or fix the old ones. Doesn't that anger you? That we're weak and stupid compared to them?'

'No,' said Luther.

'Why not?'

'Because we're alive and happy and they're neither.'

'I'm not happy. And my mother's not alive,' Lilly said. 'And I think it's because we're weak and stupid.'

Luther did not reply.

No one had assaulted the Stadium in numbers in more than a hundred years. There had been skirmishes beyond the walls that killed a dozen or so a year, of course, but nothing in numbers. There were bandits and wandering tribes; Roamers and Ghost Talkers. There were some distant colonies with whom they traded and sometimes people's tempers flared and blades were pulled. But on the whole, there weren't enough people left alive for a proper war. Luther considered this to be a product of the Stadium's philosophy: silence and secrecy. Don't make yourself a target and don't become one.

The population of the Stadium was under two hundred souls.

In Lilly's view, however, it was only a matter of time before the Stadium would fall. Her mother's death had proved that to her. She could feel a stirring in the winds and she knew in her bones that a day of reckoning was coming, so they needed to prepare. The outside world was growing more dangerous and more daring. If the Council of The Few chose stagnation as a strategy for survival it would mean death. Only relentless, unerring and attentive progress would save them. If the Council of The Few didn't have the brains to lead them in that direction, Lilly was going to grow up and do it herself.

'When are we going to start making new things, Chief?' Lilly asked him.

Luther's arm and hammer were swinging to a rhythm now. Twenty years of body memory, arm and hammer worked as a single machine, a beat as steady as a horse in canter. He ignored her, knowing his silence would be heard as an invitation to speak. Then again, so would any of his words. So he saved the words.

'I'm talking about things that don't exist yet,' she went on, 'or maybe things that once did exist but don't any more. Things like this,' she said, picking up a mystery object from beneath a work bench and handing it to Luther, who stopped hammering with a sigh and accepted it only because rejecting it would have required words.

'Guess what it is,' Lilly said with a smile.

It looked like an enormous fish hook with a small steel ring at the end.

'It's an enormous fish hook with a small steel ring at the end,' he said.

'No. Use your imagination. Picture a rope tied into the ring. What could you use it for?'

Luther didn't like using his imagination. When he did the pieces never lined up the way two pieces of metal lined up. The metal he could bend gracefully. The ideas came out twisted and misaligned.

'I'd rather not.'

'Please.'

He took it. Turned it around.

'We could . . . sit on the walls and dangle it over the edge and catch giant desert monster fish.'

'Desert monster fish?'

'You told me to use my imagination. You understand the danger now?'

'If you hold the rope,' she said, demonstrating, 'you swing this around so you feel the force of the spin in your hand and at the right moment you release it into the air and it flies up along the wall and hooks itself on! And then you can climb up! It's a climbing hook. Get it?'

'Why wouldn't I take the stairs?'

'Maybe our enemies are on the stairs and we want to encircle them, so one team scales the wall while the other fights from below. Then we pinch them like tongs. See?'

Luther's mighty shoulders dropped. He raised his hand and made a fist against the sky. The sun was two fist-lengths from the wall. Two fists was the same as for ever with Lilly around.

'You can break for lunch,' he said. The sun wasn't in charge of her apprenticeship, he reminded himself. He was.

She stood her ground.

'The Council,' he said in a last-ditch effort to talk sense into her, 'wants buckets so we can carry more water from the clean part of the river at the base of the falls back into the Stadium at the top of the falls. It isn't weapons work, but it's helpful. Why don't you want to be helpful, Lilly? Isn't that why you chose to be a blacksmith for your apprenticeship?'

'Helpful? Yes – and I could be so much more helpful if they let me invent better ways of doing things. The Stadium could grow bigger and better and smarter and . . .'

'Safer?' Luther offered.

'Yes! I'm going to learn everything there is to know and I'm going to make us more powerful than everyone else in the world. You watch me.'

Lilly looked at Luther to see if her appeal had meant anything to him. Disappointed, she tossed the poker to the ground and looked into his enormous, passive face.

'Who even built this place?' she asked, sounding resigned to the need for this conversation. 'The plaque on the wall says *Olympic Stadium*. What does that *mean*?'

Lilly was referring to the brass plaque on the outer wall by the Main Gate:

Olympic Stadium MMXCVI [2096]
Bicentennial Summer Olympics
In Accordance with the Kyoto Treaty of 2085,
this Stadium produces zero carbon emissions
through its use of Circular Energy powered by
solar, hydrodynamic and human-kinetic force.

'Two-zero-nine-six looks like a year,' Lilly said, 'because two-zero-eight-five is being used like a year in the sentence and we know that a treaty is an agreement. So they built this Stadium to fulfil an agreement. To do . . . what? Who was Kyoto? Why did they name a treaty after her? If there were Summer Olympics, does that mean there were Winter Olympics too? Does that mean there's another Stadium out there that's for the winter? Maybe it's also full of people. Maybe it's closer than we think. Maybe it's just beyond the desert—'

'There's nothing beyond the desert.'

'If we go west, where The Few came from, legend says we hit a massive ocean.'

He was ready for her to stop talking now.

'Can we stop talking now?'

'For God's sake, Luther! What happened to the Old World? And what's going to happen next? What if the same event is going to happen again, the way the sun passes overhead every day and we're unprepared but could be prepared if we only knew more? Are we really going to just sit here and wait for it while making buckets?'

'Stop,' Luther said to her. 'Enough. Something terrible happened to you, Lilly. It's put smoke in your eyes and now all you see is fire. But the fire is inside you. *You* are what's changing and I'm not going to help you set us all ablaze. You have to control it. You think we need to protect ourselves from the world. Right now, child, the world may need to protect itself from you. So go, don't come back until you're calm. That's an order.'

'Yes, sir.'

'Chief. Yes, Chief. I'm a Chief. Now go.'

As Luther started hammering away again, a commotion formed at the Main Gate and four soldiers armed with pikes and swords – and one with a pulse rifle – ran to the gate to take up position. The pike soldiers stood to either side of the gate and the rifleman knelt behind a waist-high boulder they'd dragged in long ago for this purpose.

The gate opened and Saavni ran in.

Saavni was Lilly's age, with raven-black hair, soft brown eyes and the build of a warrior. They'd come up together in school and were friends. Saavni wasn't inventive like Lilly, but she was extremely resourceful, didn't like fools and had an adventurous streak Lilly admired.

Saavni ran straight past the guards to Lilly, who was sitting under the shade of a tarp and drinking warm water from a tall bottle. She couldn't imagine why her friend was in such a rush.

'Adam,' Saavni said, doubling over at the waist to catch her breath when she arrived. 'He finally did it.'

Adam was Lilly's slightly younger cousin. She didn't like him very much.

'Did what?' Lilly asked.

'He made a Black Jump, Lilly. In the Gone World. He's . . . gone.'

Lilly stood there, incredulous. Adam was fifteen and, in her view, a little stupid. Where Lilly was beautiful and powerful and smart, Adam was feckless and skinny and strange. It wasn't that he was bent like the Ghost Talkers, it was more like his mind was weak and the more he tried to be like other people, the more strange he became.

'What happened?' she whispered. Luther was banging away at his metal and had no interest in Lilly's conversation, but she didn't want him to hear. Lilly knew the power of loose words; how rumours could turn the whole world against people. Secrecy was better, certainly where Adam was concerned.

'You won't get angry?' Saavni asked, keeping her own voice low.

'I really don't know.'

'We slipped out again.'

'I figured.'

'There were four of us at first – me, Verena, Sheku and Reed. Adam heard and wanted to come.'

'Because of Verena. But she's not interested in Adam, trust me.'

'I know,' said Saavni, standing up now and reaching for Lilly's bottle of water. She drank half of it before putting it back on the wooden ledge. 'But he wanted to come and we couldn't stop him, so . . . well, he came. We left with a band of Traders this morning when they opened the gate, then we hooked up with an encampment of Roamers down at the edge of the Gone World—'

'That's dangerous,' Lilly pointed out. 'Bandits often dress as Roamers and the Roamers can be foul-tempered and unpredictable when things aren't going well for them.'

'In this case, they gave us lunch in trade for carrot seed.'

'Roamers don't plant seeds.'

'No, they *trade* them,' said Saavni, irritated and wanting to get on with her story. 'So we finished and we slipped into the Federal Building through the gap in the fourth window on the south side – you know the one. So we're messing around in there a floor down and Reed dares Adam to go down three levels to see the first skeletons because we know Adam hasn't taken the Dare of the Steps before. Three levels down, though—'

'It starts getting dark because you're under the sand at that point,' said Lilly, arms now crossed.

'Well . . . Sheku went four down but he came back up all freaked out saying that the bodies had all fallen head-downwards

164

right on the stairs, just like the old people said because – you know.'

'The Sickness.'

'Anyway, we all went down to see, but we didn't go any further because we didn't want to die. But this time,' Saavni continued, her tone saying that Lilly really needed to stop interrupting, 'we used mirrors to bring down as much light as we could – you know how at a click after Sun-High the light hits the stair shaft at the perfect angle? So with the mirrors we could reflect down five, even six levels and see much more. Anyway, we could see the Otis Shaft doors were open down there, and then Reed – because he's an asshole, he really is – dared Adam to go down. Of course Adam looked at Verena, because he always does, and she immediately told him not to, and she said it was time to head home because the sun would close the light window soon, but instead of going back up, your idiot cousin jumped off the edge onto that metal rope that hangs down and just . . . he just slid into the Black. Lilly,' said Saavni, her voice shaking a little, 'he's gone.'

'When?' Lilly asked.

'I rode here straight away. The horse is drinking now.'

'You're coming with me,' Lilly said, grabbing Saavni by her lavender shirt and pulling her across the courtyard.

'Where are we going?'

'Storage on level five and then back to that tower to find Adam.'

'It'll be dark—'

'That's why we're thinking ahead and taking what we need to make light.'

Lilly pulled Saavni by the sleeve of her fancy new shirt straight through the corn, spelt and wheat fields, past the row of berries and herbs and into the South Gate at the far end of the court-yard.

'I just got this!' yelled Saavni.

'The world is full clothing. I only have one cousin.'

'You don't even like him!'

'That's not the point,' Lilly said, pushing her down the stair-case to the lower level.

At the southern end of the Ring Road inside the Stadium, an inexperienced guard named Wax armed with a short spear stood looking bored in front of the storage room he was ostensibly guarding (from what, Lilly had no idea).

'I'm with Weapons,' Lilly said. 'I need . . . stuff. Get out of the way, Wax.'

The guard looked at the dirtiest girl he had ever seen. He looked at her blackened hands and face and her angry blue eyes. He wasn't sure whether this was what blacksmiths looked like, but he was pretty sure it was what they smelled like.

Lilly something, right? He'd seen her around. Her hair was weird. The sooner she went away the better.

'Okay,' he said, unmoving and unmoved.

Lilly pushed past him into the room.

It was dark inside, with only the light from the doorway illuminating the goods stacked on the shelves.

'What are you looking for?' Saavni asked her.

'Here they are,' Lilly said in reply, opening a coarse canvas bag. Inside were two cardboard boxes. One of them was open, which was no surprise because she'd been the one to open it a few weeks ago when she'd been in here rummaging around for interesting things to take back to Luther. What she'd found had been as close to magic as anything she had ever seen, which was why she'd kept it to herself and hadn't told Luther. She'd made a mistake, however. Aunt Sarah had invited her

166

to dinner and with so little else to talk about she'd let slip the news of her secret stash. Adam had heard. What she hadn't appreciated was that he actually been *listening*.

'You'll never guess what I found after a trade,' she'd said. And then she showed her aunt.

Stupid. You don't *share* secrets. You *keep* them.

The open box was still there and untouched and the identical second box was there too, but not the third, because Adam had taken it.

'Little shit,' Lilly said, picking out both boxes. 'He was *planning* to do it. He didn't jump on impulse, Saavni. He planned on making a Black Jump.'

'Lilly,' said Saavni, who had no idea why they were in that storage room, 'what are we doing?'

'Gearing up for the urbanscape. Now go and get that rope.' She pointed. 'And those knives. And that leather jacket and those gloves, and that bottle too – we're going to need water.' As Saavni did as she was bidden, Lilly glanced at the door to make sure Wax hadn't suddenly developed an interest in anything, then lowered herself to the floor, rolled onto her back and slid herself under the steel shelf at the far end of the room.

The black bag was still where she'd hidden it. She pressed it to her nose to smell the fresh oils inside. She jiggled it and felt around. Everything was there.

When she re-emerged, Saavni was looking down at her, those brown eyes curious, the lustrous eyebrows raised.

'It'll all make sense later,' Lilly promised her, adding, 'I'm not going nuts.'

Saavni frowned. 'What are nuts?'

'I don't know,' said Lilly. 'But if you put them together, they can replace your mind and it's apparently not good.'

Saavni wasn't interested in old words like Lilly was. What Saavni was interested in was Lilly's intentions. 'We're not seriously going after him, are we?'

'We're going to see if he fell and whether we can get him back. More than that,' she said, 'I don't know.'

The sun was still high in the sky when Lilly and Saanvi slipped out of the Stadium through a gap in the wall at the north end, not far from Luther and the furnace. Saavni's horse, Costello, was tethered to a smooth, weather-beaten log down on the flats below the Main Gate. It was possible a spotter on the tower, high up on the rising oval of the Stadium, was watching them even now, but Lilly didn't care. Unlike Saavni, Lilly didn't have parents any more. The worst that could happen was that rumours would spread about Adam being gone, so better for her to be seen trying to save him than not.

Saavni held the reins and Lilly sat behind her. They were both experienced in the saddle, but Saavni had taken to racing when she was twelve and she was now the best rider of their generation, such as it was given there were only thirty-five of them, so the climb to the top was limited. Saavni pressed them across the rocky and hilly expanse and out into the flatter desert beyond as Lilly sat behind and opened the black bag which contained her Colt .357.

Pulse weapons were extremely rare but they were also incredibly durable. When placed in their charging cradles under the Stadium, where The Few had first found them hundreds of years ago, the Stadium's Big Electricity recharged them, the green lights climbing up the spine of the magazine proving their worth. Whether dropped, smashed, submerged in water or frozen in ice, the pulse weapons could still be relied on for a hundred bursts to stun an enemy or thirty bursts to blow a hole in their chests or knock their heads clean off at two hundred metres. They had forty weapons, and each weapon had three magazines, making the Stadium the most powerful military force in the known world. With the Stadium walls rising protectively around them, General Mino thought they were invincible.

Lilly knew otherwise.

Less rare, however, were guns. Guns were everywhere: pistols and semi-automatics, short barrels and long ones. At the age of fourteen, Lilly had taken it on herself to start collecting pieces of them, oiling them, assembling the ones that looked as if they fit together best. The ancient six-shooters were the least complicated and therefore the most reliable. Hers was a Colt Python .357 and unlike the vast majority of guns left in the world, hers had bullets.

Luther had told her that most of the ammunition had probably been used during the Unspeakable Years after the Gone World fell and before the Long Quiet started, which was when The Few stumbled on the Stadium and created 'this paradise', as he called it. Today, most of the ammunition that anyone finds and trades is corroded or rusted or cracked or won't explode. And the ammunition that does work almost never matches any of the guns that work.

Fingers or whole hands have been blown off trying to match ammunition to guns, and after a while someone decided precautions had better be taken.

'Every so often,' Luther told Lilly, 'you come across some boxes where the owners had put them in special bags that somehow had all the air sucked out of them. If those wrapped bullets were kept in a cool place, they can still shoot today, even after hundreds of years. Sometimes we found giant depots of them. We think they might have come from an army.'

Lilly's mother Rachael had collected fifty rounds that looked good for her Colt. Lilly herself had found almost a dozen more once she learned what to look for in size and markings.

Now, Lilly checked the cylinder. There were three live rounds still inside. The other three she had fired at her mother's killers. She had no memory of whether the bullets had found their marks. She removed the spent shells and pocketed them, then carefully reloaded.

Lilly and Saavni approached the landmark near the end of the Gone World's territory: the tail end of an airship or a spaceship, entire and unmolested, that rose at a slant thirty metres into the raw blue sky.

AIRBUS.

There was no debris around it.

People said that whatever kind of machine it was had been eaten whole by the rising earth and that inside – like in the towers – was Sickness. The teachers said it had floated in silt and wet sand in the same way that sinking boats point sky-wards, until, somehow, the thick waters had become hardened earth and all that had been moving came to rest. The curious had looked into the glass windows to see the bones fastened tight into seats by straps around their torsos. Some had fallen apart, heads rolling off and disappearing into the dark where the windows were covered.

The world was full of Raw. No one needed the metal. Better to have a landmark in this barren place.

*

Seven towers rose out of the desert sands. Tumbleweed and brush had collected into massive piles on the eastern side, from where the wind came most often in the evenings. People considered that proof that the deserts went on for ever.

Each building had a name. This one was called The Federal on account of the words etched into the stone at the top. The other towers were higher than this one, which rose eight levels up from what was now the ground.

The rest of the Gone World was wiped out or buried. Whatever happened here, long ago, had happened fast.

Saavni dismounted and tied the horse to a pole jutting out of the ground. Lilly followed her as she led the way through one of the windows that had been destroyed when something fell from the sky, crashed through the floor and disappeared into the dark below. All the other windows on all the other buildings were intact. They were tough things: impossible to remove, except for this one, impossible to break.

Inside was the usual assortment of steel chairs and desks, drawings on the walls and the smell of urine that Lilly was convinced would last for ever if it soaked into concrete.

She followed Saavni down the stairs into the ever-darkening passage until they were on the fifth floor. It was widely known that the old Ground Level was eight floors down.

'The next one,' said Saavni, stepping over bones.

Lilly reached into her pouch and removed one of the sticks. She tore open the paper covering with her teeth, and then snapped the short stick so the tubes inside broke.

She shook it.

The entire staircase burst into a greenish-yellow glow. Saavni backed away from Lilly's glowing hands until her back was against a wall.

'It's not dangerous,' Lilly said.

171

'It's burning.'

'It isn't hot.'

'How can something be burning and not be hot?'

'I don't think it's burning. I think two different liquids mixed together when I snapped it. When they came together, they made light. Someday I'm going to find out how it works. There is an answer to everything.'

'It's like magic.'

'That word is death because it's where questions end. Now, where's Adam?'

Saavni led her to the Otis Shaft.

Lilly had never seen the doors fully opened before – no one had. Everyone knew the shaft was there because they'd pried the doors open just enough to look. But Saavni was right: now the doors were wide open, revealing a tunnel dropping straight down into nothing.

'We thought of tossing a torch down,' Saavni said, 'but the wind would have put it out as it fell and we didn't have oils.'

'Adam!' Lilly yelled as loudly as possible.

There was no response except from her own voice returning to her.

Lilly tossed the glow stick into the shaft and watched it drop sixty feet until it was nothing but a tiny green square, smaller than her thumb.

Saavni hung her head over the edge and looked down.

'Lilly . . . he's gone. He's really gone.'

The next day, back at the Stadium, Lilly went down to the inner ring, circled it underground until she arrived at the Western

Window overlooking the clean river that flowed out from under the Stadium, and made for Adam's apartment.

Lilly's Aunt Sarah and Uncle Grayson slept in two rooms behind a small plaque that said 'Equipment'. She knocked, entered and found Sarah there.

She told her what had happened to Adam.

For an hour, Sarah wept and talked, saying again and again that something like this had been inevitable because Adam wasn't right in his head. He was prone to being impulsive; to falling for ideas and for love and for excitement too easily. He was never a thoughtful boy, never cautious enough. 'Not long for this world,' she told Lilly.

When her breath returned, Lilly left her there with the truth and the consequences.

With no solutions and nothing else to do or say, Lilly returned to the forge with Luther and tried to be a comfort to her aunt and uncle as they had tried to be a comfort to her when Rachael was murdered.

For eight days word spread throughout the community about the loss.

On the ninth day, Adam returned.

Lilly was alone at her favourite spot behind the Stadium near the waterfall. There was a rocky ledge beneath the Western Window that was close enough to the wall itself that no one could see her when she sat there. Her favourite time of day was sunset. The orange ball would hang over the river, and in the reflection, there would be two suns. As it sank it would touch itself, merge, then become a perfect circle before falling into the river and vanishing. This is where Lilly would sit to think of her mother and try and imagine what her father might have looked like. Her mother had raven-black hair and fair skin – so how did she get cursed with hair so yellow? Did her father have yellow hair too? What would that even look like on a man? How could he have been attractive enough to find love with her mother?

Lilly never had got around to asking and now she'd never know.

As the sun burned below the water and the sky turned to purple, Adam turned the corner on the ledge.

At first it was only a figure; no one she knew. She looked and tried to determine who it was. The idea of Adam came to her before the truth of him. It felt as though the ghost of him was – in that moment – taking possession of whoever the person might have been. This is the way Ghost Talkers have explained themselves in the past. How spirits of the dead possess the bodies of the living for brief moments and a wall between worlds falls away. This version of Adam, in front of her, was skinnier than ever. His eyes were vacant and his skin pale. His hands were covered in caked blood and dirt. The shoes and clothes he wore – the same ones he'd been wearing the day he took the Black Jump – were filthy, as though he had been walking in mud.

The same shoes and clothes?

This must be how it happens, she had thought, *how the Ghost Talking begins for some people. Thousands, millions, billions – all dead below the sands and the waters. It is impossible for so many people not to hear their voices, their screams, their longing and their pain. Ghost Talkers are to be feared because they have lost their minds, but pitied too, and comforted, if they can be. They are often the kinder souls: the ones who cannot push back the emptiness of the entire world.*

Until that moment, Lilly had never thought of herself as one of them.

When Adam started walking closer it was affirmed to her that she was not.

They were the same shoes and the same clothes on the same boy.

Adam – *alive* – walked closer to her but did not speak. He did not smile or show any joy in having seen her or in having been seen. He stopped when he was close enough for Lilly to smell him, to know he was a person and not a vision, and when he did, he raised his right hand and showed three fingers together. Then he rotated his hand so they were horizontal.

'There are three worlds,' he said as though he were speaking from the grave. 'The world we see. The world buried by the sand. And a third world: a world below their world. And they are all connected.'

Adam turned and walked back the way he'd come as the waterfall continued to crash below them.

Lilly sat trying to recover from the shock of seeing him. When the moment had passed, she sprang to her feet and quickly navigated the rocky ledge to where it widened and met the flatter land on the northern end, then ran up to the Western Gate to get back inside the Ring Road.

In the cool of the Stadium, Adam was nowhere to be seen.

Without considering the implications, Lilly sprinted for her aunt and uncle's home, burst into their rooms without knocking and found her Aunt Sarah sitting on the edge of the bed in a kind of trance.

She was wearing a lovely orange dress with flowers that must have grown somewhere before The Rise. Lilly vaguely remembered seeing it on the rack on the last Trade Day a month before.

She wore no shoes. Her feet were flat on the floor and her hands were in her lap.

'Aunt Sarah?'

'Hello, Lilly.'

It occurred to her only in that moment not to ask the question she wanted to ask. Some part of her still thought Adam's appearance might have been a kind of vision.

'How are you?' she asked instead.

'Adam's alive,' Sarah said, Attesting.

'Yeah. He just found me on the ledge by the waterfall.'

'Something's wrong with him,' Sarah said.

'What do you think is wrong with him?' Lilly asked.

'I think,' said her Aunt Sarah, 'that the boy I raised is gone.'

'Where did he go, Aunt Sarah?'

'He's . . . away.'

Lilly had heard this phrase used for men or women whose minds were for ever broken by circumstance or pain. That hadn't been what Lilly meant, though.

'But . . . where is he?'

'The Thunder Room,' she said, still looking forward at the wall, her hands still resting on her lap as though movement were superfluous. 'He said he was working down there.'

Lilly left Sarah sitting on the bed in her flower-covered dress and went to find her crazy cousin.

Lilly ran, across the Green, though the harvest, past friends and old people, to the staircase no one used because it led to a room that served no purpose; a room that once-seen was ignored. Some said it had a strange power, an odd energy. They didn't like the way sound moved in there. It wasn't natural.

Of course Adam went there.

It was growing dark. The purples and greens of the sky were

176

not entirely visible as the last rays of the orange light fought to remain. The water outside the giant window – almost silent, as the Ancients had evidently wanted it – shimmered against the walls and across their faces.

Adam had lit two torches and placed them on the massive table.

He stood there drawing.

Lilly watched her cousin, who looked more like a shadow than a boy. His arm moved frantically and his concentration was intense. He had not even looked up when Lilly entered the room.

She had never known him to draw – he had never been one for the arts or other creative pursuits. He was in his last year of studies and hadn't excelled at much. For his apprenticeship he was thinking about farming because he liked the smell of fresh earth and watching things grow. Lilly had told him it was a good idea.

'What are you doing?' she asked him now.

'I'm drawing the world below the world that's below our world,' he said, wide-eyed. 'It's all connected. I have to draw the routes before I forget them.'

Lilly stepped closer to the table. He had somehow acquired a giant white sheet from one of the storage rooms and a vat of purple dye that some traders had made from cabbage, beets, flowers and oils. Using a medium-sized brush of wood and horsehair, he was drawing curves and lines and circles: squares that connected to other squares; what seemed to be steps leading upwards or downwards. He scribbled notes in places – words that made no sense, a grammar that didn't exist. He was drawing as though the lines were there already and all he had to do was copy over them to reach the other side of his mania.

'What is that?'

'The map of the underworld. Like I said.'

'Adam. How are you alive?'

'I brought the glowsticks. Each one lasts half a day. Two a day. Nine days. Eighteen sticks. I'd brought twenty. I was lucky to find the exit. Very lucky. Had to keep moving. Keep going. Stay away from the silent people. Watching me. All the time. Still too. Very still. I painted my name on one of them. *Adam Was Here.* Like on the walls in the Gone World. Tell us they once lived. Ghosts now. Bones. Dust. All the dead. They were all there. Now only their names are here. Our names too. We use their names. Our names are their names – living names of dead people. I used my blood because there was no ink. That will never go away now. He'll always remember me, standing there like that on his chest. *Bam!* Thought he could scare me but I showed him. I found the Hard Room – found all the Hard Rooms. Tunnels behind the walls. Sneaky tunnels. Most of them hidden. Not all, though. Some gave up their secrets to time and so I found the pattern. So much water down there. So much stick and rot. I'll never stop smelling it. Little dead children skulls. They don't float. You step on their heads and they're slippery so you fall and then you get angry so you reach down and find out what it was. It was a baby! Someone's baby! Slippery baby skulls in the green light with those big black eyes. "Hello, Adam!" They didn't talk – that was me. Nine days alone but it felt like months. No windows or light. I found a dry room, had a nice bed. I slept there. I wanted to go up and I found a staircase but I wasn't done. I have to make the map. The map is going to make me famous. The map is going to make them stop laughing at me. This,' Adam said, looking up at her for the first time, 'this is going to be my legacy. No one's going to pick on me any more. "Why aren't you more like your cousin Lilly?" everyone asks. "She's so beautiful. She's so smart. You're not beautiful or smart," they say to me. But I know things no one knows. My map – the Adam Map – this is the truth of things.'

He put down the paint brush and stood upright. He placed his three fingers together again.

Adam's words were only whispered but in that room, they thundered in her ears, travelling across the slick ceiling like ripples on the water and then dropping onto her like a storm. No one used this room because of that. It was impossible to be here when different people were speaking, making teamwork maddening and – who works alone? The passage down was too narrow to carry large objects and the stairs were too long for heavy ones to make their way back up.

Lilly became keenly aware she was watching a madman draw a map of nothing for no one. It frightened her.

'Adam, I'm sorry you went down there. Obviously, you saw some terrible things. You clearly haven't eaten anything proper in a week and you haven't bathed either. I'm sure you were lost and it's a miracle you found a way out. But what you're saying makes no sense. And no one,' Lilly said, pointing to the drawing, 'can memorise that much information while moving around underground in the dark. I have an exceptionally good memory, Adam, and I wouldn't be able to do it. That map doesn't mean anything. You need to stop now and get well.'

Adam put down the brush and pointed at her. 'You don't believe me, but I have proof! I have proof!' From beneath the giant table, Adam pulled up a bag of green fabric, unzipped it and removed two objects that at first looked like guns.

These were the objects that Lilly had placed on the table for Birch to see.

Back then, Lilly continued to explain, she had studied them as she walked closer to him.

The artefacts didn't look like guns so much as rifle receivers: there were grips and guards, but no barrels or stocks. The one in his left hand said PRIME and the one in his right hand said ACTIVATE. The triggers inside the guards were long and red, as though two or even three fingers would be needed to pull them. Each was covered by a plastic guard and at the bottom of each guard was a kind of safety device so that it would be impossible to pull the triggers by accident.

'What are those?' Lilly asked.

'Proof.'

'Of what?'

'That I was there!'

'They watched you go down, Adam – they can all Attest to the fact that you were there. It's the other craziness that's the issue.'

'It's proof the underworld exists, that I found the Hard Rooms. That I found a new world – an old world – a new old world!'

'You have a couple of broken guns and a bent head. These prove nothing. You could have found them anywhere. There's shit everywhere. You can't pick this world clean, there's so much junk and so few people.'

'They were in a special cabinet marked DANGER. WARNING.'

'Guns are dangerous. You were warned. So what?' She took the objects from Adam's hands. They looked like any other bit of Gone World junk, albeit shinier and cleaner. Nothing they found ever did anything, nothing ever worked – nothing except knives and hammers and other simple tools. Even objects that had been found in the most perfect condition, things that lit up when given electricity from the Stadium, did absolutely nothing. It was like they were waiting for something, something that never came.

Lilly flicked off the safeties and placed her hands on the triggers.

'They're for you,' Adam said. 'You're the inventor, Lilly. You are the creator. Use them. Make something!'

Lilly pointed them towards the staircase on the off-chance they were loaded and might discharge – though without a hole for a pulse or a bullet she couldn't imagine how. With a pitying look at Adam, Lilly pulled the triggers at the same time.

Nothing happened.

Convinced nothing ever would, she placed them on the table and looked up at Adam, ready to berate him, when she stopped and gripped the edge of the table because the earth beneath them, in that moment, began to rumble.

When Lilly caused the tower in the Gone World to fall by activating the fail-safe detonation using Adam's Finds, the depths were cracked open to the light and a wonderment rose like a plume over the Territory.

At the time she didn't know why the Ancients would build a mechanism to kill themselves and bring a tower down. That she would learn later.

After the earth shook, Lilly went running up the steps like an athlete and shot out onto the Green. She sprinted to the upper wall, following the eyes of others who were also watching in disbelief as the smoke blocked the green swirls in the night sky. They stood in silence.

To Lilly, it looked as though the spirits of the dead had been freed from their unholy prison and let loose into a world already vanquished and parched.

When the sky was fully black and green and there was nothing new to see from this distance, Lilly returned to the Thunder Room. She collected the trigger-machines and walked as quickly as possible to her hiding spot in the storage room. Pushing aside the stone, she hid the evidence of her actions even though she didn't understand them.

A Scout named Amelia Stone was sent by the Council to view the wreckage. She reported back two days later that the activity around the site was like 'maggots to meat'. Desperate hands had been carried there by worn feet to arrive in droves searching for something of worth in the rubble.

Word of her briefing got out. The population was smaller then, and secrets even harder to keep.

They learned that there had been two buildings of similar size. The first, Amelia explained, had fallen inwards and down, straight into the hole, as if the very foundations had been destroyed. There was speculation about whether the ground-water might have weakened the lower levels, causing the collapse. They had seen the results of erosion before.

Why now? was the most common question

Why not now? was the most common reply.

Any 'now' would have evoked the same question.

This thinking satisfied many.

But the shape of the fall – to fall inwards and down and not tip over – what does that?

Nothing does that.

And so some remained unsatisfied.

The building beside it also collapsed, but not in the same way.

The rumbling and destruction of the next-door tower weakened its upper floors but not the lower ones. As the first fell, pieces broke off and battered the other, shattering what most had considered unbreakable windows. As a flower bends towards the sun, so the standing tower had bent towards the falling one until it too tumbled over and exposed its innards to the new.

That was the tower that beckoned the adventurous, its gaping hole now exposed to the world like an animal whose stomach had been ripped open by a giant claw.

Stairs, said Amelia, lead the intrepid into the dark.

Working at ground level for the next few days, scavengers pulled silver-streaked, gleaming objects from the building. Everyone called them 'shinies'. They were beautiful things that had once done something but no longer did. Without names or known purposes, the people of the Territory would ascribe new value to them.

At first there were fights among the Roamers and Traders, bandits and local tribes, which included attempts to cordon off the hole and claim it, but that proved impossible because those who tried – those who placed themselves between the hole and the angry mob – soon ended up skewered or down the hole themselves.

People made pulls: chairs and desks, pencils and paper that was miraculously white and still dry. Artefacts with numbers and words etched into metals, clothing that hadn't rotted or dissolved.

They took anything that could serve a purpose, even if that purpose was only to wave something unknown around so the traders could convince the gullible of its worth.

This lasted until a new whisper came on the wind, the rumour that there had been something foul in the air down below. A smell. A stench. Bodies. Something that had killed people at the bottom of the building. The deeper they ventured, the more bodies they found. It was not only the existence of the dead that mattered: that had been expected, because the remains of the Ancients were everywhere. The sun had bleached bones by the billions.

What had surprised the spelunkers was the sheer number of bodies. 'Piles of them,' Amelia reported. And more: most had died with their heads downwards in the stairwells. 'Something killed them as they walked,' everyone noted, but not bullets or blasts; not falling rocks from above; not maniacal gangs of murders or man-eaters. These people had died on the move and in mid-breath.

What does that? people wondered.

A Sickness, they surmised.

There were children's stories and songs and poems and folk art about a great sickness that had wiped out the Ancients. Could this be the proof?

There was sickness in the world now, too; death that came from nowhere and could not be named or stopped. Maybe it was the same; maybe not. Maybe it was the same, only weaker after centuries had passed. Maybe the living were more immune than the Ancients had been. Maybe that was why people now survived.

Maybe. Maybe. Maybe.

It was just words. There was no way to Attest.

However, the Tracollo confirmed what everyone knew: the Gone World was deep and dangerous.

'This is the wisdom that's passing from voice to voice now,' Amelia explained. 'People are thinking that the Sickness had become trapped inside the buildings with the unbreakable windows. Now that the buildings have come down, the air has escaped like a breath that's come out of the earth. No one,' she said, 'is going to the bottom except dogs. They're being sent down to see if the air is safe – to see if monsters are down there.' She laughed. 'People are discovering that the dogs have no reason to go down the stairs, so they have to be encouraged. People have been dropping food in to make the dogs follow, but the dogs decided they weren't that hungry.

'Then they started throwing small animals down there, critters the dogs liked to hunt. I guess they thought the prey would run deeper on its own and the dogs would follow. It took a while for people to start thinking more clearly. After all, what does it prove if a dog does not return?'

Nothing.

It proves nothing and wastes dogs.

Lilly already had her proof. Adam had gone all the way to the bottom and survived there for nine days. His mind was going, yes, but his breathing was fine. His colour was normal. His hands didn't shake.

Adam might have been crazy but he wasn't sick.

This was Lilly's first secret; her first proof that the truth of a thing and the story about it can diverge so forcefully. The question in her mind was whether to bring the truth and story back into alignment or ... *perhaps* ... continue to set them apart.

Was it bad for the Territory to stay away from the depths? If there were secrets down there, might they not be better protected by silence or lies than truth?

Lilly hungered to go and see what Adam might have seen, to grab her glowsticks and explore the subterranean spaces. She might have controlled this burning need if Amelia hadn't told the Council about the box.

*

'I heard about it at the Tracollo,' she had reported (and her report had leaked out). 'Later, I saw it for myself at the Bridge to Nowhere, which is where it is now; in the possession of a crazy-ass Roamer named Cardo. It's a storage chest of some kind. He claims he pulled it from the lowest level – a Hard Room filled with water and the dead. I'm not sure it's true,' she'd added. 'He has muscles like a horse and a brain to match. He's the kind who aggrandises himself. Word is that he carried it out on his shoulder by himself, hitched it to a horse and dragged it to the Bridge to Nowhere. No one believes he went to the bottom and came back with only a box, but no one wants to tell him that either.

'I went there and saw it myself,' Amelia said. 'It's silver, like the best and shiniest metal. There's not a blemish on it. It's large enough for a child to curl up inside with the lid closed. Cardo has hauled the box to the top of the bridge inside the Pavilion like a trophy. I was there in time for the show because once he had an audience, he pulled out a big knife and started going at it. At first he tried to chisel into the lock – which was no kind of lock I've ever seen before – but that didn't work. Then he tried going after the hinges, but the metal was too strong. That led to him smashing it with a giant hammer. He didn't even dent the thing. At that point, the crowd started muttering, so he tried anything he could get his hands on. He bashed it with rocks, mashed it with his rifle stock, but *nothing* worked.'

She took a swig of water to wet her throat before resuming her story. 'It was kind of a joke at first. All the biggest men took a try, and there was a woman there with a pistol – she shot the lock but it only left a scar. Cardo was getting frustrated because he's that kind of animal. He offered a reward for anyone who could open it, so for the next few hours, practically everyone

186

there had a go. When that didn't work, he raised the stakes: he offered a slice of whatever was inside, but that didn't make any difference. That damned box was sealed tight. It was all becoming a bit manic because now the box was hurting his pride – people were starting to laugh at him.'

Amanda looked around at her audience. 'Turns out, Cardo's cleverer than people give him credit for. He sensed the change in the crowd, so he turned it into theatre. He dragged the chest up to the highest spot on the bridge, and the crowd was getting into a real frenzy, placing bets on whether he would really chuck it off, and if it would break open if he did. He took off his shirt and waved it like a great flag, then he hefted the box and hurled it over the edge – and down it went, crashing into the ground . . . and *nothing happened.*

'It sat there, unbeaten, unopened. The betting ended because everyone had learned the lesson. The chest had won.

'Everyone became pretty moody after that,' Amelia said. 'People began swearing about the Ancients, cursing them for being unwilling to surrender even a few of their secrets to the living. What right did they have to take everything to the grave? Last I heard, Cardo had retrieved the chest and is now trying to sell it. Problem is, there are no takers, because word had got round about its invincibility. I left him imbibing a dizzy drink with his men.'

When Lilly heard this she knew she had to have the box. And she had to hurry. Amelia thought the story ended there, but Lilly knew better. That box was going to become a symbol soon: a totem of invisibility or something. Someone would want it.

The next day was warm, the skies blue. She rose early and found Amelia on guard duty at the top of the Stadium wall facing east, over the gully and towards Yellow Ridge. She was alone and looking through her binoculars, her pulse rifle resting against the wall. There was no activity below.

Lilly skipped the preliminaries. 'I want it,' she announced. 'I want that box.'

'It's indestructible and it's locked. It's useless, Lilly.' Amelia was ten years older. They knew each by name and family.

'Anything indestructible,' Lilly said, 'must have been made that way for a reason. It's locked because it's useful, and it's heavy because it's filled. Whatever's locked in an indestructible box, hidden at the bottom of the Gone World and unfound for hundreds of years must be interesting. Very interesting. I want it.'

'It's locked, Lilly,' Amelia repeated, 'and I watched a hundred people try to open it in every conceivable way. You'll never be able to open it.'

'I'll be able to.'

'What makes you think you can when no one else could?' she asked, lowering the binoculars and staring at Lilly. 'What are you going to do that everyone else in the Territory hasn't done?'

'What they should have been doing all along if they were half as smart as I am.'

'Oh yeah?' Amelia said, 'and what's that?'

'I'm going to find the key,' Lilly said.

Lilly set out in the afternoon with a box of glowsticks, her Colt Python revolver, enough food and water for three days, and Saavni's horse.

She crossed the deep gullies and rifts below the Stadium

that had been formed by waters flowing across them for decades or longer. Luther had crafted leather guards for the war horses to wear on their legs, protection against all the sticks and spikes and discarded raw they had to trot through day after day.

For five hours she rode alone and undisturbed, her gun at the ready. She passed the time humming to herself and counting the plastic bags that were for ever blowing in from the east and sticking to the browning shrubs. Some of them bore the most exotic words and pictures.

As she hummed, she considered her options. She had set off like a gunslinger into the wild, not knowing if her plan to find that key had any merit, but in that saddle, moving with the gait of the horse, hours with only vigilance and quiet, she had time to think.

Where was the key?

It was clear from Amelia's story that Cardo didn't have it, and by her reckoning no one was looking for it, so the pressure was off in that regard. Still, though. Where on this earth was she headed?

Down didn't feel like enough to go on.

Lilly considered the objects the Stadium's people had found and recovered from the desert sands over the decades, and also those that had washed against the walls as the traders lapped at the gates and left behind their wares.

She rolled her ideas around for hours, welded them together and pulled them apart. She looked at the bridle on the horse and the saddle; the hanging stirrups and her own position as a rider: it was all working together to make it possible for her to get from where she was to where she needed to be. Each object wasn't simply an achievement or solitary instrument; everything supported the other parts so that, through a kind of

189

teamwork, they could form a machine – a system where every part needed each other to make something happen.

As more hours passed it became Lilly's conclusion that the triumvirate of box, owner and key formed a distinct system. If that was so, it stood to reason that they would not have been far away from one another during the cataclysm that set the world asunder. The box had been moved to the bridge, but the owner and its key had not.

She knew the rumour of where the box came from so all she needed to do was find its owner. Amelie might not have been convinced by Cardo's story, that he'd gone all the way down into the waters of the lowest levels, but after listening to Adam's ramblings in the Thunder Room, Lilly was.

And that meant finding this so-called Hard Room he'd talked about. She'd have to go straight down the stairs to the very bottom. That was the kind of linear thinking a man like Cardo would have: bigger, stronger, faster, further. Fighting, drinking, fucking. If he couldn't climb to the top he'd prove his worth by going to the bottom.

What else?

When she stopped for the night the wind was heavy with the fine grains picked up from the Empty Quarter to the east; it left golden shadows in the folds of their clothing. Above, a vulture gawked while soaring on a tuft of rising air in front of her. It twisted left, swirling upwards, and turned in search of whatever was not there.

Lilly camped but slept little. In the desert her mind turned to danger. The danger made her angry and it flamed the hatred in her heart. It was her character that forged the anger into courage.

*

Lilly slept and dreamed of throwing her wall-climbing hook to the sky and pulling down the secrets of the Ancients as the floodwaters rushed through the wadis and bathed her dry and battered feet.

The sun rose yellow and dull behind a haze of dust. When she had come for Adam, this dead place had been unmoving. Now there was life everywhere. The scavenging may have slowed but in the glow of the dawn, Traders and Spaders were still sifting through rubble for shinies and raw, their mood and voices tempered, their expectations low. They knew – because everyone did – that the bones of former treasure had been picked clean over the centuries and long before the Stadium rose as a colony.

That truth, however much it was known and accepted, was not enough to stop more than three dozen people from working away, each hoping to find an object that would change their destinies.

Lilly sat and watched to sense the patterns. She looked to see if anyone emerged wet from the depths, but no one did. Hers was a race that would not be won with speed alone and she knew it.

At midday, when people stopped to eat, Roamers set a camp on the edge of the second building. They were not possessive of the site and they paid her little attention. They ate their food sitting in a circle and watching a young girl dance to total silence in the middle. The girl was graceful, and the more her own dance turned inwards and soulful, the more graceful and beautiful it became.

The arduous work of removing the debris from the staircases had been accomplished, allowing the bright sun of day to shine into the lower remains of the tower. Lilly had never seen a building sliced in half – no one had. She had not known about the thick steel tubing inside the walls or the way the electric wiring had been thoughtfully placed throughout, creating a kind of mechanical organism. Simply studying the subject from above would be a worthy way to spend months and she planned to recommend it when she returned.

Lilly turned from the hole and approached the Roamers. She opened her palms and walked forward as though pushing an invisible wall, a common gesture on the road. A woman from the circle stood up. She was heavy in the hips and her face was wrinkled from years under the sun. Her dirty hair was light brown in colour. She was probably in her fifties and looked as though she had few reasons left to smile and wanted that known. She raised her hands in the same manner. They did not touch.

'I'm from the Stadium. You know us?' Lilly said, letting her hands fall to her sides.

'We know you,' the woman said, lowering her own hands. She wore oiled leather britches and a brightly coloured green jacket that was hard to come by but favoured when it was found because it sealed against rain and wind and sand. 'I wouldn't have taken you for Stadium Folk,' she said. 'They keep quiet in there. You're not a quiet one. I've never seen anyone watch the world louder than you. You've got a growling hunger in you, girl. There's something you want.'

'And what's wrong with that?'

'The Ancients were hungry too. They made all this and got so hungry they tried to gobble everything up. Everything gobbled them up instead,' she said, nodding at the earth.

'We don't know what happened to them,' Lilly said.

'We sure do. They died.'

'How do you get into it?'

The woman looked at a red rope that was tied securely to a girder that ended in a coil on the stairway landing.

Lilly followed her eyes.

'People here want to make some pulls,' the woman said, brushing her dirty hair from her face. 'I think you want something else. What is it?'

'I'm curious, that's all.'

'Curiosity killed the cat,' the woman said.

'What's a cat?'

'Something dead because it tried to learn too much.'

'The cat probably asked the wrong questions,' Lilly said.

Even with the structural damage, sunlight did not penetrate the stairwell more than five storeys. Making her way down and down and further down – more stairs than anyone had ever walked in living memory – she also learned that there was no respite from the dust she was pulling into her lungs and that clung to the sweat on her face. She wrapped a scarf around her nose and mouth, but it did nothing to shield her from the smell of the stairwell: chalk and smoke and the sweat of locals.

On each landing she found the embers of fires that had been recently lit to illuminate the path of the workers excavating and scavenging for finds. Doors on each landing had been propped open and the scuffmarks through the dust were testimony for what had been dragged and hauled up into the daylight for the first time in centuries.

Eight floors down she came to a door that opened into the grandest lobby she had ever seen. The floor was a material she would later learn to be *marble*. There were mirrors rising to the ceiling and magnificent lamps that hung low and glittered. The chairs were stylish and they all matched one another: a stunning combination of aesthetic perfection, harmony and balance. This was a place to feel at rest and greet old friends or meet new ones. To share the news. To rejoice in life. This was the old level of the earth. Eight floors down.

She closed the double doors and descended further, cracking a glowstick to light her way.

The deeper she went, the more skeletons she saw.

The final flights scared and disheartened her. There were more bodies, more dead, the pelvic and femur bones pointing downwards like the rumours had claimed. Skulls had rolled. These people had not been shot or stabbed; no arrows pierced them. They were not dismembered by explosions and they had not suffocated while sitting on the ground, for surely their positions would have been more varied.

A sickness? Maybe. But it was no natural sickness; nothing natural could kill a person as fast as a bullet. Whatever had done this was something *un*natural; unnatural – and no longer here.

The temptation towards fear, though, was great. The need for answers can outweigh one's capacity for reason; such is the urgency of Knowledge. Lilly had sympathy for this.

But little time – because she wasn't dead, and neither was Adam.

The deeper she went, the worse the stench grew. Below the Gone World's 'ground' level, the air became sticky and damp. By the time she reached the bottom, she was standing on skeletons and wading through water that came up to her thighs. It was much colder than she had expected – it felt like bathing below the waterfall in autumn, not freezing but bitterly cold.

At the bottom she pushed through the water down a long corridor, her feet slipping off the bones of the long-dead, making her way towards a thick metal door that was wide enough ajar for a giant man carrying a box to walk through.

Lilly's heart raced and her breathing was laboured. It was easy to understand how Adam's fears might have manifested in a place like this, sending him running home with tales of ghosts and souls trapped in the walls. It was easy to imagine him getting lost on the way back up, too. Adam hadn't fallen into the *Tracollo* (that was the word used by the Roamers). He'd made a Black Jump down an Otis Shaft, so who knew where he'd ended up? There were so many doors into so much darkness.

In the Hard Room, the walls were thicker than any she'd seen before. Once-locked doors were now open and room after room contained machines no one had bothered hauling up. Storage shelves were now empty, as were massive barrels that might once have been filled with water. It was a *shelter*: a place to live, a safe zone of some kind. It had been set up at the bottom of the building, so she reasoned that people would have been fleeing here to escape danger from above, maybe far above. Maybe planes really did fly – her mother had not been lying. And after all, Lilly had seen the tail of the AIRBUS. Did those same planes carry weapons? Were they once weapons of war? They would have been formidable things. And if every building had such a room as this, the threat must have been palpable and real.

She spat out the dead and raised her scarf.

Instead of sorting through the detritus in the sleeping quarters or the kitchen, she passed them over for an open door that read *Communications*. Whatever had not dissolved into the water over hundreds of years was under it or floating on it. The stench was burning her nose and the back of her throat and she was starting to feel the depth of the earth and the weight of the building and the deepness of the darkness on her mind. The skeletons she had tried not to think about now moved and reanimated in the rippling green light all around her.

Eye sockets seemed to be watching her. She wanted to get out – but she would not go without her prize.

Every step she took moved the putrid waters, moved the light, moved the shadows.

She breathed through her mouth and tried to focus on the task.

How had Cardo found the box? It must have been under the water. The crazy bastard must have been wading through it and kicked it.

I'm one to talk, she thought.

A dog barked somewhere. It was in the building that was pitch-black. It was lost. It was best not to think about it.

Lilly was starting to panic. Water dripped from the ceilings and objects long stationary were now knocking against the walls, pushed by the ripples that she left in her wake, every one sounding like a person who was going to close the door and lock her in, turning this treasure Trove into a tomb. She too would die here. She too would dissolve into the water and her bones would become like all the other bones and she would be as forgotten as each one of the Ancients.

That was when she saw the desk. The image seared into her mind, where it would stay for fifty-four years, long enough for her to be able to recount it in perfect detail to Birch, Master of the Order of Silence, who would be born more than a decade later.

The water was making an island for the dead man whose upper body rested on the flat desk as though he had died from exhaustion, even after making it to dry land. His head rested on his arms in permanent sleep. He wore a kind of suit she had never seen before. The colour was indeterminate because of the green glow of the stick, but the letters on the shoulder patch were clear: HCG®.

It was not a word, and the letters and symbol meant nothing.

Unlike the scraps of cloth that clung to the shelves and floated around her, his suit was intact, holding in place all his bones except his head.

On the desk, directly in front of him, was a perfectly smooth rectangular surface raised up on an elegant steel trellis. Unlike the desk beneath it, which was flat, this was angled gently towards him. Though everything was the colour of her glow-stick, Lilly knew that its surface was perfect and uniformly flat. Later, when she removed it to the surface, she would learn it was white. There was not a stain on it or a discolouration. There was also no mark, no word and no button. The only interruption to its paper-smooth surface and character was a black glass eye encased in metal and centred on the edge of the board at the far end which appeared to be looking at the corpse.

Lilly rubbed her hand over the surface. She wasn't sure whether it was her imagination but it felt as though tiny grains of sand, infinitely smaller than those in the desert, gently rippled like water as she moved her hand across the surface.

Whatever this thing was or whatever had been on it, Lilly knew only that it had been the centre of this man's attention in his final moments – and it must therefore be very, very important.

The only other object on the desk was a metal platform, to the left of the board with the glass eye, and on top of that was a more familiar-looking electronic box with the equally familiar – if otherwise meaningless – words above the various knobs and buttons that adorned its face: LOADING, PLATE, PRE-SELECTOR, MODE, GAIN.

197

Lilly had seen some metal boxes like this in storage at the Stadium and a few others brought in by traders in their wagons. Those at the Stadium did nothing and there was little market for new ones that came in. Often, the sheet-metal backs would be removed and given over to the blacksmiths to cut or re-cast into arrow heads, knives or spear-tips, among other things.

What made this box different from all the others she'd seen was a black coiled rope that ran from a silver hole in the front and disappeared under the water.

Lilly pulled at the submerged cord until she felt it snag. Undeterred, she yanked harder until the resistance gave way and up came the man's boney hand. It was clutching some kind of black device with a button on it.

Using both of her hands, she snapped off his bones and removed the little box.

Lilly looked around again to see if she had missed anything. She reached down into the frigid, stinking, poisonous water and felt around, but there was nothing. She tried with her feet as well, and then surrendered.

The board was remarkably light. If it had commanded the Ancients' attention at the very end, it deserved hers too, and so did the other thing he'd been clutching. Like the stirrups and reins and saddle, like the box and key and user, this had all comprised a system too, once: man, flat-board and cord-box. It was a solution to a question she would need to discover.

Quickly now, because her eyes were hurting and her lungs were aching and she wanted to scream but didn't dare because of what it might awaken down here, Lilly unslung the pack and tossed out the water, the food, the knife and the change of clothes to make room. She knew very little about electricity, but she did know that objects that used it didn't like water. There was no telling whether the water used to be higher and had already ruined everything. If she had more time she could check the walls for marks, but her claustrophobia was growing. She needed to get out of here.

With some strain, because it was much heavier than it looked, she managed to fit the machine and the flat-board into her backpack.

After pulling it back on, she turned her attention to the man. She pulled him backwards until that the front of his suit was visible. There was a name tag in a reflective material on his chest that read HARRINGTON.

There were stripes on his shoulders indicating a high military rank.

The suit was made of some sort of iridescent material that didn't feel like any fabric she had ever touched before. The long zipper on the front was partly opened near the collar. Lilly pulled it down, exposing the remains of his torso.

Around his spine was a necklace.

On the necklace was a key.

She pulled it off him, placed it over her own head and made for the exit.

The Bridge to Nowhere appeared to Lilly through the mist rising from the wetlands below it. She had ridden here with her mother more than once, just to gawk at it. It rose from sand, arched over a patch of woodland made green by freshwater hidden far beneath, and returned to the sand again. It was stupendous, awe-inspiring and utterly useless.

Children liked walking on it and looking down through the glass.

Horses did not.

In the past few days, since the towers had fallen, something had changed. Because of the many pulls and the desires of the Roamers and Traders to profit from them, small stands and shops had started to pop up on the bridge. At first, Lilly could see, it was to become more visible to the shoppers, to literally lift themselves above the competition. That, unsurprisingly, became a competition in itself, with new shops rising to higher ground up the bridge.

But that was not without its own problems. Why go up so high when you can stay at the bottom? The shopkeepers at the higher ends solved this by encouraging traders to take a journey all across the bridge.

'*Rise wanting. Return flaunting!*' they advertised.

It was weak talk, but this was not Lilly's business.

She spurred Costello on and together they made the climb up the glass surface, passing over the trees to the Pavilion at the top, where she heard male voices yelling and laughing, where her box was waiting for her.

As she rode she considered the finds and the offers around her. Some of this must have come from the Tracollo. The rest? Maybe the prospect of a market alone had attracted the sellers. Though her mind was firmly fixed on her mission, Lilly could not help but look at the finer things and think of her mother. The magnificent clothes and stitching from the old fabrics, the brightly coloured wires and cables, the mirrors and carpets, polished stone building materials, even the occasional bicycle. One man had set up a table selling children's toys, including plush pillows shaped like magical animals that had no names.

Everything around her was a clue to what the world of the

Ancients might have been like and what might have led to their destruction. And no one here cared at all.

'You there,' shouted a brave man willing to talk to someone as filthy as Lilly, 'come see this.' He held up a small object.

His smile was warming so she approached.

'It comes from a fabled lake in the north, before you reach the forest. It's bottle glass,' said the bearded man with a smile. 'Worn down by sand and time. All the rough edges are gone, nothing left but the pure fact of the thing. A rounded beauty alone in a cold world. Each one the same; each one unique. Each a soul,' said the man, 'just like us.'

Lilly's horse didn't care for the glass. It bayed and snorted. Lilly, however, loved it.

'I'll trade one for an idea,' Lilly said.

'What kind of idea?' asked the man.

'A way for you to sell more.'

'You'll have to risk telling me first.'

'I choose to trust you,' said Lilly.

'Well, have at it then, young thinker.'

'They're beautiful, but in a pocket no one can enjoy them. Take some thin Raw and wrap it around the glass. And then hang it from a string so it can be a necklace,' she said, thinking of Harrington and his key. 'Match the right colour of glass with the right person's skin. And keep a mirror here,' Lilly added, 'so people can look at themselves.'

The seller laughed, delighted. 'It's a deal. What colour for a fine mind that needs a shower?'

'Blue, please. I dream of big water.'

The bridge road divided as she approached the apex, the two arms gently wrapping around the Pavilion and then rejoining on the other side.

Her parents had taken her there once when she was eleven. A circular viewing station had windows all around. The gap that opened from the splitting lanes became a free drop into woodland. There was no other way to die like this in the territory.

Some, it was said, had chosen this death for themselves.

On the flat in front of the northern door were four tethered horses. Lilly had been expecting more activity; surely the box was a draw? It was when she saw the thick smear of blood leading from the door of the Pavilion to the far edge of the bridge where someone had been hurled off that the limited gathering made more sense.

Lilly looked more closely at the horses for signs of who might be inside. One of them had a harness with two long metal tubes holding a cloth that was folded cleverly to create a stretcher. The fabric held the outline of a box like a footprint in the sand.

Lilly removed her backpack and left it on her horse. There was a risk it might be stolen, but that was minor compared to her need to be fast once inside.

She slipped her Colt into the back of her waistband.

With a deep breath, she stepped inside.

For the past half-century, the story Lilly told was one of self-defence and attempted rape. She was attacked, she shot her way out of it and left behind three dead men, two of whom were at least double her weight. She returned with the box and became a hero when she opened it 'with the key Cardo had been hiding'.

Why had he hidden it?

No one knew. Lilly speculated it was to draw attention to himself. The unopened box gave him power. An open box? Merely the contents.

It sounded reasonable and with no one to Attest, it became the truth.

'What I want to tell you,' Lilly says to Birch in the Map Room, decades later and in a whisper that hugs the ceiling like a lover, 'is what really happened. I want to tell you,' she says, 'because it explains why I told no one that the Sickness wasn't real. Why I told no one about the flat-board – the White Board – and its relationship to the radio. Why I never told anyone that it was me who knocked down the towers using the detonators that Adam brought back from the underworld. Why all of this convinced me to found the Order of Silence and ask Saavni to run it.'

Birch says nothing.

'There were three men,' Lilly says. 'One was Cardo – I knew him at once from Amelia's description. The other two I didn't know. Cardo was wearing a shirt, but he had ink drawings all over his muscles and there were scars on his face. His head was shaved and he wore rings on his fingers. I didn't recognise the tribal markings, but I did recognise the box he had his feet on.

'The man on his left was long and lean, like he didn't eat enough. His teeth were bad and one of his eyes had clouded over. He was chewing dried meat with his mouth open when I walked in. The other was hunched over with his elbows on his knees. He had a sword across his thighs.

'I had wanted to buy the box and I said as much. "I heard it's for sale," I said to Cardo. "What do you want for it?" This is part of the story I always told and all of that was true. But here's where I lied. The story everyone knows is that Cardo looked me over and started to laugh. He said I was the dirtiest whore he'd ever seen and he wasn't sure he wanted to put his dick in me, but he'd be willing to try. He stood up and adjusted a big knife he had sheathed on his belt. He put a foot on the box.

'"For this box?" he said, "we'll bend you over it four times, twice for me, and once each for them. For that I'll give you the box. We'll be done by . . . tomorrow night. I'll even feed you between now and then. You'll need your strength." He laughed and they laughed, as you'd expect. He told me I should consider myself lucky, because he was the bravest man in the territory. He'd been to the underworld, he said, he'd gone where no one had been in hundreds of years, because he had the biggest balls on Earth.

'I told him that I was from the Stadium – that we have seed and clothes and tools and water and maybe even a horse. I said the box was useless to him and he was in no position to drive the price because there were no other buyers. I asked if he was going to continue to act like a fool or whether he wanted a deal.

'Cardo laughed at me. That's the story I always told. But that isn't what happened. Instead of attacking me, he laughed and then he pushed the chest over to me and said, "Have it. My gift. I don't need it because I know the secret."

'"What secret?" I asked, and he said he had been down to the very bottom – he had touched the waters of death and swum in them. He said he pulled the box from a dragon made of water and bone and here he was, alive to tell the tale. Others might doubt it but he knew the truth.

'I thought that was going to be it, but then he surprised me because he put the ideas together. He said, "You know what that means, don't you? It means there is no Sickness. It means that whatever killed the Ancients is long gone and whatever else is down there is mine. I am going to be the King of the Underworld. I am going to put together a crew of the strongest men and we are going to make the greatest pulls the world has ever known. I am going to control the world beneath the world." He actually used the same phrase that Adam had.

'At first I didn't know why he was telling me this – why share your secret? And then I realised it was because I was a girl. Maybe he thought I was weak, or maybe he was going to kill me and he needed to brag to someone before he did because it was in his nature. But in that moment I had my understanding: I realised that the one thing bigger than walls or weapons or inventions is Knowledge. You see, Birch? The one with the Knowledge is the one with the power. Down below – unreachable until the Tracollo, unapproachable because of the story of the Sickness – was the last undiscovered country we could reach. Since then our Explorers and members of the Order have gone further and mapped more, but at the time this was the next frontier. The only thing keeping people from invading that place and learning its secrets and finding its Troves was that story.

'Once I realised that, I knew what I had to do. I pulled out my Python and I shot Cardo right between the eyes. His two idiots stood up and reached for their guns but I dropped them before they stepped. I left with the box. I told everyone they'd gone mad with the Sickness – that they were foaming at the mouth, that when they'd made a move to rape and kill me I had no choice. No one questioned it for a second. I was a hero when I got back.

'I look back now,' Lilly says, concluding her story, 'and wonder how I was so brazen. Anyway, it all amounts to this: the tunnels are real. The Sickness is not. Consider it, Birch! All the books, all the music, all the pictures – they're all gone. Either the Gone World decided they didn't need them any more, or they put them out of our reach. I simply cannot accept that

205

they chose a life without them – not with everything they accomplished. So if they put it all beyond our reach, it either still exists or it does not. There is no alternative. If it does exist, even a fraction of it, there will be enough to jump the Central Archive ahead by a thousand years.

'It is entirely possible that Elimisha has found a room like mine but better preserved. She has a radio and I'll bet you she has a White Board. I think the books and the music and the pictures are in the White Board. Or . . . or it's a door to find them. I don't know. It's all part of a system that we can't even imagine – and God knows I've tried. But if that little girl can make Knowledge rain down from the clouds it will change . . . *everything.*'

During the time Lilly has been recounting her tale and admitting her secrets, the sun has set and the Map Room has become dark. The waterfall behind the window has nearly vanished; now the torches reflect off the perfect surface. Without a word, Birch stands and walks to the northern edge of the window. She reaches into a simple wooden box and removes four more torches for the walls.

Though Lilly's story has been long, she feels a tremendous sense of urgency to make decisions and get moving. They need to find this girl before the Keepers gather, control the Gone World and deny them access to everything they have been working and fighting and dying to achieve since the Harrington Box was first opened and the Great Books were revealed, setting them on a course to ensure that the Knowledge of the world would never again be forgotten.

It is agony watching Birch drag the torch stands to the giant table, place them, try to light them, fail, try lighting them again, and finally sitting down again. It is all Lilly could do not to scream at her.

When Birch finally settles, she reaches beneath the table and – to Lilly's surprise – removes two enormous scrolls as well as an open wooden box filled with fist-sized stones.

With an expertise born of repetition, she unrolls the first map and places the stones on the corners to keep it open. Satisfied with the placement, she does the same for the second map, placing it directly to the side. From Lilly's angle and distance she cannot see what they are, but one looks more like art and the other like a technical or schematic drawing of a machine.

Still standing, Birch, the third Master of the Order of Silence, says to Lilly, 'I'm forbidden to tell you any of this. If you repeat any of this, one or both of us will die.

'This,' she says, placing her hand on the artistic scroll, 'is the Adam Map. Saavni found it and hid it away. I don't know why she didn't tell you but my team discovered it inside this desk about six years ago. And this,' she says, placing her hand on the second map, 'is what we have learned in those six years by studying the Adam Map for clues and using those clues to explore the Gone World. Because you're right: there is no Sickness. Saavni knew it, you knew it, I know it. We have perpetuated your first lie to keep people out, because Adam was also right. There is a world beneath the world, and a world beneath that too. The Rise is eight storeys high. But we all failed to imagine what should have been obvious from the start: that most buildings are less than eight storeys tall and are still there, buried entirely below the sands. And most of them have multi-storey basements.

'And there's more. You and Cardo went straight down and straight back up. Adam, though, stayed down there. What he learned, and what we now know, is that all the buildings are connected.

'The Ancients,' she continued, 'knew the world was going to end, so they set about building a vast underground network so they could be safe from what they foresaw as the danger. They didn't have much time so the tunnels are rough. Also, it turns out that they were wrong about their odds and solutions. Something killed them that they hadn't been expecting. So the catacombs remain: tunnels connect all the Gone World buildings together – or most of them, anyway – and the network is vast, but very, very hard to map.'

'He wasn't insane?' Lilly asks.

'I don't think that's the question, Chief,' says Birch. 'You were there and looked him in the eyes. Only you can Attest. What I know is that sixty per cent of this map has proved sufficiently accurate to guide us, or at least orient us towards passages that we might not have found on our own. He was down there only nine days, so the space he mapped out is limited compared to what the Order has subsequently explored and noted. But he got us thinking about how things were laid out, not only where they went. As for the other forty per cent: the rest is either too poorly drawn, incorrectly remembered, or . . . yes, he made it up. What he saw broke him and threatened the cohesion of the Commonwealth. That's why he was sent away to the east.'

'Do we know what happened to him?' Lilly asked.

'No, but there were rumours that he survived for many years, spreading his stories. And there is still a contingent of thinkers who believe that we should have killed him immediately rather than let him spread loose talk across the deserts. But this was long ago, Lilly; long before my time.

'Something else,' Birch says, turning back to matters at hand. 'Three Runners are missing and one of them is Elimisha. She was supposed to Signal from Blue Crest the night of the

Tracollo. Henrietta Wayworth insists that she heard three explosions before the Tracollo. No one can Attest but I believe her. Elimisha was on the Orange Route which crossed that tower. It is possible she went down – and it is possible she survived.'

'Are you telling me that we know where she is?'

'No, we never found a Hard Room under that tower. But we do know' – she points at the technical map – 'that the Ancients sealed some tunnel entrances or hid them, while leaving others exposed and clearly marked. We're not entirely sure why, but from uniforms and the linkages between hidden rooms and passages, we think there might have been a military logic to it.'

'Are we going to go find that girl and the internet or not, Birch? Because if we're not, I need you to tell me so I can lie to your face, tell you that I understand, and then find a way to do it myself. Because I'm not leaving this one to the amateurs.'

'We're going.'

'I didn't mean me. I'm seventy-one years old. Getting back up those damn stairs is probably going to kill me. You need someone young and strong and fast and willing to sneak out of here against the Lockdown Protocol, and it ought to be someone Elimisha knows and trusts for about a hundred different reasons. It also needs to be someone we can trust; someone who knows the route and has a mind for improvisation. I'd say a member of the Order, but I worry that if anyone gets caught they'll have to answer to General Winters and implicate you and we want to avoid that. This place isn't as big or secretive as we'd like to think it is. So who does that leave?'

'We need an outlaw.'

'What does that mean?' Lilly asks.

'I'm thinking Wayworth.'

'Henry or Graham? Because while Graham is a pain in my ass he's not exactly—'

'We need one of the kids from the Urban Explorers,' explains Birch. 'I'm thinking Alessandra.'

MISSION

Alessandra Wayworth stands in front the radio at eight o'clock the next morning, eyes wide and staring at the colours flickering on the front panel as her friend Elimisha talks about plants. She listens under the strictest rules – from both Lilly *and* the Master of the Order of Silence – to say *absolutely nothing*.

Birch has never spoken to Alessandra directly. Being approached by her and told to 'follow me' is like learning that God knows your name and wants a word in private.

As Alessandra listens, Birch, in her usual black leather, is leaning back against the table, her arms folded.

Lilly is sitting with her legs crossed, sipping hot water with a twist of lemon. She is refreshed from a night's deep sleep and watches Alessandra's face as Simone and Bruno are entrusted with writing down everything Elimisha says, no matter how little sense it makes.

Photosynthesis can be represented using a chemical equation. The overall balanced equation is $6CO_2 + 6H_2O$ which yields $C_6H_{12}O_6 + 6O_2$. As everyone listening knows: CO_2 = carbon dioxide, H_2O = water; $C_6H_{12}O_6$ = glucose. O_2 = dioxygen. I'm joking, as no one knows this, but you'll have to hear me now so that we can all make sense of it later. All I can promise is that it's important for learning how to start growing new crops out there. Now, let's touch on the word glucose this time to see what that is. *[Pause]*. I'm thinking that I should have started reading inorganic chemistry first and then moved to organic chemistry but if I did that I probably should have backed up all the way to basic chemistry and biology, at which point, where are we? Might as well just do the whole curriculum. Which is what I'm reading: The High School Curriculum for . . . let me see . . . Cape Elizabeth High School in Maine, whatever and wherever that might be, last updated in 2085. Which is older than the Pirelli calendar, but that's another conversation. What did I say I was going to look up? Oh yeah. Glucose.

Lilly turns down the volume and snaps her fingers to get Bruno's and Simone's shared attention.

'I need the room, please.'

'But . . .we'll miss stuff,' says Simone.

'Yes.'

'If we miss it, it'll be gone for ever. We'll be letting Knowledge slip through our fingers like—'

'Like sand falling back into the desert. I know the metaphor,' Lilly says. 'You'll make an excellent Evaluator someday, Simone. In the meantime, I'm willing to sacrifice a little Knowledge for a bit of privacy. Okay? Now, get out. Both of you. And you,' she says, raising her chin to indicate Alessandra, 'you stay.'

After Bruno and Simone have left the room, Birch checks the door to ensure it is properly closed. Elimisha continues to talk utter nonsense as Lilly turns down the volume and directs Alessandra into a chair across from her.

212

Sitting, she continues to stare at the radio as though it were a fire.

'What do you think?' Lilly asks her.

'What?'

'That,' Lilly says. 'What do you think about that?'

'What do I think?'

'Snap out of it,' Birch says.

'Yes, Master Birch. I'm sorry.'

Lilly tries to soften her tone. 'We asked you in here because we need your help and we think you can handle it. But you look like you've hit your head on a rock. Can you focus?'

'Yes, Ma'am.'

'Chief,' Lilly corrects her.

'Yes, Chief.'

'Do you recognise that voice,' Lilly asks again.

'Yes, but . . . it's impossible.'

'Who is it?'

'Elimisha. She's a year younger than me but . . . you know . . . she's good. Fast. Smart. Strong. Likes rules. Maybe too much. Where is she? How did she get a radio? Is she in the Stadium someplace? Is this a test?'

'It's a mission,' Birch corrects her, resuming her cross-armed pose by the desk again. 'What I'm going to tell you is only known to me and Chief Lilly. No one else knows and no one else *can* know. Not your parents, not General Winters, not members of the Order. Are you still a member of the Urban Explorers?'

'I . . . um . . .'

'It's a yes or no question, Alessandra. You'll want to answer truthfully here,' Lilly says.

'Yes, Chief. I mean . . . yes I am, Chief.'

'Do you consider yourself an Adamist?' Birch asks.

'Well . . . no. Not really. I think some people have gone a

little crazy with those old stories. Everyone knows it's D3 down there so there's a limit to how far we go. I do think there's more to explore, like the Adamists do, so rather than go down, what I like to do is go up. There's a break in the northeast window of Landmark Five Tower and if you step off the Green Route at Marker Eighteen there's a staircase to the right and the thirteenth floor is wild! I don't what those Ancients were doing in there but—'

'We know,' Birch says.

'I don't. What does D3 mean?' Lilly asks.

'Dangerous, Dark and Dead,' Alessandra answers.

'We want you to find Elimisha,' Birch says, impatient with the chatter. 'Wherever she is, she's trapped with enough food and water to keep her alive; enough electricity to power the radio and – how do I explain this? – a very special kind of Archive that we want to retrieve.'

Alessandra looks at Birch, who hasn't moved and still wears no expression. She isn't entirely sure what's being asked of her. 'Me?'

'Yes.'

'Um . . . why?'

'Because,' says Birch, uncrossing her arms and gripping the table on either side of her, 'we don't want anyone to know we're looking for her. Which means if you're caught, you will lie. To everyone. We have confidence in your ability to get the job done and keep your mouth shut. Are we wrong?'

They are not wrong, but Alessandra has questions. She has never been in a room with people like this before. Yes, she's known Lilly since she was a little girl, but this is no social call. She has always thought her experiences in the Urban Explorers would get her into trouble some day, maybe even prevent her from rising through the ranks. It never crossed her mind that the Master of the Order of Silence might be watching the Urbanists for talent.

Thinking about it, though, it makes some sense. The Order needs people who don't fit into the system perfectly – the sort who can not only follow routes like Runners, but can also build routes from their imaginations. They need people who have a different kind of personality and character: the sort who want to push beyond the boundaries, not merely follow the rules.
Wow!

Alessandra looks at Birch. She is unable to suppress her own conclusion: 'You protect the Urbanists from the Military so you can find people for the Order! I cannot believe this – you've been watching us the *whole* time? It's a kind of test, isn't it? To see who to take in? It makes total sense now.'

'We also watch to make sure you don't get yourselves killed. There was no Order when Adam made his Black Jump,' Lilly says. 'I founded the Order afterwards.'

Can we get back to the topic, please?' Birch asks.

'Why don't you send the Dragoons and secure the site and just dig her out?' Alessandra asks, but as she finishes her question, she realises she isn't sure she's supposed to ask anything. Are there rules she doesn't know about?

How could she know?

'Alessandra,' says Birch, 'I'm going to answer your question and after that, we're going to work on the assumption that Chief Lilly and I have thought through the problem with more information than you have, and that we're coming to you for this solution already wise to our choices. Okay?'

'Yes, Master Birch.'

'Last night,' she says, 'I sent someone to the tower. There

215

is no way to get to Elimisha from there. We have to come at her from other passages from other entrances. If we secure those sites now, it will notify the Keepers that something is happening, and that might encourage them to attack – so if that's the case, we'll need to divert more troops away from the Stadium to fight or to cover the retreat if we're severely outnumbered. Both are bad options. Secrecy and stealth and quiet are all better strategies. We have selected you for reasons that we think are well-considered. So that's all you need to know about it. You either accept this mission or you don't. We don't want your opinion. Now choose.'

'I'm in.'

'You are going to enter through the Open Tower. That's the one that only partially collapsed beside the first Tracollo from fifty years ago, which we call Tracollo One or T1. At the bottom of the Open Tower building—'

'Bottom?'

'Listen. At the bottom of that building there is a passage that was built along the ancient power line that connects all the buildings in the city to the original electric grid. T1 is six hundred metres away from T2, which is where we suspect Elimisha is trapped.' Birch raised a hand to ward off Alessandra's potentially pedantic objection. 'We understand that T2 did not cave in completely like T1. We don't care. We call it T2 anyway. Now. I will talk you through the details in the Map Room. Assuming you find her – and this is the part you need to remember even if it makes no sense to you – you need to confirm whether or not the internet is real. If it is, ideally, you should bring it out with you. We don't know how big it is, or how heavy, or how it works, so if you can't bring it out for any reason, we're going to need to secure it in place. This is what you have to tell us on the radio, and if that's the case, we'll secure the site and come and get you. But we'd rather you escape unnoticed with it. You should probably bring a bag.'

'Do not leave the internet unsecured. Do you understand?' Lilly added.

'I honestly don't know,' Alessandra says.

In the workshop, Bruno and Simone are sitting together at their usual bench. Eight other engineers are busy stitching together a new type of balloon for hot air invented by a man called Foggy. Almost as old as Lilly, he is one of their cleverest inventors. Noting that hot air rises and having proved it through a series of tests, he now has a plan to heat the air inside very thin sealed bags that will make them rise far beyond the height of the Snake Tower. Using three different balloons secured to strings, he wants to create a coded language based on their relative heights. Low-high-low could mean 'enter through the East Gate' for Explorers, Traders, Runners, Raiders and others working the Territory, whereas high-high-low could mean 'hold position and wait for an escort' or whatever High Command preferred. The messages are unimportant now. The issue is the engineering. He needs to figure out how to raise and sustain the balloons. Everyone is very enthusiastic about the idea, but they haven't yet solved the problems. This is currently absorbing all his attention, as Simone complains to Bruno while Bruno himself is straining to hear what's happening on the other side of the door.

'You heard what she said a few weeks ago,' Simone whispers, not even pretending to work. 'Seven voices over half a century and never in our own language and always a weak signal at night. Here it is, a voice, early in a work day with the sun up and it's loud and clear *and* in the Common tongue. And then Master Birch shows up? And we actually *stop* securing the new Knowledge so they can have some privacy? What kind of insanity is this?'

She looks at Bruno for an answer.

Lana, one of the young Engineers, suggests that maybe the airbags would rise if Foggy were to talk into them for a while, which makes everyone laugh.

None of them are at all interested in whatever's happening in Lilly's office; only the apprentices are ensnared.

'Why did they let us in?' Bruno asks.

'To write it all down. Obviously. Lilly's hand cramps up if she writes too—'

'No, that's not what I meant – why let us know all this is happening?'

'Why not?'

'The radio is working and it's saying incredibly complicated things about important subjects like how plants turn sunlight into energy – but we don't even have a research plan on that topic, and neither does the Food Centre. And then Master Birch arrives? And some kid? Who's the kid?'

'Alessandra Wayworth.'

'Wayworth as in . . . daughter of the Raiders?'

'That's the one.'

'Is she famous for something?'

'No,' says Simone, 'but her parents are legends. Maybe she's going to share a secret with them.'

'Why not invite them directly?'

'I don't know, Bruno,' Simone says, annoyed now. 'None of that is our business, is it?'

The door opens and Alessandra is the first to leave the room. Birch follows and together they exit Weapons and Communications. With Lilly's office door left open, everyone can hear Lilly turn the volume back up on the radio. The girl is still talking:

—since glucose is a basic necessity of many organisms, a correct understanding of its chemical makeup and structure contributed greatly to a general advancement in organic chemistry. This understanding occurred largely as a result of the investigations of Emil Fischer, a German chemist who received the 1902 Nobel Prize in Chemistry for his findings. I don't know about all of you, but I want to know what the Nobel Prize is. So let's take a little journey over there. Poke!

'I need to use the toilet,' Bruno says, removing his apron and placing it on the table. 'Good luck, Simone.'
'With what?'
'Everything,' he says.

BLACK JUMP

Four hours later, as the day approaches sun-high, Alessandra squats low in a wind-carved valley among three of the tallest of the remaining fourteen towers. There is no breeze now and the sand is motionless. There are, however, sounds.

Sound carries well here in the Gone World but sourcing them is nearly impossible. So many surfaces are smooth that sound ricochets the way a stone skips on water, bouncing off the windows, the solar glass, the steel and the struts.

She was taught by her parents to trust the *existence* of noises but not their perceived directions. That was when she was a little girl, maybe six or seven, when her parents had introduced her to the mysteries and unique qualities of the desert and the Gone World.

Animal cries, hoofbeats, weapons-fire, birds, people talking – these things are real and give you information. But where they are? What direction? How far away? There is no telling, so play it safe, be slow. Running, they had told her, is how we attract the young into the glamour of the work – although most Running is slower than walking.

Creeping, really.

No one would sign up to be a Creeper, though. *Might as well call us bugs.*

It is hard for Alessandra not to pull back from the reality of what she is doing and fill her own head with trivialities. Her father always said that repetition – of routes, of fighting, of running and jumping, of multiplication tables or signal codes – moves Knowledge 'from outside to the inside', until it is no longer simply Knowledge but part of us; like the food we eat and the light that passes into our eyes.

'So when you're doing something very familiar,' he had said, smiling, 'it tends to leave the mind free to wander. It's not necessarily a bad thing. But don't lose your purpose.'

This from a man who could sit speechless in a saddle for a month – with even the horse standing stock-still.

Obedient to her first mission as a Member of the Order (which she thinks she is now, but was too afraid to ask as Birch led her to the tunnel that let her slip out under the noses of the Commonwealth's Spotters), Alessandra is staying low and quiet as she makes her way to the first Tracollo, hoping no one is there. It is on the far side of four low buildings only three to five storeys high that rise out of the earth.

'No one will be there,' Birch had said.

'How do you know?'

'Because the Order has made sure they would be too afraid.'

There are birds in the sky today below the wispy clouds far above. They pass in a V-formation travelling westwards. Nothing obstructs their path.

The air looks bluer up there. Cooler. Fresher.

Better.

*

When Lilly's Tracollo fell and the second tower snapped in two, the otherwise pristine desert floor became littered with the debris of ten storeys of building. *There are surely other dead cities*, she was taught, *and it may be that the land there did not rise. We simply don't know. If the land did not rise, we can wonder what their own streets and High Roads might have looked like. What kinds of animals or vehicles might have wended their way through the towers in those Gone Worlds. What else might have lived or worked or remained there. But for us, here in our Territory? Between the sealed towers is only sand and the few plants that grow in it. Here are tiny animals that the birds prey on and we occasionally put into soup. But when the Big Tower snapped, it splashed its insides and outsides across the desert floor like a person throwing Raw and shinies out of a bucket.*

The Order created routes through the debris. The one that passed the first Tracollo was called the Purple Route. It led to an Archive in the deep forest to the north called *Narnia* after a book found there in a Trove. However, this time Alessandra has only three hundred metres left to travel.

Checking her lines, listening to movements and hearing only a distant rattling of metal, she sprints for a cave created by a plank of concrete falling across the pile of a rubble. They call it Marker Nine. In the back, tucked in the corner beneath a half-clothed skeleton covered in ragged cloths, are two litres of fresh water and a flare. Or that's what Runners are taught, at least.

Each of Alessandra's steps falls on an object: a rock, a piece of fallen metal, a half-buried wheel that was once carried in on a tide. When she reaches the cave she has left nothing behind, not a single footprint – which is helpful, because around the Tracollo comes a column of men moving in her direction.

They march three abreast and are led by a man of average

height but very strong build. Their clothes do not match; they are wearing nothing that clearly distinguishes them from any other tribe or clan or community or colony. No headdresses, no jewellery, no paint or piercings or colours. What does distinguish them, however, is this discipline.

Armed with swords and spears, bows and arrows and the occasional rifle, the men all walk softly and in rhythm with one another. They do not talk, cough, sneeze or spit. They flow, the way smoke flows from under a door, following one another the way one ripple in a puddle follows another.

Alessandra backs further into the darkness of the ruins. From an external zipped pouch in her sling-bag, she withdraws a thin fabric the colour of the sand and dirt and covers herself with it as she drops slowly to a prone position and becomes part of the earth in a place where no one would bother to step. From here, and in this way, she waits.

One of the men in the column closest to her breaks from formation and walks directly towards her.

Alessandra cannot lay any flatter. She cannot retreat into the dark of her cave any further and the small exit at the far back behind the skeleton is narrow.

The man stops less than a metre in front of her. The weave of this fabric lets her see out enough to realise that the man could bring his sword down on her head in a flash and she will not have time to know she is dead.

She holds her breath and waits for discovery.

Alessandra once saw a column of men. She was ten and at the top of the Snake Tower above the Stadium. She stood between her parents and watched a thousand souls – not Roamers, but people they had never seen before – pass the flats before the Commonwealth gates and, without a sound, move onwards.

223

'They are disciplined,' said her mother. 'We are lucky this time. Disciplined men are hard to fight. That's why we are disciplined too.'

It was the first time she had ever seen the Stadium prepare for war. But there was no war, only a Crossing, her mother had said: the brush of one tribe against another with no Union made and nothing exchanged, nothing left behind but disturbances in the sand when they were gone.

It had been, however, a sight to see, with fires on poles and the horses pulling the long trains of gear behind them.

Together, they watched the procession.

After a time, Henry muttered to herself.

'What?' Alessandra said.

'Men,' she repeated.

'What about them?'

'In some tribes it is only the men who fight. You see them?' She had pointed. 'The women are with the children in the middle.'

'Why?'

'We're not sure.'

*

It is not a sword that presses down on her covered head; it is something worse.

A heavy, acrid stream of urine hits the ground in front of her, splashing onto the fabric all around her. As he pisses he sways and, to pass the time, draws pictograms. Quickly bored of that, he adjusts his aim and blasts the top of her head.

The sounds of it – dampened, lower, with a richer splash and a pleasing gurgle from the fabric – clearly appeals to him, so he keeps at it, drilling a nice dent into whatever he thinks he's pissing on which is, in fact, at the exact spot where the two halves of Alessandra's skull are welded together.

The fabric becomes so soaked that the warm liquid flows through the stitching down into her hair, around her forehead and into her eyes, stinging them, then down further still around her nose where the rivulets gather and then drip off from the inner edges of her nostrils.

She has to open her mouth to breathe. The wet stings her lips.

He must be draining his own bodyweight of water.

Alessandra wants to take her boot knife and slice off his hose, but drawing blood would draw attention and get her captured and killed, or worse.

When he is finished he splashes the remains everywhere like a battle-dog shaking itself after a rain. He stomps his right boot three times before he spins in the sopping dust and returns to the line.

Angry, stinking and disgusted, she distracts herself by counting the rows as they pass. The foot soldiers are followed by cavalry. She estimates the number of horses. With a Runner's eye for detail she notes the weaponry. Under explicit instructions from her trainers and her parents alike, she looks for Gone World firearms and explosive weapons.

There are few, but the few are noteworthy.

In all she counts sixty rows but the smell and her disgust and her immobility may have thrown her off her concentration. Maybe there are more. Or fewer. Three columns gives her 180 troops, though. Enough to take command of the entire urbanscape if they want to.

When the men and horses and dogs have passed she continues to wait until the dust settles and the sounds have moved off.

*

Alessandra tilts her head so the remaining urine runs off the side of the fabric before removing the cloth altogether. She decides to abandon it. It might be washable but the memory will be a permanent stain. Out in the sunlight again, she notes that she is coated in filth from face to foot and utterly disgusting.

For a moment, Alessandra looks around. Behind her is an army only she has seen, an army that is marching towards the Stadium. Ahead of her is a pit into darkness and her first mission as a member of the Order: to locate Elimisha, communicate the status of the internet back to Lilly via radio, and secure the Trove one way or another.

While doing that she'll rescue Elimisha and report back on that army too.

There is a low route to the first Tracollo from here but Alessandra has opted for a high one of her own design. Armies don't always march together. Sometimes they come in waves, she's been told, and sometimes troops arrive late to guard the back. Better not to remain here among the snakes and brittle grass. Better to take to the sky with the birds instead.

Leaving the cave behind, Alessandra darts to the narrow alley between the two buildings and wedges herself into the gap. After flipping her pack around to her chest, she presses her back to one side and her feet on the other. This is why there is armour against her back. This is why her boots stick and her gloves are thick.

She slides up and then walks her feet. Practised in this manoeuvre, Alessandra can cover one metre in ten seconds. At twenty metres there is a ladder she has been told is secure which will take her directly to the roof. The door up there is locked and cannot be opened (they've tried with everything but explosives, which they can't risk) but it joins the Green Route at Marker Nineteen and from there she'll be on safe ground.

She needs two hundred seconds or three minutes and twenty seconds to reach the ladder. It is a long time to be exposed, but the passage is rarely trafficked and when it is – who would look up?

Reaching up, finally, Alessandra grabs the ladder with both hands and lets her feet slip. She dangles there by her two gloved hands, almost sixty feet up, but not for long because she needs to turn around. Taking a deep breath, she releases one hand and pivots her entire body so she is facing the building she is attached to. As quickly as she can, she replaces her hand on the bar, flips her other hand around and using her feet to help, muscles her way up three cross-bars on the ladder until her feet finally find purchase and she is safely on.

Three more metres up she reaches the top of the building and takes a breath. Her trainer has instructed her to always pause when there is a safe moment and bring the heart rate back down.

Deep breaths.

The body wants air.

At the corner of the building there is a mythical stone creature with wings, much like one of the beasts on the iron door leading into the Map Room. Together, Alessandra and the flying dog stare over the rooftop's iron edge at the distant marauders, who continue to march on.

She strains her eyes against the glare off the smooth sands and glass towers. The sun is high and ignites the alluvial plain beyond the edge of the urbanscape.

*

She leaves her rooftop friend with a pat on its stone head and meets up with the Green Route marker. All Runners have been warned that rooftops can become soft – people have been known to fall in. That's one of the reasons the Order establishes routes to follow. In this case, discreet nails have been placed into the roof, then hammered over and made to look unremarkable, giving Alessandra a path to follow across the building.

At the far corner there is another steel ladder that drops all the way to the ground. Quietly, so not to draw attention, she glides down to the risen earth, where she stops at the bottom, drops to a knee and takes a long pull from her canteen.

Not far – maybe the distance of a rock thrown by a strong boy – is the hull of a boat gleaming a lunar white. Its top third sits perfectly on the ground, turning it into a hut. The rest is below the sands of The Rise like the AIRBUS and so much else.

Alessandra meanders slowly to the boat's hull, knowing that motion attracts attention and a person sprinting is a sight to turn any head. Once there she takes shelter from any prying eyes. The stink of her hair is worse now that she's been sweating.

The entrance to the underworld is close.

When Alessandra was ten years old, her mother woke her long after moon-high on a winter night and told her to dress for the cold. Her entire class was going on a march. She wasn't prepared, but she had been raised to always be ready to flee or fight. It had been freezing. She and her classmates walked in disciplined silence. They walked for two full days with only brief stops to rest and eat during the night between. Their socks became wet and their feet swelled and their bellies begged for the unleavened bread they knew the Officers carried in their packs, but the walk taught them to suffer and to know and appreciate when they were not suffering. *This is a life of continuous readiness and warfare*, it was explained. There were other lessons:

- *The Knowledge will not keep itself safe.*
- *The Stadium is only a home.*
- *Only the Commonwealth is eternal.*
- *Socks can be replaced.*

If there were others, Alessandra cannot remember them now.

A wind is picking up. It is channelled between the buildings into a chilling blast. In her boat, a coolness finds the edges of her damp clothing. Moving again will restore warmth.

Dogs begin to bark. It's hard to know their direction and what happened with Alan Farmer means they might not be wild. Alessandra smells ripe and is upwind: she needs to get underground.

Where the tower broke in two, all those decades ago, there are still jagged edges of shattered windows. The sun, far across the southern sky, reflects its daylight through them, casting rainbows on the sands in front of her. A slat from the roof makes a ramp to the lip of the building where Alessandra is expecting a red rope that she can take down to the staircase inside.

She can't see anyone, and there are no dogs, despite what she's hearing.

Sometimes, she thinks, Runners run.

After checking that her sling-bag is secure, leather boots zipped to the top and gloves snapped tight, she sprints like a stallion across the sands to the remains of the Mutual Building. Committed, she locks her vision on the distant DANGER symbol on the ramp, willing herself towards it as though it were pulling her. Alessandra is as tall as her mother and her stride is long and powerful.

'Poise' her father calls it: a body sleek by form, her tied-back black hair streaming behind her as she runs.

Flat here, the ground. Why the ancients built their towers so far apart from one another in some places and so close in others has never made sense to her. There was usually so much pattern to their thinking when she looks at what they once made; what they once did.

Card number one hundred and forty-four of Trivial Pursuit *asks, 'What planet did the* Mariner *spacecraft visit?'*

Answer: Venus.

The Ancients had reached another *planet.*

She ran as though the world burned around her. As though fire itself was chasing her. Alessandra Wayworth, Runner of the Commonwealth, Member of the Order of Silence.

Two horsemen in black burst over a hill two hundred metres behind her. They are riding side by side. Between them is a net.

On the Green, Alessandra can cross a hundred metres in the time a water-filled jug takes to drop from the top of the flagpole to when it snags on the rope, inches from the ground. She is the second fastest woman and the eighth fastest person overall at the Stadium. The memory in her bones lets her measure the distance from here to ramp on the Mutual Building while her instincts do the maths based on the speed of her pursuers.

She isn't going to make it.

*

Alessandra slides to a stop, pulls Lilly's Python from the chest holster as fast as she can – but before she can pull the trigger, there is a crashing sound and both horsemen and their mounts disappear into a hole that their own weight and motion have created, breaking through whatever had been making this part of the Gone World flat for hundreds of years.

Twenty metres away, in a cloud of dust, the riders are . . . gone.

She hears the thud of their bodies hitting something below. The horses start baying and screaming; their legs and bodies are surely broken. What has become of the men she can't say.

For a moment Alessandra is alone.

She stands there knowing she is now supposed to go to the ramp, swing down the rope and into the gaping hole of the Mutual Building. The world – the Fates, the Gods, the Ghosts of the Ancients, the Values that whisper their promises and warnings into the ears of the people – all agree that she should exploit her dumb luck and get going.

But the blackness of the hole in front of her calls out. She has to look.

How can she not look? It pulls at her. Just a look – a glance to know what's down there, what no one has seen in living memory. Hers could be the first eyes—

Slowly, as if approaching a scared animal, Alessandra walks across the flat surface she now understands to be the roof of some buried building.

At the edge, she cannot see inside. The angle of the sun is all wrong and what light does try and penetrate the hole – a hole jagged with glass and steel struts – is captured by the dust and sand that takes hold of the light and refuses to let it pass.

With one flare she could see it all.

These are Alessandra's thoughts – until three more riders

turn the far corner of the Mutual Building, denying her access to the ramp and her rope and her Mission.

These riders have no net. They have intention in their eyes.

When one of them raises a rifle to his shoulder, Alessandra looks down into the swirling dust below her. Thinking of Elimisha and the internet and her mission and her parents, she makes the Black Jump.

MUSIC

When Elimisha saw the Earth spinning in front of her above the White Board she became breathless. She had never seen the Earth before and yet, as though awaking an ancient memory, she knew instantly what it was: a child returning to a lost home. There was a terror in seeing a physical object hovering in front of her but the fear was calmed by the tranquillity of the scene itself. The Earth rotated, unique and whole, leading Elimisha away from loneliness and outwards towards wonder.

As she looked and watched it slowly moving, she remembered that she had heard something too – a greeting.

'Hello,' a voice had said. 'How may I help you?'

'Hello?' Elimisha says softly, looking past the sphere to the girl on the wall and after, to the open door behind her.

'Hello, how may I help you?' it repeats.

This is a man's voice. He is an adult. His voice is deep and comforting, like listening to her father when the lights are out and the bonfire on the Green flickers over the ceiling in her bedroom.

'Where are you?' she asks.

'Right here,' he answers.

'Right . . . where?'

'With you, to assist you.'

'Assist me with what?'

'Whatever you need.'

Elimisha removes the glasses. The Earth disappears.

'Can you still hear me?' she asks the voice, testing an idea that the glasses and the voice are connected, just as the images and the glasses surely are.

There is no answer.

Her trainers would tell her to breathe and control her fear. Her mother would tell her to steel her heart and remain brave. Chief Lilly would tell her to reason through the problem. 'Ask a question, think of a possible answer and then *try and prove yourself wrong*. If you fail to prove yourself wrong, it does not mean you are right. It means your confidence in your answer has gone up. That's all. Only when no one can prove you wrong can you be properly confident. But even then, you must hold onto the possibility that you might still be wrong. Why? Because maybe no one can find the flaw in your reasoning. Maybe you've reached the edge of your capacity for logic but . . . sadly . . . not the end of logic itself. Maybe, simply put, you don't know *how* to prove yourself wrong.'

This, she admitted to herself, did not sound simple. In fact, engineering logic and science were rather complicated.

'Welcome to Weapons and Communications,' had been Chief Lilly's response.

Willing to test her idea further, Elimisha repositions the glasses on her ears and nose and speaks. 'Is this is a radio?'

'The object to your left is an ICOM HAM radio, circa—'

'So . . . *you're* not a radio? That's a radio. What are you?'

'I am an artificial intelligence entity rooted in a Prometheus system, tasked with providing knowledge and services.'

'And you're . . . here with me?'

'Yes.'

'You're not a person?'

'I am an artificial intelligence entity.'

'How can someone be artificially intelligent? Doesn't that mean stupid?'

'In this case it means inorganic.'

'You're inorganically intelligent?'

'Yes.'

Elimisha could tell that Lilly – if she were standing over her shoulder – would not be impressed with Elimisha's line of questioning. She would be directing her to get focused. *Get to what matters*, she would be saying.

'Can you hurt me?'

'No.'

'Do you want to hurt me, whether or not you can?'

'I am tasked with providing knowledge and services. I have no motive or capacity to cause you deliberate harm.'

'What about unintentional harm?'

'I cannot fully anticipate the consequences of providing you with requested knowledge or services.'

'So you can partially anticipate it?'

'Some images, video, music and information have been known to widely cause distress or be age-inappropriate. As I get to know you, the better I can provide you with knowledge and services that will not likely cause harm, if that is the setting you prefer. However, the consequences of learning cannot be predicted. Will you permit me to learn your preferences?'

'Yes. What's a video?'

'A moving image.'

'How can you move an image?'

'By taking hundreds, thousands, millions or billions of images and displaying them at a frame rate that exceeds the human eye's capacity to distinguish one from another as separate images, thereby creating the illusion of motion.'

'Show me a video.'

'Of what?'

'Something interesting.'

'I don't know your preferences well enough to anticipate your interests. Would you like to start a new profile that allows me to learn your interests and preferences?'

'Sure.'

'Would you like me to restrict harmful content as I come to determine it?'

'No.

'What is your name?'

'Elimisha.'

'Elimisha. Swahili for "educate", to be a giver of knowledge.'

'What's Swahili?'

'Swahili, also known as Kiswahili, is a Bantu language and the first language of the Swahili people. It is commonly spoken in the African Great Lakes region and in other parts of eastern and southeastern Africa, including Kenya, Tanzania, Uganda, Rwanda, Burundi, some parts of Malawi, Somalia, Zambia, Mozambique and the Democratic Republic of the Congo, also called the DRC. At its height, it was spoken by tens of millions of people.'

Elimisha knows what a language is and she knows what a lake is. Beyond that, none of the words mean anything. However, that isn't the interesting part.

'How do you know all that? And so quickly?' Elimisha asks, continuing to watch the Earth spin and realising it must be a 'video'.

'My systems have access to numerous archives and can access them rapidly.'

'You're a Librarian?'

There is a pause before the Prometheus system says, 'Yes.'

'How big is your Archive?'

'Approximately one hundred and forty exabytes. Unfortunately, access is currently limited because of severe damage to the sub-oceanic cables, wide-spread hub- and storage-failures and the inaccessibility of the satellite networks.'

'Uh huh. So . . . it's big but used to be bigger?'

'Yes.'

'Bigger than the Central Archive at the Commonwealth?'

'I have no information on that facility.'

'What's in your Archive?'

'Everything.'

'Let me ask it differently,' Elimisha says to the globe, for lack of anything else to look at. 'We classify knowledge into geography, entertainment, history, arts and literature, science and nature and sports and leisure. Do you have information on all those things?'

'Yes.'

'So you have six flags on . . . everything.'

'Images, videos, books, music—'

'Wait,' Elimisha says, 'you have music?'

The voice of Lilly – over her shoulder – tries to get a word in again to redirect her to what's essential but this time Elimisha is not interested and pushes her away. She wants to know this.

'I have more than one hundred million songs dating from Édouard-Léon Scott de Martinville's performance of "Au clair de la lune" in 1860, through Riddhi Chakma's *Hip-Hop Renaissance Volume Four* uploaded from Bogra, Bangladesh in—'

'Okay, okay,' Elimisha says, overwhelmed by the words, the speed, the spans of time, the new names, the foreign languages, the presence of a disembodied voice – and the dawning understanding that here, with a White Board and a pair of glasses and her Haptic Command Gear, is a gateway to an Archive that has no walls, no shelves, no Librarians, no paper or boxes or towering ceilings, no Scribes or Evaluators or Archivists or Runners. An Archive that appears to have no limits.

Elimisha removes the glasses for a moment and rubs her face.

She pushes her curls out of her way and replaces the glasses, telling herself, *Get a grip on yourself.*

The building, she knows, has solar windows like the Stadium. One of the questions at Weapons and Communications, when she apprenticed there, was why had the Towers no electricity if they could create it from the sun? Surely the power goes into a battery made of water, like it does at the Stadium, right? But clearly not, because the intact towers were dark inside. Perhaps all the lights were broken? But that seemed unlikely, when the illumination panels at the Stadium still worked.

Foggy, one of the senior Engineers, had a theory that the building didn't generate electricity for itself, like the Stadium did. Maybe it contributed to powering everything and used only a bit of what it produced for itself. In that case, maybe the tall towers are all part of something broken; they collect electricity but have no means of sending it to its final destination.

Foggy said the answers would lie underground, in some kind of physical connections between or among the buildings. Lilly agreed and said it was a pity, therefore, that no one would ever learn the answer.

Except this 'Prometheus system': this still worked.

'Why are you working when everything else is broken?' Elimisha asks.

'Because I was designed to survive,' it says.

For several moments Elimisha sits and watches the Earth. She had no idea it was covered by so much water; that there were so many stretches of land unconnected to others. The top had a little snow and the bottom had a lot. Many sections were beige like the desert but other parts were green. The scale was beyond her comprehension. The atmosphere was so thin.

From her perspective – out in space, where she sits – there are no people. If she were to move closer she would find some, those in the Territory, at least, and a few in the northern forest and maybe out at the colony at Anchorpoint where the Traders go to collect salt and whatever might have washed ashore this year. But Anchorpoint is a month's journey to the northwest and no one really knows how far the waters stretch.

Looking at the planet, it occurs to her that she has no idea where they actually live – which part of this sphere is hers. She is tempted to ask, but the solitude is playing on her mind more heavily than the expanse in front of her.

'You said you had music. I want to hear some.'

'What music would you like to hear?'

Elimisha had never heard music that wasn't being played or sung directly in front of her by musicians. The very notion that she could listen to it in their absence was wild. She had heard music echoing down corridors, though, and she had heard it come through her window from the Green when she wasn't looking. Maybe it would be best to think of it like that.

'What music did other people request?' Elimisha asks.

'When and where?' asks the Prometheus system, always aiming towards precision.

'How about here, at the end. What music did people want to hear when everything was . . . ending?'

Instead of an answer using words, a gentle piano chord fills her ears, a sound Moishe might create. That chord rings and is soon followed by four other notes rising up a scale as though climbing a short hill together. The final note plays again – and a second piano plays two soft accompanying notes as though it were a bird song in the background. When they fade, the chords walk back down the hill to rejoin the first. It is when that note repeats and steps away from the little hill that Elimisha feels she has been invited into a melody she has never heard before. Inside the doorway of that new experience is a chorus of men's voices that rise up behind the gentle piano, making way for the warmest, most gentle, most kind singing voice that Elimisha has ever heard. He sings to her and to all the people who are facing death. After a gentle introduction, the man's voice blows through Elimisha's soul like the white light of eternity and tears race from her eyes as her chest constricts and he croons, '*Lean on me . . .*'

For the next four minutes she is exposed to poetry, rhythm, tenderness, love, pain, memory, hope and the terrible and vast expanse between what was lost and what little remains.

As Bill Withers' voice sings out the last notes, Elimisha stands, picks up the axe, drags it down the corridor and beats the concrete wall beside the blast door, trying to get out with everything that is trapped inside until she collapses into a sweaty heap and sobs.

Over the next two weeks Elimisha gains a rudimentary understanding of the White Board and the glasses and suit; of nanotechnology and how the nanites of the White Board are taking their commands from her operator cues, creating tactile surfaces that allow her to type or steer or feel or use tools that were faster by hand than voice. She comes to see how the artificial intelligence listens and learns from her; mimics her use of terms, metaphors and analogies to help her better accomplish her tasks in the most natural ways. The disembodied man's voice speaking to her learns her accent and inflections and comes to feel like a companion sent directly from the Commonwealth to rescue her.

In the morning she rises and exercises and beats at the hole, trying to get out. After that, she showers and eats. Once her body is calm and her mind clear, she sits down with the internet and explores.

One afternoon she flies like a bird across the Mediterranean Sea, south of Piraeus in Greece, to where Sparta's and Athen's forces had once clashed. She watches a re-enactment of the battle as though she is hanging over it one minute and in the fray itself the next. Another day she strolls through the Louvre, circa 2051, on a five-hour tour guided by the professional curator who speaks Elimisha's language but with the most delicate of accents. Jumping to 2073, she enjoys a laser-light show of the Pyramids at Giza celebrating the hundredth anniversary of *The Dark Side of the Moon*, a record album by a rock and roll band called Pink Floyd.

She drives a car at Le Mans; SCUBA-dives in the Comoros Islands before the coral reefs died; goes sky-diving over Shanghai; sits at a clam shack on the coast of Maine watching the Atlantic Ocean lapping the craggy rocks as the light fades behind her, then sees that same sun set into the Pacific Ocean between the twin rocks at Rockaway Beach in Oregon.

There is nothing she cannot experience with the internet and the Haptic Command Suit, no place she can't go . . . no place except home.

'Do you know another way out of here?' she asks it.

No.

'Why can't you contact people for me?' she asks later.

Because there is no one else using the system.

'If you were designed to survive, why isn't anyone else here?'

Because, it explains, *people were not.*

After days of this, days of deep loneliness and fear and occasional bouts of hopelessness, she would sometimes close her eyes and tell the computer to put her on top of a mountain above a forest and then feel the air all over her body and pretend she was outside and free.

Eventually, her spelunking through the Archive led her to wonder about how it had all ended. The man's voice answered her simply, because the greatest mystery in the world now was no mystery at all when it happened. With time to learn the new vocabulary, Elimisha came to a basic understanding: On November 19, 2097, at 08:02 UTC, a single if extraordinary flare from the sun knocked out a network of mission-critical orbiting satellites, cutting off vital communications and data systems and setting the world ablaze with geopolitical recriminations. Governments and corporations were quick to accuse one another of capitalising on the flare's unbalancing effects. A century's mismanagement of diplomatic relations and multilateral processes, and the de facto abandonment of global institutions – all designed to prevent and manage catastrophic destruction – had left the planet fragile. Accusations quickly escalated into military actions which fuelled reprisals until one state – arguing that a first strike was the only rational response left – unleashed a bio-engineered nanotech weapon that targeted people with specific genetic markers. The victimised countries promptly launched coordinated nuclear strikes on the antagonist, obliterating the population and triggering a programmed retaliation from sea- and space-based weapons. The biogenetic weapon – which had never been fully tested – quickly mutated and spread from the targeted population to everyone else on Earth.

Forests decayed into deserts and land gave way to waters. Particulates from the bombings transformed the night skies from black to green.

Everything that had once been connected now stood alone.

They called it the Solar War. Less than twenty-four hours into the crisis it became clear that it was going to threaten all life on Earth. The military in this part of the world started rapidly carving out emergency tunnel systems to link buildings and utilities below-ground, in case large populations needed to move into conjoined shelters. Robotic excavation was advanced at this time, Elimisha learned, and commercial androids were immediately re-tasked, becoming efficient digging machines – until they too fell apart.

In the expectation of biohazards and contamination, bunkers were fitted with fail-safe devices to seal in the affected and destroy the bunkers so that others might live.

How anyone survived at all, Elimisha didn't know. The records stopped.

What Elimisha does know is that she is trapped, alone, and now responsible for the greatest repository of Knowledge in the history of human civilisation.

*

243

This is a Trove: Knowledge at rest. One way or another, she is duty-bound to protect it. Looking at the radio, she decides that if she can't get out, at least some of the Knowledge can.

ADAM WAS HERE

A Black Jump is the worst of all choices that comes at the end of all the worst outcomes because the only time a Runner faces a Black Jump is when everything meant to support her in the field – the educators, the Agoge, the trainers, the Order of Silence, the military troops – has failed. A Black Jump is literally a jump into the unknown. It can go down for ever, or end in anything – water, rubble, spikes ... It is an act of utter desperation, which is everything the Commonwealth is structured to avoid.

Alessandra has no time to think about any of this as she jumps into the dark pit.

She falls in preparation of a drop that will last for ever. If she lands at all, she will need to buckle her legs and roll out of it. Arms crossed as if in death, she lets the air out of her lungs and tries not to scream or close her eyes.

But she does both.

Down ...

A five-metre fall ends on something soft and forgiving.

Knees bent, her legs absorb the hit and Alessandra rolls off the dead horse onto a floor made of stone. In the room now, not above it, she can see. What's hard is breathing.

The dust is chalk-white and blacks out her view in most directions.

Head still dizzy, she crawls back to the horse and pulls Lilly's revolver out of its pouch. It has three green markers for sighting: when she aligns the two in the back with the one in the front they form a perfect line showing her that she has taken aim.

Her mother is the expert shot but it was her father who taught her to fight in enclosed spaces. *Lean into the fight*, he would say.

Gun up, Alessandra quiets her breathing and tries to calm her heart, which is still pounding from the fear of the jump. Time isn't making sense any more; she cannot tell if she's been down here ten seconds or two minutes. She isn't sure what's still in motion from the drop and what motion belongs to something else – something with motive.

There is a noise to her right that is terrifyingly close.

Figuring *everything* is hostile, she twists to her right, throws her back against the soft stomach of the horse and fires.

The bullet blows a hole in the other horse's head. The flash from the barrel lights up a man on his knees, one hand closing around a fallen rifle.

She shoots twice more and the report is absorbed into the vastness of the building, a room as large as the Sharing Room in the Central Archive.

That's three bullets fired. Three more in the cylinder. She *must* keep track. But that's not all: now she has to move.

Positions, her father had explained, *get used up, just like ammunition. People make the mistake of getting too comfortable when things are working out. If you're firing from an exposed position, change it up. Especially in the dark, because of the muzzle flash.*

246

His advice saves her life. She rolls away and takes to a prone position by the second dead horse as three bullets riddle her old position. The man has not only missed his mark, he has also given away his own position in the dust. Alessandra kills him with one shot.

That's it. Two men on two horses. They're all that's down here. *Not up there, though.*

As fast as possible, she scampers away from the dead all around her to look for a staircase to take her down, because there is no point in even trying to get back up, not with an army wanting her dead.

Knowing other men will soon be looking down – and maybe with those flash-bombs her mother had said preceded Elimisha's Tracollo – Alessandra hustles to the edge of the room, away from the hole in the roof.

This is some kind of great hall or maybe a party room. Her back is pressed against a tall glass wall that looks out onto dirt and sand. In front of her is a fountain with a spiralling sheet-metal sculpture adorning the centre. At the centre of the wall to her right is a wide, elegant staircase going down, and in her liner pocket is the map of how to get from Lilly's Tracollo to Elimisha's.

Though it is only a guess, she is pretty sure that the journey from one to the other passes through this building, and if it does, the answer lies beneath.

As Alessandra stands and runs across the polished, perfect but dust-coated floor to the staircase – and, hopefully, the resumption of her Mission – three men emerge at the rim of the hole above. As one of them tosses down a rope, Alessandra disappears down the stairs, taking them two at a time into the unknown.

*

The Harrington Box has a book of ancient Greek myths. One of them tells the story of the Labyrinth at Knossos. As Alessandra descends into the black without a light, trusting that the stairs will go on and on and that the directions she memorised from Birch are correct, she finds herself thinking about Theseus.

In the introduction to that story, it says the word for a ball of yarn in Middle English was *clewe*. Later, as the years passed and language changed, the spelling became clew, losing its final 'e'. The homophone was clue, and, 'Today,' said the book, 'we use *clues* likes balls of yarn in the labyrinth at Knossos to find our way through the maze of our mysteries.'

The lesson for that day at the Agoge had been that the current world is always built on the foundations of the past and that civilisation rises, layer on layer, to new possibilities: word building on word, story on story, but constructed less like a tower and more like a mountain. 'What is built,' said the teacher, 'cannot be so easily destroyed.'

There are skeletons and bodies as she arrives at the bottom. Water has collected there and she hesitates before accepting that she has to step in.

When she does, her foot slips on a femur and she falls into the black water and rises freezing and cursing and angry. Very angry.

It is too much. She removes a glowstick from her jacket and cracks it, revealing a massive puddle or water reservoir. The room is long and rectangular, with a hallway on her right and a series of doors to her left. There are pictures on the walls, abstract images that may have once been considered 'art'. A thick algae has grown up the walls and over the surfaces of tables.

Glowstick up, the pistol and its remaining bullets pointing

ahead, she whispers to the dead around her, 'There had better be a fucking tunnel down here.'

The switch-backs of the stairs disoriented her but she is reasonably certain she's moving westwards now, back in the direction of Elimisha's new Tracollo. As she walks, Alessandra looks for an Order Marker called Albert Wormwood, the name of an artist carved into a brass plaque under one of the paintings on her right – and she finds it.

Yes.

If she had reached the first Tracollo, headed to the bottom and followed Birch's instructions, she would have passed through here. So she is back *en route*.

The surface of the water is covered in dust. It doesn't move like water as she walks through it; it is more like a giant bedsheet roiling up and down with the wind.

Theseus was looking for a Monster. Alessandra is hoping to avoid them.

The recent collapse, she tells herself, shook up the nearby structures and weakened the glass ceiling that the riders fell through. It was dumb luck – or, seen another way, it was the inevitable result of the Gone World falling in on itself and being attacked with explosives. Of course it was weakened. What else?

Alessandra follows the route in her head. She follows trust: trust in Adam and his map. Trust in Birch. Trust in Lilly. Trust in her own memory. Trust that the ground has not shifted under her feet – beneath the water – yet again.

Moving through a series of open doors, past old machines that were once used for washing clothes, she arrives at a wall with a hole in it that is shaped like a coffin with rounded edges. This is not something that was part of the building when it was erected; it was added later. It appears to have been blasted out, or somehow carved. Though different in shape and texture, it reminds her of the tunnels beneath the Stadium used by Soldiers and Traders and Runners.

Alessandra follows the water into it, running her fingers along the wall as much for support as to connect to something beyond her own fears.

At almost the same instant, she hears two distinct sounds from opposite directions. The first, ahead of her, is a whistle: air is passing through a small opening with enough force to leave a note. There is also a kind of throbbing. It is even and – if the idea isn't too preposterous to consider – actually sounds like drum beats.

The second sound is footfalls on the stairs behind her. The bastards are still coming for her.

Being inside the tunnel is a risk; maybe an unacceptable one. Behind her are Keepers and ahead of her is – *what*? It's impossible to know. She could back out and stand her ground, try and fight but she doesn't know how many are coming. Sound, she well knows, can be deceptive. Or she can continue and hope for the best.

Back to trust again.

A black cable appears on the ceiling, running away from her. It's held in place by U-shaped clamps hammered into the stone at regular intervals. The Ancients not only dug this tunnel but ran electricity through it.

It must go someplace, she reasons. *There has to be something ahead.*

Alessandra commits to going there – but not with the glow-stick. That only makes her a target. There are four more in her sling-bag, so she tosses it behind her into the water and walks on.

They'll still know she's in the tunnel, but when they're standing over the green glow, *they* will be the targets.

The water behind her is illuminated. The first feet splash towards the glowstick. Ahead of her is the black shape of the tunnel itself, where the sound grows louder and louder as she rushes forward. There is no way it could be but – if she had to put a name to it – she would have to call the sound . . . *music*.

And in that music is a man's voice telling her to 'stay alive'.

Alessandra moves as fast as she can in the dim light until a shape begins to take form in front of her.

It is a half-naked, fully-grown man with steel claws for hands.

SPY

Bruno is not an experienced rider. When he was a child he occasionally rode in front of his mother during their long journey from the East, but that only acquainted him with the challenges of being in a saddle. Speed, command, pursuit – these were not his special skills. When Alessandra stole out of the eastern-most tunnel he was able to follow her because they were both on foot. After several kilometres, in the burn of the late morning, she met her contact, Aaron son-of-Shauna, a horse wrangler for the Dragoons, who placed her on a horse used by the Order. He'd seen this one in action before. It was scared of nothing. As she rode off, Aaron and his horse were left behind.

Not being observed in the exit tunnel had been hard enough. He'd had to hide in the shadows, then jog across the desert to make up for the time he'd lost. But fighting Aaron for his own horse was harder. Although he was a Keeper by birth and belief, Bruno had grown soft during his ten years at the Stadium. It turned out apprenticeships with the farmers and Scribes and archers and Chief Lilly had done little to teach him how to walk into a fight.

Luckily for him, Aaron was no better.

'Bruno?' he'd asked, seeing him approach. 'What are you doing here?'

There was an answer – one that no one had suspected and he'd had to keep to himself for year after painful year as he waited for the rest of his people and the Leader himself to arrive – but it was not, even now, an answer he wanted to share.

He walked up to Aaron and said, 'I need your horse. There's something Alessandra forgot. I'm to give it to her.'

Turned out Aaron wasn't quite as gullible as all that. He started, 'I have my orders from—'

So Bruno struck him with a rock on the side of his head, dropping him to the earth with one blow, where the blood ran thick into the sand. It should have been easier. His heart shouldn't have raced the way it did and there should have been no hesitation or guilt. But there was, and that was because the softness of the Commonwealth had entered him. So much talk about the past and what used to be there and so much more about the future and what should come next . . . it was spreading him thin, making him lose focus, allowing Time to play on his mind.

Aaron lay on the ground. Whether he was dead or not was of little significance. Bruno needed the horse to confirm Alessandra's destination, which was the one part of the story he wasn't able to guess. He'd been able to piece things together well enough to know that now was the time for him to report back for the final time. The radio worked again and Lilly had heard something she considered so secret that she needed to see the Master of the Order of Silence rather than General Winters. It was something so important that she needed to recruit someone who was outside the chain of command. It was something so urgent that Alessandra daughter-of-Henrietta needed to leave immediately. And it was all because of a voice on the radio that was close and sitting on a Trove that could 'change everything'.

The return of Alessandra's parents flying all six flags had been a spectacle, one that Bruno had thought significant, but still he had stayed. It had been a good decision to wait and see if any more came out of the ground. Apparently, the single fuse mattered a great deal more than the flags.

On horseback, following Alessandra, he is finally free. This is the end of his time as a spy – no more pretending to be an Urban Explorer so he can sneak off with information for his people while the others break minor rules and try to add lines to a nearly worthless map to test their own mettle.

No more lies. No more deception. No more pretence of helping these people bring back the horrors that killed so many people.

They were not *bad* people. Some were good and kind. But they were misguided, and as the Leader always said, 'Our mercy is their greatest weapon.'

It became clear after half a day tracking Alessandra that her destination was the first hole in the ground that went to the bottom. What wasn't clear to Bruno was why Alessandra was going to look in that hole for the voice on the radio – but the Leader might know the answer and that was enough for now.

An hour ago he broke off his tracking and headed to Yellow Ridge to meet his people.

Now, he rides up to greet them.

The camp at Yellow Ridge has massively expanded since last Bruno visited, four months ago. The tents are spread out and wide enough for four soldiers to engage on any avenue as needed. There is no effort being made to hide their positions, but fortifications have been built using Raw to protect it in case the Stadium becomes expeditionary. Bruno himself has carried the message that an attack here is unlikely. It runs against the General's character and her beliefs that the Stadium is smart and the barbarians are fools and will eventually break themselves against the walls the way birds fly into the windows of the towers and never learn.

Still in his mourning robe, the Leader walks to greet him as he dismounts. He will hand the horse over to the *caballero* later. For now, holding the reins steadies him. It is quite a moment, knowing he is back for good, that he has decided for the second time in his life to turn away from everything he knows for a cause greater than himself.

'How are you?' the Leader asks him.

'I'm well,' Bruno reports, wiping his face with the clean cloth handed to him by a child he doesn't know. 'I have no injuries. I'm shaky, though, and emotional. I have important news. Because of this news and how I left, I won't be able to return to them. I am here now.'

'I see,' the Leader replies. A crowd has gathered around them and the Leader makes no effort to send them away. What Bruno has to tell him privately will come later. For now, they are all one.

'Tell us: in all those years, have they changed you?' the Leader asks him.

The horse snorts and pulls on the reins. Bruno calms it with a touch. 'Yes,' he admits. 'They think differently about so much that the only way to stay present within myself was not to fight the ways I was changing. I found pleasure in their rituals and their company. I found loneliness too. I grew from being a boy of seventeen to a man of twenty-seven. These were important years. There was love and loss during that time too. Coming back is . . . wonderful, and also painful.'

255

The people listen. Some nod.

'There are good people there,' he says, repeating himself to explain it better. 'Some are kind and funny – I was in love with a girl for three years. Some are cruel, they would walk over the bleeding to serve themselves. In this way they are like all other people: no better and no worse. They are systematic and imaginative and I admire that. They have a hunger for happiness and rejoicing that I will be sad to see end because there isn't enough of it.'

'Have they convinced you of their way?' the Leader asks him.

Bruno, having anticipated this question, nods, acknowledging it, then shakes his head as an answer.

'No, Leader. They accumulate knowledge believing that it will teach them how the Gone World ended so that the same mistakes might not be made. But really, they hoard what they learn and don't become any wiser. They speak about the Gone World constantly, but they don't humble themselves to what they don't know; they simply keep pressing and pushing for more, as though their own ability to ask questions is enough reason for answering them. It never occurs to them that their path might lead to the same weapons, the same relationships, the same errors, the same consequences as those they fear. I think this is because they lack humility. They are arrogant and single-minded and have organised themselves to go only one direction without questioning whether they should be going anywhere at all. They cannot stand aside from themselves and see what they are doing and imagine the harm it may bring.'

'This direction they are going,' the Leader asks, 'does it follow the Ancients or does it lead another way?'

'Their future seems to be the world's past. If they are taking their learning in another direction, I don't know what it is. As

256

best I can tell, they don't know either. They simply press on. A horse with no reins.'

'And we know where that road leads,' he says.

'Yes, Leader.'

'You feel sorry for them?'

'Yes.'

'We're stopping them, Bruno, not punishing them. If words were enough, we would use them.'

'Have we had those words yet, Leader?'

'What do you mean?'

'Is there no last conversation to be had? One final chance to stop what comes next?'

'Their Archive is a seed,' the Leader says, 'that will grow into the plant that strangles the life out of the world. Surely it needs to be stopped now.'

'Yes, of course,' Bruno concedes. 'But what if they could be convinced?'

'Come back to the tent. We can discuss the rest with the Deputy. Take your time,' he adds. 'There is no rush.'

The Leader turns to go, but Bruno stops him with a hand on his arm.

'Actually, there is,' Bruno corrects him. 'Time presents itself again, Leader. There's a girl travelling through the desert. I think I know where she's going but I don't know why.'

He speaks of the radio and Alessandra and the voice and the Trove, trying to explain Lilly's insistence that this changes everything, though he can't find the meaning in her phrase. He tells the Leader about Master Birch being consulted and the girl's secret departure, speculating that Alessandra is going underground to find the source of the radio.

'The bottom can't be reached,' the Leader says. 'There is Sickness there. They're looking in the wrong place.'

'There are those who believe that tunnels connect the deepest places in the Gone World, Leader. Alessandra might be trying to use them to reach her destination even though it's buried.'

'What about the Sickness?' the Leader asks.

Bruno knows that the Leader's daughter died from illness, and the wife too, a most generous and kind woman with a beauty that could break a young man's heart. So he tries to phrase his idea as gently as possible. 'Perhaps the Sickness of the world now is not the same as the one that killed the Ancients,' he says. 'Perhaps,' he says, not looking the Leader in the eye for fear of causing him unnecessary pain, 'there is only a Sickness above the ground, although most of the dead are beneath.'

The Leader knows his people killed two Runners and he had thought the third was killed in the building's collapse. Perhaps she survived – and if she did, he knows where she is, although getting there is another matter.

'We have troops coming here from the north, but they don't know the Territory. I'll send men,' the Leader concludes.

'They'll need a net,' says Bruno.

STAYING ALIVE

The Librarian provides Elimisha with almost three hundred and fifty years of recorded music, including pieces written much earlier and recorded centuries later, which amounts to a thousand years or more of musical exploration – almost none of which she'll hear before she dies down here and all of which will be buried unheard if she does.

Once again, per her daily routine, she stands in front of the hole with her axe, sweat from an hour's work dripping down her skin and her eyes shining with determination and hostility. She pulls the axe back with her gloved hands and yet again lets the blade hack into the chalky concrete in time to the beat of her latest musical selection, 'You Make Me Feel Like Dancing' by one Leo Sayer.

Despite the Librarian's protestations about limited access and the destruction or inaccessibility of many mirrored sites and data centres, there are a dozen-times-a-dozen lifetimes of music for her to listen to and even after taking an eight-hour music-appreciation course (she should have slept, she knows it, but it's so hard to rest with so much to learn at her fingertips) she doesn't entirely understand how one era of music differs from another. What she does understand is that the beat really picks up in the 1960s and then it all gets 'funky' in the 1970s.

And funky is good.

From then on the beat never really stops. She's been trying to take it in order but it's been too much.

When the Librarian offered to 'curate a playlist to her interests' and she said, 'Sure—' it asked what kind of mood she was in. Elimisha didn't know what kind of mood she was in other than bitter, angry, resentful, self-destructive, hopeful, overwhelmed, sad and dutiful – for which there seemed to be no single word – so it asked her what she planned to do while listening.

'I'm going to break out of a bomb shelter with an axe.'

So the Librarian made a playlist for that.

What she has learned – and is now the only person in the world to know this – is that if you're trying to chop your way through a four-hundred-year-old wall, music by the following people and bands really helps: ABBA, Lenny Kravitz, Gin Wigmore, Beyoncé, Stevie Wonder, Kool & the Gang, Aretha Franklin, David Bowie, New Order, and her favourites so far – The Bee Gees.

'Stayin' Alive' is what she listens to most often.

As Elimisha hammers away to the dulcet wailings of Barry, Robin and Maurice Gibb, two gunshots pop from the direction of the kitchen, followed by a woman's scream, an explosion and a massive crashing sound from inside the kitchen itself.

'Librarian, turn off the music,' she instructs, lowering the axe and looking back at the T-junction. She knows that she heard something, but after a month alone underground she isn't sure that what she heard was real. There is always a chance she is losing her mind.

There is nothing – not a sound . . . at least, not until she hears someone kick a pot across the concrete floor of the kitchen and swear like a drunk Dragoon at the midsummer party.

Axe tight in her grip, Elimisha limps to the corner of the hall that splits to the kitchen on her right and the Communications Room far down the hall to the left.

If this is a hallucination, she thinks, *it is so obvious as to be trite.* 'I can't get out so my brain has made another door. Obviously. And the person in the kitchen is going to be a version of me. I wonder if anyone's studied dreams before? I'll bet someone has.'

Her hands throb to the beat of her heart inside her leather gloves. Her muscles twitch from an hour hitting the wall.

Axe in hand, leg dragging, she limps to the kitchen door, pausing every now and then to listen for any sounds; any confirmation.

Quietly, and with minimal pressure, Elimisha presses down on the handle to unlatch the door and with a gentle hand she pushes it open – to find a young woman with a pistol standing in front of her over a dead body.

Elimisha isn't sure if the vision is real. The girl is wearing a Runner's uniform and looks to be her age. Her face is red with blood and her eyes are fierce.

She looks familiar. She sort of looks like the girl in the Pirelli calendar if the girl in the Pirelli calendar was muscular and bathed in blood and pointing a gun at her chest.

The girl raises the gun at Elimisha and shouts, 'Drop the stick! Now!'

Elimisha looks at the girl, who doesn't fire. Her reactions and her eyes and her speech and that gun – she admits to herself – are awfully life-like for a hallucination.

'Are you real?' she asks.

'Am I what?'

261

The girl really does look familiar. She both is and isn't a version of Elimisha herself: same Runner gear, same age, almost the same height, but lighter skin and her hair is much, much filthier. Whatever issues Elimisha might have been having with her curls earlier, they are long gone.

She may not be a ghost after all.

'Who the fuck are you and how did you get in here?' she asks.

'I'm Alessandra Wayworth, Archive Runner for the Commonwealth.'

Elimisha knows the name – she knows such a girl – but she isn't at all sure that the beast in front of her is really Alessandra Wayworth. But that's only of passing interest compared to her second question.

'How did you get in here?'

'The . . . tunnel,' Alessandra says, looking back the way she'd come in.

The metal shelf with the poisonous canned foods has been pushed over to reveal a tunnel. It is crude, the edges rough, but the dimensions are perfect: a passage out carved by a machine.

'Elimisha,' says Alessandra, 'you know me. Can you put down the axe, please?'

Elimisha grips her axe tighter. 'Are you real?' she asks again.

'I was sent to find you. I was followed. They tossed some of those little bombs after me – the ones they must have used on you. The tunnel collapsed behind me, so now I'm stuck in here with you. I assume we're stuck?'

The look Elimisha gives her removes any doubt.

'Is this an Archive?' Alessandra asks, because she was instructed to ask.

'Yes,' Elimisha answers, lowering the axe as Alessandra lowers the gun.

'Is anyone else here?'

'Not . . . exactly,' she answers.

'We heard you on the radio. That's how we found you.'

'You heard me?'

'You were talking about plants.'

'Why didn't you answer me?'

'Lilly's microphone doesn't work.'

'Who did you kill?' Elimisha says, looking down at the body below Alessandra and realising she probably should have asked about this earlier but – when? Everything feels equally important at this point and the dead can wait.

'Don't worry about him. How big's the Trove, Chief?'

'Chief?'

'This is an Archive at rest and you're securing it, right?'

'I guess so. Yes.'

'Then you're the Chief, Chief.'

Chief Elimisha releases her axe and feels a buzzing, prickly sensation in her palm as her fingers finally unclench. On instinct, after years of drilling, she looks at the Runner on the floor and asks, 'Do you need food, water or medical attention?'

Through the damp, the grime, the smell of gunpowder and urine, Alessandra hears the words of order and structure come from a girl even more trapped and scared than she is and begins to laugh.

Elimisha, hearing her, begins, slowly at first, to laugh too. And once the emotion fills her chest, she starts to cry. The muscles in her shoulders seem to collapse like a falling tower and she drops the axe as she sobs.

Alessandra rushes over to embrace her.

Behind Alessandra and in front of Elimisha is the half-naked and well-shot-up body of the claw-man. Alessandra not only hit him twice but also stabbed him through the neck with a dagger.

He's lying on his back.

Elimisha, calmer now, wipes her face and stands to examine the body.

'It was dark and I was very scared,' Alessandra says from behind her. 'Those guys were coming up fast behind me and this guy was about five metres from me. I fired. I think that's why they stopped following me and chucked in the grenades instead.'

The body looks like a man in his thirties, with skin like Alessandra's – what people at the Stadium call *leaf-brown* – and eyes much darker than Elimisha's. They stare, wide-eyed and open, at the ceiling above him.

He isn't a person, though. It never was.

He – it – is dressed in workman's overalls, unsnapped to reveal a bare, hairless chest of fine but not unusual definition. He wears thick leather boots. Instead of hands attached to the wrists, there are thick metal claws with blunted ends. Alessandra is examining them closely as Elimisha tentatively pokes the chest with her finger. There is some kind of dried blood on the chest, but not splattered from the shot. It looks more like a decoration, as though it was painted on for some reason. The blood has flaked off, so Elimisha is having trouble finding meaning in it.

'The shape of these claws are the same shape as the tunnel texture. I think this thing carved the tunnels out somehow,' Alessandra says.

Elimisha can now see that the blood on the chest is definitely writing of some kind. Alessandra steps over the body and straddles it for a clearer view. The writing is very old and very smeared and what is left has turned to a blackened crust. Once her eyes see the words, though, there is no mistaking the message.

'It says "Adam was here",' Elimisha says.

'Oh,' says Alessandra, 'you're right – it does. I see it now.'

'Adam was Lilly's cousin. This is the proof! The tunnels are real! The Adamists were right.'

Alessandra stops looking at the claws and gives Elimisha a pathetic look. 'I just came out of the tunnels. The *tunnels* are the proof that the tunnels are real. Not the graffiti.'

'That's . . . also true.'

'Master Birch already briefed me on this. That's how I found you – and why we're not dead from the Sickness.'

'Why aren't we dead from the Sickness?' Elimisha asks.

'There isn't any.'

'Oh . . . no, there is. Or there was. There's no question about it. I've seen them – in the Inferno Room.'

'The what?'

'I don't want to talk about it,' she says, walking over to the tunnel and starting to crawl inside.

'You can't get out that way. They collapsed the tunnel.' Alessandra sticks a finger into the hole she made between the claw-man's eyes. 'So amazing.'

'What the hell is it?' Elimisha asks.

'It's a machine shaped like a person. Maybe it was meant to act like one too.' Alessandra looks up. 'Maybe these are the ghosts everyone talks about.' She raises one of the legs. 'It once walked around – look, see? The boot's soles are worn down. Maybe it kept walking after everyone died, the way some machines kept going. Are you okay?'

'You just stuck your finger into its brain.'

'It's . . . a machine.' Alessandra taps its bare eyeballs. 'See?' She sticks her fingers up its nose. 'It's a thing. A weird thing. But a thing. What happened to your leg?'

Elimisha looks from the claw-man to her leg. Her bandage

265

is hidden by the Haptic Command Gear but the limp is too obvious to hide when she moves.

'Got hurt.'

The mechanical doll-thing at Elimisha's feet looks forbidding. As it was never alive she is not sure it can ever be dead, either. It seems to be looking towards a sky none of them will see again if they can't find a way out.

'Too bad I shot it,' Alessandra says. 'It's a tunnel-maker – maybe it could have tunnelled us out of here. Where's the Trove?'

'What?'

'The Trove you found – that you were reading from. It's the internet, right? Master Birch and Chief Lilly want to know if it's small enough that we can take it with us.'

'We can't get out at all.'

'We'll get out somehow. They know where we are. Or they will once I tell them over the radio. That still works, right?'

'Yeah.'

'Is there something else I can wear? I've been in water and . . .' She winces.

'You can take a warm shower and then put on the Haptic Command Gear. I'm wearing a small. You might need a medium.'

'Looks like it was made for you.'

This makes Elimisha smile. She points Alessandra to the showers and fitting room as she bends down to start cleaning up.

Alessandra leaves the messy kitchen and walks down the long hall as instructed, looking for the showers. There is a room marked 'Habitat'. She opens the door and goes inside.

There are no showers.

The lights are off in the room but a red bulb is glowing brightly, casting a bloody hue over four skeletal remains. One

– an adult – is crouched over a desk on the right side of the room. In the bones of his hands are two devices that look like the grips of guns. Between them, under the head, is a book. The three other bodies are against the far wall directly in front of her on the floor. The one in the middle had been an adult. She sits bolt upright, the empty sockets of her skull staring at Alessandra, but whether in plea or accusation, she can't tell. But in her stomach she feels it's about fairness and unfairness, sorrow and pain, the eternity of the space between love and emptiness.

The woman's arms are around the two smaller bodies. Their skulls are resting on the remains of her lap.

Alessandra backs towards the wall.

'They came here to be safe,' Elimisha says, behind her now. They thought this place could protect them. But it wasn't built for what killed them.'

In sight of the four skeletons, Elimisha tells Alessandra a story that she has now memorised by rote:

'There was a historian in 2099 who wrote a retrospective on the century. Dr Antonio Molinari. He said that a global collapse was coming because the institutions which gave peace its structure were being eroded by neglect and malevolence. He predicted that as the institutions were dismantled, civilisation's resilience would be too, until we finally became fragile enough that even tiny events could cascade into Armageddon. He called that cascading process a *Tracollo*. A collapse. It's from a language that used to be called Italian.

'Years later there was very bad space weather and Earth was caught in its path. There was a Coronal Mass Ejection, a massive one, so enormous that the flare charged the particles throughout interplanetary space and changed the night skies from black to green. At that time, the entire world was electronically connected but politically divided. So when the Sun took out the satellite systems around the world and fried the grid, which is what they called the connectivity, everyone blamed each other. It was like their emotions caught fire.'

Alessandra stands there, watching the dead. She has seen bones before, hundreds of them, but never a family, never resting in their moment of death. And Elimisha's vocabulary is almost incomprehensible. *Italian? Armageddon? Particles?*

Elimisha continues as though in a trance, 'The damage wasn't irreparable. There was terrible data loss and many dependent systems failed, but it was hardly the end of the world. The trouble was, countries started accusing each other of using the disaster to gain advantage over one another – small misunderstandings led to big attacks, which led to a series of regional wars. An untested and unstoppable biological weapon was mated to nanotechnology and it spread, killing people almost immediately. The heavily populated centres went down first, then some of the bioweapon bled into the food supply, causing genetic-level damage. No one knew how to turn it off.

'They had a few days' warning. They didn't know exactly what was happening, so they prepared tunnels and shelters and evacuation plans. They put fail-safes in the biggest buildings so they could be destroyed if the virus – or whatever it was – got in. It was the only way they knew to isolate it. They put military personnel in charge, believing they had the discipline necessary to do what might be needed when the time came. Colonel Harrington was one of them, but he didn't do it. So was he,' Elimisha says, pointing at the dead man at the desk, 'and he couldn't do it either. How do you murder your own family?'

'Not everyone died,' Alessandra says, looking around the red room. 'We're here.'

'A few turned out to be immune. Others were isolated and they outlived the bugs. This was more than three hundred years ago. I've been eating rice and bee honey. I read about some archaeologists who found honey from Ancient Egypt three thousand years old. They said it tasted exactly the same.'

'Are you okay?' Alessandra asks.

'That's the first time I've ever told that story to someone else. I've been practising it over and over and over, in case I'm the only thing that gets out of here and I have to recount it. No one would be able to Attest, but soon you'll see the proof too, and then you can Attest, and because we both saw the same thing and our reputations are—'

'How do you know all this?' Alessandra interrupts.

'Go and shower. Put on the Haptic Command Gear. Make sure you bring the gloves and the glasses from the belt. After that, I'll show you the Archive. When you see it,' she adds, 'try not to freak out, okay?'

MISSING

It is a clear night. The view from the Crow's Nest at the top of the Eastern Wall is sublime. The wind has settled and if Henrietta were to make a shot from here it would travel the world as if pulled on a string.

She only lowers the scope from her right eye when the final rays have disappeared from the top of Yellow Ridge. Once the sun is gone Alessandra won't be able to use the Signal Mirror, and that means she isn't coming back tonight.

She turns to the Spotter whose position she'd taken. She can't quite bring his name to mind, although she knows it's something everyone else would remember. 'If she had signalled, which tunnel would have received her?' she asks him.

'I don't know, Commander,' says the young man, who has unusually long hair. 'I get the signal, I send a messenger to the Gatekeeper and he makes the choice depending on what else is happening out there. I only know once the messenger comes back. Then I can sometimes see what's happening, but usually not. We can only watch a small number of the entrances from here.'

'What happens now?' Henry asks.

'Alessandra was assigned a Signal Mirror by the Buried Clown near Blue Crest. A few weeks ago we cut off his hat, installed some flooring over the hollow parts and then mounted a new double mirror, so if she climbs the back of the Clown and removes the hat she can use it at sun-up and sun-down. It's interesting, because Weapons and Comms worked with the blacksmiths to create a latching system for the hat so when it gets windy—'

'So Alessandra has to sleep out there?'

'Yes, Commander.'

Henrietta looks through the scope again. The fires are burning with impunity over Yellow Ridge. If the brightness of the glow is any indication, their numbers are growing, but still Winters won't make a move; she continues to talk about the Battle of Cannae and how she's going to draw them down into a trap; how she's going to encircle and kill the barbarians.

Lilly, as usual, had been the one to speak up, reminding her that it was the barbarians – under Hannibal – who'd won that encounter. His strategy had been based on the Romans being arrogant.

That was the sort of thing that got her booted off the High Command. Now that she *was* off it, there was no stopping her.

'Calvin,' she said. 'Your name is Calvin, right?' that fact returning to her from nowhere.

'Yes, Commander.'

'Of Calvin and Hobbes fame, I presume?' Henry doesn't much care, but the silence is annoying her. Any distraction – even Calvin's mouth – is an improvement at this point.

'Yes, Commander. My parents were in their twenties when the High Command released parts of the Harrington Collection to the Museum. There was a lot of interesting stuff – you know, the Gibbon book, Thucydides, Homer – but just like everyone else, they really wanted to see the 200th anniversary edition of *The Complete Calvin and Hobbes*. The last one was published on 31 December 1995, so the 2095 edition is the one that Harrington packed away. You know all this, of course . . .' His voice trailed off.

'Tell me the story of your name, Calvin,' she says.

He looked relieved. The small talk comforted him as well. He'd never stood this close to someone so famous. 'Okay, so the four volumes amount to one thousand, four hundred and forty pages, and you remember how every day the Curator would turn a page in the glass box? That meant we could see two pages at a time – but it still took almost two years to see the whole thing. What was so interesting to my parents was how no one here at the Stadium had ever imagined telling stories with pictures before. Or imagined that written stories could be funny because we took every Find so seriously. My mother said that watching Calvin and his parents changed their entire world view.'

'Oh yeah?' Henry says. The sun has been replaced by Keeper fires now. Life with death.

'It made them think that maybe one kid would be enough.'

It was a good joke. Henry would have laughed had the mood been right. As it is, her mind is too far away.

Comedy wants intimacy, not distance. The sky here is too big to fill with laughter.

She returns her scope to its pouch and tries to calm herself with the view, although it is poor comfort, because without the scope everything – and Alessandra – is even further away.

It doesn't make sense. When Alessandra didn't show up at dinner, Graham was the first to say something was wrong. Without needing to discuss it out loud, they both went to find

Lian in the Central Archive. The soaring windows along the Southern Wall had been sealed tight and the lighting inside had been set low. She and four Scribes – two elder and two younger – were debating.

As they walked in, a younger scribe was saying, 'The lesson here couldn't be more clear. Thucydides said it directly: "The strong do what they can and the weak do what they must." This is how decisions are made, by seeing the world with clear eyes and making the reasoned choice. The Melians made the wrong choice and so they were defeated. It's a simple story about power.'

When the four scholars reached agreement, Lian had smiled. 'That is General Winter's reading of the conversation as well. It is not, however,' indicating Graham, 'his reading, as I recall. Commander Wayworth here used to be a Scribe long before becoming a Raider. Tell us your reading of the Melian Dialogue, Commander.'

'We're trying to find Alessandra.'

'I'm told she's on a Run. Tell us – while you're here.'

Henrietta crossed her arms. She knew Graham was powerless to resist sharing his minority views of the world. Hopefully, it wouldn't take long. It made no sense that Alessandra would be sent on a Run during a Lockdown. Something was off. Her ears heard Graham but she was watching Lian for clues.

'It is no surprise that the strong usually win over the weak,' Graham said, animated by this rare opportunity to share thoughts, not only information. 'In fact, it is so unsurprising one might wonder why someone as astute as Thucydides would bother writing it at all. That's when I realised it wasn't what he wrote – you see, the story isn't about Athens winning over a tiny island with a tiny military. It's about how Melos, even knowing they would lose, chose to fight anyway. *That's* what's interesting. If you want to win, by all means be stronger. But if you want to avoid war, being stronger isn't enough. You need to know how the other people think. That, in my view, is what Thucydides was trying to tell us. In my other readings – before I changed career paths – I was working on an unfinished theory that defies common sense and it's this: losers start wars. Consider the ones we know about in the twentieth century. Germany started and lost World War I. It started and lost World War II. North Korea attacked the south and lost. The Arabs attacked Israel three times and lost—'

'Japan attacked Russia and won in 1904,' Henry said, 'and North Vietnam attacked the South and won.'

The other Scribes stared at them, wide-eyed over their acumen.

'We've had these conversations before,' Henry explained.

'I'm not saying the losers always start the wars. I'm saying it happens so often that being stronger evidently doesn't stop others from attacking. In all my travels,' he went on, 'I have learned one thing: peace needs as much of a strategy as war. Given that we're the strongest in the Territory and clearly don't understand the Keepers, I think the conversation is relevant.'

Graham smiled the world's most undefeatable smile – a smile that Henry had to cut short.

'Lian, a moment, please?'

As Graham strutted among the Scribes, Lian walked over to join Henrietta in a private conversation.

'Commander?'

'Did you send her on the Run?'

'No. I was told by a messenger that she was out.'

'Sent by one of the other Evaluators?'

'I was busy and didn't ask. I'm sorry. It didn't seem

significant. We have Runners going out periodically throughout the week.'

'Not during a Lockdown Protocol.'

'No, I suppose not. Who was the messenger?'

'It was Eric son-of-Danielle. You're going to find out who sent the message?'

'Yes. My daughter's missing, allegedly outside the walls during a Lockdown – and that after three Runners have gone missing and Alan was murdered.'

'The boy is only ten, so don't bite his head off, okay? It wasn't his idea.'

Henrietta found Eric asleep in his parents' quarters. They were not pleased to see Commander Wayworth, but she outranked them.

The answer to her question was *Chief Lilly*.

LOVE

Seventy-one-year-old Lilly sleeps alone. It wasn't always this way. When she returned with the Harrington Box, she agreed to turn it over to the Council on the condition they made her Chief Archivist. This done, she was invited to join the Mid-Command where Section Chiefs gathered each month to coordinate action. Though only a teenager, she became a participant in government where the Chiefs educated each other and learned from each other and put their knowledge to the service of shared goals; turning existing conditions into preferred ones. It was at one such meeting in Lilly's mid-twenties that her relationship with Verena Roughsea deepened.

Verena was twenty-eight and a bit older and more experienced than Lilly. She came from a family of sea-dwellers who had journeyed inland to the Commonwealth for trade and met resistance on the Road. Her mother, like Lilly's own, had been killed, although that was where their similarities ended. Lilly's father had never been part of her life, whereas Verena's was worse than absent: he tried to sell her to the Stadium. But the Stadium back then did not buy children – not until later, when Lilly recommended they start so they could build their numbers without having to worry about spies.

Even without payment, the man left Verena there and never returned.

Five-year-old Verena was placed in the Agoge with the other orphans and rose through the ranks. By the time Lilly met her in her mid-twenties she had become a Chief of Movement, in charge of all transportation outside of military operations, all comings and goings, all horses and manner of motion. She worked for the Mayor and coordinated with High Command. In secret, she coordinated with Saavni in establishing the Order of Silence.

Lilly was attracted to Verena's confidence, her clarity of argument, the way she moved. Verena noticed and they become lovers. That lasted for four years, ending abruptly when Verena informed Lilly that she was leaving.

It had made no sense.

'Leaving . . . me?' Lilly had asked.

'Leaving the Stadium.'

'You mean the Commonwealth?'

Verena did not answer immediately. It was as though the two were not the same in her mind.

Lilly pressed her. 'You're leaving here with me in it?'

Verena had a tendency not to answer questions with an obvious answer. It was not a stance; she genuinely thought people spoke as a means of catching up rather than informing themselves.

'Leaving to go where?' Lilly asked, also ignoring her own question.

They had been in bed. They shared an apartment above Door 3, Section 2, Ring 8, which caught the morning light. The rays were sliding through the partly open slits of the shutters, across the blankets and Verena's sandy skin.

277

'I can't say. I've been asked to do something. The Commonwealth has secrets that run wider and deeper and . . . further . . . than even you know.'

'That's no surprise,' Lilly had said. 'Nor is it an explanation.'

Verena's calm voice sounded more like a teacher's than a lover's. Lilly hated it when she spoke like that. It was the only time she felt at a distance, and it was compounded by Lilly almost always being the smartest person in the room: she didn't like being condescended to and she felt condescended to now. She wasn't used to it.

Verena, however, was not in a conversation. She was imparting information. Lilly could hear the distance in her voice – a distance she often saw in Verena's eyes, learned from being an abandoned child who had had to make her own way. That distance, however, had closed dramatically and passionately and even comically during their time together. It was painful to see it return. It was a surprise to know that Verena had reserves of it that she could call upon when circumstances demanded.

They were beside each other in bed in gowns of soft cotton but Lilly heard Verena as though she were sending coded signals from a lamp on a ridge. As she spoke, explaining the facts but revealing nothing, Lilly remembers looking at Verena's shoulder and imagining it gone from her bed, the warmth removed, the dialogue of their love silenced.

'Will I ever see you again?' Lilly asked.

Verena paused too long to answer, which made it one.

Lilly stood, dressed and left the room.

Three days later Verena was gone.

Five years later there was a man. Lilly tried taking lovers pretending she was as bold as her mother while learning that she was not. Her courage was manifest in other ways. Her heart, however, needed protection. She settled into this truth of herself and both slowed and lowered expectations.

His name was Gideon and he was older, almost forty. He had a sharp mind and an easy way of talking. His humour was gentle and his manner quiet. She felt at ease in his presence and they became good friends. She fell into the rhythm of his company and decided she was better with it. They tried for children. There was a brief flowering but it lasted only two months and, in its course, went away.

The doctors and the healers sat with her. 'A water baby' was what they called it. She was instructed not to deny the sense of loss.

She did not deny it, but she could also not define it. She pictured a cloud – a smear, a distortion in the wind – that became a place for the person who might have been. A daughter, someone to talk to; someone to sit with without talking. That would never be.

She ended the relationship with Gideon, who was heartbroken, but did not resist. Three years later he met a woman named Jennifer, who already had a child.

Lilly was happy for them.

Two loves were enough for her. Later, and by her fifties, she was not beyond the reach of intimacy but her mind had been turned upwards and outwards, away from the body and more towards the stars. Some Evaluators say the peak for the creative mind – a mind like hers – is in the rich and imaginative period of one's thirties when there is both enough knowledge to work with and enough energy to use it. To this, Lilly only laughed louder than a hailstorm on the Stadium's roof and when she recovered, turned her still active mind to ever greater challenges.

*

She sleeps alone now, and lightly; that is a function of age and she accepts it. She does not feel it in her mind but she does in the bladder and so too in the patterns of restlessness without cause.

Tonight, though, the cause is external. There is a knock on the door and a rapid entrée even before her invitation to come in.

'Of course it's the two of you,' Lilly says, sitting up and rubbing her face. 'Is it morning?'

'Pre-dawn. Start talking,' Henrietta says.

Lilly looks at Graham, who does not come to her defence. There is no lightness to his mood.

The Wayworths. They form a phalanx around each other no matter the odds or circumstances.

'Close the door,' Lilly says.

Henrietta does as she's told and then crosses her arms to avoid strangling Lilly, which would be unproductive because that's where the knowledge is.

'She's working for Master Birch and the Order now. We sent her out to the Gone World. We heard a voice on the radio – thanks to Graham here – that I'm certain is Elimisha daughter-of-Cara. I believe she's sitting on a Trove important enough to affect the direction of the future. Given all Alessandra's personal skills, including but not limited to her speed, her brains, her judgement, her capacity to fight and improvise – not to mention her head being packed with seventeen years of information from the two of you that I'm absolutely certain you weren't supposed to tell her – she was without a doubt the best person for the job. Also, she's not technically a member of the Order yet, so Birch can look General Winters directly in the eye and say that no members of the Order are unaccounted for. Which will be necessary because Birch and I are running a conspiracy. Welcome to the revolution. May I put on some trousers, please?'

Lilly dresses and leads the anxious parents out of her apartment, through the Ring and down to her office. Yes, yes, they're nervous and worried for their daughter, but the question is whether she and Birch had been right to make the decision at all and if so, if they've chosen the best person. As the answer to both is affirmative and unequivocal, all that remains is dealing with the fallout.

Walking downstairs before sunrise is not a joy for her legs. Each day she works to strengthen them, climbing stairs and even jogging slowly around the Green, and as a consequence, each day her legs are both stronger and more sore, meaning that her efforts to walk better are preventing her from walking better – so whoever created the human body had done a terrible job and she wanted to have words.

It isn't as though Henry and Graham are the only concerned parents here. Elimisha has a mother too, and two siblings, both promising and who both adore their sister. But at least Cara has the good sense not to burst in demanding answers to decisions made long ago.

Everyone serves, Lilly thinks. *Everyone plays some part in the Stadium's survival, everyone plays some part in moving us forwards. Everyone has some role to play in learning, delivering, archiving and protecting the hard-won Knowledge of the Commonwealth so we can rebuild the world in the event of catastrophe, precisely what the Gone World never did. They went digital, the digital failed and now humanity knows nothing after The Rise except the scraps we reclaim from Spade, Raid and Trade. It all depends on Knowledge. How can you get anything done if you don't know how to do it?*

'What?' Graham asks as they approach the door to Weapons and Communications.

'What do you mean, "what"?'

'You were mumbling.'

Was she? Lilly does have a tendency to do so these days.

'I was talking to myself and I won't apologise for it. I'm interesting. Now get in there.'

Lilly had left explicit instructions for the radio to be attended at every waking moment and for the fewest number of people to know about it. Birch had asked Javier to place extra guards at the door, guards known to be especially discreet.

The limited personnel, unfortunately, meant extremely long working hours for both Simone and Bruno and Lilly was only half-surprised on entering to find Simone with her face down on the desk, sleeping soundly on the White Board that was continuing to do its characteristic 'nothing'.

'Morning,' Lilly says, touching Simone gently on the shoulder.

'Chief.'

'Where's your partner?'

'He's not here.'

'I see that. Where is he? I thought he was supposed to relieve you three hours after moon-high.'

'He hasn't been here since yesterday.'

Graham and Henrietta enter Lilly's office. Graham pours himself a dram of Lilly's Lizard Poison, knowing she can't say a word as this is only the first part of her punishment – the one he knows she doesn't think she deserves, and therefore isn't consulting her on the matter.

The radio is silent. It glows impressively but does nothing.

'When was the last time you saw him?' Lilly asks Simone.

Simone can sense the situation has changed – not only

because the Wayworths have entered the room but because Lilly is sounding concerned. This is rare.

'He said goodbye soon after you and Master Birch and Alessandra left the room. Is it okay that I'm saying this?' she asks, looking at Graham and Henrietta.

'What else did he say?'

'He said "good luck".'

'With what?'

'He said, "with everything".'

Lilly looks at Henrietta, who knows immediately what this means. Lilly, however, isn't willing to accept the unacceptable conclusion so readily.

'How did you vet him?' Graham asks.

'Usual channels. He'd been here for years – seven years. Ten years, maybe. I don't know.'

'He wasn't Stadium-born?' Henry says.

'Neither were you.'

'And yet it's relevant.'

Lilly looks into the blue glow of the radio for no other reason than to fix her eyes on something. Could she really have been duped by a spy? And Winters? And Birch? And Javier? And everyone else? This is a place of secrets and lies and she knows that because she has been the progenitor of much of it – but to be played? By a *child*? The implications were more than she could embrace. They went beyond her own pride.

'The Keepers would have had to drop off a teenager, alone, and leave him here for a decade of his adolescent life. A life that involved – well, *everything*. Growing up, love, sex, hate, fear, honour, courage, learning, studying, debating . . . everything. And through all of that, he would have had to keep his convictions that the Keepers are right and we are wrong. That's preposterous.'

'I think it's the correct conclusion,' says Henrietta.

'If it is,' says Graham, 'we have no idea how much or in what ways we've been compromised, and it underscores yet again that we know *nothing* about the enemy.' He restrains himself from mentioning Thucydides and the Melians.

'What do these animals believe that deserves greater loyalty than we do?' Lilly asks. 'Look around! We are the greatest civilisation—'

'Something,' Graham interjects, uninterested in Lilly's shock. 'They're loyal to something. A way of life, a belief, a philosophy. I don't know. What I do know is that you and Birch have a confession to make to Winters, right now. And Henry and I won't be there to hear it because we have other things to do. Tell me,' he says, leaning forwards, all gentleness in his voice gone, 'where's my daughter, Chief?'

CAPTURE

'Leader?' comes a small voice. It belongs to a girl of fourteen, a distant niece of some kind; it can be hard to keep track of them. Her name is Mora. She likes new clothing too much in his opinion, which he has kept to himself.

Is it dawn? Already? *These days are so full.*

He reaches out his hand in bed to wake his wife before remembering.

'Yes, Mora?' he answers.

'Word has come from the riders who were sent after the Runner.'

'Let them in.'

She is confused by his use of the plural but allows the single man inside.

The Leader sits up and pulls the tanned skin of a once-white sheep over his shoulders for warmth. There are other clothes – ancient clothes with vibrant colours – that work as well, but this one reminds him of other times.

His face drawn, he listens to the rider recount how two horses and two men fell into a new pit and how a girl in black leather bested them, shot them in the dark and disappeared into the depths.

The Leader resists the impulse to try rubbing life back into his face or else raise his voice.

'There is no way out,' says the man, certain everything will work out. 'We followed her down, despite the Sickness, and sealed off a tunnel she was inside. I think we got her, but if not ... where can she go?'

'Why couldn't you catch a couple of girls?'

'They never misstep, Leader,' says the man, now on his knees. 'We don't understand it.'

How many days and weeks since he started this by dropping the first building? How many days since his wife's last breath? Already he cannot count them because the number speaks nothing to the feeling and therefore the truth. The Days of the Dead and the Days of the Living are not the same. For her – for their daughter – time slips away like rain from oiled leather. Counting their days, his wife and his daughter's, as though they were the same as his diminishes them all. He will count nothing and carry the weight, without number, alone.

The man continues to kneel, unable to answer the Leader's question.

His mother had told him that the Ancients had machines that could fly. She knew this because she had once seen a field of machines with wings, far away from here.

'Imagine it,' she had said. 'I was excited, but I didn't see any people to enjoy them. It is better to have the people without the machines than the machines without the people,' she explained. 'A kind of joy is lost and we don't deny that to ourselves. Flight! Like the birds! But in forsaking it, all other joys remain. Why? Because joy can only exist where there is life, and so life comes first. That is what we must keep. That is why we are called the Keepers.'

All the greatest virtues, she said, put the needs of others first. Loyalty and duty and sacrifice are greater than desire and passion and even wonder. *So we must choose. The soul only matures in the act of choosing,* his mother said. *The Ancients,* she explained, *either did not choose or they chose poorly. It is better to remove the temptation than to untangle the knot.*

Even now, he still dreams of flying.

Eyes closed, the Leader takes flight in his own imagination, not as a machine but as a bird. Beautiful and alive, he soars from the rock on which he sits and catches a thermal that hoists him far above the company behind him and outwards across the scrabble of the earth to the Gone World. With the eyes of a hunter he studies the ground so that he might understand the movements and meanings of everything below.

It is easy to feel the wind through his feathers when he closes his eyes. It is easy to sense the slight flutter in his belly when the wind changes and he drops unexpectedly before . . . tilting, ever so . . . he catches the edge of the wind-river that he rides to find that peace again; that necessary control.

Looking down, he can see the two Tracollos staring back up at him like black eyes gouged out of the earth: one from the time of his parents and one that his men created a month ago while chasing the curly-headed girl across the Gone World, the girl who slipped through his fingers as his wife slept beside him on her last night.

This is the wounded face of a dead city. Beneath it now are two girls who sit on a Trove that will raise the dead and kill them all over again.

And that needs to stop.

The longest tunnel out of the Stadium is known, sarcastically and without affection, as the *Funnel*. It begins in the site of the original Communications room at the northeast quad of the lowest Ring. That Comms room was looted long before The Few arrived and little more than the name on the door remained. The tunnel is the width of a narrow doorway and as tall as the tallest man with his arms outstretched. The edges are rough, chiselled and perfectly uniform. They were cut by a machine – the Order knows about the mechanical people with hands like claws. Beyond the edges of the shared maps, Explorers have reported on ravines full of them, lifeless as the day they were made. You enter the tunnel and travel two kilometres straight ahead. There is no turning back if others are following, and if anything – or anyone – has found the tunnel's exit and is coming, whoever is in the front will do the fighting until the end.

There is nothing fun about the Funnel.

The Order controls the access and generally Birch doesn't send Runners through it, or Explorers, or Traders, or anyone else with normal business outside the walls. She is too worried that the exit will eventually be spotted because wherever it had been intended to terminate, it now opens onto the side of a cliff that requires either a dexterous fifteen-metre climb to the surface or a ten-metre rappel to the bottom of a ravine that is too exposed for her liking; once inside it, there is too great a chance of being surrounded by an enemy from a superior and elevated position, especially if they choose to bring forces in from either side.

This morning, however, is an exception, and not only because she is pretty certain that Henrietta and Graham Wayworth will kill her and hide her body if she doesn't obey them and get them safely and undetected through the Commonwealth's perimeter to find their daughter.

The Funnel Room is now a storage space for winter gear, including blankets, sheets and outerwear for military and civilian personnel and equipment like shovels and torches and oils. The room is seldom visited and because the rattier blankets are stacked in front of the Funnel entrance, it is well hidden.

Birch closes the door behind them and turns on the electric lights.

'I obviously can't stop you, but are you sure about this?' she asks. 'Alessandra might be fine and we haven't heard anything on the radio yet.'

'Her mission was secret,' Graham says, 'and now, because of the spy, it's not. They will go looking for her and they probably know exactly where to start. The greatest chance of her completing her mission is for us to find her and escort her and the other girl – Elimisha – back here, or to take them elsewhere, to a safe location of our choosing.'

Birch does not answer. What he says is true, but she knows his motives are to protect his daughter. On the other hand, what difference does his motive make if the solution remains the same?

'Are you going to tell Winters?' Henry asks.

'Once you're long gone. In four or five hours, late morning, and by then I expect we'll hear something from Elimisha. Either she'll continue her regular pattern of Sharing on the radio or else she'll say or do something to signal that Alessandra is there and knows the plan. In any case, my hope is that you two can get the girls back with the internet or as much of it as you can carry on foot.'

Graham tightens his empty backpack.

'If you make it back, you'll be the only team in history to return with all six flags twice.'

The two parents look at Birch, expressionless.

'Right. When you get out of the tunnel and start the Run, return the canvas blanks to their original position to cover the exit. The Yellow Route will give you access to the most direct path until it links with the Red. Send up one flare to signal return and three flares to request assistance. I'll be alerting Anoushka and the archers to your excursion, and Javier and the Dragoons as well. Try not to come back before I do.'

Birch hands them both a canteen of water. They each drink half.

'Godspeed,' she says as they disappear into the pitch-black of the Funnel.

Five hours later, Lilly ascends the Western Stairs to the ground-level ring, which she follows to the direct stairs leading to the Snake Tower. Two silent Praetorians permit her entrance to the ten gruelling flights of stairs she needs to mount.

She's not sure if Birch is already there, but she knows they are both are expected because Winters accepted Birch's request for a high-level meeting. *There is no way the conversation is going to go well,* she thinks as she walks up, holding onto the polished wooden bannister on the way. Winters is going to be angry that Birch and she made decisions without her; she's going to be testy over their evident insubordination, and if she didn't have a good sleep and a big breakfast, she'll use the occasion to chew them out in front of everyone else in a bid to reassert the authority she obviously doesn't have, because if she had it, Lilly and Birch would have gone to her in the first place.

Fucking politics.

According to some signs in the Control room, this place once had 'air-conditioning'. No one is certain what the phrase means, but if air can be conditioned in some way, it probably means the temperature can be altered. That means the Snake Tower staircase would be even cooler, which would have been nice.

Then again, if the elevator in the Otis Shaft was working she'd be able to ride up and down with a view. That would be even better.

Oh well.

No longer one for ceremony, Lilly is wearing baggy green cargo trousers, a black leather jacket and ancient Engineers' boots that buckle on the side. She carries a Leatherman like Graham (his gift to her for her sixtieth) in a pouch on her belt. After the sixth flight she slides her gold-rimmed sunglasses on top of her flaxen hair, the arms fitting tightly against her scalp inside the ponytail, and swears.

When she's finished, she returns the glasses to her face and continues humping her way up the stairs despite the pain in her hip.

Two Praetorians in black garb – the kind of guard who will kill you if General Winters orders it, no matter who you are – are stationed at the top of the stairs before the closed door. Their assault rifles glitter with the oils Lilly invented more than thirty years ago.

Lilly raises her invitation medallion and the faceless guard on the right reaches behind him to open the door for her.

*

291

The top of the Olympic Viewing Station – the Snake Tower – is a half-moon with an unobstructed view of the entire Green below. The glass windows are three metres high and angled outwards at the top. A technology understood by no one, including Lilly, dims the windows when the sun is at its peak. When night comes it not only accommodates the few stars in the sky but illuminates them.

Like The Crossing, the floor here is smoked glass – a glass so strong bullets cannot break it and wars cannot damage it, as is known from experience. From here the High Command can view all 360 degrees of the Stadium Wall and its defences. At this height, they can see the desert beyond Yellow Ridge and to The Crossing; all the way to the hills where the Empty Quarter begins and all life that drinks water ends.

Lilly, a bit winded, finds General Winters sitting beside her assistant, who is placing small red bricks on a map on the table in front of them. As Lilly walks closer, the numbers present themselves and performing quick calculations in her head, she realises that whatever she thought was happening beyond the walls is not what she is looking at now.

'You have a thousand troops on that board,' Lilly says. 'That's more than our entire population and a two-to-one battle ratio against our professional soldiers. If they have explosives, it is a game we could lose.'

'It's not a game,' Winters says.

Winters has her hair cut short now and, unlike Lilly, she has grown a bit thick around the middle despite being four years younger. To Lilly, this means she's expended more effort climbing political ladders than actual ones. She is, objectively speaking, a good engineer and a clear thinker, but her capacity to adapt to circumstance has been always weak. Eyeing Winters and the board at the same time, the mismatch is too stark to ignore.

Lilly scans the room for the first time and is shocked to see Henrietta Wayworth, her back to the proceedings, staring out the window, her best scope detached from its rifle and pressed to her eye. She is scanning the ridge for movement.

'Henry? Where's Graham?' Lilly asks.

Henry turns and there is fear in her eyes.

She has never seen Henry scared before.

Henry does not answer Lilly's question with words but instead crosses from the window to the war-board, reaches into a wooden box beside the Territory Map and removes a small blue block that she slams down in the centre of all the red ones.

'He's here,' Henry says.

Lilly spins to survey the room properly. Winters, her assistant (she can't remember his name), Javier, Henry, Birch (long leathered legs crossed on a red chair), Lian, and – ah, no, as usual, the Mayor is missing.

Lilly waits for Birch to say something, to take the lead and state what's already known, but she doesn't move, so Lilly has to assume the worst.

'Why?' she asks.

'He was captured. Giving me time to escape.'

'And you decided to come back here rather than continue on to your mission objective?'

'They were waiting. It was an ambush.'

A fast and brutal ambush that Henry does not want to relive right at this moment. They had left the ravine below the Funnel exit directly where the route begins, emerging between the skeletons of two Gone World land-vehicles. From there, the plan was to follow the wadi into the garden of towers and make their way to the first Tracollo, which

293

was supposed to have been Alessandra's entry point to the underworld. Instead, ten horsemen came on them from two directions at once.

Graham was the first to react, flicking off the safety on his rifle, dropping to one knee and killing five men and a horse in two seconds. His magazine empty, he pulled his sword from Abraxas and charged into the other fighters, going for the horses' legs to drop the men and then cut them down.

'Run!' he yelled.

She knew why.

She had never left his side in a fight before, never abandoned him, and she was prepared to die to protect him. This was her one life and her one man and their Union was stronger than ever before because they had explored the very heights and depths of life together and there was no replacing or moving beyond what they had.

He would joke with her, 'You're supposed to be the Roamer – and unlike everyone else here, you're the one who stays.'

'I love you,' she said to him.

And instead of joking, his eyes filled with tears and he turned away.

He did not turn away now, though. He charged at the Keepers expecting death.

She would not have left his side even then but for their daughter, and for their vows to each other and to the Commonwealth. And the internet and what could change if they had it; change that he valued and trusted.

So she captured a horse from a fallen rider, turned it and left him.

Henrietta fired three flares into the sky once she was clear and a squad of twelve Dragoons dressed in the beige robes of battle came out to escort her home.

'Are those numbers real?' Lilly asks, pointing at the war-board and taking a seat at the table after hearing about the ambush.

'They're based on the Order's estimates,' Winters says. 'The numbers are a best-guess but the deployment patterns are certain. When I decided not to attack earlier, I did not anticipate force levels this high.'

She looks at Javier and he nods, admitting that he had been consulted on the decision.

'What do we know of their intentions?' Lilly asks.

'Nothing we can Attest to. However,' says Winters, her voice demonstrably losing interest in this casual conversation, and – because Lilly knows the move – putting her back in her place, 'we're fully prepared. Meanwhile,' Winters says, looking out of the window to where the problems are mounting, 'Master Birch has told me everything – about the girls and the Hard Room, the radio, the Trove, even this magical theory of yours about an Archive that can fit in a bag. You know it's ridiculous, right?'

'Either the Ancients stopped reading books, looking at pictures, listening to music and sharing information with one another or they stopped using Indie solutions,' Lilly says. 'There's no alternative logic. And if their technology moved on, some remnant of it has to exist. To find it, we would need a perfect alignment of electricity, portal, a way to—'

'Oh, spare us, Lilly,' Winters says. 'The girl found a Trove and some food and water and – by some miracle – there's a bit of electricity left to power the radio. I don't dismiss the importance of finding a second radio and I want to get it, but the rest is preposterous. And we have real problems outside

295

the window. The only reason you're here is because I have an assignment for you and Birch.'

'An assignment,' says Lilly. Her voice is as flat as the land outside the walls.

'I need you and Master Birch to prepare The Drop.'

Lilly looks to the others for reactions but they are expressionless.

'Aside from all the challenges and risks, General, Commander Wayworth and I both think these people have access to explosives,' Lilly says. 'We think the Keepers used them to set off the Tracollo last month. Likewise, I'm told one of the Spotters saw flashes the other night.'

'When?' Henry asks.

Lilly raises a hand. She wants to get through this. 'The Stadium's defences,' she says to Birch and Javier, 'will be limited if the Keepers have acquired explosives, because the walls won't hold against them. Our entire defensive model – the one you and I designed together, Marsha – was based on the presumption we'd be facing bows and arrows and the occasional bullet shot from limited enemy forces who haven't read the military strategy of the Greeks and Romans like we have. In this case, we're looking at the greatest force we've ever seen, ever *heard* of, with discipline that appears to match our own, with the distinct possibility of explosives. The best way to win here is not to fight.'

'You'd have us surrender, Lilly?' Winters says, sarcastically.

'No,' Lilly says, barely containing her anger, 'I would give them a reason to go away.'

'And how would you propose to do that?' asks Javier, finally joining the conversation.

For years, Lilly didn't understand why Winters had elevated Javier to Chief of the Dragoons. He was, she would readily admit, the best rider in a generation. He had a masterful understanding of the training of horses and riders, crafting manoeuvres for mounted fighting and supporting the phalanx, and for setting relays to carry messages. But this was a kind of thinking that was close to the ground. He was a man who was at his best when his boots were dirty, not when he was a mile high in the Snake Tower, trying to use his imagination without the aid of his hands.

But at least he had the good sense to ask questions when he didn't know the answer.

'The missing piece in all of this,' Lilly says, addressing him directly, giving him the respect of her full attention, 'is that you don't create a tribe of thousands without something very significant at the centre holding them together. In my time as a Scribe, as an Evaluator, as an inventor, as someone who has read almost everything we have, I believe that nothing holds people together better than a shared idea: something so fundamental and explicable that people willingly gather around it because it feels right to them. They call themselves Keepers – so what are they Keeping? How are we a threat to that? Is there anything we can do about it? Our best military strategy right now is finding out how these people think and using that to encourage them to go away. I suggest we send someone over to talk to them. Or,' Lilly says as she stands and walks to the one blue wooden block in the middle of all the red ones, 'we use the man who's already there.

'Henry,' Lilly says, 'if we could get a message to him – your scope has a laser for marking and signalling, doesn't it? – perhaps if—'

'Our big idea,' interrupts Winters, 'was once your big idea, Chief. It's to overwhelm and kill our enemies with superior force and better weapons, thereby establishing our dominance of the territory. You know the stories of the dark years after The Rise. You know the fighting. The absence of mercy. The reason The Few took the risk to come this far into the desert. You and Master Birch will now go and prepare The Drop. We will lure the enemy onto the flats and then end it all in one strike. The survivors will tell the story for a generation.'

'The Drop,' Lilly says, in a very, very quiet voice, 'took nine years to build and fifteen years for everyone to forget we built it. Yellow Ridge is there because of all the earth we moved. General, what is the point of having the greatest Archive in the known world if we are so resistant to using that Knowledge to solve our problems?'

'My husband and my daughter are out there,' Henry says. She speaks softly, but her voice is crystal-clear.

'There's no reason to believe Alessandra is at any risk,' Javier tells her. 'She's probably well on the other side of the enemy force. Your husband is a legitimate concern, but for now I am more concerned for the rest of us. I suggest we mobilise the full civilian force. We number seven hundred at strength. With our walls and weaponry we have the advantage.'

'That includes children as young as ten,' Chief Lian says.

'Everyone has a role to play when our survival is threatened. That is what the Agoge teaches. There are tasks even for the children,' says Winters. 'The Stadium was designed to be defended.'

'The Stadium was designed to be a fucking sports arena.' Lilly sits back in her chair and folds her arms.

'But the Commonwealth,' says Lian, trying to calm them, 'is not the Stadium. The Commonwealth, I will remind everyone, was designed to survive with or without the Stadium. That is our Big Idea, General.'

There is a knock at the door. One guard draws a pulse weapon and takes position behind a thick metal barrier as high as a table with a slit in the middle for firing. The second guard opens the door.

A teenage boy with almond eyes and black hair like Lian's looks up at the unsmiling guard and hands him the black tablet book used for sending written messages around the Stadium.

'For Chief Lilly, Sir,' says the boy, backing away until he is standing outside the doorway.

Winters looks annoyed that Lilly is receiving mail in the Snake Tower but says nothing.

Lilly takes the tablet. The message in Simone's hand is admirably clear and brief. She reads it silently. When she is finished, she wipes the chalk away and closes the cover of the tablet.

Henry's eyes are burrowing into her and so Lilly turns to her first. 'Simone says that radio contact has resumed. There is a message here from both girls. They are trapped together, the Keepers know more or less where they are and I was right about the internet,' she says, not even bothering to turn to Winters to gloat.

'We need a new plan.'

RICHES

Graham's hands are bound in front of him as he sits cross-legged on the floor of a large tent on Yellow Ridge, surrounded by hundreds of Keepers, several of whom are his guards. He suffered only scrapes after Abraxas was knocked out from beneath him and he fought his way through a wall of Keepers with his shortsword before being tackled and bound, but he had given his wife what she needed: time.

The Keepers had encircled him, jumped him and pressed his face into the earth, his cheek flat against the fine-grained sand and white quartz, before being hauled to his feet by a mountain of a man.

They walked him through a camp that was orderly and clean and armed. Not a soldier made a sound, not a song, not a murmur.

He was brought to this tent, given water, which he drank, and then he waited.

After what may have been an hour, the tent flap is folded open and a man wearing a white robe and a red sash walks in. He is carrying two small folding stools. He is not mighty in appearance, nor scarred from battle, and there is a softness to his eyes that Graham reads as both sadness and resolve. He lifts his head and the soldiers around him back off but do not leave.

The man places the stools across from one another and sits in one. He motions for Graham to rise from the floor and use the other. He does and without words, they regard one another.

They sit in silence for a time, far longer than would be normal or expected at the Commonwealth, but Graham is widely travelled. Customs vary and he adapts; speaking first is rarely correct.

The soldiers behind Graham do not move. Their presence is calm. None are restless.

A woman enters, bearing an earthenware jug and two mismatching cups. She pours water into both and holds them out. The Leader reaches for one and drinks, then nods for Graham to do the same. It is fresh and carries the slightest taste of apple. He drinks three cups.

'What's your name?' the Leader asks. His voice is husky and low. His accent is different from the Stadium-born. He has heard something similar once, to the east, months away from here.

'Graham Wayworth.'

'What does your name mean?'

'The first was chosen by my parents. I was named for a friend of my father's who's dead now. The second has been the name of my family for three generations. We are Trackers and Explorers and Raiders: it means that we are worthy to set the path, to find the way home.'

'That's a good name,' he says.

'What's yours?'

'I was born with one but I have none any more. It was used by my wife and my parents. It would have been used by my daughter if she had survived and carried it forward. Now I'm alone, but I have a role and a duty. I am Leader. My name and my role are one. What I am is who I am. What I was is forgotten because it no longer matters to the Now.'

'Who we were always matters in who we are,' Graham says, 'even if it is forgotten.'

The Leader looks at Graham intently, listening carefully. 'How?' he asks.

'In our language. Our dreams. Our decisions. In our values, our virtues, our vices. In our fears,' Graham says.

Two bowls of hot food arrive: the meat of a bird in broth with potatoes and onion. Two spoons are provided and at the Leader's gesture, they eat.

'The woman you were riding with. What is she to you?' the Leader asks.

'My wife. The mother of my daughter. My partner. My lover. My friend. She's a thinker and a warrior.'

'She survived the attack, I'm told,' he says. 'She was joined by your mounted forces and returned back to the walls.'

Graham eats to give his mouth something to do other than say what he feels.

'We have had little contact with your people,' the Leader says.

'From what we can see,' Graham says, 'you've had more than enough.'

'What are you doing in there?' the Leader asks.

'You've had your reports from your spies. Nothing that should bring us to war against each other,' Graham says.

'How do you know that?' the Leader asks.

'We solve mysteries and we solve problems. We learn. We recover Knowledge that was lost. We make things possible. We enrich our lives and the lives of others and we become better for it. We share a great deal of what we know. We have helped this Territory become what it is. We turned the Bridge to Nowhere into The Crossing and gave it worth. We provide clean drinking water to everyone who wants it. We are the centre of all regional trade. We are a force for peace in this Territory that was once barren or else full of bandits on the High Road. You should come and visit. See it for yourself,' Graham suggests, wiping his mouth and sitting back.

The Leader's face is placid. 'Life is not rich enough for you?' he asks. 'You need more? You'll find it in the past?'

He waves a hand and a young woman with far-away eyes places a small table no larger than a stool between them. On the table she places a bowl. From the bowl the Leader lifts a large flower, recently plucked. It is bright yellow at the centre and the dozens of small pedals around it are an unearthly pink, darkening into fuchsia. They grow off the cacti.

'This flower grows near the Stadium – and here, and under The Crossing. What richness of life can you not find within it? In the smile of a pretty girl? In the laughter of a child? In the muscles of a horse, the dancing pillars in the desert? How is all of this not enough for you?'

'It's a nice flower,' Graham says.

'The reason you're here is to give me some insight that will allow me to make a decision about the fate of your people. Answer my question.'

'The fate of my people,' Graham says, 'isn't your decision to make. It's ours. I suppose the fate of your people might be. But I warn you, we're prepared for war. And the woman who prepared us ... not the General, the other one ... well, she's got a mean streak.'

'Forget war,' the Leader says. 'Why isn't the world as it is enough for all of you? Why do you need more?'

'Because ...' says Graham, not entirely understanding what

the Leader is asking. '. . . because there *is* more – much more, out there, buried in the sands, hidden in people's minds, hinted at in old songs, written on walls and scraps of paper. There was once a universe of unlimited human potential and creation. Humanity once travelled to other planets. We cured disease. We wrote music and stories, and . . . and the Commonwealth is recovering what we can, keeping it safe and using it to move forward.'

'But . . . why?'

'Why what?'

The Leader is a having a hard time making the man articulate his motivations. The frustration forces his mind to try something else. 'You are committed to finding and saving old knowledge. I understand this,' the Leader says. 'But my people look around at the world and know two things: the Ancients knew more than us. And that knowledge led to this,' he says, waving his hand. They are inside the tent but his gesture is perfectly clear to Graham. 'I tell my people,' he continues, as though talking to a child, 'if one thing leads to another, and that state of being is undesirable, don't do it. So we look at your actions and we look at what they will lead to and we say to ourselves, why would they destroy the world all over again? These people who consider themselves so learned? There is either something wrong with their minds, or with their souls.'

'Your premise is wrong,' says Graham, equally exasperated. 'Knowledge does not necessarily lead to the destruction of the world. Knowledge makes new things possible – not only objects and systems and solutions, but new kinds of happiness. New ways of *being*. New kinds of joy. It expands the very meaning of what it means to be alive. Don't you see? You don't see, do you?'

Graham leans forward on his stool. His hands remain bound because he is a killer, but the Leader does not break Graham's silence and does not hurry him into words. The guards, the girl – everyone is patient as Graham explores route after route, knowing this conversation is consequential.

He decides to speak about himself. 'A month ago – a moon ago – Henry and I returned to the Commonwealth from The Crossing with a piece of paper – well, three of them. It was sheet music for a piano. Sheet music teaches a person – if he can read the language – how to turn the instructions into sounds using an instrument. We have a man at the Commonwealth who can do this. He is very gifted. He doesn't only read, he listens with his whole heart. He seems to connect to the minds of the dead and he brings the truth of their experience back into the world for all of us. It's like watching the dead rise. The music was written by a man named Bach. When Moishe played that music, it was like . . . I remembered what it means to be alive. I remembered why I sacrifice. I remembered how much good there is and how much of an obligation we have to recover it. To make the world whole again.'

The Leader leans forward too. He looks at Graham. 'Why is that needed?' he asks.

'Why is what needed?'

'Piano music.'

'It's . . . beautiful,' says Graham. 'It is a testimony to what people can achieve – what we can be at our best. I'm guessing you've never heard piano music.'

'These feelings you describe, of feeling alive, knowing the value of living, finding again your purpose. I understand these feelings. I share them with you. But you are not explaining to me why you need this Bach music to feel it, why you cannot find it in a flower. You say the music is beautiful and I believe you. Perhaps I would even like the song myself. But how does the beauty of that song compare to a flower?'

305

'I don't know,' admits Graham.

'Or to that of your wife?'

'It depends on her mood, to be honest.'

For the first time, the Leader smiles. It is brief.

'My people see a flower growing on the side of a mountain and we find beauty there. We see the crystals of ice forming on the sands at night and we see beauty. We see the Auroras dance and the pillars form in the night winds and the children smile and the women flick their hair in the breeze and we see beauty. Maybe you do too. I am heartened that your people care about such things, and maybe there is still some hope for you. But unlike you, we are fulfilled, and in being fulfilled . . . we harm nothing. We endanger nothing. We risk nothing. We live in the Now. You, however – your Commonwealth – you ignore the Now and live in both the past and the future. You chase after Ancient knowledge to create a new future that endangers us all.'

The Leader looks intently at Graham. He wants him to understand this. 'Whatever they knew – whatever is under the sand – is what destroyed the world. If you continue to learn, there is every reason to believe that you will do the same. And you risk this . . . why? Because you cannot find enough beauty in a flower or a girl or a horse or a sunset. The restlessness of your spirit is what threatens to kill us all. Can you not see the foolishness in that? Why it needs to stop?'

Graham had been told these people did not care for Knowledge or ideas. It is dawning on him that everything he had heard was wrong. They care about both – they just think completely differently about them.

This man, this Leader, is forcing Graham to question what he has taken for granted since birth. The Harrington Box was opened before he was born. Lilly had already set their course.

306

Having never even grappled with his own beliefs, he is struggling now to build a convincing case for them. How can that be so? The Leader, though, is certainly right about one thing. It comes down to *life*.

'Some of the seeds aren't taking to the soil any more,' Graham says. 'If we understood the science of seeds, we might be able to fix that. What you're not accepting is that doing nothing also has risks. It is not the way of nature to remain stable and strong. Things fall apart unless we struggle to put them together. We swim forward at the Commonwealth because the current of the river is naturally against us. We learn to govern ourselves, to feed ourselves, to save ourselves from disease and discomfort. To build better defences and fight back against the decay all around us. You lost your family. We might have been able to help prevent that if we'd worked together. There's still time for others.'

'They died to save us all.'

Graham sits back. The pace is too fast. The ideas too rich. The Leader's pain too deep. Everything the man is saying is worthy of more discussion. But his philosophy is hardened by the loss of his family. To abandon it would be to admit that they might have lived. This is now a journey too far. If only they had all used their time more wisely.

'You are describing a world without change and without risk,' Graham says very quietly. 'But here it is the Roamers who are right. Everything changes and love itself is risk. You are trying to make the wind stop blowing, the children stop wondering, the eye stop seeing and the heart stop seeking. This ... this cannot be done. What you are choosing is not sustainable. Time will win because life itself *wants*. We have to submit and proceed wisely. Is this why you're called the Keepers? To keep things the same?'

'To keep us alive.' The Leader is unmoved. The distance is too great. He gestures to the people outside the tent. 'There are many people who choose life – many people willing to fight for life. More than you think. So that we might all live.'

'We're not your enemy,' Graham says.

'I believe you don't want to be, Graham Wayworth, but you are. And the truth is, you are also your own.'

VAULT

Alessandra and Elimisha sit together with their internet glasses, staring into the holograms and watching videos while sucking brown syrup off their fingers. A bluish tint reflects off both their glass lenses and their unblinking eyes as they twinkle with astonishment in a world so vast, so expansive, that all they can do is bounce from possibility to possibility without plan or direction – children in a room of toys, unleashed and unashamed.

They had started with the problem of the robot and asked the Librarian to explain it to them – but only after Alessandra had wanted to answer one question herself.

She'd stood over its body and hooked a finger in the waistband of its trousers.

'Wanna look?' she asked Elimisha.

'At what?'

'You know.'

'No.'

'You're not curious?'

'Not really, no.'

'I'm curious.'

'I'm not.'

'You're not curious. Have you ever . . . done it?'

'No. Have you?'

'Once,' Alessandra said. 'With Drake.'

'Son-of-Estelle?'

'Yeah.'

'Do you love him?'

'No. I was curious. I'm counting to three and then I'm looking.'

'This is pointless compared to what I'm about to show . . .'

'. . . two . . . one . . .'

Alessandra peeked but at an angle that make it impossible for Elimisha to see.

'Oh my God,' Alessandra says, appalled.

'What?'

'There are two of them!'

'Oh, bullshit.'

'You're right,' she said, whipping down the trousers to show a smooth, asexual surface. 'But I proved you *were* curious.'

Later, after Alessandra had settled into the shock of the internet and been coaxed back to normalcy after taking off her glasses and standing in the corner of the room for almost ten minutes, they learned about the *thing* Alessandra had killed.

What they learned was that the Ancients had committed themselves to the invention of many types of robots and humanic machines. And they also learned conclusively was that their own unit was really, *really* broken, and no amount of repair was going to get it to help them dig their way out of the bunker.

'You had to shoot it in the face?' Elimisha asked once the conclusion was clear.

'I really, really did,' said Alessandra.

*

For the morning broadcast, Elimisha decided that secrecy was useless now, so it was time for full disclosure. The Keepers knew where Elimisha was and they had chased Alessandra into a nearby basement too, so if they chose to dig them out, there would be nowhere to go. They'd have to stand and fight and – somehow – destroy the internet. Given that she had no idea how to do any of that, it was better to ask for help and hope that someone was listening.

'They'll be listening,' Alessandra said. 'They said so.'

After their morning session they lost themselves in the metaverse.

Together, side by side, they watched pictures in motion. They listened to music – at first, randomly, and then – once Alessandra had acclimated to music with a beat – 'pop charts'.

They looked at the world from above; from the windows of the Apollo missions, the International Space Station, the Marriott Space Hotel and eventually from the viewing windows at the top of Tranquillity Tower on the moon.

They had never known that the sky was black and the universe was filled with stars.

Alessandra took them car racing at Le Mans, but become more interested in the motorcycle racing at the Isle of Man TT. She watched from the eyes of Natalie Coin as she navigated curves at 300 kilometres an hour.

Elimisha wanted to go SCUBA diving. By the late twenty-first century most of the coral reefs had been either destroyed or were protected from human intrusion, but early HCG® IMAX dives had been recorded off Australia, in the Red Sea, and in specialty wreck dives including the 2046 sinking of India's Mysore guided-missile cruiser off the shallows of Goa.

At midday, they decided to visit their home. Neither had never seen the Stadium as it had been used during the Olympic

Games. Through the gear they heard the roar of the spectators and lived the experience of athletes who had recorded their every movement, experience and emotion in their Olympic-approved HCG® suits, allowing everyone in perpetuity to experience the events as they did.

On what is now the Green, Alessandra pole-vaulted with Miriam O'Conner, who won the gold medal for the United States, and Shira Voy, who took the silver for Canada. Elimisha pulled Alessandra into the modern pentathlon, a sport the Librarian told them was meant to replicate the skills of a cavalry officer behind enemy lines. Together they experienced the heartbreak of three-time champion Abigail Evans as her horse tumbled on the third jump, sending her flying from her saddle, breaking her left wrist and ending her Olympic dream.

Pushing away a bowl of rice in disgust, Elimisha is ready to make an announcement to everyone gathered: Alessandra, the Pirelli girl, all her friends on the other pages, the dead robot and all the Ancient spirits still trapped inside the internet.

'I'm making a copy of everything,' she says, tapping a small black box with a single glowing blue light. 'It's called a Quantum Drive. It's all going in *there*. Everything we see gets copied into the box. I'm Archiving. The Librarian explained how to do it, so ... it's happening now. I don't know how much, but we can put a lot of the internet into that box and then take the box with us to plug into another workstation even if it isn't connected to the internet. Lilly has one of these in her lab. I can't think of any reason it wouldn't work. At first I'm filling it with what I choose. Later, before we go, I'll instruct the Librarian to copy whatever it wants and fill the box. This,' she tells Alessandra, 'is now the Central Archive of the Commonwealth.'

Alessandra hasn't considered that.

'The invisible spiderweb that Lilly always suspected must have once held everything together is actually the internet. All the things that don't work? All the Deps? To be able to work, they needed to access the internet and they used to do that in a thousand different ways, like satellites and relay-stations. When it all went down the Deps lost their connections and became bricks.'

Alessandra's confusion is evident and Elimisha doesn't understand why at first. Then, 'You never apprenticed in Weapons and Comms, did you?'

'I just hung around there a lot because Lilly and my parents are friends,' Alessandra admits. 'I don't understand half of what you're saying.'

For a moment, during their lull, everything stops. They hear the thin hum of the generator and the wisps of air moving through the ducts. Instinctively, like any animal looking to escape, Alessandra turns to look at the door in to the hall that leads to the blast door or the kitchen tunnel.

There's no getting out. There's only being discovered by the Keepers or rescued by the Order. Until then, all they can do is sit.

'Want to see something cute?' she says to Alessandra, who at first doesn't hear her. Elimisha waits until she comes around.

'What?'

'Cute.'

'What does that mean?'

'It's a word describing lovable animals. It means you want squeeze them until they pop but you also don't want to hurt them. Apparently, you deal with the conflicting feelings by making little noises and shaking.'

Alessandra doesn't seem to care, but Elimisha has been through these moods with the internet too. It takes her on an extraordinary journey and she feels the escape – then she remembers she's trapped and all the Knowledge along with her and she returns to the desk feeling distant and moody and depressed.

'Here,' Elimisha says. 'Watch this.'

Waving her hands over the White Board like a magician, Elimisha loads a five-minute compilation reel of cats purring, eating, scratching, climbing trees, falling off tables, being startled by dogs, chasing mice, being chased by mice, sleeping on people's heads and being blow-dried.

'What are those?'

'Cats.'

'They're great,' Alessandra concludes.

'They really are.'

'What else is cute?' Alessandra asks.

Elimisha shows her:

> Raccoons
> Koala bears
> Pandas
> Ducklings
> Baby seals
> Kittens
> Ezo Momongas
> Baby snow weasels, and
> Puppies.
> Lots and lots of puppies.

A child of the desert, Alessandra is drawn to the polar bear cubs frolicking in the snow. 'Where did those live?' she asks.

'Svalbard, Norway,' comes the answer.

'Where's that?'

The Librarian provides a map and a location.

'Tell us about it,' Elimisha orders and a few minutes later the girls are looking at a rectangular structure built into the permafrost in Svalbard. At the top there is a square of broken crystals that glow in the night sky. There is writing on the side of the small building. The words are vitally important to the future of humanity, but there is one they don't know.

'What's a vault?' asks Alessandra.

PREPARATIONS

Lilly and Birch have work to do if The Drop is to be ready for a Keeper attack which could come at any time or never. Neither are convinced using the weapon is a wise idea, but they have been given their orders.

Birch descends the stairs from the Snake Tower with the agility of a teenager, barely making a sound as she skips from one step to the next. Lilly used to have better knees and hips, much like she had better patience, but as all are now wearing thin, she lands on each step with her black leather engineers' boots like she is crushing the skull of an enemy.

Birch stops on the fifth landing and waits for her.

'What are you looking at?' Lilly says.

'I can wait.'

'Kiss my ass.'

At the bottom Lilly follows Birch across the Green, where new battle preparations are underway. Anoushka is placing her archers in a new formation. The Spotters have fortified their locations with the shields that Lilly invented three decades ago: two equilateral triangles made of metal, joined at one edge to create a free-standing structure to deflect incoming weapons that can be rotated to accommodate the movements of battle. Pulse rifles are being distributed. The youngest children are herded indoors and moved into protected shelters in the lower ring.

Together, Lilly and Birch walk into the catacombs that are off-limits to all but the Order of Silence.

Lilly watches Birch as she follows her. Her leather trousers flatter her proportions as she walks. Lilly does not feel a longing for sex or affection any more, although she knows both men and women her age who do. What she does miss is the sense of longing, the hunger for contact. Something vital feels lost with it gone.

Is it odd to stare at someone's ass and think of yourself? *No, she thinks, it's normal.*

Is it strange to think about sex on the eve of battle?

Of course not. The mind turns to life when faced with death.

Question and answers. Questions and answers. The tide goes in, the tides goes out.

She wonders if the ocean is a real thing.

Birch stops and turns back to look at Lilly, as though sensing that her mind has drifted from their task.

'It's nothing. Keep moving,' Lilly says, waving her on.

They have entered the subterranean structures of the Flats through a blue door guarded by four silent Centurions. It is known as the Hollows. In three steps they have passed under the outer walls of the Stadium and into the Hollows covered – above – by the artificial earth Lilly created from pillars and wood, steel plates and unbreakable glass from the first Tracollo. This land was once a valley between the Stadium and the hills, but Lilly changed all that. What a project it was – and what

317

a passion for destruction she once possessed, so sure was she that safety could be achieved by strength.

She seldom visits the mechanical world in the Hollows these days. It is a vast, dark, empty space filled with high explosives tied to the load-bearing supports and buckets filled with sharp-edged shrapnel to rip apart the soft loins of anything above when the earth falls downwards.

There are a lot of bugs; a lot of snakes. It's damp, too.

Even if none of that were true, Lilly still wouldn't want to come here. This was the largest and most intense engineering project she ever oversaw; this now feels like a step back to an earlier period of her life when she was angrier and even more self-assured, and wildly creative but also misdirected. War destroys, she knows that, but it also creates.

The Drop was an impressive idea. She is just no longer sure it's a good one. What she has learned since then is that any weapon built will eventually be used. So yes, war creates, but it also creates destruction. It would be odd for the Ancients not to have learned this lesson too.

'Are we actually thinking of using this?' Lilly asks Birch.

When Birch turns, her look says it all.

'Don't you sweat in those things?' Lilly adds.

For the first time Lilly can recall, Birch smiles before turning back to one of the primary explosive chambers. She runs her fingers over it and holds up her hand, which is glistening in the light, demonstrating how damp everything is.

'There are redundancies in every fifth sector,' Lilly says, 'because I assumed a twenty-five per cent failure rate on detonation. The actual design needs only twenty per cent of the columns to blow up to kick off a cascading failure that will start at the centre and simultaneously work back to the Stadium walls and outwards. I assume we're within that margin?'

Birch slides her fingers along the wires that connect the charge to the main power grid. Lilly looks at them as well and sees them as an answer: every wire has been replaced over time and there are no discolourations.

'Why did you build this?' Birch asks. It is the first time that Lilly can recall her starting a conversation.

'To save us in case of a massive attack that we couldn't repel or outlast.'

'I think it was because of Verena,' Birch says.

'I hope you've enjoyed this conversation because now it's over.'

The ceiling here is wood covered by earth. Birch was a child during the construction, but she remembers the trees being brought in – more trees than she had ever seen. The smell was glorious.

Birch sits on a stack of planks and crosses her legs. Here, in the dim electric light, her eyes are a glistening brown and Lilly notes an unexpected softness to her face; she would not have expected that from one with such a solitary and hard life.

'I know that Verena left you to serve the Commonwealth,' Birch says. 'She didn't run. She didn't leave you.'

'I know that. I don't need you to tell me that.'

'This,' Birch says, opening a palm as though it could hold the entire Weapon, 'will not save us from what's out there. I actually think that even if the Keepers are defeated on the battlefield, they still might not be deterred from coming back.'

'That has crossed my mind as well,' Lilly says, hands in her pockets.

Birch still wants to talk, which surprises Lilly. The Drop, they both know, needs no preparation. You activate it or you don't. Lilly got the idea from Adam's detonators that set off the first Tracollo. Birch and her team have maintained it, and it is Birch alone who will start the detonation when so ordered by the Head of High Command, in this case, General Winters. That Birch wants to *chat* is a first for Lilly.

'Our assignment is to carry out the secret functions needed to sustain the systems of the Commonwealth. You know this: you started the Order with Master Saavni. But over the decades,' Birch says, 'we've had to become far more nuanced in learning how to go about doing it – and that nuance has not always received a welcoming ear from High Command. It sounds technical and unimportant, but it isn't. The Order doesn't simply wander through the world with cans of paint marking out routes and setting traps. That's the easy part. What's hard is learning how other tribes and clans and bands all use the land, where they go and don't go and why. Where and how they shelter. Where and how they travel and with what . . . with whom. We've learned that watching the daily habits of unfamiliar peoples teaches us a great deal about their life-and-death commitments. Our people are not only slipping between the rocks, Chief Lilly, they are slipping between ways of life. Once – in the days of The Few – those ways of life were far apart from one another. Today they are overlapping.' She places one hand partly over another. 'There are fewer spaces in between and someday, if the populations continue to grow, if the radios connect us, if our Knowledge changes the dynamics of time and space, we will be living on top of one another. And what was once a secondary function of the Order will become its primary goal: to understand the minds of others and prepare the way. I'm telling you this because I think a new era is beginning and I don't yet know what to do about it.'

This is the most Lilly has heard Birch say in one sitting.

'Winters won't be the solution,' Lilly says at last.

'She's your fault, you know.'

'I beg your pardon?'

'General Winters sees everything as attack and defence: barriers to erect or barriers to overcome. It is the mindset of a mechanic or an engineer. You are the one who set us on that path. Out of everything that could have been learned from the Harrington Box, you focused on machines, and everyone else followed along. General Winters rose through the ranks on the values you emphasised. You know that, right?'

'I was seventeen years old, Birch.'

'Not when you built this place. I was a child then. You stood on the walls like a queen directing the construction.'

'What's out there?' Lilly asks, moving away from the subject of her own complicity. 'What life-and-death commitments?'

'There is . . . passion,' says the Master. 'Tremendous passion, Lilly, that runs as deep as our own. Passion for what, I don't know, but for *something*. We've put up walls to keep ourselves in and others out. We collect Knowledge and hide it away. We're a powerful fortress, but we're not a movement. We collect, but we barely use – we barely even teach. The Keepers' message, compared to ours, is very simple: *we're alive and the Ancients are dead. Let's not make their mistakes.* And so their numbers are growing. It gives them something to live for . . . and, perhaps, to die for.'

'So we have a problem,' Lilly concludes.

Birch says nothing.

'Why doesn't the High Command know all this?'

'I told them. They think it's a military problem.'

'So what do we do?' Lilly asks.

'Find the internet,' Birch says, 'and take it away.'

'To where?'

'There's a place.'

A soldier dressed all in white enters the vast chamber. He calls to them and the echo repeats his words.

'The enemy has been spotted. Their advance has begun. You are ordered to take your posts.'

Graham Wayworth's captors have led him to the edge of Yellow Ridge and unbound his hands. He has been positioned to look down on the flats, where he will be allowed to witness the destruction of his home. If he fights, he will die, and if he runs, he will catch an arrow in the back.

The Leader rode beside him. Their conversation in the tent is over and there will be no returning to it. They stand there together now, overlooking the battlefield. The mounted troops and the infantry have moved to the edge of the Ridge.

War is imminent.

In the full light of the late morning Graham can see the entirety of the Stadium below. He is relieved to see that it has been locked down and they are ready. The Spotters in the Crow's Nest have been removed and placed behind their mobile barriers and the Mirror System and deflector plates are up. The Main Gate is sealed. The steel shutters on the windows and over the apartments on the far Western Ring are all closed to resist in-coming arrows and other missiles. The pikes have been raised from the underground chambers to repel any oncoming force who have the nerve to approach across the ground.

To the uninformed, it is a tortoise with its head pulled in.

To Graham, it is a cocked pistol waiting to discharge.

What is new is the flag hanging from the Snake Tower. It is as long as six tall men and as wide as three. It is noticeable from every angle of approach. The flag is as white as innocence; the symbol it carries is blacker than death.

It is the universal symbol of danger:

Graham turns to the Leader and says, 'They're ready. There is no way you're getting through that gate or over those walls.'

The Leader scans the valley and is satisfied. 'It's only a wall,' he replies.

'No, it's Lilly's wall. That makes it an instrument of death,' Graham says. 'She's the finest mechanical and strategic mind we've had in five generations and she had a rocky childhood and then a bad love life. You don't attack something like that. You run away from it.'

'You people have a colourful way of speaking.'

'You go there, you die.'

'You eat too much.'

'What?' Graham says, looking at his own stomach. 'No I don't. I'm no heavier than you are.'

'Your people: they bring in more food than they send out. Even with the farms down by the freshwater. If you don't trade for food, you starve. We have blocked your trade.' He points to the Stadium. 'They are already starving. It will take time, but eventually, they will have to leave.'

'We have stores of food. And we have tunnels that you can't imagine.'

'We know all this. Our spies have told us.'

'Yes, of course – but it doesn't matter. The form of warfare you're talking about is called "a siege". It can work, but it won't work on us.'

'It will.'

'We produce our own food, so below a certain population, we are sustainable.'

'You have no stomach for that amount of death, especially among the children. Our will is stronger.'

'Our tunnel system is secret and extensive. You don't know where they go and you can't block them. And so the siege will never work.'

'Yes, we do know where they go, and yes, it will.'

The Leader raises his hand. He extends his finger to the valley and the Flats and the place Graham calls home where right now his wife might well be watching him through her scope from the top of the Snake Tower with its blacked-out and one-way windows. 'We may not know where your tunnels come out,' the Leader says, 'but we know they all return to the same place. They all go there.' He points to the Stadium. 'You are going to destroy them all for us with your giant weapon. You are going to cut yourselves off from the food you need and you are going to starve or you are going to leave. Either way, with your numbers diminished, your people weak and your leaders weaker, your way of life will end. You will be stopped from gathering the knowledge that threatens the world. And even if some of you remain, your work – your path – will be over.'

III
INFERNO

GAMBIT

General Winters stands at the window of the Snake Tower holding Henry's scope in her hand. Henry is beside her. Lian has left to secure the Central Archive by hiding the most valuable books, paintings and scraps in hidden compartments, just in case the Stadium is overrun. Javier, as quiet and obedient as ever, joins Winters on her other side. Together they look down at the archers gathered in the rear quadrants of the Green and on the lower ridge of apartments, now emptied of non-fighters and under the command of the military.

'I don't see the Master Archer in position,' says Winters.

'She's scaling Ladder Six now, General.'

'Have the scouts reported in with enemy numbers?'

'They have, General.'

'And?'

'They estimate around a thousand. Maybe two hundred horses. A few hundred dogs.'

'How are they arrayed?'

'They aren't, General. We're anticipating a mad, savage rush down the hill.'

'And their armaments?'

'A few dozen rifles. Mostly we saw shortswords, bows and some lances on the horses. A few are on bicycles, which, given the flat terrain actually isn't a bad idea.'

'Won't help them.'

'No, General.'

'I see no reason to open the gates and take to the field yet. I say let them bash their heads against our walls until they're weak and close.'

'Unless they have explosives, General,' Henry reminds them.

'If we get a hint of any,' says Javier, 'we use The Drop. That's why Lilly built it. If they come down in a rush we can kill a thousand in an instant. Our Archers can take out the survivors from behind our walls. I say we send the Dragoons through the tunnels now, take a distant position behind them, and once we activate The Drop, we'll have the survivors surrounded. A hammer-and-anvil solution. This is what Hannibal did at Cannae, causing utter devastation. It will send a resounding message throughout the Territories about our power. We will then establish ourselves for what we really are: the dominant military force in the Territory.'

'Unless,' Henry says, 'we're not.'

Winters looks at Henry. 'What are you doing here?'

'You wanted to borrow my scope.'

'I can use mine now.'

'This is a sports centre, not a castle.'

'You're supposed to be in Sniper Location Echo. Once it begins, you kill the leadership on downwards, not just anyone. You are dismissed, Commander.'

Anoushka Sunrose, Master of Archers, reaches the crest of Ladder Six and slides onto the top of the stadium wall on her belly to avoid line-of-sight detection. She too is dressed in armoured leather, like a Runner, but unlike the Runners, hers is brown from neck to ankle, lighter than her hair but darker than her eyes. She wriggles her way to the base of a giant pole angled outwards that extends high above her. The DANGER flag is at eye-level far behind her. She wonders whether it will prove to be a message the savages will heed or a target for them to shoot.

Anoushka is forty-two years old. Her face is long and thin, her hair is tied into a ball on the top of her head. The fingers on her right hand are hardened and rough from years pulling at bow strings. She was among the best of the Commonwealth archers and, as always happens with everyone truly good at something, she was promoted out of it and into management. Now, instead of her trusted weapon, she holds an ancient Indie compass with which to take bearings and a small red flag to issue orders.

She's facing an incoming army of a thousand with nothing but her opinions and she doesn't like it.

'You,' she says to a messenger, a boy of about twelve. This is his first proper job.

'Master?'

'Go down to the Green and find me a bow and a quiver of thirty arrows. Tell them it's for me. I want a good one. Go now.'

The wind at the top of wall is not the same as the breezes across the Green below or even the Flat beyond. She has discussed this problem with Lilly, explaining that arrows are subject to directional changes, especially on the return arch to the earth when they have lost most of their power. Lilly's solution was to place diaphanous fabric at key locations on the battlefield, best viewed from Anoushka's angle and not the enemy's, so she could better judge and direct the barrage.

329

The archers on the Green are blind to the enemy. It is Anoushka's eyes alone that will command three hundred bows.

Lying still and breathing calmly, she stays very low in the protection of the viewing wedge. The sun today has turned the Flat to a lovely gold. A pool of sunlight ripples over the long approach to Yellow Ridge. She hasn't seen Moishe in nine days – they had a fight and she stormed off, leaving him fragile. She did try to find him before her deployment to the wall but he had already been assigned to his Crash Team, ready to repair any breeches or weapons failures during the battle.

She hopes word has reached him.

Anoushka twists on her belly and slips to the edge so she can see her Deputy Master below. He is a first-generation soldier with eyes like a falcon. He's holding a long red pole and looking up at her from ten metres below. Around him is the Great Compass Ring. It is ten metres across and marks out 180 degrees of arc. She will take the bearings on her compass and share them with him. He will redirect the Company by angling the pole to the bearing, and three hundred archers will shift to mimic his gesture. They are a machine: together, they will own the air, so the sky can command the earth to cease all movement.

Henrietta Wayworth has assumed her position inside as a sharp-shooter. Her rifle scope is charged. She looks through it periodically, but prefers to watch the entire ridge with her naked eye to better appreciate the entirety of the problem. The scope only focuses more attention on a smaller part. With Alessandra and Graham both out there somewhere, looking through the scope feels like crawling under a rock.

She is lying on a metal table. A few small rags have been left there, at her instruction, so she can position the rifle at her cheek. The constant, annoying wind in her face from the hole in front of her dries her lips and eyes, but there is no real solution for this other than placing a piece of glass there until the battle begins. It's not a bad idea, but for now she'll suffer the breeze.

Henry hears the shuffle of feet behind her.

A ten-year-old girl has taken a position by the door like a tiny guard. This girl has fair skin, blue eyes and red hair, all of which is unusual enough to be memorable. She wears a bag with a red cross on it; it is packed with medical supplies. She is positioned here to be Henry's message-carrier but it looks like she's also being trained as a First Responder.

'You look familiar. What's your name?' Henry asks.

'Bee.'

'Do I know you?'

'At The Crossing you told my parents to bring me here when they went looking for the city to the west. I was sick so they did. They haven't come back.'

'You look better.'

'I am.'

'How are you doing?'

'I need to pee.'

'Everyone needs to pee during a war. No one ever talks about it.'

The girl looks scared and now Henry does vaguely remember her. It's not an unfamiliar story, nor even a sad one. Assuming she survives the war, she's better off here.

'Pee in the corner,' Henry tells her. 'I won't tell anyone.'

She turns back to the hole in the wall and looks out again, scanning the hill, waiting for the first indications of enemy action as Bee's urine hits the floor behind her with a force that threatens to leave a dent. This is the standard indignity

331

of conflict. When civilisation breaks down, the bladders are always the first things to go.

Henry catches movement and re-activates the scope.

A shadow, a head, a torso arises as a phantom from the ridge. It is the only face she can see. She amplifies and across 1.2 kilometres of quivering air she is looking at the face of her husband. He is alive, and if the swagger of his body is an indication, he is unharmed. His hands, she can see, are not even bound. She can tell that he is looking directly at her, although he can't possibly see her.

He knows the battle flag is flying. He knows they have taken up war positions. He knows where she is stationed and he knows where to look. So he is looking at her, even if he cannot see her – because he knows that his wife can see him.

She zooms in as close as she can and points her rifle directly at his chest so she can read his lips and see his hands.

A man emerges and stands next to him. He is wearing a white robe and a red sash.

Henry activates the sighting-laser on her scope and takes a new aim at his hands. She taps out a coded message that flickers on his interlocked fingers resting by his groin. She tells him where Alessandra is – or might be. He's to get there if he can.

She repeats the message, and then repeats it again.

In the middle of the fourth attempt, Graham's hands move. He places the thumb of his right hand between his first two fingers. He then encloses his left hand around his right as though protecting the shape he formed. He whispers into the wind and hopes her eyes are sharp enough to read his gestures and words.

Protect the tunnels, he says. *Don't use The Drop.*

Acknowledged, she replies. *Alessandra?* she taps out.

He makes a face she knows only too well. It means, 'I'm working on it.'

332

'Bee,' Henry says in a soft voice so as not to frighten the child, 'go to the Snake Tower and tell General Winters I have contact with my husband. He is instructing us to protect the tunnels at all costs and not to use the weapon. Your message changes the course of our history. Do you understand what I've said?'

Bee repeats the message.

'Go now. And go very, very fast.'

As Bee rushes out the door, Henry moves the scope from Graham to the man in the white robe and red sash who is standing beside him. She moves her finger from the right side of the receiver to the trigger.

As she does, the man's hand points to the valley below and with that small gesture hundreds of troops rush over the edge of the ridge and charge screaming into the valley and onto the Flat, swords drawn, spears set and hate in their faces.

Henry gently squeezes the trigger and shoots the man beside Graham.

CROSSINGS

Above the Main Gate Anoushka watches the oncoming assault, dumbfounded by the numbers and the rage. The tribesmen and the horses and the dogs roll over the ridge and across the flats like a flood and there is no end to their numbers. She has seen battle before, but not like this.

The sounds issuing out of their throats are not the war-cries of beasts. There is an anger and a self-righteousness to those calls; a genuine and deep hatred of the Commonwealth that stuns her.

Under their feet and their hooves is a sound she has never heard – a sound that no one has ever heard: the rush of an army over the Hollows.

She looks up at the unbroken blue sky. It is clear of birds and undisturbed by the turmoil below. It is still peaceful there, but that will soon change, because the sky is her domain.

The Keepers cross into range, trampling the directional pole and its cloth to the ground, but it is no longer needed, because the dust kicked up by their many, many feet tells Anoushka everything she needs to set her archers loose.

Anoushka holds out her compass and points it in the direction of the stampede with the greatest concentration of enemy. She adjusts the mirror so she can better see the compass bearing and rotates the plastic glass until north is captured in the small arrow. They are coming down at forty-eight degrees east by northeast. With hand signals and her red flag, she relays the information to her Deputy Master, who takes the instruction and points the tip of his giant pole at the proper bearing on the giant compass at his feet.

Three hundred bodies shift their position to match his own.

Leaning back so she can meet his eyes, she slices her hand downwards, as though it were a sword upon a neck, and with the precision of an ancient machine, a volley of three hundred razor-sharp arrows meet the sky, forming a dark rainbow over the Stadium wall, and fall with wicked intent onto the heads and bodies and silenced throats of their attackers.

They re-notch and release a second volley.

Again iron meets flesh and again the foot soldiers wash over their own to press the assault.

As Anoushka prepares her fighters for a third round, she sees the first arrows coming back towards them from the oncoming Keepers. A quick sideways slash of her flag signals the danger and the waiting Phalanx and her Sagittaris raise their shields in defence.

A head pops up beside her from the top of the ladder: a certain piano player she recently broke up with. He is not supposed to be here.

'Have you abandoned your post?' she says to him, wishing she had said something different, but she didn't and she can't take it back.

Moishe smiles at her.

'I told you to stop smiling at me like that,' she says, unconvincingly.

Moishe only smiles at her more: a smile as incongruous to their relationship as it is to this moment of war and potential annihilation.

It is a smile she fears more than the barbarians on the Flat. It is a smile that speaks to the depth of his emotions, the taste of his lips, the kindness of his heart and the bliss she will fall into and never emerge if she accepts his love as completely as he is offering it. She fears it will confine her and this is not what she needs as a Master, as a soldier, as a woman. She needs to be elevated above it all. Bliss is not the motivation she needs.

The trouble is, he is offering her wings to soar above whatever is base and low in this world but she is too prideful to accept them – too worried that happiness will rob her of her ambition.

Which it might. Isn't all ambition driven by some discontent? Isn't that discontentment therefore needed? Doesn't it need to be nurtured? Happiness sounds stagnating to her. And this is a place of motion.

Maybe we'd be better off as Roamers.

Moishe is not smiling to distract her or trap her. He is smiling because he is happy to see her.

It's so linear it drives her nuts.

'Go and do your job!' she yells at him.

Scooting past her, he jogs along the wall. He's needed inside the Main Gate and this is the fastest way to get there . . . while passing Anoushka.

In the Snake Tower, the elevator opens and Javier wipes his face with a cloth as he approaches Winters.

'Report,' General Winters says, watching another volley of arrows and a lone figure running across the wall of the stadium in the direction of the Main Gate. She's not quite sure who it is. It might be the piano player.

'I've sent the divisions through the tunnels,' says Javier, 'and they're emerging at Lawson Point. They have orders to come back around once The Drop is activated.'

'So that's the last of the Keepers? Concentrating themselves on the Flats? You're behind them now?'

'Honestly, General, we don't know. Anoushka is giving them hell from above,' Javier says, 'but these numbers . . . we don't know how deep their line is. They're chopping through the pike barriers now and they're almost at the walls. We have no casualties and they're taking dozens but there is no let-up in their attack.'

'Do we have them surrounded or not?' Winters asks.

'Surrounded . . . yes. But that's not the issue,' Javier says, wiping his face for the umpteenth time. 'We don't have enough forces to press a rear attack. We are *massively* out-numbered, General, so we either commit to staying behind the walls and hope they don't have more explosives to punch through, or we take advantage of their concentration of forces out on the Flat, right now, and use The Drop. We can use the Dragoons to secure the perimeter and prevent any survivors from regrouping.'

Winters stares at the Flat. It is filled with the enemy and the walls still hold. If there are indeed more on the Ridge or beyond, they can bear witness to their brethren's folly.

Now is the time.

She sends Messenger Harishma to issue the order to Birch. She is thirteen, with very dark skin and the strong legs of an athlete or Dragoon. She has cut her hair short like a boy's and

337

while too young to be a Runner, she wears a leather jacket like the uniform she soon hopes to don.

She is fast and, to her parents' consternation, fearless and ruthless. Nothing will stop her from delivering the message. This is why she is Winters' personal messenger.

Harishma flies down the Snake Tower steps until they connect with the central stairway. She swings around first one ban-nister and then another, practising the moves she has seen the Runners perform on the Green. As she whips around the second, she bashes into a slight girl who reeks of urine and is wearing a medic bag. She's seen this girl before: she's small and weak and her red hair makes her look like a freak.

'Watch where you're going, kid,' Harishma says as her shoulder checks the little girl, who falls backwards and bumps her head against the wall; her chin slams upwards and she bites her own lip and cheek, which start to bleed.

Harishma disappears into the basement through the tunnels and carries on to Birch, who is the warrior she will someday become.

Bee hoists herself up, blood on her lips, and hobbles outside to the Green. Her head throbs, and so does her ankle. The rounded bone on the side of it that has no name is hurting and she winces as she runs. As she passes through the archers, the buzz from the twanging strings reaches the same perfect pitch as the ringing in her ears; in that moment the world is in perfect harmony.

She reaches three soldiers manning the elevator to up the Snake Tower, the fastest way to General Winters.

'I have to use the elevator. I have a message for General

Winters from Commander Wayworth. It is very—' she starts, but that is all she can say because her last words become inaudible when suddenly the ground shakes, an explosion splits the air and a fire lights up the sky beyond the walls.

WAVES

The explosives ignite, but the land does not drop. It rises into the air, higher than the darkest ambitions of hell.

At the moment of the blast Henry had been acquiring a new target from her perch at Sniper Location Echo. In a harrowed breath, before the sound even reaches her ears, the vista before her eyes is replaced by blackened earth. That is the last she sees of anything before a shear of wind and debris rips through her viewing hole in the wall and tears open her left eye, which is unprotected by the scope.

In anger as much as pain, she drops the rifle, clutches her face and rolls off the table, landing hard on her left shoulder. As her head strikes the floor she knows that Bee has not delivered her message, that the tunnels Graham told her to protect are no more and everything is . . . somehow . . . lost.

Moishe's job had been to release the cables that dropped the weights and snapped shut the Jaw Gate that both rose up and slammed down outside so any breach would be impossible. For some reason, the mechanism was stuck and he needed to sort it out. The Main Gate was closed but the Jaw Gate was impenetrable and needed to snap shut. Once there, he is to take shelter behind of one Lilly's triangular shields to effect the repair.

But he is too slow and he stands too tall. For one last time he extends his left arm and waves to her.

Anoushka watches as an enemy blade blown into the air by the force of the blast slices off Moishe's left hand at the wrist and sends him toppling over the wall and onto the Green below.

When Moishe opens his eyes he sees a beautiful little girl with hair like a sunset wearing a bag with a painted red cross. She has a touch of blood on her lower lip. Wordlessly, she is already applying a tourniquet to his stump. He stares into her perfect blue eyes as she performs her job. Blood sprays across her chest and neck as the veins on his arm are constricted by her twisting a stick in the bandage with all her might. She keeps going until the flow finally stops, then she ties the stick to his forearm, places a clean bandage on the stump and wraps it carefully.

When she is finished she sits and places her arm around him and pulls his head to her chest. 'Don't worry,' she says to him. 'I'll protect you.'

Graham crouches down beside the Leader, who was shot before The Drop was ignited. Though debris is raining down on them, Graham is unharmed by the blast. Rather than run or take advantage of the confusion, he drops to one knee and crouches by the Leader, who reaches up to grasp Graham's hand.

He will be dead soon and they both know it.

'Your wife?' the Leader asks about his chest wound.

'Yeah.'

341

'Mine would have done the same,' he says to Graham.

'I believe you,' Graham says.

The Leader's voice is raspy. Blood is trickling from his mouth. 'I am remembering my daughter and my wife. I dishonour them in my final moments by living in the past.'

'No you don't,' Graham says to him, 'because love is always in the Now.'

The Leader nods once, before he releases Graham's left hand and dies. When he does, Graham closes the man's eyes because that is the way of the Commonwealth. He sits beside the man's body and for a moment, wraps his arms around his own knees and surveys the carnage and catastrophe of their collective making.

Where once there was a cragged valley of rocks and brush that Lilly had turned into a flat, there is now a valley again: but this valley is filled with fire and smoke. Graham looks down on it like a premonition of what's to come. In the roiling black smoke, the closed gate flickers into view and then, like an apparition, it is gone again.

The danger flag still hangs from the Snake Tower.

The walls have held.

The fortress, such as it is, remains.

He watches as Anoushka's arrows fill the air again, even after that blast. Winters shows as little mercy for the enemy as she does understanding.

Bursts of sapphire-blue from pulse rifles fall like starlight into the remains below and Graham is filled with a terrible sense of lost possibility.

There is a canteen on the ground beside him. From habit he lifts it, opens it and drinks until it is it empty.

*

342

Graham turns away from it all and looks eastwards. The setting sun behind him turns the towers of the Gone World a fiery orange; further off, the rays are burning through The Crossing, turning it to a half-ring of crystal and fire.

Alessandra is out there and he is outside the walls, beyond the valley – even beyond the Keepers. This war is lost to them now and if he can anticipate Javier's moves, there are probably Dragoons circling around to the Ridge now. He doesn't want to be caught in the middle when that happens. If he can find a way to escape, he can start his search for his daughter and the internet and maybe do some good.

As he stares off into the distance, however, he sees a dust storm kicking up from the ground. It is not blowing in because the skies are clear; instead, it is coming up from the earth. It takes Graham almost a minute for his mind to allow him to see what his eyes are already staring at: a second wave.

Like the dogs that brought down Alan Farmer.

Before Graham can make his move to leave, the Deputy on his horse joins him beside the fallen Leader.

Looming over them both, the Deputy asks, 'Did you close his eyes?'

'Any reason to kill me will do. You don't have to start making things up.'

The Deputy dismounts and stands in front of Graham, albeit at a little distance. They do not speak for a time as the second wave comes into view.

'Only now are you starting to understand what we mean by sacrifice,' he says to Graham.

'You might be right,' he says. 'And yet, all of this . . . *all* of it' – he gestures in a half-hearted way – 'is purposeless. It all could have been avoided with a little wisdom. A little understanding.'

'Your tunnels are broken. The Stadium is cut off from its food and supplies. The people of the Territory will abandon this place and move north through the forests or south to the smaller colonies. Like a thousand others before you, your colony has failed. Your people are trapped by their own decisions.'

'Aren't we all,' Graham asks sarcastically.

'How did he die?' the Deputy asks Graham.

'My wife shot him. Maybe she'll kill you too.'

'Perhaps she will,' he says calmly.

'You people wrap words around fear and call it philosophy. If you want to know what probably destroyed the Gone World,' Graham says, 'that's a good bet.'

Birch and Lilly return to the Snake Tower without a new plan. They stand shoulder to shoulder with the rest, looking down at the pool of death below the fresh army on the Ridge up above.

Anoushka has also seen the new wave of troops, and when she did, she stopped her assault on the survivors in the pit. She did it for mercy. She did it to stop the provocation of the new troops. And most importantly, she did to save their arrows.

Inside the tower, the High Command viewed what everyone below was seeing. Winters spoke first: 'We defend the wall. We defend the Commonwealth until the end.'

It is Lian who speaks this time. She is, after all, the Evaluator. 'They tricked us into using The Drop, General. They concealed their second wave. They were willing to let the first thousand die as a gambit to destroy our tunnels and they have outsmarted us because we never thought anyone could do that.

We also thought that an army this size could never be raised against us. Now, if my sums are correct, we starve or we leave. Because they aren't going to attack.'

'Why won't they starve instead?' Winters asks.

'Because they can come and go as they like and we can't. There are outposts and smaller trade routes that will welcome their business, especially having lost ours. Simply put, they're free and we're trapped.'

'You're making all that up,' Winters says. 'Look at them: packs of wolves on a hill, ignorant, unlearned, disorganised – they'll attack us again and they'll crash against these walls and we'll burn them alive, this time with liquid fire from the parapets. You would have us think you know what they'll do, but all you're really telling us is what you would do.'

'I am making a reasoned argument with what we know. If we had more Knowledge, we could make better arguments. That's why we collect it,' Lian says, with a clear edge to her voice.

Lilly snorts.

Winters turns to her. 'What are you even doing here?'

'Thinking. I thought someone ought to.'

'As you consider the options, General,' says Birch, quickly, 'I will remind you that there are . . . alternatives. Grand alternatives that the Order of Silence spent many decades, at great cost, making possible.'

THE ASSIGNMENT

The detonation of The Drop rattles the bomb shelter and Elimisha and Alessandra both instinctively slip from their seats and hide under the table.

The shudder is not strong but they can feel it: a dusting from the ceiling, a rumble of shocks, followed by a groan as from the Earth's own pain.

'What was that?' Elimisha asks.

'I have no idea.'

'Are they trying to get in?'

'That wasn't close. It was far away and big,' Alessandra says.

'Another Tracollo?'

What else? they both think.

'How many bullets do you have left?' Elimisha asks.

'Three.'

Elimisha had asked the Librarian about guns and ammunition that might have been stored with them in the bunker. There had once been a dozen assault rifles and eleven pistols, not counting the one strapped to the waist of the skeleton in the other room – but those weapons hadn't been maintained in four hundred years and the stockpile of ammunition had suffered corrosion. The only active weapon is Alessandra's.

The lights flicker and then stabilise.

'Okay, okay,' Alessandra says aloud as an answer to the moment. Or possibly an appeal.

Neither one is inclined to crawl out from the meagre shelter of the sheet-metal table. They both know it offers no protection from a building falling on their heads, but as Runners they've both been taught to hide when the surroundings or the route become uncertain; to think it through, to adapt and innovate. This is all better accomplished while hiding in a small, dark place.

Has anyone *ever* had a good idea in a large and well-lit room?

'Okay. What are we supposed to do now?' Alessandra asks Elimisha forcefully, as though the question itself is a decision.

'We're going to prepare for Breach Protocol,' Elimisha says in a whisper.

'Like at the Stadium?'

'Yes.'

'How? I have three bullets and neither one of us has ever done this before.'

'You took Mr Whitaker's class on Stadium operations, didn't you? You're a year ahead of me.'

'Well . . . yeah. But he only explained them, he didn't tell us how to do them. And not in a bomb shelter.'

'The idea's the same,' Elimisha murmurs, her voice low. 'We need to secure the Knowledge and we need to prepare for the enemy to get in. We don't let the Knowledge fall into enemy hands: that's the first rule. Chief Lian is under orders to destroy the entire Central Archive if it's overrun – the rumour is that Lilly has filled the floor with explosives.'

347

'That's a myth,' Alessandra says firmly, but Elimisha is shaking her head.

'Why?' Elimisha says. 'It makes sense. If whoever's attacking us knew what the Stadium knows, they could become even more powerful. Plus, all the Knowledge stored there is saved elsewhere, which is the whole point of all this. Our problem is that – well, this *is* the Central Archive. So we need to do what Lian would do. We need to plan to break the internet in case they get in, and we need to take with us as much of it as we can when we get out.

'Up on the desk—' Elimisha starts to say, but Alessandra is a step ahead.

'Can we get out?'

Elimisha doesn't answer, which is the answer.

Choosing to go first, Alessandra slides out from under the desk and sits back on the chair, feeling better for it, if not safer. She reaches out her hand and helps Elimisha into the second chair.

Glasses on, Elimisha waves her hand over the White Board to activate it. She lifts the small black box with its curved edges, no markings and the one perpetually glowing blue light along the edge. She places it on the White Board and the nanites immediately reach for it and clamp down. The blue light begins to move back and forth, from edge to edge, as though it is looking at them.

'We'll need to work fast,' Elimisha says, her priorities now clear: 'Librarian? Copy all disco music to the drive.'

'Done,' came the voice through the glasses.

'What does it mean, "done"?' Alessandra asks, who heard it too.

'It means,' says Elimisha, 'it's done.'

'It didn't do anything.'

'You didn't *see* anything, but now all the disco music is in the box. So if we take the box with us, connect it to a functioning White Board and glasses that have electricity, we can listen to it, even if there's no connection to the internet. So if we're breached, we destroy the internet, grab the box and run.'

'What if the bad guys get the box?'

'Honestly? I don't think they'll know what it is and there's no obvious way for them to learn. I mean . . . Lilly still has no idea and she's been thinking about this for ever. There's no obvious reason to put the Quantum Drive on the White Board while wearing a pair of glasses, is there? Might as well put half a coconut on your head while wearing a raincoat.'

'Are you okay?'

'Not really! No!'

Alessandra decides not to poke her any more.

'You can tell it what to copy by just talking to it,' Elimisha explains. 'It seems to understand everything if you speak normally. I'm going to check the tunnel and the generators and stuff, see if I can find places for us to hide in case we're breached. I'm thinking that if we can't fight we might be able to hide and wait for them to go away, then follow them out afterwards.'

'The Commonwealth is coming for us,' Alessandra says. 'They got the message. I'm sure of it.'

Alessandra, now in charge of Archiving, tells the Librarian to play 'music that'll make me happy' as she sets about exploring the internet on her own, trying to find things to copy to the box.

Perhaps it would wiser to tell the system to make its own choices, but for the moment Alessandra doesn't like the idea of leaving everything to chance.

Aloud, but not necessarily to the Librarian, she adds, 'Okay, let's get this party started.'

When the music begins, Alessandra realises that the AI had combined her request with her encouragement to herself. A song called *Get the Party Started* begins with a girl giggling and then a thick, loud, pounding beat that Alessandra loves. The lyrics start: 'I'm coming up, so you better get this party started.'

Which is depressingly appropriate.

'Far out,' she mutters and wonders as she does whether that phrase too is new or old.

Connected to music and released from time and space and gravity, Alessandra engages the entire sensory experience of the HCG® system and glides and dips on a blanket of wind, rising and soaring through the remains of the internet. Much of it is down, but she has no sense of what is missing – only what is found.

Now she is a Runner through a library as vast as an artist's imagination and she can climb any surface, leap over any space and arrive anywhere she wants with just a wave of her hand or a click of the button that is projected into the air in front of her eyes.

Every time she jumps from a word to an object to an idea that lands in a place populated by a million souls who – somehow, out there – still exist, she feels as though she is leaping across stones a thousand metres in the air. She can start anywhere, go anyplace, linger or sprint. There are no set routes, because they form beneath her feet as she runs. There is no Order of Silence because there are no secrets. She is alive in the minds of every person who has ever been and created anything at all.

The sensation is utterly joyful – until it takes a turn.

Starting with a childish curiosity about the Olympics and

following connections almost randomly, she arrives at moments of horror:

Olympics – Greece – Mediterranean – Crete – Knossos – Labyrinth – Jorge Luis Borges – Geneva – United Nations – Universal Declaration of Human Rights – Nuremberg – Holocaust.

She arrives at a photo of a line of soldiers raising their rifles at a line of women holding babies beside a pit.

And then come the videos.

Alessandra removes her glasses.

The system resets so the Earth spins silently in space.

Graham does most of the cooking at home, leaving Henry and Alessandra in charge of the washing up. He takes a certain pleasure in varying their diet, surprising them with new foods to take their minds away from the dwindling options that are coming from the soil, and the women enjoy that. Sometimes they eat on the Stadium's wall, watching the sunlight. Sometimes, in the fair months, they cook down at the base of the waterfall. Most often, they sit at their little round table in their apartment on the ring, talking together.

Alessandra once came from a class where a Deputy Archivist had been lecturing on The Few. He talked about choice: the choice to venture out into the unknown, their luck in coming across a structure with power and fresh water and enough seclusion to fortify it before they were challenged and overwhelmed. He talked about how they faced internal threats too, and how discord or failure to compromise could have weakened their early resolve. And he talked about how it was a near-miracle that The Few had been able to solidify their control over the territory before being attacked by wandering tribes or bandits or Roamers.

It was a cheery picture of their origins: the women who led them through foresight and cooperation, and the men who rose to the occasion.

Alessandra had been outside the walls with the Urban Explorers by then. She'd seen the devastation close up. Her parents had wanted her to know about it. Her mother in particular viewed the Commonwealth's Choosing Walk with suspicion; she always said it was designed to scare young people into returning, rather than equipping them with the resources needed to become independent and wise.

Alessandra, like all young people, was being trained and prepared for war, but no one ever explained to her why wars happened at all. And no one ever seemed to devote attention to preventing them, either.

'There aren't enough people left to worry about it,' was the pat answer.

'You told me,' Alessandra had said to her parents, 'that there's plenty of stuff out there – plenty of clothes, plenty of animals to hunt, more than enough places to make shelter, maybe not right around here in the desert, but out into the forests and where the Big Waters begin. So why do people fight?'

'Honour, interest and fear,' her father said, quoting Thucydides.

'Colonies or nations might fight for those reasons,' her mother had added. 'But people will fight for any reason.'

Courage regained and the glasses returned to her face, Alessandra braves the history and images of mass slaughter and genocide and slavery and terrorism and torture. She watches children taken from their parents and sold like animals into bondage and permanent misery; gas attacks and mechanised warfare; concentration camps and mass murder and gas chambers; planes used as missiles; cars used as battering rams against whole families; explosives dropped on food lines; chemical weapons dropped from aircraft over hospitals and schools; genetic marker-targeting with bioweapons for ethnic cleansing; the weaponisation of space and the Moon; the eradication of entire political parties – of entire *categories* of people.

So many categories of people, all attacking other categories. White and black. Jew and Gentile. Christian and Muslim. Democrat and Communist and Nazi. Japanese and Chinese and Korean and Philippine. Indian and Pakistani. Hutu and Tutsi. Turkish and Armenian. Catholic and Protestant.

Categories of people who don't exist any more.

She looks at the black box: a vehicle of remembrance.

Should we really remember everything? No matter the consequences? Won't that bring the categories back? – bring all of this back?

'Chief?' Alessandra yells.

'What?' Elimisha yells back from down the hall.

'Have you found ... all this other stuff?' Alessandra shouts.

'What stuff?' Elimisha answers from another room.

'The ... bad stuff.'

'There's a lot of that,' Elimisha shouts. 'A *lot*.'

'Should I save it?' Alessandra asks.

'Yes.'

'Have you been doing it?' Alessandra shouts.

'It hasn't been Breach Protocol yet, so . . . no, not yet. I only started copying things a few days ago and it's mostly been science and a lot of maps so we can start to grow new seed and discover and recover things that might still be out there. I only learned about the Quantum Drive just before you showed up.'

'Why should we copy the bad stuff?'

'It's Knowledge.'

'We're assuming all Knowledge is inherently good?' Alessandra asks. She is not certain Elimisha can hear her properly. 'Can you get in here? This feels important. I don't like yelling,' Alessandra yells.

As she waits, she copies across thousands of maps, hundreds of languages and dictionaries and translator tools and both high school and university courses in medicine, biology, chemistry and physics. She has just started collecting material on astronomy and cosmology when Elimisha arrives covered in a dust that changes her skin from its normal *bark-brown* to an eerie shade of grey.

'What have you been doing?'

'I was under the cabinets in the bedroom.'

'Why?'

'Looking for hidden passages and stuff.'

'The one with the dead people?'

'No. Obviously.'

'Maybe you should be looking in there.'

'I don't want to.'

'That's not a good plan, Chief,' then, 'Fine, I'll do it later,' Alessandra says, turning back to Quantum theory – whatever that is.

'Did you solve that problem?' Elimisha asks, plunking herself down into her chair again. Alessandra notices that Elimisha has changed the dressing on her leg. The wound has not become infected, which is very lucky, but she was impaled through the meat and neither girl thinks she'll ever walk properly again, let alone run or climb.

Neither mentions it.

'It doesn't make sense that all Knowledge is inherently good,' Alessandra says. 'Haven't you ever lied to anyone?'

'Not really.'

'Not your mum?'

'Well . . . her, obviously.'

'And the Urban Explorers? Every time we go out, we're lying. Turns out, by the way,' Alessandra says, 'that the Order of Silence is depending on us to break the rules and lie so it can find the best talent for the Order. It's weird, but I think lying and telling the truth and remembering and forgetting – they aren't all lined up and obvious like I thought before. I think it's more complicated than that. I'm thinking we might have to consciously decide what to put on the box and what not to.'

Elimisha shakes dust from her hair, creating a cloud they both brush away – ineffectually – by waving their hands around. 'You might be right, but I think that's for the Evaluators to figure out. Runners protect Knowledge in motion and the Archivist protects Knowledge at rest. The internet is all Knowledge at rest, so we protect it. When you copy things, you're like the Scribes. And when we carry the box, it's like we're Runners again. You see? We just need to do our jobs.'

Alessandra looks across the room to the Pirelli calendar girl in the leather jacket and no trousers. She never blinks. She never moves. She has no ideas, no opinions, no family, no history, no tastes, no needs, no desires, no friends, no decisions to make. She just fucking stands there . . . looking pretty, weak, and hungry.

'I'm sick of her,' Alessandra says.

'She's been there in the dark for more than four hundred years. Isn't that amazing?'

'I think that's long enough.' Alessandra stands up, walks over to the girl and turns the page. Next in line is another skinny, previously sick girl of about the same age with the same sad look on her face. This one wears a diaphanous cloth of some kind that's being caught by the wind as she walks barefoot across sand, her hair blowing in the breeze and her pale skin exposed to the harsh rays of the light.

'What the hell is it with these girls?' Alessandra asks.

'She's going to step on something,' Elimisha says. 'Barefoot in the sand? Can you even imagine?'

'That was before The Rise,' Alessandra says, trying to make sense of it. 'I'm sure there was less metal and stuff.'

'Yeah but still . . .'

They both look a moment longer.

'Under what circumstances does a woman wander around naked in the desert?' Elimisha wonders.

'Maybe she was attacked. You know the dangers.'

'She looks fine. There are no bruises. And the picture's kind of . . . pretty.'

'Ghost Talker?'

'That's all I can think of.'

Alessandra turns and looks back at Elimisha and the spinning Earth between them. 'Until you found all this, the only thing Evaluators did was determine whether something was true. They didn't decide whether it was valuable. We simply collected whatever we found and worried about whether it was valuable later.'

'What do you mean, valuable?'

'I mean,' Alessandra says, throwing up her hands, '*good* – I mean good for us. Like . . . the way food is good for us. Or whether it's poison. We're putting Knowledge into ourselves and we're not wondering what might happen to us. Evaluators don't know how to do that. There was never enough to worry about it before. Now there is.'

'And?' Elimisha asks.

'And I'm saying maybe we shouldn't copy some of this. Secrets can be good.'

'I don't think that's our choice to make. I think it's a worthwhile question, but for the Commonwealth. For . . . you know . . . adults.'

Alessandra does not agree, not at all. 'Some of these ideas are crazy and dangerous. There are places where they used to take knives and cut off girls'—'

'I know. I know. I saw. I know . . .'

'Well,' says Alessandra, 'they don't do it any more, do they? And I really don't want to give them the idea. Do you?'

'Not really.'

'So let's not!'

Elimisha is unconvinced. 'If we don't remember, who will?'

'Maybe it would be better if we forgot,' Alessandra says, coming to the inevitable conclusion of her line of reasoning.

'Are you agreeing with the Keepers? Who tried to kill us?'

'The Keepers have some kind of philosophy,' says Alessandra. 'They don't actually know anything. I'm looking at real stuff that will actually hurt people. It's not the same thing.'

'You're still recommending that we throw out the past and lots of Knowledge. Like them, you're suggesting that we forget.'

'I guess I am. Yes.' Alessandra removes her glasses and starts to pull off the gloves. They fit snugly and it takes some time. 'You said the Gone World ended because people didn't trust each other when something bad happened, and they didn't have ways to work together to solve their problems. If that's true, it's not really about remembering or forgetting, is it? It's about how we work together with whatever we've got. If some Knowledge will make it harder to work together, I say we leave it out.'

'What if it's the opposite?' Elimisha says. 'What if knowing all that is what brings us all together? What if that's the proof we need to scare us into cooperation? Or what if there's something that seems useless or harmful now but in the end is what saves us all? Or, what if people already remember and we just don't know it? Then we'd be the ones to forget and they'd be the ones to remember and we're throwing out what we need the most! We can't know any of this just sitting here,' Elimisha says.

'People used to *own* other people!'

'Maybe, out there someplace, they still do. And maybe all the best reasons for not doing it are sitting right there!'

'I think the risk of doing harm is greater than the possibility of doing good. I say we copy the science and the great music and forget all the history and literature and religion and anything that makes people hate each other,' Alessandra concludes.

'All that stuff was supposed to make people love each other,' Elimisha whispers.

'And it didn't work – perhaps you've noticed!'

Elimisha isn't convinced. And she's the Chief. 'I think that if you bury the truth on purpose and someone finds out, there will be hell to pay. Copy it,' Elimisha says. 'That's an order.'

That night, Alessandra lies in her cot, unable to keep her eyes closed. She is picturing the family in the next room and feeling the weight of their presence. If she could be anywhere now it would be with her mother on the Western Wall, facing out over the river that gushes out from deep underground and meanders into the far distance where no one ever goes. She imagines that it was a big sky tonight, a night without clouds when the colours fade with a softness and warmth that is nothing like fire.

Like the presence of the family in the next room, though, Alessandra feels the presence of the Keeper army in the distance of her daydream. Watching the sun set is not enough. There is a danger lurking out there and she has to attend to it. It would be wishful to think their intention is to walk past on their way to another place like the troops she and her mother watched when she was little.

And yet that sound last night, the one that caused the ground to shake yet again . . .

Alessandra looks up at the mattress above her. There are hatch marks there that seem to move in the poor light; they are disturbing her vision and that's more than she can take, given the silence, the family, the Keepers.

She slips out of bed in search of a new mood.

Out in the hallway she stands in front of the door that hides the dead family inside. As she stares at it a thought occurs to her. She walks to the Communications Room and sits at the Throne. The system comes alive when she puts on the glasses.

The Librarian has told them about retinal scans and voice recognition passkeys, barriers that once prevented people from sitting down and simply using an access point like she is doing now. Knowing that the entire world was ending, a 'Presidential Executive Order', whatever that was, banned all barriers to general internet access in the final days. If that one last act of foresight hadn't happened centuries ago, she and Elimisha wouldn't have been able to use the internet and radio now. Not for the first time, she reflects on the impossibility of knowing how much is owed to the dead.

'Librarian?' Alessandra says, waking it.

'Yes, Alessandra?'

'Did you know the family inside this bunker?'

'Yes.'

'How long were they here before they died?'

'Four days.' It provides the date and local time.

'Is there a record of their experiences?'

'There is a video diary.'

'What's a diary?'

'A diary is a record of the creator's experiences, thoughts or attitudes, often produced daily and intended for means of catharsis or record-keeping. Diaries were historically produced in written form, but later were created using a variety of multi-media, including but not limited to audio or visual recordings, biometric data entry and automated or programmed self-surveillance.'

Alessandra doesn't know many of these words but she has grown used to that and is currently not in the mood to care. Every question is like a Black Jump into endless exploration on the internet; the only thing that breaks the fall is remembering why you asked in the first place.

'Can I see the last entry?'

The Librarian says yes and then produces it. As soon as it plays, Alessandra realises that she has made a mistake.

Replacing the spinning Earth is the face of a man, perhaps a little younger than her own father, with pinker skin. His face looks careworn and there is a tremendous anxiousness in his eyes. His hands are busy beyond the edges of her glasses. It is clear that he recorded this from the very seat where Alessandra is now sitting.

He has well-cut thick black hair and his eyes, a cold blue like deep ice, are as bright as her own when she looks into a mirror. The detail and texture of him are as real as looking into her father's face as he bends to kiss her goodnight. She is looking at an Ancient as though he is here, speaking directly to her from a seat across from her own.

He is afraid but controlled. She has never seen an adult so scared, but he is not a soldier now: he is a father.

'They say,' he begins in a weak voice – and his accent is much like her own – 'that the sub-sea conduits are being attacked and we could lose connections to Europe, Asia and Africa any time. The satellites are ... off-line. The solar flares and the EMP did a real job on them. After that, the suicide satellites moved into position beside mission-critical systems and self-destructed, which took down almost everything else. The debris is in orbit, we're told, so they're predicting a cascade failure greater than anything we've ever seen. The whole civilian grid is going to be destroyed. The missiles have landed, but they weren't nuclear – not yet. I'm told they released a neurotoxin or possibly a nanotech bioweapon that kills ... immediately. I don't know if we'll be safer in here or not, but the kids feel better in the bedroom so we'll ride it out there. I brought a few books with me.'

The man rubs his face.

'I never read the classics – I wasn't interested. Now I feel like I want to be close to something eternal, something that's already lasted, so I know it will be here later too. We got so much wrong.'

There is another explosion in the video. It sounds like a heavy thud. Dust falls into his hair. 'I have to go. Abigail and William are scared. May the Lord have mercy on our souls and forgive our folly.'

The man stands and the screen becomes empty. Without Alessandra prompting it, the image changes and she is watching the family from inside the room where they are going to die. Alessandra watches the two children cowering under the arms of their mother. The man kisses and hugs them. He touches his wife, who says to him, 'Read to us. Anything.'

He sits at the desk and opens a book and says, 'This is the Longfellow translation of Dante.'

The woman is not listening to words, only to the sound of his voice and the heartbeats of her children.

> *Midway upon the journey of our life*
> *I found myself within a dark forest,*
> *For the straightforward pathway had been lost . . .*

The man reads as though getting the words out and into the air somehow matters, is somehow an act of necessity.

The children cry and with every subsequent shake, the dust falls from the ceiling. Alessandra listens to his words and, like the children, tries to be soothed by them. But they cannot because they are scared and young and she cannot because she knows how the story ends. As the man is compelled to read, she is equally compelled to listen. A bond – a duty – has been awakened in her that feels like it would be unholy to break. She must bear witness, even if doing so breaks her.

The language is opaque and much has been lost over the 1,200 years between the writer's own voice in the year 1300 and her own ears now, but there are moments of transparent understanding that flow into her; pure and complete:

> *Of those things only should one be afraid*
> *Which have the power of doing others harm;*
> *Of the rest, no; because they are not fearful.*

Soon after reading this verse a thunderous boom shakes the camera and, moments later, the children begin to cough, followed by the wife and then the man. A drop of blood flies from Abigail's mouth and the man becomes frantic as the woman tries to comfort her children while her own coughing becomes uncontrollable.

His hands shaking, the man removes a key from around his neck and opens a box from which he removes two yellow and red devices that look like the receivers of a rifle but without a stock or barrel. He breaks the seals on them as the little girl spits blood and the mother screams, her eyes darting to anything – *anything at all* – that might save them.

He holds the detonators, shaking from pain inside himself, one pain of the body and another of the soul. He is meant to squeeze the triggers and collapse the building to end the excruciating pain instantly, bringing forward the end that cannot be stopped. He turns and watches his children as blood trickles from down their eyes instead of tears and his wife clutches them to her breast in an effort to return them to the body that built them from the very stuff of her own; a body that was once a fortress that protected them.

Alessandra knows for a fact that the man cannot and did not pull those triggers, because she is sitting in the room that otherwise would have been rubble. She knows the children will cough themselves to death; a cough so violent she imagines their souls trying to escape their dying bodies to find new hosts.

All of this is coming next and it will happen before her eyes – across the centuries – and Alessandra starts to cough and gasp for breath too because she is so choked with fear and terror and empathy and love and she yells, 'Stop it! Turn it off!' and that fast – an eyeblink – the glasses return to the silent, distant spinning Earth. Four hundred years vanish in a heartbeat, leaving Alessandra rocking in her chair like a baby, with her head down between her knees in the hope that she can vomit this Knowledge out and it will become something separate from herself that she can wash away and forget.

'No,' she says to herself.

She *will* bear witness. She will Attest. She will be strong and see the past, but she will not pass on the sickness of *mind* that caused the Ancients to kill their own, to do this to one another *on purpose*. She will not leave these decisions up to Evaluators who might lack the empathy to know the pain of what they might cause.

He was unable to bring the building down and spare his family their excruciating deaths. So Alessandra, centuries later and in her own way, will do it for him.

When she has recovered, she orders the Librarian to find the bad memories that might already be on the Quantum Drive – the memories of human destruction and malfeasance and murder and inhumanity; the literature that made sense of them; the videos that documented them – and erase them all: the racism, the nationalism, the anti-Semitism, the sexism, the ideologies that would have separated the people at the Commonwealth into groups they have never even heard of and filled them with ideas they would never have dreamed on their own.

The Keepers are right about one thing . . . you can stop the plague, or you spread it, and Alessandra is not going to be the source of humanity's second Apocalypse.

Alessandra returns to her cot to sleep. The ticks on the mattress are still moving, but she no longer cares. She falls into a deep sleep and dreams of a kitten who walks, uncertainly, across a thick rope between two soaring building and – despite almost slipping off many times – successfully reaches the other side.

RESCUE

It is dark when Henry wakes on the cold slab of stone beneath her shooting perch at Sniper Location Echo. She does not realise how dark it is until her right eye adjusts to the moonlight streaming through the shooting window in the wall. With a shaking hand she reaches up to touch her left eye and feels thick blood caked all over her face. She cannot see the hand that probes her. It is only her right eye, the one that was protected by the shatter-proof scope, that can see the dust as it drifts across the moon light.

The girl – Bee – is not here. Henrietta is alone.

If the room is still, it is not silent. Wails of pain float through the air – not her own; they come from outside somewhere. The Flats, she assumes.

Henry too is in pain, but it is not unbearable. The debris that blasted through the window struck her face and her open eye, but the rest of her had been protected by the leather. There is no mirror, but she is certain the scratches and other wounds are deep.

There is a dull pain in her side from the fall off the table. Her ribs, perhaps. She is bruised too, but those will heal.

366

Henry braces against the table to push herself up. The dizziness compels her to hang onto the table leg. Feeling unsteady and light-headed, she finds a piece of cloth to cover her left eye, creating a patch.

The room smells like woodsmoke, rotten eggs and burning meat.

When she is ready she stands and looks outside to assess the battle.

It is night. Yellow Ridge is a black mound traced by a meandering line of orange torch fires stretching for miles, separating the black earth below from the white stars peeking out from the rising greens swirls of night above.

If every light is a soldier, there are *thousands* of them. Somehow The Drop did not kill them off. Henry wonders if Winters set it off too soon. Whatever the reason, an enormous, organised army awaits them at dawn.

Her rifle is on the table. She checks its condition. It is filthy and covered in grit and dust, but there are no scratches on the unbreakable crystal of the scope and nothing indicates that it can't fire again. She will have to test it later.

As the shock starts to wear off her eye socket starts pulsing with pain and she thinks of Graham and Alessandra.

Henrietta slings the rifle and hobbles to the doorway. She uses the walls for support and holds the bannister of the stairs on her way down. There is a long, torch-lit corridor full of people on missions to fulfil their tasks; they ignore her as she progresses gingerly. She is not the only one wounded and she is not requesting assistance.

When she breaks out into the Green the smell hits her harder. The Phalanx formations still stand and the Archers remain at their ready but there is an uneasy quiet and their formations look slack.

She grabs a Lieutenant Colonel she knows as he is walking by. He looks perturbed when he sees her.

'Rodriguez,' she says.

'What happened to your face?' he asks.

'Where's Winters? The High Command?' she says, ignoring his question.

'We're told they're building a new strategy.'

'What the hell does that mean?' Henry asks.

'It means the old one didn't work. That's what it means, Commander.' Rodriguez is old for his rank.

'And in the meantime?' she asks.

'We've been told to defend the walls at all cost until they get back with something better. So while we remain poised for battle waiting for the hammer to fall, the enemy is resting and sleeping and eating and gathering their strength for an attack that could come now or never.'

'Where are they building this new strategy? Up there?' she says, nodding towards the Snake Tower.

'The Map Room.'

Birch and the High Command hear a pounding at the door of the Map Room, which is rare because usually the guards restrain anyone from doing that, most often by killing them.

As that didn't happen, it means it is probably Henry Wayworth, because no one else would dare.

Except Lilly, of course. But she's already in the room.

Birch winces at the noise pounding her ears because of the domed shape of the ceiling. As quickly as possible she waves her hand and signals the guards at the door to open it before they all go deaf.

As expected, it is Henrietta – but the sight of her injuries holds Birch's tongue. Even Winters says nothing.

'What happened to your face?' Lilly says as she stands and moves across the room to meet her

'It's nothing.'

'Let me see it.'

Lilly removes Henry's makeshift dressing and stares into the frosty lens of what remains of the eye. She knows, having seen such wounds before, that it will never heal and Henry will never see through it again. 'I'll wrap it up so it doesn't get worse,' she says gently.

Henry looks into Lilly's face for an answer to her unspoken question and, reluctantly, finds it.

Birch looks at Winters for the right to continue and she nods, knowing that sending Henry away now is pointless.

Javier and Lian are there too, leaning over a very large map of the region.

'The situation,' explains Birch, 'is that we have food reserves for sixty days for seven hundred people, after which we starve. That's two months. By three months, we're dead and have lost the Stadium, unless we regain access to both the farm-land by the river and a critical mass of trade supplies. We might do the first. We'll never do the second. The fact is, the Commonwealth is not sustainable if the Keepers maintain a siege with that new army. What I want to propose is a way that will possibly save the Stadium, will definitely save the Commonwealth and preserve our way of life, and should save most of the people. Despite this,' Birch adds, 'it will sound like failure.'

369

Winters places her hands on the table and slumps. When she saw the Keepers charge across the flat she had been certain the day was hers and the battle would become the poetry and fire-songs of the territory for decades to come. Now they're planning to flee and the fault is hers. She still doesn't know what she did wrong.

Lilly has her own thoughts on the matter but for a change, holds her opinion.

'Speak,' Winters says to Birch.

'I'll start with the Stadium. I suggest we take six hundred people away and leave a hundred behind to defend it. That would give them a year or more of food reserves. Not all our tunnels are down; those left will allow them to smuggle in smaller quantities, which might be enough, especially if we leave a contingent of the Order behind. We've not only been storing Knowledge: we've been packing away rice, dried meats, water, seed and more. The Few – long ago – were able to farm on the Green and with the pulse weapons and explosives and their training, we believe a small contingent of a hundred people can defend the walls even against these odds.'

'And where would these six hundred people go?' Javier asks.

'I'll get to that. But the first part of the plan is finding the girls and rescuing the internet.'

'You mean,' says Henry, 'rescuing the girls and finding the internet.'

'Yes. Of course,' says Birch, though her face says otherwise.

Using a detailed map of the Gone World buildings which Henry has never seen before, Birch explains how there is a good chance that the Otis Shaft in Elimisha's building, which goes all the way from ceiling to cellar, might still be accessible. The shafts, she says, are extremely durable because of their shape; they are often the last parts to fall. There is also an air vent, apparently, that might connect the Otis Shaft to the bunker, and with an extremely long rope . . .

Henry's face throbs and she's unable to focus on the details. Her eye pulses and burns with every beat of her heart as she fights back the dread that surrounds her like a black cloud of smoke, threatening to engulf her if she makes the mistake of thinking about it.

She needs to not think about it because Alessandra needs her, and so does her husband. So if there's a mission outside these walls to save them, she's going.

'I'd like to return to my question,' says Javier, less interested in the rescue plan than the entire crazy strategy itself. 'Move on to *where*? We've been here a hundred and fifty years because there's nowhere else *to* go.'

Birch looks to Winters for approval and she, in turn, looks non-committal about the release of their greatest secret and for which countless lives – Members of the Order, Explorers, Runners, Archivists, settlers, soldiers – have been lost or destroyed.

'I need verbal permission to release this information, General, so others can Attest.'

'Granted,' Winters says in a resigned tone.

'South,' Birch says. 'We will go very, very far south.'

'That's a Black Jump into nothing,' Javier says.

'What I'm going to tell you,' says Birch, 'is our most closely guarded secret. And Lilly . . . it is going to pain you.'

Birch instructs the assistants to make space for a second map to sit beside the detailed Territory map now at the centre of the table. 'The Commonwealth is larger than any of you know.

Our Stadium,' she says, trying not to be dramatic, 'is not the Commonwealth's only home. In fact, there are four hundred more souls who are part of the Commonwealth. They live in a Museum built by an architect of the mid-21st century named Emilio Rubinson. It is located in a mountain range in a place called Mexico in an area once called Veracruz.'

'What are you talking about?' Javier asks.

'Forty years ago an Explorer came back with news of a community who lived there. The path there was ... perilous ... and it took years to get there and back again. These Explorers became our first Cartographers. The Order of Silence got the idea of charting the coastlines from Card number 106 from the Trivial Pursuit deck.'

Lian, who long ago memorised them all, quotes, 'Which 16th century cartographer created a map designed to simplify navigation?'

'Right. We used it to build a route,' Birch says, moving on, 'which we now call the Blue Route. Originally, it started with a climb over the mountains. Our Explorer – David Shoreman – earned the trust of the Museum folk by teaching them how to stitch nets to guard against flying bugs, how to deliver babies more safely and how to clean water using recovered bottles and the light of the sun. The Museum language is called *Espanyol*, but many of them spoke ours too. A bond was formed and a relationship began. It turned out they had a small Trove of Knowledge there too and they were like-minded as to its value, but unlike us, they didn't have a Harrington Box and a Lilly to give that impulse some structure. We taught them our classification systems, Scribe processes and archiving solutions and they mirrored our efforts. We started to exchange Knowledge, which is why, fifty years ago, the Central Archive began growing so rapidly. It was too far away for our Runners, so we had the idea that the Museum should have their own Runners and Evaluators and Scribes and all the rest. Coordinating our efforts while keeping them completely secret meant they needed to meet us halfway and we each needed a liaison, a representative from here to live there, and one of their own to live here. At first we were the teachers, but that didn't last long and now their people know as much as ours, and in some subjects, more. Our treaty-bond commits us to helping one another. They are – and always have been – waiting for us. And we have been waiting for them. And now . . . now it's time to send our people there.'

'There's another Commonwealth?' Lian says, trying to draw out the logic of this.

'We like to think it's the other part of the same Commonwealth, Chief.'

Fifty years ago. Lilly does the maths in her head.

'Who did you send? This Liaison?' She doesn't really need to ask.

'Verena,' says Birch. 'But it wasn't me – it was before my time.'

Lilly does not move a muscle. She holds her face perfectly still. 'Is she . . . ?'

'She died two years ago.'

'How far away is it?' asks Javier, ignoring the drama.

'About two thousand five hundred kilometres,' says Birch, her voice flat.

'How would that even work?' Javier yells, opening his hands in appeal. 'We'd have to fight our way through barbarians from here to there and feed six hundred people, some old,

373

some young, some injured, some weak. We'd be a drawn-out line of exposed civilians, because we'd be leaving our best to defend the Stadium. It's a fool's plan. Exciting and bold, yes, but foolish.'

'In all our wanderings,' Birch says quietly, 'we have never come across a territory with more people than here. It's a dead world, Colonel. If we take to the road, we will be the most powerful army on it, even with only two hundred armed troops. All our children, our elderly, our infirm, are trained for war. We go slow, we keep the lines tight. We dig in and fortify when necessary. If these Keepers let us go, our chances are better out there than here because time is against us, Chief Javier. We need to prepare the departure while a team is finding the girls and the internet. I will be leading that team.'

'I'm going too,' Henry says.

'There's no sense in denying your condition—'

Henry ignores Birch. 'I'll meet you in the stables.'

As Birch and Henry walk towards the door, Lian moves back to study the map. It shows a coastline along an endless ocean stretching thousands of kilometres down a country that has no apparent end.

'Mercator,' she says to herself, running her fingers along the unbroken line as though it were the curve of a lover. 'Gerardus Mercator.'

On the way out of the Map Room, Birch takes Lilly by the arm.

'Get away from me,' Lilly whispers.

'There's a letter for you.'

'What letter?'

'I was only allowed to release it if the secret of the Museum became known. It's part of my—'

'What *goddamned* letter?'

'From Verena.'

DECOYS

When darkness falls, Graham watches the Keepers light torches all along the Ridge around him. It is an extraordinary display, given the scarcity of wood in these parts. At first Graham thinks the lights are a ritual, a ceremony for the dead below.

They are not.

Each Keeper is carrying two or three torches to exaggerate their numbers. They keep moving, on foot or by horse, handing them off to others, making it impossible for anyone at the Stadium to count them or track individual movements. It is, he can tell, both a practised dance and a sophisticated military manoeuvre. Graham is developing a grudging respect for these people, who are brave and self-sacrificing, if strong-headed and unyielding in their immutable beliefs.

The Deputy, who had left him unattended for hours, now returns on a horse, dismounts and stands beside him again.

'Are you going to bury him?' Graham asks.

'No.'

'You think so little of life?'

'We think that little of death.'

'How about,' Graham says, standing, 'I go home. And when I do, you all go home too. It's been a day. Let's be done with it.'

The man snorts like a hog.

'He was a better leader than you,' Graham says, resigned to what he knows must be done next and knowing it will have to be uncompromising and fast. 'He had questions. He *wondered*. He was pained by the cruelty of the choices he faced. There was a humanity to him. You, however, have no questions and so you'll never learn anything.' He tosses a pebble at another and hits it. 'I don't see you lasting long in this job.'

'He had no questions.'

'The bullet didn't kill him immediately,' Graham says, choosing his words carefully. 'His last words were about the memory of his wife and daughter. His final thoughts were of the past. He betrayed your religion and therefore all of you. He chose love. A bit late, if you ask me, but it was touching all the same. You should have been there.'

'You lie.'

For the first time Graham hears a tension in the man's voice. What he tells the Deputy is not what he believes in his heart, but there is work to be done and he is a Raider, not a diplomat. Now is the time to weaken his enemy because the chance for peace is as dead as the past.

Graham looks around and sees that for all the movement, all the activity, all the torches and preparedness, no one is paying any particular attention to them or their conversation. Which means the time is now.

He dusts off his boots and stands, brushing himself clean of the dust and the day. He steps to the old Leader's dead body and kneels down. With care, he unties the red sash and removes his white robe, which is red at the stomach with blood.

The Deputy, confused by this foreign ritual, stares on.

Graham, undressing the body, asks a question. 'There was a girl approaching the Gone World. What happened to her?'

'We buried her,' he says.

'That girl is my daughter,' says Graham, 'and she survived. Unlike you.' Without raising his voice or blinking, Graham shoves the long slender knife from his boot up through the man's chin and into his brain.

As the Deputy's hands reach instinctively to his own neck, Graham pulls him in close and eases them both gently to the ground. He does not say a word as they lock eyes, but he follows the Deputy's gaze until the distance is too great.

Alone with two bodies, Graham works quickly. He dons the white robe of the former leader and ties the red sash around his own waist, which covers much of the blood. He is hoping the darkness and the movement will cover the rest.

There is a hood, which he pulls over his head before mounting the Deputy's waiting horse. A touch of the heels spurs it to movement and together they gallop along the ridge in the direction of the Gone World where Alessandra – he can only hope – is still waiting.

The Tribesmen look at the determined rider racing across the Ridge. His robes are illuminated by the orange flames of their own torches. There were rumours among the newcomers of the Leader's death but they are people who have been taught to trust their eyes and there in front of them is the man himself.

As he rushes past them, his face and features are obscured by his mourning shroud but they recognise his body and the quality of his riding.

A lone figure in white, he bursts from their ranks on the Ridge and for reasons of his own, tears across the desert sands towards the Gone World, leaving a rippled cloud of spreading dust in the moonlight behind him.

The Spotters see the new movement on the Ridge.

Anoushka, below on the Green, is covered in Moishe's blood from carrying him on her own shoulders to the medical ward, where she had to leave him in the care of a child whose head barely reached Anoushka's own chest. Having returned to her post, she hears the rhythm of warning on the steel drums used by the Spotters to signal an enemy change of position.

She's heard it almost a dozen times already tonight, and while the Spotters are good at their jobs and ten of those times she's agreed with their assessments, the relentless pacing is wearing her down. She tries not to think of Moishe's missing hand, which is lying . . . somewhere. But to not think about it, she has to think about it first, making her curse her own mind.

Anoushka grips the sides of the ladder which will take her up to the top of the wall (for the twentieth time today, at least) but she pauses to lower her head, catch her breath, clear her mind and regain her focus.

They are saying there is something new to see. She needs to be able to see it.

Knowing she is alone and that her face is concealed in the dark, she allows herself a few precious moments to sob, then she shakes her head and breathes it off, steels her eyes and mounts the ladder.

Around her neck is one of the ten night-vision monoculars issued to the division Masters. She cradles it like a newborn as she climbs and crests the wall.

Lying flat on her stomach she turns on the Infrared

Illuminator and the night becomes hers to command. Each monocular bears the symbol of the inter-locking Olympic rings of the Stadium. They were found here by The Few. She was told they were for watching sporting events.

She and Moishe, two years older than her, are both Stadium-born. They didn't see each other as possible mates until about five years ago. They met as adults – with hearts equally open – one night after he finished playing his piano at a spring festival. She told him that he concentrated too hard when playing music. She hadn't yet realised that she was already jealous for his attention. This had made him laugh. It reminded him of a story his grandfather used to tell of a rabbi who would concentrate so intently that one time a bird passed over his head and burst into flames.

'What's a rabbi?' she asked.

He didn't know.

'What was he concentrating on?'

'You,' Moishe said. 'He just didn't know it yet.'

He told her that night that every song is a story that carries a promise of a resolution and a happy ending. He said his ear told this to the heart without it ever passing through the mind. It had learned that only recently and hadn't told anyone yet.

She was worried from the beginning that she might drown in the depths of him.

She places the monocular to her eye. The Keepers are not coming down the hill; instead, there is a figure in a bright white robe riding north on the ridge as though the horse's tail is on fire. She magnifies and presses the monocular against the pole for stability. She can see him riding towards the Gone World and counts twenty riders following him. She can't see his face but she is certain she has seen those robes before.

The Leader.

If the figure in white is the Leader of the enemy force and he is leaving the field of battle in a hurry, the High Command needs to know.

Anoushka's senior messenger is a lanky boy. Although he is fast and reliable, he is rubbery and his limbs flail as he bounces off the torch-lit tunnels below the Green. His arms whip around him after every turn and he skids around corners with the unpractised skill of a foal on blue ice.

When Birch finally sees the source of the commotion she wonders how he was chosen for the job at all. He would make a better decoy than a silent messenger – he wouldn't last long in the new job, but he'd be good at it until the end.

'Quiet,' Birch says to him when he comes into view.

She is clad in black leather, standing in the underground stables that were untouched by the blast. She is soothing a black horse that is calm already. She slips a shortsword into her backpack and a pistol into a holster at her side. Henry, beside her, is already mounted and she too is all in black. Her rifle is harnessed at her side and she is chewing dried meat, not having eaten in a day.

There is a new – and proper – patch on her eye. She is not the first to have lost one.

'From General Winters,' says the boy, talking to the dirt between his knees.

Birch and Henry say nothing.

'The enemy leader,' he announces, 'has taken a contingent of soldiers to the Gone World. About twenty of them are riding in his wake, moving fast. They're ten minutes ahead.'

'Where are they going?' Birch says.

'They ran off the Ridge in a hurry, making a straight line towards the urbanscape.'

'That doesn't make any sense. Who's the source?' Henry asks.

'Anoushka, Master of Archers.'

'She's very solid,' Birch says to Henry.

'General Winters thinks the Keepers know about . . . wherever it is you're going,' says the boy, panting and clueless.

'Leave,' Birch instructs the boy and in haste, he is gone.

Once the excitement leaves the room and no one is sucking the air out, they consider what they heard. Henry says, 'I put a bullet in the Leader's gut. I accept that Anoushka saw someone in a white robe, but it wasn't the man I shot.'

'Maybe it's the new one,' Birch says, mounting her horse and motioning for their escort team to prepare themselves.

'Not in the same white robe it's not. He was the only one wearing white.'

'Maybe it's the colour of leadership. The new one dresses like the old one?'

'Maybe,' Henry says.

'If they know about the radio or the internet, why not take a hundred troops and secure it? Why only twenty? They have people to spare and no counter-force in the Ridge,' Birch asks.

Henry considers Birch's question and, turning her horse towards the tunnel entrance off the stable says, 'We don't know. We don't have enough information.'

'That,' says Birch, 'is the correct answer.'

Henry and Birch wrap black scarves around their faces and ease their own horses down into the tunnel, where they fall into line with two columns of Dragoons dressed in black robes.

Each carries a lance that is long and heavy and rests on the shoulder of the rider in front.

The mission leader, at the front on the right, clicks his tongue once, twice, and on the third they all move in unison at a walk. The horses know the pattern; they are trained for this exit manoeuvre, which is known as a Cruel Birth. He clicks again and they all advance at a trot in the dark of the tunnel as the orange light of the Stadium's interior fades behind them and their own shadows ahead grow long and then faint and then vanish altogether.

Their speed rises to a canter, with less than a metre separating each one in the dark. They are moving fast, like a building wind. Henry is finding her right eye starting to tear, which it has never done before, and she realises she cannot judge distance any more, meaning that she will never be able to shoot properly without the scope's instruments to be her missing eye.

She concentrates, again, on her family.

The Dragoons ride to the sound of the hoofbeats and their own thighs slapping the saddles, the horses' breaths and their enormous lungs echoing out like thunderclaps.

'How's your face?' Birch, beside her, asks Henry as they gallop.

'What possible difference does it make?' Henry answers.

She can feel Birch continuing to look at her.

'What?' Henry asks.

'We're clear on the mission, right?'

Henry has no time to answer as the party rips through vines and a diaphanous gauze that conceals the exit.

Like a porcupine backing out of a cave at the speed of sound, the Dragoons – singly, on cue and dancing as one – lift their lances from the shoulder of the rider in front and hold them outwards.

In moments they encounter five enemy soldiers on patrol, drawn by the curious sound they could not locate or name; their lives immediately end, impaled by the Dragoons, leaving no witnesses to the midnight venture.

Moving fast as a unit, the columns break to the right in front of the two women, those who had been riding behind them joining their fellows.

The practised choreography means the two women are now riding to the left of the Dragoons.

'Make sure the Leader in white sees you and follows you,' Birch says to the mission leader, 'but don't make it too obvious.'

'Yes, Master,' he says.

'Godspeed,' she says to him as the columns peel away to the east and she and Henry veer away from them and set off clandestinely for the Gone World ahead.

BREACH

Elimisha rises early and looks at her sleeping friend on the facing cot. Alessandra is lying on her side with the pillow tucked comfortably beneath her head. To Elimisha, Alessandra looks much older than her seventeen years. She's more womanly than Elimisha feels. She doesn't have the same soft-edged, baby-smooth skin. Alessandra has a confidence and certainty and independence that Elimisha sees in people in their twenties or older.

Then again, maybe all girls think this about the other girl across the room.

When she stands to stretch she feels an immediate stabbing pain in her leg, which collapses beneath her, forcing her back to her cot. Blood has soaked through her sleeping gown and there is a tingle all the way down her leg to her feet. Something is really wrong and she has no idea what it is or what to do about it. At the Commonwealth, the doctor's usual advice is, 'Leave it alone and keep it clean and let the body do the work.' That's better advice than most people get at The Crossing but it doesn't always work.

It's not working now.

Elimisha struggles to her feet anyway and performs her morning routine. She checks the time with the Librarian. It is only 5:30 a.m.

Elimisha sits in the communications room with her morning tea, a drink she discovered here in the bunker and which has become a blessing. At this early hour she seldom broadcasts; in her view it is better to keep to a schedule. However, now that she knows the Stadium is listening, she figures everything has changed. It feels strange, speaking to a stranger in Weapons and Communications, but maybe it's no stranger than speaking into the void, which is what she was doing before.

Feeling lonely, the silence becoming too heavy, Elimisha pulls the microphone towards her, depresses the grey button and starts to talk:

'Good morning . . . Stadium. I know someone's there but I don't know who. I wish I knew what was going on out there. I feel like I'm trapped in that tent – do you know the story? It was a Commonwealth storyteller who wrote it. My father used to tell it to me – I was still pretty young when he died, so it always makes me a little sad, but I'm sad now, so maybe sharing it is what the sadness wants from me. I don't always know what the sadness wants. Anyway, it's called *Wilful Creatures*. That's what he used to call us, me and my brothers. Do they know I'm okay? Has anyone told them? And my mum? You need to tell them – they must be going crazy. Okay, so, there were once four children who lived in a tent in a deep forest. But the forest was so dangerous they weren't allowed to go out. So every night, when their parents fell asleep, they would each place their hands on a tent wall and together they would push it until the tent grew a bit bigger. And as the tent got bigger, more and more of the world started to grow inside it – more trees and animals and relics from the Gone World. Each morning the mother would wake and say, 'The world looks so much bigger today!' and the father would say, 'That's because the children are growing,' and this happened every day until the tent was as wide as the world itself and the children became adults, and there was nowhere else to go because the world was now full and endless. But that didn't matter because on the day that the world became whole and complete, a little tent appeared in the centre of *that* world and inside it was a family with four little children, fast asleep with their parents.'

Elimisha pours more tea.

'I didn't know if they were called Wilful Creatures because they tricked their parents, or because they had the will to change the world and explore it and make it bigger, or whether it was because it was somehow a story about how all of us will survive because life promises to start over even at the end. I like it, though, knowing that nothing really ends. I guess the big question is whether or not it repeats in an endless circle or whether that circle can be broken somehow. Who knows?'

She pictures her father kissing her on the forehead and both cheeks, the way he did every night, then calling for their mother to come in and do the same.

'Anyway,' she says, after another sip, 'I used to picture the trees growing inside the tent – and this is kind of funny actually, because—'

There is a *BANG* and Elimisha spins in her chair to look behind her. She hears bare feet slapping against the floor and knows it is Alessandra, but she is not running towards her. She's is running from the bedroom to someplace else.

She hears Alessandra scream, 'Get the gun – *get the gun!*'

Elimisha opens the desk drawer and removes the pistol. She

struggles to her feet and moves as quickly as pain allows down the corridor, listening to thumping and banging inside the kitchen.

When she arrives, she sees Alessandra in her nightgown holding up the axe and shaking.

A man's voice comes from inside the caved-in tunnel. It is eerily calm, the accent different from their own.

'We have already won the war. There is nothing you can do.'

'Fuck off!' yells Elimisha.

Alessandra looks at Elimisha and sees her holding the gun.

'Are there really no more weapons?' Alessandra asks.

'None that work, and bluffing won't work here,' she whispers

'We have to get out of here,' Alessandra whispers back.

'We have guns,' Elimisha yells at the man, bluffing. 'We're armed and we'll kill you all!'

Alessandra gives her a look.

Strong arms start swinging tools in the tunnel. Their progress is aggressive.

Elimisha grabs Alessandra and pulls her to the side and whispers, 'You have to hold them off. I have to destroy the internet.'

'Yeah, okay. Go fast.'

Elimisha pulls away but Alessandra doesn't let go. 'Wait – then what?'

'I don't know!'

Hopping down the hallway, her heart pounding with fear because they are trapped, Elimisha shouts, 'Librarian!'

'How can I assist you?'

'Can you destroy yourself?' she asks him.

'No,' the Librarian answers.

'If I break the White Board, is the internet broken?'

'No. The interface provides access to the internet. It is not synonymous with—'

'If I break the board, can I permanently prevent access to the internet?'

'Internet access can be restored by reconnecting another device capable of performing a handshake wi—'

'I don't know what a handshake is.'

'May I assist you in finding definitions for the term handshake?'

'I don't want to make the internet work. I make to break it!'

'Breaking the internet is a colloquial phrase from the first years of the twenty-first century meaning—'

Elimisha unplugs the Quantum Drive from the White Board and kicks the board from the table, smashing it on the floor. She drops her glasses too, smashes them and brushes the remains away from the desk so there's no obvious relationship among the pieces.

Alessandra appears at the doorway to the Communications Room. Her eyes are wide.

'Holy shit, what did you do?'

'I destroyed the only device with an interface that can perform a handshake with the internet.'

'You . . . what the fuck are you talking about?'

'I broke it. But it's still here, somehow. I don't know how it works!'

'They're going to get through,' Alessandra says. She is wearing her tight blue and gold HCG suit and her leather running boots now. The pistol is gripped in her right hand.

'Take this,' Elimisha says to her. She extends her hand with the Quantum Drive in it.

'What are you doing?'

'This is still an Archive and I'm still the Chief and you are still the Runner. We both have jobs to do and we both made vows. Put this in your bag and get away. If you can't get away, you must destroy it and everything on it. They don't know how many people are in here. We were stupid enough to yell at them so now they know there's at least one. I'll lure them down the hall and barricade myself in here. You'll hide in the hole in the kitchen and when they all pass you, you'll slip out after them with the Quantum Drive. You take the gun because . . . you know.'

'Elimisha—'

'You respond, "Yes, Chief!" That is your sworn duty. You are holding all six flags and the future of the world in your hand – literally. And,' she adds, for Alessandra's sake, 'they might capture me and not kill me. We don't know. So this is the only plan where we both might get out alive and save the Knowledge. Right? So let's go.'

Alessandra lifts her sling-bag from the floor, opens the main compartment and places the box in the middle of her rain gear for protection.

They both move back towards the hammering in the kitchen. The Keepers are not through yet, so there is still time for Elimisha's plan to work.

But when they pass the Control room, there is a new sound: a clattering of something heavy and metal hitting the floor from behind them; it's coming from inside the Inferno room.

'We're surrounded,' Elimisha says. 'Hurry – go and hide.'

Alessandra, though, freezes in place, whether from fear and indecision or because she knows – in some way that does not involve language or thought – that she is the one with the gun and the only one capable of fighting because of Elimisha's leg.

A person emerges from the Inferno room. That person is dressed in black and speaks in a soft and calm and female voice which is not supposed to be there. It says, 'I have a way out. We have to move fast.'

But Alessandra is so ramped up and tense she cannot make sense of the image or the words. She only knows that Elimisha had a plan, they are surrounded, and she needs to go and hide.

Aiming for the centre of mass, she shoots.

OUT

Alessandra's bullet hits Birch in the stomach.

Her hands drop to clutch the wound as she staggers back two steps before lowering herself to the floor and shaking her head.

All these years of sneaking around past enemies and trudging through dank tunnels only for this.

'I'm with the Commonwealth. Don't shoot me,' she says and, after inhaling for more breath, adds, 'again.'

'Who the hell are you,' Alessandra demands as the chipping of the walls starts behind her again. The woman's face is familiar but right now, at this very moment, nothing is familiar.

'I'm Master Birch. I'm here with your parents, Alessandra. Henry and Graham. It's a long story and we've had a very hard night. There's a vent near the ceiling that connects, eventually, with the Otis Shaft and comes out on the roof. There's a rope and your parents will pull you up. Hurry up. Please.'

'You need to go first,' Elimisha says. 'You *need to go.*'

'I can't leave you here,' she says to Elimisha.

'I'll come after you.'

'How?'

'Go,' Birch interjects. 'We'll find a way. Go – and leave the gun, please.'

The chiselling and hammering change their pitch. Rocks and concrete are breaking out and flying across the kitchen floor. The hole is getting bigger.

Alessandra grabs Elimisha by the arm one last time. 'There's something I need to tell you – something I did. Something you won't like. Something you told me not to do but I did it anyway and now I'm not sure because—'

'Tell me later.'

'I'm afraid you'll hate me.'

'I won't hate you. Go!'

'Yes, Chief,' is all she can say.

Alessandra hands Birch the gun and rushes into the room with the skeletons and the rope and the way out.

Elimisha helps Birch to her feet, both of them bracing against the wall for support. The bullet is a 9mm and it is lodged in her gut and though she is accustomed to pain from a life of constant exercise, training and war preparation, this one is debilitating because it is not only pain – it is injury.

The Inferno room is only a few metres down the hall. Birch pushes Elimisha inside the room she's been avoiding for more than a month. Birch herself stops in the doorway and leaning forward, takes aim down the hall.

With only a moment to talk before the Tribesmen breach into the kitchen and come looking for them, Birch asks, 'Is it real? The internet – is it here?'

'Yes, it's real.'

'Can I destroy it?'

'I've tried. It's . . . hidden. But we can't destroy it.'

'That's too bad,' Birch says as she sees the first man, holding a crossbow, turn the corner into the hall. She shoots him dead before his eyes can focus on what killed him.

'You need to get yourself out,' Birch says to her. 'I'll secure the site.'

Alessandra is long gone. Elimisha looks at the rope leading to the vent and the vertical shaft inside it.

'My leg—'

'I know. You're going to have to continue to do your best. You've done a very, very good job.'

Elimisha takes hold of the rope and yanks it. A moment later she feels it gently tug back and a man's voice, weak and far away, yells something but it is too distant for her to make out the words.

Gun in hand, Birch slides out of the Inferno room, focusing down the barrel and attuned to any new target, and hobbles forward into the Control room, where she closes the door behind her. She is looking to kill the power.

Once inside, Birch buckles at the waist for moment from the pain of the gunshot wound. She doesn't know enough about the insides of the human body to know what was hit, but she has seen enough injuries to know which are least likely to heal.

She breathes shallow to catch her breath and recover her anger, which is all that is going to help now.

Birch has spent a lifetime silently moving through tunnels. It is little surprise to her that she will die in one, although she never thought it would happen for being too quiet.

The control room is not unfamiliar. She's passed through rooms like this before. She reads the labels and signs and flicks everything that is in the *on* position to the *off*. The lights go out all around her and are replaced by the red emergency lamps.

She finds a switch to turn those off too, turning the shelter into a pit of black.

From her hip pocket she removes a night vision monocle, removes her boots, takes another breath and opens the door.

Bathed in the green light of her night sight, Birch sees three men standing back to back in the middle of the hall.

But not for long.

Birch was a member of the Urban Explorers at fifteen. She was approached by the Order at eighteen. 'We want you to use your Choosing Walk for something else,' they said to her. It was something never attempted by someone so young: a six-month Run due south, long past the end of the guarded Road.

The Blue Route, they called it, because, 'on it you will touch the sea and the sky'. She was told, 'At the end you will meet a man named José. You will exchange bags and then you will come back. You do this,' the bearded Explorer with the inked arms said to her, 'and we will welcome you to the Order. You have a week to decide.'

She kills the three men; two with the remaining bullets from Alessandra's gun and the third with a long, thin knife she'd received as a gift from Graham Wayworth long ago.

She's now out of bullets.

A thirst is building in Birch's mouth. She knows what it portends. Returning to the Inferno room, she steps in and closes the door behind her.

Elimisha is gone and up the shaft. Birch can hear banging inside it: the injured girl making her way up. Distantly, a man's voice – surely Commander Wayworth's? – is shouting something to her; his voice is too muffled for meaning.

For a pause – for a long, deep breath – Birch considers how to use her remaining time. More Keepers are coming and she cannot follow the girls.

She turns to the desk where a steel-backed chair is occupied by a dead man. His arms are splayed across it and his head rests on a book that does not interest her.

What does catch her attention are the two handles in his bony grips: ones which resemble what Lilly described to her in such detail.

'Oh, Lilly,' Birch says to herself.

She places the now useless gun on the table and pries the detonators from the skeleton's hands.

Birch stares at the door. It is only a matter of time. Pushing the corpse off the chair, Birch sits down, pushes the detonator safeties off and presses both pieces against her stomach to relieve the pain of the gunshot.

An internet of all remaining human Knowledge.

A Library of limitless wonder.

A chance to know everything humanity has learned until now, and to apply it to the challenges of the day for the betterment of the world.

To have had such a treasure and squandered it.

It would have been nice to grow old, Birch thinks as someone starts to pound against the door.

Graham sits in the sand, his feet hard against the edge of the concrete circle that leads down into the shaft. The Order poked a hole in the roof here – it drops down into the Otis Shaft – but the idea that anyone would have voluntarily gone into it strikes him as madness. Then again, he knows he's trying to adjust to more than forty years of believing that the depths will kill you with Sickness. It's like being told that urine tastes like lemon; the ears hear, but the mind rebels.

He wears riding gloves. Inside them he can feel that he's starting to bleed. An annoying wind has picked up and it's chucking sand against the right side of his face, which was covered by the hood but that's been blown off and there's no putting it back on without letting go and he can't do that because there's a girl dangling down there with a hole in her leg who is – he hopes – climbing as best she can, but he knows that he won't have the upper body strength to lift her, and he knows she can't climb the steel cables without the use of her legs, because her right leg can't wrap and pull, so for right now she's dead weight and he's hoping against hope that the rope won't snap because he has no idea how strong it is.

Alessandra is on the roof now and behind him, her feet also planted in the sand, also pulling. He can't see her but he can hear her grunting, giving everything she has.

And she must be exhausted.

He should be feeling much worse than he does, but he doesn't because despite all the odds – of escaping the Keepers, of anticipating the Dragoons' deployment, of riding them into an intercept and not getting killed by either the Keepers or his own people, of fighting his way through that and linking up with Master Birch and his wife at the rendezvous, of Birch saving Alessandra using maps that started with the Adamists and ended with his daughter climbing out of a pit of doom – he and his family are together again, with only Henry's eye as a casualty.

It's a serious casualty, but it's not life-threatening.

Graham heaves harder and he knows Alessandra is doing the same, but it's slow and he's not sure it's going to work.

'Henry, would you *please* get over here and help us?'

'No,' she says for the third time.

She is perched on a rock surveying the hills and the windows in the higher towers and the approaches to their position and the morning sky for birds that might signal ground movement. She is not losing her family again. They need her remaining eye and rifle more than her strength, which is limited now in any case.

Vows or no vows, this world can burn so long as the three of them ride it out together.

Alessandra's groans are unsettling Graham. His daughter's sounds have always unsettled his calm. When she was a baby, the slightest cough or sleepy moan used to have him on his feet; even before Henry woke up, his hands were inspecting her for rational discomforts before lifting her to provide irrational and unconditional love.

There is a thud: a deep, powerful, concussive thud.

'What was that?' Graham yells, turning to look at Henry.

Her face tells him that he already knows.

Graham lets go of the rope.

Spinning around, he grabs Alessandra's left foot and yanks it towards him and then, quickly, he falls on top of her to shield her from what comes next.

For a second – for a pause – Alessandra is apoplectic. She tries to prevent the rope from slipping back down but she can't; the weight is too much.

The pause – the paradise of not knowing the truth – ends when a flame bellows up and out into the orange morning, cuts through the rope in a flash, relieving Alessandra from bearing the full weight of her friend in her hands.

Her father is shielding her from the black ash and debris that rain down on his back and legs. Underneath him Alessandra is no longer struggling; her body is immobile and her eyes are fixed on the fire in the sky.

When the first stone sears through his jacket he decides he'd had enough. It's time to go.

Pulling his daughter to her feet, he grasps her chin and speaks to her unblinking, unbelieving eyes. 'We have to go. The roof could give way. There is nothing more we can do here.'

IV
LEAVING

SOJOURN

When Henrietta was a little girl and her parents died, the Roamers taught her a term for her state of mind: a *Sojourn*. The mind, they explained, tries to follow the dead by leaving the body behind. The body carries on doing what living things do, but it falls into a state much like the animals – proceeding, acting, functioning, but never speaking or thinking or reasoning in quite the same way. The mind of the person on a Sojourn lives in a perpetual state of wonderlessness, trying to follow the dead to where the living can't go. As a result, they become much like the dead.

In many ways, said the Roamers, the animals are better off because unlike the Sojourner, the animals can still feel a range of emotions from joy to fear, from excitement to malaise. But for the Sojourner who leaves the body behind – often to chase after a Union that has ended – there is no range of emotions, only a flatness to sound, a greyness to light and a coldness in the companionship of others. This was how Henry felt as the Roamers moved off, leaving her to guard the graves of her parents with her father's rifle, alone in the desert.

*

403

With the bunker destroyed and the Gone World on fire again, Alessandra rides on her mother's horse, clutching her sling-bag in her arms as though it were a baby. Henrietta can tell from Alessandra's body language that her own Sojourn has begun.

On the fifth day of riding north, away from the Gone World, away from the Keepers and The Crossing and the Commonwealth, Henry decides to unhook the clasp at the top of Alessandra's shoulder and free her trapped hair from beneath the strap of her sling-bag. When she does, Alessandra flinches as though struck. She hugs the bag tighter, pulling it to her chest. Henry opens her palms to signal calm and decides to leave well enough alone.

Even now Alessandra has not asked her mother about the eyepatch. That, to Henry, is proof of how far away her mind is.

At this distance from the war, there is no sense that the world is anything but peaceful and quiet and bright. Sea Glass Lake is less than a kilometre from the edge of the Great Forest and as they approach, it glitters its rainbow of colours, a vibrant and magic spectacle that has been a source of artistic and poetic inspiration to the Territory for generations.

Despite Henry's injury and general fatigue they have made good time, and without pressing their mounts or themselves. Henry and Graham decide to let the horses linger and graze. They are off the Road now, travelling mainly in the wadis and gullies and lowland to stay out of sight. They are nine days north of the Stadium. The trade road curved westwards three days earlier, and there are no paths here. The only reason to venture into the depths of the forest is to hunt for food or to collect wood. There are paths and better ways in than here but Graham has his reasons.

'Look,' the father says to the daughter.

Alessandra looks with her eyes but not her heart.

'We were here when you were nine,' he says. 'You must remember it. Tens of thousands – maybe hundreds of thousands – of bottles once broke here. Our best guess is that massive ships capsized, losing their cargo, and the unbroken bottles floated here when this area was full of water. They must have all fallen over that outcropping over there to the northeast, smashed at the base and then piled up, over and over and over again for – well, who knows. A long time. We think that the constant lap of those long-since-vanished waters wore the edges of the shards into gems and pebbles and now it's this glimmering sea of jewels. It's gorgeous by day, but we should stay and see it by moonlight too, when the reds are pulled back and only the greens and blues light up. It transforms from one place into another at night – and then when the dawn hits it, all the reds and oranges and yellows light up too, as if the sunlight were falling like raindrops. I just love this place.'

Graham looks at Henry after his speech. Though their eyes meet, they are seeing their daughter.

That night they pitch their black dome on the far side of the lake at the edge of the forest where an upturned boat hull rises like a hollow tombstone. They feed and water the horses and do the same to their daughter, who opens her mouth mechanically, an invalid willing to receive warm food. They put her to sleep in the dome clutching the bag the way she used to clutch the stuffed animal Graham gave her for her fourth birthday, acquired from a travelling craftsman with a gentle profession. He called it a *lion*.

'There were animals that looked like this?' Graham had asked him.

The craftsman had smiled and shrugged. 'Either that or someone out there has a wonderful imagination,' he had said.

At dawn the morning sun is warm and good and strikes their dome. Henry awakens first, flushed by the heat. She has never liked the weight of the dome air in the morning and so steps outside, letting Alessandra sleep on. There is a pleasant smell of grass and leaves here; a feeling of growth and life and water and the suggestion of far-away ice. Above, an arrow-head of seven birds pass in formation that is a song in routine.

She clicks her tongue twice and Graham appears from behind a small knoll with her rifle.

He silently shakes his head and she nods her own.

When they are close Graham removes Henry's patch and the gauze and inspects her face. 'No infection,' he says quietly, 'but no improvement.'

'The eye is dead,' she says.

'You look sexy with a scar,' he tells her.

'And an eye the colour of Sickness?'

'Patches can be very stylish.'

She grabs his nose and wiggles it.

'Where are you taking us?' she asks as he washes her face with a soft cloth and applies a new dressing.

'The Abbey, assuming it's still there. I told you about the colony that made the *vin* back when I was on my Choosing Walk. It isn't on a Commonwealth route and there's no trade road. Nothing crosses the forest there and there are no finds mapped nearby. If they're still there, they'll take us in and keep our secrets. We need to stop moving and rest someplace until Alessandra comes back to us.'

'What's an Abbey?'

'It's a place of solitude and reflection. Or if you're feeling less generous, it's a place for misfit men to live together out of the reach of history.'

'What do they do there, these solitary misfits of yours?'

'Mostly they argue, do magic tricks and tell bad jokes.'

'So . . . your people,' Henry says.

'Exactly.'

ABBEY

Abbott Francis has his eye on Frere Jacob, who is finally coming around to hating rabbit soup. It has taken a long time and more trips to the outhouse than should naturally be required. Jacob had made the mistake of declaring his love and passion and commitment to rabbit soup one night, stating at the Big Table, 'I could live on nothing but rabbit soup!' Abbott Francis, in charge of the education and welfare of his Abbey companions, had said, 'and not by every word of God?'

'God,' answered Frere Jacob, 'in the few scripts we have to understand Him, never mentions rabbit soup. I am happy to include the words of God in my eating of soup,' he had boldly asserted, 'but I will not remove my soup from the words of God.'

And so Abbott Francis took Frere Jacob at his word and put him on a nothing-but-rabbit-soup-and-water diet until Jacob came around to admitting that he had probably overstepped a bit – but Jacob was a stubborn one and it was Francis' conclusion that Jacob was secretly hoping that his decimation of the local rabbit population would create a *fait accompli* and

408

God – in his wisdom and mercy – would remove the rabbit from his soup for him so that Jacob might save face and get on with eating other things.

By this point, however, he has come to realise that if God doesn't help him he'll have to relent and help himself by admitting that unreflective faith in anything which is not moderated by wisdom and reason is probably a bad idea, which, he has come around to realising, was probably the lesson the Abbott had wanted him to learn in the first place.

Abbott Francis didn't hear Jacob say these words, but he could see how he stirred his soup for a long, long time before putting more of it in his mouth, which was proof enough that *some* lesson had gone in.

As it happened, the Abbott didn't know much about God and wasn't really that interested anyway, because the few scraps they'd cobbled together from the Bible, from the New Testament, from the Talmud and the Koran seemed to have only thing in common: God didn't really want anything *from* us; he wanted things *for* us. And what he mainly wanted was peace and for people to be good to one another. Acts of harm or extreme were the general no-nos at the Abbey and failing a theology that was more sophisticated, that seemed a reasonable way to live.

The big surprise, over the years, was finding out how many people disagreed.

Meanwhile – because measurements can be helpful – Abbott Francis has started a count of how often Frere Jacob has taken to squatting and moaning in the poo-shed. His final analysis was that Jacob's pride was – literally – wearing him thin.

The Abbott knows he should call an end to all this and consider the lesson learned but . . . it's amusing. And how do you simply end something amusing in a world gone mad? It was a good question.

A question worthy of a glass bead.

Francis is at the Big Table this morning. He is playing a game of chess with Frere Vince when there is a knock on their heavy wooden door.

It is rare for someone to knock. The Brothers come and go, guests are accompanied and enemies usually walk right in.

The Abbott stands and, thinking twice on it, sits again. He has an ingrown toenail that's bothering him and pressure on it makes it worse. He knows he'll have to go after it with a sharp knife at some point but . . . better tomorrow.

Instead, he calls Jacob to go and answer it. Jacob is in the kitchen looking at his latest batch of soup. He has deliberately overcooked it as a means of punishing the rabbit – twice – for his own mistakes.

It is an unkind gesture towards everyone, including himself, and he's ashamed. Still, he's doing it anyway.

'D'accord,' he yells in response to the Abbott's request. After tossing his hand towel to the wooden cooking block, Jacob passes the long table and the Abbott and opens the unlocked door. Before his eyes is a sad family.

'Je m'appelle Graham Wayworth,' says the man. 'Je suis un ami du Frere Francis. Pouvons-nous entrer?'

Despite the man's reprehensible pronunciation of the Français, he extends his arms to the woman with the wounded eye and the girl she's supporting and ushers them all in. Jacob is only twenty-two but he knows the ailment on the girl's face better than the mother's. He has seen it many times. She is *away*. It is not an uncommon state of mind here. Many people who come to the Abbey – for a day, for a lifetime – look like

410

this on arrival. When Jacob was sixteen he became aware that his own father was *away* and would likely never return. That is when he decided to come here, to a place where people are always present.

'My wife and daughter don't speak the language. Can we use the Common?'

Brother Jacob hates the Common because it sounds as flat as a raccoon pelt and his own mouth doesn't like the shape of the sounds. But hospitality demands sacrifice, and many of the scripts about God they have found are in the Common. The general consensus is that it was written in this way so as not to overwhelm the reader with its beauty.

Jacob opens the door fully and the late-afternoon forest light floods the room and reveals the smiling Abbott, who has already recognised his old friend's voice.

Trying not to wince with discomfort, he embraces and kisses his old friend on either cheek, and Graham returns the gesture and sentiment.

'I said I would visit your Commonwealth. I didn't. I am ashamed and I apologise,' says the Abbott. 'It's just so ... big.'

'I'm glad to see you all well,' Graham says. 'You look stronger and thinner. Younger. Doing absolutely nothing all day clearly agrees with you.'

'Everyone out there is in such a hurry, but I can't see where they're going,' he says.

The Abbott is tall, in his early sixties and has a broad chest. Wordlessly, he grasps Henry by both hands before he reaches out to Alessandra, whose hands are weak. Her eyes stay low.

'You are welcome here, daughter-of-Graham.'

Henry smiles at this. It has been a long time since she has heard anyone mention the name of the father. She knows it is a common practice in some places, but it makes no sense to her. It's a matter of logic: you always know who the mother is.

But . . . men.

Francis draws them all inside, closes the door and seats them at the table while gesturing for food and water.

'So,' Graham asks, 'have you figured out what religion you are yet?'

'Not quite,' Francis says. 'We only know about Catholics, Protestants, Jews and Muslims, although we suspect there are more. We like how the Catholics recognise sin and both enjoy and apologise for it. They're the most fun. The Protestants are less distracted by such things, which can be handy if you need to get anything done. The Jews ask the best questions and then search for answers with both passion and moral intent by arguing. It's most fun to be Jewish when we're drinking. Although being Catholic can be fun too. It's never fun being Protestant. And the Muslims, who don't drink so this is an issue, have the most wonderful way of breaking up the day into these segments of activity and then prayer and reflection, which seems wise and comforting and communal. Unfortunately, they wake up a bit early for our tastes.'

'So really, it's nothing but work around here,' Graham posits.

The Abbott uncrosses his arms and places his palms up towards Alessandra. 'And who is this powerful young woman?' he asks.

'Our daughter, Alessandra,' Graham says, introducing her formally, although he's already spoken her name. 'She fell into a hole with a friend. She came out alone.'

'I see,' says the Abbott, his thick leather boots scuffing against the wooden floor as he settles into a new position.

'You know about the war at the Stadium?' Graham asks.

'Yes – we've been tracking the troop levels and monitoring the traffic on the roads to see if they are putting up stops. So far it's clear, but it's only a matter of time before that ends. I heard about a weapon?'

'Yes. That was us.'

'I see,' he says.

'We had no idea a force this large existed,' Graham admits.

'I'm not surprised. With these Keepers there's a . . . simplicity. *Look around at all the destruction*, they say. *The Ancients did this. The Commonwealth is the ally of the Ancients. Join us and resist a new destruction.* It is clear and noble, if misguided.'

'You've become better at our language,' Graham says.

'A necessary evil.'

'Are we safe here?'

The Abbott nods and smiles. 'We have more than enough food and water out in the forest. Fewer rabbits than before,' he says, raising his voice slightly, for some reason, 'but still more than enough. We stay quiet and there's nothing people can take from us they couldn't find elsewhere and at less risk. We're better armed than we look and we whisper it in our trades to make it well-known. We're safe, but we're hoping the mood of the world will change.'

'It is not only a passing mood, Francis.'

The Abbott looks at Graham. 'Can you still do the trick with the coin?'

Graham smiles. 'It's been a while.'

The Abbott digs into his right pocket and pulls out a coin that is silver on the outside and gold at the centre. On one side there is a bear on a rock with the words, 'Canada 2 Dollars.' It is worn from being frequently handled. He slaps it on the table and slides it across.

413

'That's my lucky coin. Keeps the bears away,' he says to Alessandra.

'There are no bears here, Francis,' says Graham.

'See? It's working.' He winks at Alessandra.

Graham picks it up and feels its weight. He then pinches it, shows it to everyone, and – quickly wringing his hands together – makes it vanish into the air.

The Abbott is delighted. 'Make it fall out of my nose.'

He does.

'That's true talent,' he says, pointing to Graham.

'I fear for you both,' Henry says.

'Stay as long as you need. Keep your weapons close. Avoid the soup.'

The Abbey comprises four buildings and there are no defensive walls, only a thin fence of wooden planks wired together to keep out the less motivated rodents. The living quarters, also made of wood, are adjacent to the stone-built Gathering House. The chapel is a library but one that would be unfamiliar to the Commonwealth, for nothing here is classified or coded, copied or formally studied. Instead, it is a place of curiosities and artefacts designed to stimulate imagination and evoke inspiration. They invent here, and create, and solve problems big and small. Unlike the Commonwealth they have no designs on perpetuity: life is for living and then it ends. All that matters here at the Abbey is trying to do good and be good and have a few drinks and laughs along the way. There is no agenda here beyond peace, but it is one they will fight to maintain.

That night Alessandra sleeps between her parents like a little girl. She twitches and calls out and mutters words that have no meaning to them.

During the following quiet days she walks in the forest around the Abbey, staring at the way the leaves are the subjects of the wind.

She goes nowhere without her sling-bag.

THE MUSIC MAN

On their twenty-second day at the Abbey, a strange man appears in the woods. Through the scope of Henry's rifle she can see he is unkempt, with a long beard and tattered clothes. His age is impossible to determine through the hat and hair and fabric. He drags behind him a small wagon that is painted on the sides with animals and musical instruments. His approach is slow and as subtle as a rockslide because the wagon is rickety and the man mutters to himself as he walks along the barely visible dirt path. If there is any deception here, then he is the distraction, so Henry scans the forest for danger.

She finds none.

Henry tracks him for another two hundred metres through the dense but thinning forest to the fence. On the way, humming a tune, he passes her unseen in her look-out perch. At the flimsy gate he stops as though it were the door to a house and taps. Receiving no reply, he loudly opens the gate, saunters into the perimeter, closes the gate behind the wagon once it is inside and proceeds to seat himself on a tree stump by the Gathering House door.

After sitting silently to catch his breath, he stands, straightens his jacket, brushes back his hair – which is no improvement – and knocks on the door. Henry watches all this from her position twenty metres away in a tree, her finger resting on the receiver and clear of the trigger.

The man waits patiently and after a time the door opens. The young Brother, Frere Jacob, smiles. Henry can hear their conversation, though she cannot understand the Français, which is both fluent and fast. Jacob looks calm and curious and eventually invites the man inside.

Henry shoulders her rifle, climbs down the tree and approaches the door to listen from the outside. She may not understand the language but heated words always freeze open hearts, whereas the sounds inside are doing quite the opposite.

She can hear men talking jovially to one another. She listens for several minutes, hearing three other Brothers joining them. Soon after, she is listening to the sound of mugs being clanked together, *spondees* spoken and libations drunk. They're having more fun inside than she is outside and at that point she suspends her suspicions and decides to join them.

The Brothers all fall silent when she enters the room – but it is not on her account. The man has started cranking a wheel on his strange wagon, and as he does, it starts to usher forth a song. It is nothing intricate, not like the layers of storytelling that come from Moishe's playing or from the orchestrations he arranges for the other musicians. This is delicate and gentle and solitary, sounding like a set of glasses being tapped by the tip of a metal prong, over and over. The notes dance and flow and overlap, their time apart separated into perfect beats: a melody, a child's song. To Henry, it sounds like rain falling on flowers from a dark but not foreboding sky. It lasts for some two minutes and ends on the note on which it began.

It leaves behind a silence as fresh as morning dew.

417

Henry is surprised but happy to see Alessandra standing in the corner.

The man, hatless now and largely bald, waves his hand and ushers Henry in as though she were a long and awaited friend. She cannot help but smile at this table of jolly folk who appear to have no other care in the world than camaraderie, and no inhibitions about a stranger arriving from a dense forest with music in tow in the midst of the war.

'*Et quel est ton nom, ma chere?*'

'I don't speak the Français,' Henrietta says apologetically. She cannot remember the last time she was in a room with only men. It feels almost comic. Is this what they do when women aren't around? What a nice thought. And would that it be true.

'Don't be shy,' he says in her language, in her accent. 'Tell me your name.'

'Henrietta,' she says. 'My father called me Henry.'

'He wanted a boy?' the man says.

'No. He wanted me. He said my name was too long and by making it shorter he could say it more times in a day.'

'To Henry's father and his love for his daughter,' he says, raising a glass, and all the men drink to her father and his love for his daughter and they continue to drink when the toast is done because no one reminds them to stop.

'You look handy,' the music man says to Henry a few moments later as conversations turn elsewhere and the drinking becomes a party that ignores them both. 'I wonder if you could help me fix a wheel.'

With Graham in the corner Henry decides the music man is no threat. She follows him to the wagon parked in the space between the table and the far window. There, he crouches down beside the hub at the centre of the back wheel. Using a metal spoon he'd taken from the table, he pries off the cap and indicates what is beneath. 'Have you ever seen something like this? I'm hoping it's a conversation-starter,' he says, pointing to the seal of the Commonwealth and the six-wedged pie.

'Yes I have,' she says. 'I think I can help you.'

EVERYTHING

The forest is filled with bugs come dusk and the woods are full of crickets. The crickets are nice. The other bugs are not. The Brothers find the limits of their own mercy when the mosquitos arrive and the constant slapping occasionally synchronises into a rhythm and a pitiless song of death, but no one is listening.

Inside, Henry and Graham join the music man in the room Francis has prepared for him. The room contains a bed and a plastic chair, a wooden desk and a large bowl filled with fresh water for washing. Beside it there is an attractive blue glass bottle and a cup for drinking. On the bed itself is a white sheet and an itchy but warm blanket. All the Brothers sleep in similar rooms, with their own personal touches.

When the door closes, the man sits on the bed with one leg tucked underneath him and his back to the wall. In private he is less vivacious and theatrical. He has not changed out of his costume: this is work for him and it will not end until so ordered.

He motions for them to sit.

'You're from the Order?' Henry asks.

He speaks quietly, his accent changing back to their own. 'There are a range of solutions for moving unseen.'

'How did you find us?'

'We didn't. We're all looking everywhere. No one knows whether you've survived and if so, whether you've collected the Prize.'

'The Prize,' Graham repeats.

'That's what High Command is calling it.'

'What's happening at home?' Graham asks.

'I do have news. But before that,' he says, turning to Henry, 'where is the Master? She left with you.'

'Birch is dead,' Henry says. 'She saved my daughter and secured the Archive by setting off the explosion.'

The man says nothing, but by his expression, he knew her well.

There is a tap at the door. Henry stands and opens it to find Alessandra standing there clutching her bag.

'I asked her to come,' says the man. 'I told her who I am. You're most welcome, Archive Runner.'

Alessandra says nothing. He waves her in and she steps inside, closing the door carefully behind her. She does not sit, instead lingering by the entrance which is also an exit.

'When I left,' he says, anticipating their questions, 'nothing had changed. The stand-off continues. The enemy forces remain on the hills. Their numbers continue to swell. There is now discussion of whether or not to evoke the Walk. Much of that decision rests on what I learn from you. It is Winters' intention for the core military to stand their ground and hold the Stadium to the end, but she's prepared to evacuate the population if you have the Prize. Do you?'

Henry and Graham both know that Alessandra is the only

person alive with the answer to that question and she hasn't spoken since the explosion.

'What is your name?' Henry asks him.

'I don't need one,' he says. 'I know that you and Master Birch departed with the Dragoons. What happened after that? How did you all reunite?'

'Henry shot the Leader and I killed the Deputy,' says Graham. 'I escaped in the Leader's robes and a tribal force followed me, which I hadn't intended. They assumed I was him and so they followed. Apparently, I was spotted by the Stadium when Henry and Birch broke away from the Dragoons for their own mission. The platoon engaged the Keepers who were trailing me – luckily, they recognised me—'

'It wasn't luck,' Henry interrupts. 'I knew I hadn't missed my shot, so I told them to verify their targets because something strange was happening.'

'Oh,' Graham says to Henry. 'Thank you.'

'You're welcome, dear.'

'Henry and I stayed on the surface to secure the site and Birch went down to find the girl—'

'Chief,' says Alessandra.

Henry and Graham look at their daughter. It is the first word she's spoken since the fire on the mountain.

It is the man who engages her. 'Which Chief?'

'Chief Elimisha. The Archive was called The Inferno. It was named after a book by Dante. Elimisha was the youngest Chief of the Central Archive in the history of the Commonwealth.'

'We think,' Henry says, not entirely following Alessandra's reasoning, but also not wanting to contradict the first words she's spoken in weeks, 'that the Tribesmen set off explosives after beating us in a race to the Hard Room, which unfortunately took the lives of the Chief and the Master,' she says.

'That's not what happened,' Alessandra whispers.

The three adults wait for Alessandra to fill the space.

'It isn't called a Hard Room. It's called a bomb shelter. The bomb shelter was retro-fitted days before the Solar War with a connecting tunnel, provisions, communications, internet access and a safeguard mechanism. If it became contaminated, the officer-in-charge was to destroy it and everyone inside it to both stop the contagion and to end their suffering, because the survival rate was close to zero. Humanic robots were re-purposed to create subterranean passages between key nodes in the underground network following the electric grids to guide them from one building to another so that military and civilian personnel could work as a community during survival and restoration, but none of that worked because they didn't understand the kind of weapon that was unleashed. The sun only broke the world because the Ancients had made it so fragile. If they had made it more resilient to harm by working together, the solar flare would have been only a gentle blow. Instead, it set the tinderbox alight. The reason the world ended is because the Ancients didn't work together and trust each other. It was that simple, really.

'The tribesmen dug through to the Archive. We were fighting them off when Birch showed up behind me. I turned and shot her in the stomach. The Chief was already injured in the leg and there was no way the two of them could climb out. Elimisha ordered me up the shaft first and I went. She was supposed to follow me and Birch was going to stay behind to secure the Archive. She's the one who set off the explosions using the fail-safe. She probably waited as long as she could to give Elimisha time, but she had to uphold her vows. It wasn't enough. I should have pulled harder.'

The adults are each beset by their own list of questions. It is the man from the Order who speaks first: 'Why did Master Birch set off the fail-safe explosions?'

'To secure the Archive.'

'You said that, but a single Archive – even if it's a reasonably large or important Trove – isn't worth the death of a Master. Commander Wayworth could have cut the rope if they started to climb after—'

'It wasn't just "some Archive", okay? You're not *hearing* me. It was the *Primary* Archive of the Commonwealth. It was a gateway to the internet. It was ... *everything*. Maybe not everything-everything, but close enough, and more than we could ever have collected in ten million full-flag runs. The Harrington Box was a seed,' says Alessandra. 'The Inferno was the forest.'

'And Birch secured it at the cost of her life?' the man asked.

'Yes.'

'Well then,' says the man. 'I guess that's that.'

He places his floppy hat on his head and wipes his face with a cloth from his pocket. 'I'll need to fill my water bottles before I go. I need to get back and report to General Winters. They have some hard decisions to make,' he says, standing. He taps the music wagon a few times. 'I'm going to be sorry to leave this tranquillity behind. You can tell the Abbott it's a gift.

'You were very lucky,' the man says to Alessandra, 'to have touched an Archive like that. To have seen what no one else alive has ever seen and never will again. You and Chief Elimisha have solved two of the greatest mysteries we have: what happened to the world, and where did all the Knowledge go. Now we know, thanks to you both. You'll have to explain it to us a few times, I fear, because I didn't understand it all, but there's time. I'm sorry for the price. I understand why Master Birch and Chief Elimisha had to destroy it. It's a pity it's gone.'

'It's not gone,' Alessandra whispers.

'What?' her mother says.

'You can't destroy it. It's a global network, like roots under a massive tree. It once connected all the Deps together and worked like a Central Archive – one that anyone could visit from anywhere. But it was all dependent on the satellites that don't work any more. And all the information between continents that didn't use satellites passed through the sub-ocean cables, most of which have been cut. Much of the Knowledge is mirrored in data centres, but there's no way to know what exists on which continent or in which part of the network and what doesn't. The internet is still there, though. It's like . . . like the waters that run beneath the Gone World. Master Birch destroyed the only access point we know. We'll find another. That's what's next.'

Graham reaches for Alessandra's shoulder and touches her gently. 'The chances of finding one again are very, very low.'

'No they're not,' she says. 'I have the maps. It's all in here.'

Alessandra removes her sling-bag from her shoulder, unsnaps the end and unrolls the top. She extracts a piece of fabric that she places on the bed as carefully as if it were a tiny broken animal in need of care. She peels back the layers and there, in the middle, is a small black box with a blue domed glass and small holes on one side.

'What is that?' the man asks.

'It's . . . *everything*,' she says. 'Everything we could save, anyway.'

'Are you telling me,' says the man from the Order of Silence, 'that in this little box is an entire Archive?'

'I'm telling you,' says Alessandra, 'that this is the Central Archive of the Commonwealth. It's not the *entire* internet, but it's way more than you can possibly imagine. It'll take lifetimes upon lifetimes of Evaluators to even see it all.'

'Is there another copy of this?' says the man.

'No,' Alessandra says.

'So that . . . that is the most precious object on Earth?'

'Yes,' Alessandra says. She wraps it up and returns it to her sling-bag. None of the adults object. 'If we have electricity Lilly can access all of it with her White Board and some glasses.'

The music man looks at the Wayworths. Even before Alessandra was born, Henry and Graham were a formidable couple, with their skills, their uncanny connection to one another, Henry's Roamer background and Graham's strange calm and humour interlaced with a killer's skills. They were universally respected throughout the Commonwealth – and now their daughter is a legend in her own right. A girl who will need a long time to recover from what she has experienced, but one – if he is any judge – who is likely to rise to the High Command faster than any before her.

All of that, however, is for another day. For now, he has his orders. With the Prize secured, their path is clear.

'We have a long, long walk ahead of us,' he informs them.

CHICKEN

In the morning the Abbott sets out breakfast, even though it isn't his turn in the rotation. Guests are rare and he enjoys the rituals of hospitality. It is a pity that their offerings are not what they were only twenty years ago. Brother Hamon – torturer of plants *extraordinaire* – has been cutting stems and grafting them to others to create hybrids that he hopes will yield new food solutions. He has a wild theory that because important crops are no longer flowering and reproducing like before, small animals can no longer eat them, which means big animals can't eat the smaller ones, and somehow the entire world is a kind of enormous machine that is winding down because the smallest parts are broken. If he can grow a flower, he can change the future of the world.

Francis is not surprised Brother Hamon sees the world this way. He arrived with a heart so broken he has yet to even find the pieces, let alone reassemble them. The cause was a girl in a village to the east and months away by horse. He said he was so in love with her that every aspect of life, from eating and drinking to walking and breathing, were infused by an awareness of her spirit. It was as though she

427

was a sea and his every gesture was a slow and deliberate journey inside her.

Worse still, she loved him too.

She died. Her death was as sudden as these things sometimes are.

He left and came to the Abbey, and fourteen years on, Abbott Francis still doesn't know her name. Even in death he doesn't want to share her, poor boy. Of course the world looks broken and slowing down. Of course a flower could fix it all. How could he see it otherwise?

The Abbott lays out dried meats, berries and a hardened flatbread they often eat with goat's milk cheese. Sometimes they are broken into small pieces and softened in whisked chicken eggs and cooked over a flame. Everything is better with salt, but that is hard to come by this far inland – and soon it will be impossible, on account of the war and the end of trading, at least for a while.

In time the other Brothers stumble in, eyes red and shoulders drooped after a night of too much happiness. (Does nature favour balance? Does the human body? Does justice and time and history? All good questions, all worthy of a new piece of sea glass. All worth remembering for later . . .) They sit at the table touching nothing until everyone has arrived. Brother Patel has a chicken joke he's been saving. The Abbott has begged him not to but the man is undeterred – he has apparently re-written the joke especially for his Commonwealth audience.

Abbott Francis retreats to the corner of the room for a moment once the table is set and takes in the full moment. It pleases him. He can hear his guests' voices from down the hall discussing the weather – a popular topic on a day of voyage. Graham has explained the situation, to a point. He will be sad to see them go, and so soon, when there are years of conversations yet to be had and entertainment for many nights. Too much passes too quickly and so much is left undone. At least, the Abbott thinks, he has been aware of this wistful truth and his heart has been open to the joy of the visit.

As Graham and his wife take their seats at the table, their shoulders are touched and patted by the hung-over Brothers. As Abbott Francis looks at them he has a powerful sense that the moment they are in is already behind them.

He looks around for the daughter, but she isn't there.

'You will love this joke,' Patel instructs his captives, pressing his palms downwards to keep the happiness that is at the centre of the Earth from erupting too quickly. 'Listen, listen,' he says, barely able to contain himself.

'A chicken walks into the Central Archive. He walks up to the Chief Archivist and says, "Buk." The Archivist looks at him and says, "You want a book?"

'"Buk."

'"Any book?"

'"Buk."

'So she gives the chicken a book and the chicken leaves.

'Later, the chicken returns. "Buk buk."

'"You want another book?" she asks.

'"Buk buk."

'So she gives the chicken another book and the chicken leaves. Later that same day the chicken returns for a third time. "Buk buk buk," it says.

'"You want a third book?"

'"Buk buk buk."

'"You read the other two?"

'"Buk buk buk."

'So the Archivist hands the chicken a third book, but this time,' Brother Patel chuckles, 'but this time,' he says, shaking

429

as the best part approaches, 'she gets suspicious. So she follows the chicken out of the Archive, across the sands, through the Gone World, to a small pond at the edge of the forest, where the chicken swims up to a bullfrog on a lily pad. The chicken shows the bullfrog the book. And the bullfrog looks at it and croaks ... "Read it."'

Everyone erupts in laughter except poor Brother Jacob. Confused, he shakes his head and says, 'Chickens can't swim,' at which point all order is lost.

Alessandra is outside the hall, walking along a worn footpath by the perimeter of the compound. The first leaves are beginning to fade and she stops beyond the Gathering House to admire them. The few trees inside the Stadium are all small and food-bearing. The surrounding desert turns no colours beyond what the sky offers and the air lacks the wild scents of the forest that have awakened parts of her that, until now, had not known they were sleeping.

Sensing movement, she turns her head, her hand moving to her knife before she sees Abbott Francis.

'Good morning,' he says. 'I missed you at breakfast. Walk with me?'

The grounds of the compound are well-manicured. As they walk, the path slowly transforms beneath her feet from dirt into an artful walkway of carefully laid flat rocks mixed increasingly with sea glass from the special lake. The closer Alessandra and the Abbott stroll to the centre of the compound, the more intricate and colourful the path becomes until, finally, they arrive at a well in the centre of a mosaic so vibrant and alive it looks like a star that has fallen to earth.

Five paths converge here, set with curved wooden benches that wrap around the well.

Francis invites her to sit down, then joins her.

'Did you build all this?'

'Me? No, of course not. I'm not that creative. Hundreds of people did this over decades. I did make two of the benches, though, and carried stones for the well. I worked on the roof of that one over there too.'

'No, I mean, did you start all of this?'

'Oh. Oh no, I'm the third Abbott. This is our seventy-fourth year here. We were once part of a large and glorious colony but we're all that remains. That's a story for another day. Next year we'll have a big party. I fear you're going to miss it.'

'Why are there no women here?' she asks him.

'I suppose,' he replies, 'that it would require an unusual kind of woman.'

'Unusual . . . how?'

'Unusual . . . weird. Men will often join a company of women, but women seldom choose to join a company of men – even if they're as charming as we are.'

'That's probably true.'

'Why,' he asks. 'Do you want to stay? You can, you know. You are welcome here.'

'No.' Alessandra taps her right foot. 'What do you do here? Other than eat and drink and laugh and argue?'

'There's more?'

'I mean . . . what's your purpose? Why live out here in the middle of nowhere all by yourselves?'

'Oh, right. You all have a grand purpose. It must be hard for someone as young as you to imagine a way of life that isn't directed towards something specific.'

Alessandra says nothing.

'Well . . .' he continues, trying to answer, 'I think it's pretty here. It's nicer than many other places I've been. I like it more

431

than the desert. It's cooler in the summer and a bit warmer in the winter because of the trees as the winds don't much bother us. We don't get many bad people passing through because there's no reason to come here. The food's okay most of the time. If I become lonely for new faces I travel, but I always come back. But I don't think that's what you mean. You want to know if we have a grand purpose too.'

'Yes.'

'There are different ways to contribute to the world. One of the most important is to be the kind of person you wish there were more of. There's no telling what kind of effect that will have, but I can promise you that the only wrong answer is "none at all".'

Alessandra looks away from him to the ground.

'What happened to your friend?' he asks gently. 'The one who didn't come out of the hole with you?'

'I don't want to talk about it.'

'Tell me anyway. We have to be brave in the face of time and I don't think our paths are going to cross again. I can't promise that I'll hear you better, but no one else will hear you the same way.'

'She was hurt – she couldn't climb up the rope fast enough. I'm sure Master Birch waited as long as she could and I don't blame her. But it wasn't long enough.'

'You're not only grieving. You're carrying something. Do you blame yourself?'

'I could have pulled harder.'

'I don't think that's it. Your hands were bloodied when you arrived and so were your father's. Unless she was a metre from the top a little extra effort would have changed nothing. The guilt isn't from physical weakness; it's closer to your heart.'

'I lied to her.'

'I see.' There is no condemnation in his tone.

'There was something she thought was important to keep and I thought it was better to throw it away, so when she wasn't there, I did. She ordered me out of the bunker so I could save what I'd already destroyed. I feel like I ... I don't know ...'

'Like you betrayed her.'

She looks at her feet.

'What did you throw away?'

'Evil – knowledge about all kinds of evil things people did to each other in the past. There was a Trove – a very special kind of Trove. I only kept the good things.'

'Why did she want you to keep the evil?'

'She thought it was best to remember. She said that the past being buried is very different from burying the past.'

'How old was she?'

'Sixteen.'

'Sixteen,' Francis repeats.

Alessandra senses of the weight of Elimisha's words by studying the Abbott's face. Does that mean she was wrong?

'I did understand what she meant,' Alessandra explains. 'If we bury the truth on purpose it'll come back to haunt us somehow. But ... we all have secrets, don't we? The Commonwealth has secrets. The Order of Silence has secrets. All the Archives in the Territory and beyond are secret. Survival of all human Knowledge is based on secrecy. I don't see why it's okay for those things to be secret and not some Knowledge about the past.'

She turns to the Abbott, wanting him to understand. Her voice cannot hide the depths of her appeal. 'The Ancients hated each other – they did awful, *awful* things to each other for reasons that don't matter any more. If we bring those memories back, people will feel shame and anger and want revenge.

433

Other people might start to adopt those words and categories and ideas and start to believe them. Remembering all that could be the reason for new wars, new evils. I realise what she said was important, but I don't see how Attesting to all that is necessarily better.'

'Do you think you did the right thing?' the Abbott asks her.

'I don't know – I thought so at the time, but now, out here in the woods, I wish we still had it so we could talk about it together. What do you think?' she asks him.

What does he think? It's a good question.

'I think,' he answers carefully, 'it's less important how much you know than what you choose to do with it. I've never entirely understood the Commonwealth's hunger for Knowledge. There does appear to be a greater emphasis on finding it and saving it than putting it to good use. I think many people share my confusion, and that's part of your problem.'

'Lilly says you can't get anything done unless you know how to do it.'

'That's reasonable,' the Abbott says, 'but it applies more to things than to people. If you want to get things done with people, you need to know their stories and what they learn from them. It's rather different.'

'My father,' Alessandra says, 'believes that art and music and stories all make us more connected to each other; they show us that we're not alone.'

'That's certainly true. But they also teach us how we're different from one another too. Understanding those differences and knowing how to manage them is better than pretending that we're all the same.'

'A lot of the differences I learned about from the Trove don't exist any more,' Alessandra says, digging the toe of her boot into the mosaic to see if any of the sea glass will move. It won't. The reflection from the sun is mesmerising. Sitting at the centre of all that color makes her feel like she's on a stage of some kind; it elevates her sense of purpose. It makes her want to talk, as though talking here will make the words and the lessons more lasting. She knows, even now, that she will never forget this feeling: the need to arrive at Truth.

'If the point of all this is to make life better for people,' Alessandra answers, 'we may need to forget things and start fresh.'

'That conclusion,' Francis says, 'would put you at odds with your entire culture.'

'I know.'

'And your parents.'

'I know.'

'You must feel quite alone.'

'Yes.'

'But not at peace with that reality.'

'I'm not sure I'm right. How can it be right to forget? To pretend massive things didn't happen to all those people? To simply wipe out their pain?'

'So if I understand correctly, you're conflicted because remembering might be a threat to the living but forgetting is a betrayal of the dead.'

She gazes at him. 'Yeah, I guess that's it.'

'Your pain is starting to take the form of a question. It's a question about your friend, but also a question about everyone else, above all, the Ancients. Can you hear it? If you can, you should voice it.'

Alessandra looks her hands. The ones which had been unable to hold the rope. 'What do we owe the dead?' she answers.

The Abbott pats her hand. He places a piece of blue sea glass in her palm. It is smooth and rounded, but for a chip in the clouded surface revealing a beautiful, watery interior. 'Take this,' he says. 'It's a tradition of ours. Once you come up with a good question, you take a glass stone and you hold it as a symbol of your question. When you feel you are ready to part with the question – because you've answered it, or outgrown it, or replaced it with a better one – you leave the stone in a special place of your choosing. Picking one up and letting one go are both acts of growth and wisdom.'

'Thank you.'

'We place our old questions in an empty lakebed. You might have passed it on the way here.'

Alessandra cracks a smile.

'Oh come on. That was better than the chicken joke. I know you heard it through the window.'

'I kind of liked the chicken joke.'

VERENA'S LETTER

Dear Lilly,

It is unlikely you will see this letter, but I have been assured that if the secret of the Southern Commonwealth is ever revealed the Order will hand it to you. The odds of that happening in both of our lifetimes is low. As I leave you the Stadium is secure and filled with a new structure and purpose and vision that we never had before. It was your courage, your Find, that unified us and strengthened us and gave us purpose. You should be proud of what you've created and what you have done for us all.

Unfortunately, what is best for the Commonwealth is worse for us and so we become victims of what we love most.

I'm writing this the night before I depart and I'm leaving it here with the Order because I'm not allowed to share this information beyond the Stadium's walls.

I'm in the Central Archive now and it's very late. I've been permitted three hours of solitary access because it's supposed to instil in me a sense of purpose and understanding about why I'm doing this.

The Archive is a special place at night. It feels like being inside the womb of civilisation itself. There is a sense of floating, like a baby, with everything we know about the world all around us. I felt both unborn and also the centre of the universe.

I have everything to explore and read and I'm allowed access to even the most fragile texts. But would you believe I'm spending the evening reading Calvin and Hobbes and writing to you?

I was once told that everything found in the Harrington Box was held in such awe that it took the Evaluators months to realise the comics were meant to be funny and it was okay for us all to laugh. It was interesting to learn that you can stare at something, even focus all your mind on it, and still not see it for what it is.

I don't want to know anything new before I leave. Instead, I want to revel, one last time, in a sense of home and domesticity: the very things, of course, I know I'll never have with you. I wish we could have had that, the two of us. We could have adopted a child, maybe two. Or one of us could have become pregnant. Probably you. I know there are some fine men you have your eyes on.

I imagine a life that is less ambitious, less curious and more contented. But still I go.

I have been asked to join the new High Command of the Southern Commonwealth as the liaison. If you are reading this, you'll know about the Museum already. Though I haven't seen it yet, I have to tell you that it is a remarkable thing. It is located in a place once called Mexico, in a region named Oaxaca. The people say there was a city with that name but it's long gone now. The people fled into the mountains to the east and took shelter at the Museum, much like The Few found the Stadium.

The population of the Museum is around ninety or so, I'm told. They have a festival that they insist dates back long before The Rise – what they call 'El Cambio', or the Change. The festival is a celebration called the Guelaguetza. Though the main languages there are Espanyol and our Common, which they call English (and I suppose we should too?), the word 'Guelaguetza' comes from another language called Zapotec. Apparently, cultures are built on the remains of other cultures, like ours

438

is built on The Rise. Even languages seem to lay one on top of another, influencing and enriching with new ideas and practices. (Oh, Lilly, there is so much to know!)

What is important about this festival – and may be essential to our survival – is that the word Guelaguetza evokes an ethos called the *obligación de la reciprocidad*: the obligation of reciprocity. They believe very deeply in the mutual and heartfelt exchange of gifts and services and blessings and it is this belief which has made their hearts open to exchanging with us. Our Explorers told them about our love for Knowledge and how The Crossing emerged as a place of exchange.

I've always thought of The Crossing as a very practical place, one driven by necessity, but they see it as a symbol and the more I think about it, picturing it in my mind rising from the sands and flying over an ancient river of green trees and grasses, only to descend back into the sands again, I can begin to see the beauty and romance of it the way they do. That eluded me before, and I think it's because I know what happened to you there, and what you did – what you had to do with Cardo and the others. I wasn't able to see past that history into what it has become. Again, Lilly, it's all because of you.

The Museum people feel that such a culture is like their own and that somehow our souls are already intertwined. They have a lovely way of talking, as though much of what comes from our minds is motivated first by the heart. I wonder if I will learn to see the world this way too. This sense of us being connected has made it easy to open relations with them and build trust. That trust, Lilly, will double the size of the known world. With this at stake, I have been asked to go there and oversee the progress of our friendship.

Can you think of anything more important, more vital? Even us?

The existence of the Southern Commonwealth is the greatest secret we possess. Should the Northern Command fall and the people need to flee, there is an escape route – we call it the Blue Route. It is the road I'm taking, in the company of an Explorer who knows it. I leave at dawn.

439

I will describe it to you, because if you are reading this, it is your future, and it will be hard.

Our Stadium, as you know, was once a major attraction for visitors. Years ago, The Few found boats behind the waterfall – this has been kept secret from everyone but the military. The hulls of these boats should have rotted over time, but they didn't because the material is particularly resilient. Visitors would ride these glass-roofed boats out from under the waterfall and tour the river which, I'm told, once looked and ran differently than it does today. The fifty boats are each named for a state in the United States (that's the region of the world where the Evaluators think we live now). Each can hold twenty people. Because of the flow of the river these days and the fact that the engines no longer work, any use of the boats would be a one-way journey, so they have been saved in case a mass evacuation is needed. The people will travel with the boats for about a month. The river water is undrinkable, but Explorers and members of the Order have created depots along the way with supplies and fresh water. This is one of the reasons we discourage talk about the Shining City and other myths to the west. The truth is, there are such cities but they're ruins and we don't want people stumbling on our caches in their search for them.

After a month you will reach mountains so high that they are capped with snow even in summer. You will leave the boats here because the waters now run too shallow. From there, you walk due west. The going will be hard and the young and old will suffer the most. Hunting will be plentiful. You'll find the hills teeming with deer, wild boar and jackrabbits. The Explorers say the ease of the hunt will be an indicator of your safety because only animals that know people are afraid of them.

There are fruits growing wild along the route; enough to sustain even a thousand people on the journey.

Eventually, I'm told, we will meet the ocean. This will be less like a body of water than it will an image of the sky having fallen to earth. I am looking forward to seeing it.

On the beach, which is much like a desert that touches the water, ancient

440

ships rest on their sides, half-buried in sand. Hundreds of massive containers rise from the shore, colourful monoliths or grave markers of giants or monsters who once roamed the coastline. There are carts and wheels, pipes and tubing, toys and artificial limbs – I am told to prepare myself for the thousands of human-like bodies that have washed to shore. Apparently, they are incredibly lifelike, with eyes staring blindly as if their attention has been seized and their minds are in rapture. They are robots or humanics, machines built to serve the Ancients which were made to look like them.

From there the route turns south and you will walk along the coast. Solar generators will purify drinking water, but now the problem of food will grow more acute. After that, it's too hard for me to explain. He tried to tell me what a selva is (in his language it means 'trees more dense than a wall'?) but that makes no sense to me.

What I do know is this: we join continents together, the north and the south – you and me.

I will not be allowed to write again because I cannot compromise the Secret. No information about us is allowed to flow north. I also think that you need to let me go. I know how you are: if we communicated in secret (I'm sure you'd find a way!), you would never move on with your life. All the same, I plan to keep a personal account of my experiences here as part of the Archive. My papers will be waiting for you when you arrive.

Dear Lilly, we have duties that are larger than our own lives: a commitment to keep the world and its memories alive, to solve the problems of the world with knowledge and passion and promise. Like you, I will keep my vows to the Commonwealth. I regret only that I did not make my own vows to you.

An artist here has written a poem for the children to memorise on the boats, before the Long Walk. It is sung to the same tune as the 'Season Song' – every child at the Stadium knows it. My heart is torn because I hope no child will ever have to learn it – but also that no child will ever forget it if they do.

As I think about it now, it is also my song to you.

We're taking a trip
We're going away
To find a new home
A place we will stay.

The walk will be hard
The walk will be far.
But we won't be alone
Whoever we are.

Remember the coast
Where water meets land
If I become lost
I will go there and stand.

And if it grows dark
I will be brave and be strong
I will scare off the monsters
Until help comes along.

I'll need water to drink
and food for my tummy
A safe place to sleep
So I can be comfy.

I might have to wait
Through sun and through snow
But I trust you will find me
Wherever I go.

Yours in love.
Verena

V
LATER

THE SONG OF US

When the refugees from the Stadium arrived, almost eighteen months later, they learned that the people of the Museum did not only celebrate the *Guelaguetza*, but also another festival called *Dia de la Asuncion de la Virgen Guadalupe*: a celebration for the goddess of life and nature.

A silver-haired woman of indeterminate age and excellent posture gathered them all into the field outside and addressed them in English. Everyone was acutely aware, after the Long Walk, that this was the largest gathering of people on this continent in four hundred years.

The woman's name was Gabriela deSoto. She had welcoming eyes.

'According to legend,' she started, 'a goddess was born, perfect and without sin, from the heart of the forest itself. Her kindness and beauty were so intense that the forest chose to give her a son so they could be happy together and her love could be directed to something good and outside herself. But sadly, the son grew heartsick when he became a man because he had no woman of his own to love, and for all the love he had for his mother, something inside him started to die.

'Guadalupe was rent by a pain inside her very soul because she had not imagined that their love would not be enough. The son chose to go away and wander the world in search of a wife. He was gone for ten years and every day Guadalupe's tears would water the earth. The flowers bloomed around her but gave her no comfort. After ten years, the son returned, as broken as his mother was elated. She sheltered him and protected him, fed him and loved him, but the space between them had become as wide as the distance between two oceans, for each was longing for a kind of love they could never have.

'Today,' she continued, 'the people of the Stadium have arrived, but our tears are not those of Guadalupe, but instead the tears of lovers who do finally meet, face to face, the authors of the poems that captured our hearts. Today is not a day of welcome or even new friends, but of unification and home-coming. This is not a new place, my friends, but the missing half of your own homes.'

As Gabriela deSoto had hoped, the hardened and weary refugees broke down and cried in their embrace, fulfilling the circle of love that poor Guadalupe had been denied.

There had been no Rise here, no deforestation, no heavy winds pushing up the sands like in Nevada, no floods leaving behind cargo planes and containers. Here, it was the sea levels which had risen, flooding the low-lying lands, and as the waters rose it felt as though the world had dropped.

El Cambio: The Change.

Lilly, by then, had a limp. She was gaunt from the irregular diet and too much stress on her ageing body. Slowly, painfully, she had walked more than two thousand kilometres over varied terrain. Once upon a time, the stairs of the Snake Tower had been a challenge – on the Blue Route, she had had to face mountains. What sustained her was the message she had received: that although Master Birch was dead, Alessandra and the Wayworths all lived, and so did the Prize, which would meet them in the south.

To lose Verena and then the Prize on account of being too weak, too old? That would have been too much. So Lilly walked.

She didn't know the word *tumour* yet but she felt that something was growing inside her. Having, so long ago, carried a water baby, she felt a change. Unlike that time – which had felt like life – this felt like death.

Three days after they had arrived and been embraced by the people of the Museum, Lilly met Alessandra in the oval 'gift shop'. With soaring ceiling and skylights and tall windows along a curved wall, it was an elegant – and empty – space. Alessandra, who had arrived with her parents four months earlier, had chosen it precisely because it was secluded and unused. This would be the new Communications Room.

When they embraced, Lilly felt frail and old to Alessandra.

Instead of asking about the Music Man, Master Birch and Chief Elimisha, though, Lilly went right to the point. Sitting herself on a white plastic chair, she said, 'Okay, show it to me.'

The Museum has a total floor area of over twenty thousand square metres, with over six thousand square metres of gallery suites for displays and exhibitions. Even with a thousand people inside, the Museum is mostly empty; quiet space is easy to find. The gift shop-turned-Comms is one of the many unused rooms that had long since been cleaned out by looters and abandoned by the community.

Still, it's clean.

'Once a year,' Alessandra tells Lilly while unpacking Lilly's

White Board and unfolding the Haptic Command Gear, 'the entire community sweeps and washes and dusts the whole place in preparation for yet another holiday. This one they call *Navidad*.'

'What does that mean?'

'Christmas.'

'Which is . . . what?'

'I don't know,' Alessandra admits. 'I haven't looked it up yet, but I know it's something to do with a virgin giving birth to the son of God in the desert and a man in a heavy winter coat who then shows up to give him gifts.'

'In the desert?'

'Yes. And the coat's red. With white trimming. And there are bells.'

'I don't care. Show me the Archive.'

Alessandra had carried it as though it were a newborn baby, with all the care of a mother holding the fate of the world. Now she extends her hands and allows Lilly to reach out and pick it up. 'Be careful,' she says.

'Well . . . obviously.' Lilly is gripping it carefully but tightly, as though it might be an object in a dream she can see but not grasp.

'It's so light,' she says.

'Knowledge doesn't weigh anything,' Alessandra explains.

'No, I suppose it doesn't.' Lilly's hands are shaking a little. She has stopped holding sharp objects due to this new affliction and has instead taken to barking commands to cover for her increasing palsy which she generally denies despite it being obvious. Seeing that Alessandra is nervous about it, she says, 'I won't drop it. My grip is good. The shaking is something else.'

'It doesn't seem worth the risk,' Alessandra whispers.

'It is,' says Lilly, 'because when you reach the end of your

448

life and there's a chance to hold everything you earned – everything you sacrificed for – in the palm of your hand, you do it. And if you can let someone else do it, you do that too, especially when it's me saying I won't drop it. You're honestly telling me that this is a library?'

'Come,' Alessandra says, taking Lilly's other hand and pulling her up. 'I want to show you the world.'

The room Alessandra has picked for Lilly's journey into the Quantum Drive is the small unused office connected to the gift shop. This will be the new Central Archive. The room that the Museum now uses, she has decided, will be called the Library. Everyone will be able to access the Library. The Central Archive will be another matter. She – not Lian – will be the new Central Archivist.

And if the adults don't agree to this, she's decided, she will withhold the password protection she and the Librarian placed on it.

The password is Redemption. No one knows but her.

After showing Lilly the basic mechanics of the Haptic Command Gear, White Board and glasses, Alessandra leaves her to explore.

Lilly emerges from the secluded room thirty hours later, her eyes red from so many tears. Outside, in the jungle, the weather is hot and humid. Gabriela deSoto, the ruling Matriarch – who is slightly suspicious of Lilly, which Lilly considers an excellent instinct – says that summers are usually like this, and winters are very, very wet, which is, actually, a blessing because the rainwater is drinkable whereas the ground water can cause terrible pains in the stomach and even blindness.

Lilly has listened to these important facts with little interest and now, after her experience with the Quantum Drive, she has even less. She is not in charge here and will not live long enough to die by anything external. Her end, she knows, is already inside her. The Quantum Drive, however, is a new life.

When Lilly emerges from the new Central Archive, she finds in the new comms room reading a book he's found in the library. He isn't waiting for her, but is the first to see her.

'Welcome back,' he says to her as she stumbles out.

'Has Alessandra explained to you what's on that machine?' she asks.

'I'll have to look myself. I find it hard to imagine.'

'It's been said,' Lilly says, sitting down beside him on a rolling chair, 'that Paradise is our questions answered. Your daughter pulled Paradise from a place called Inferno.'

'She's a great kid,' Graham says.

'She has planted a seed that will restore civilisation itself.'

'That's great. I'll definitely take a look. Unfortunately, the suit Alessandra brought with her doesn't fit me. I think I'm a large.'

'You can use the glasses alone,' Lilly says, rubbing her eyes again. 'And I think we have a large in stock too.'

'I was making a joke.'

'Oh yes, I'd forgotten about your sense of humour. It turns out,' she says, thumbing over her shoulder, 'there used to be funnier people than you. They used to stand before an audience and tell humorous stories, sometimes for up to an hour. It was called "stand-up comedy" – although some were sitting down.'

'Uh huh.'

'Graham,' Lilly says, changing the subject, 'I know Gabriela deSoto is the Chief of the High Command here, which is fine, but she has a rather relaxed attitude towards security. In fact . . .

there's no security around here,' she says, waving her hands for emphasis. 'No procedures, no armed guards, no perimeter defences, no walls. It's like the early days before I found the Harrington Box and we got organised. I thought Verena would have locked this place down.'

'It's quite peaceful, Lilly. I rather like it.'

'It's great until all of a sudden it's not.'

'One could make a pretty strong argument,' he says, 'that this place is so nice and peaceful because of whatever it was Verena did. One thing I've learned is that there's always more going on than meets the eye. Have you, for example, actually talked to anyone yet?'

'I'll get around to it.'

'Uh huh,' he says again. 'Meanwhile, Chief, there's no one out there.' He puts the book down. 'We just walked a thousand miles and we saw barely anyone – a few colonies, the odd bandit. There's no force out in the woods here. The Museum is also armed and Gabriela has a Rapid Reaction Force – I've already talked to them. They're called *los Agradables* – the Agreeables. Isn't that great? They're sharp. I'm not worried.'

'Charming. Here's what we're really going to do,' Lilly says, forgetting that she's neither twenty-six nor in charge.

According to Lilly, the first task was to use the maps and schematics from the internet Find to help them locate more HAM Radios so they could establish communications with the Northern Command. The artificial intelligence known as the Librarian on the Quantum Drive helped them find locations where HAM radios were either once sold or repaired, or had been used in Mexico in the final years before *El Cambio*. Expeditions would be sent out to retrieve as many as possible – at least one and up to thirty; Lilly had plans. Using a term coined by Elimisha, these operations were to be called Discover and Recover, or D&R missions.

Second, but concurrent, was to find another empty Quantum Drive (or as many as possible) and copy the full contents of their own. The Commonwealth would still need Runners and it would still need off-site locations to store the Archives, but they probably wouldn't need Chiefs to command them any more, because the Archives could be hidden and also (they learned) password-protected, so the Quantum Drives would be worthless if found by anyone else. Each one would be a Harrington Box that was completely secured, even against people as smart as Lilly.

The new structure of society was already taking place in Lilly's mind. The pieces fit together with symmetry and purpose, designed to achieve a condition in the world that Lilly alone could see but everyone could be made to understand.

A fine piece of engineering.

It was not only the Quantum Drive that revitalised Lilly after the Long Walk and the growing awareness of her own limited time. It was the opportunity to *think* again. Here was the quickening in her chest she'd been missing; the sense of driving purpose that was nearly sexual in its capacity to fulfil.

Ah, to stop making buckets with Luther and imagine the unimaginable again: to go forth into the future with the confidence and clarity of youth.

Yes, this is what got her into trouble the first time: a supreme confidence in her own conclusions, driven in part by personal trauma. Then, it had been her mother. Now, to a lesser extent, it was the Long Walk and losing Verena a second time.

It was hard for her to learn from these lessons, though. Maybe if she knew how everyone on the continent east of Yellow Ridge had somehow heard about the Commonwealth and decided to hate it, she'd have a better grasp of what she'd done right or wrong. But that was an unanswerable mystery, at least for now. Perhaps, someday, if there was ever peace with those people and they could talk to one another in confidence about their mutual errors, she'd learn how word had travelled to them and prejudiced their minds against her and hers.

She was in the comms room explaining her master plan to Graham when the thought struck her: could it have been *Adam*?

They'd ostracised him even though he was only a boy, saying his visions and character were a disturbance to the peace. Even his mother, Lilly's aunt, hadn't been able to plead for him, for her argument had been based only on love, not reason. She'd had no argument left to make, which is why she'd left too.

Lilly had never heard from them again. She hadn't known where they went, until Birch told her that Adam had gone east, and that some of the Order had been concerned about his loose talk.

What if he had met people, Lilly wondered, *and what if these people had believed him? What if the Keepers believed him and learned of the Commonwealth and came to see the Commonwealth as a threat? What if* Adam *had created the Keepers?*

Could Adam, Verena and Lilly – all of them, and in their own ways – have started all this? Had the three of them been the cause that took fifty years to reach its effect? Had this drama always been destined to play out like a Greek tragedy?

'Lilly?'

The voice is familiar and calming and warm, a voice she knows and recognises and loves.

'Lilly? Have you finally snapped?'

Graham.

'Not yet.'

'You drifted off there.'

'I had an idea I've never had before. I don't know how it never occurred to me.'

'Something you want to share?'

'Graham . . . did you talk to them? The Keepers?'

Graham is still sitting with a leg crossed, his boot up on a chair. He no longer carries the knife, not since arriving here.

'Yes.'

'Do you know why they attacked us?'

Graham draws a deep breath of the lush air into his lungs, air filled with the smells of plants and rain and sunlight and life. He would hold it there for ever if he could, but each time he exhales it is an opportunity to draw it in again. It's strange the way this place has made him more sentimental.

'We all want things to be better, but we're all at odds on how to achieve it and that is a terrible, terrible pity.'

'How did they come to us, though? How did they gather such forces against us? What made it start?'

'I don't know. Why?'

'I think I might know,' Lilly says, 'and if I'm right – and I am beginning to suspect that I am – then I have seriously overestimated the power of walls and weapons and seriously underestimated the power of words.'

According to the Librarian of the Quantum Drive, the Museum was founded in 2048 with a grant from the Organisation of American States – the OAS – to celebrate one hundred years of regional solidarity. Inspired by Frank Gehry's Guggenheim Museum in Bilbao, Spain, the sweeping steel and glass building of irregular curves perches on the top of a glorious hill in the Sierra Madre of Oaxaca that faces east over the plains of Veracruz and out towards the Gulf of Mexico far beyond. Ground was not broken for construction, however, until 2069, because of tardy payments, new hostility towards multilateral cooperation, financial skimming, corruption and political backsliding.

Five years later, the Museum's basic structure and interior were completed, but at sixty per cent over budget, and almost immediately the project faltered and became a symbol of internecine conflict.

By 2080 the OAS was rendered irrelevant because of growing 'localisation', which was the term given to the revolt against globalisation, the counterforce that claimed to resist 'imperial homogenisation' and 'culturcide'. Countries and cultures wanted their own languages and religions and ways of life back. Cooperation was mistakenly thought to be antithetical to those goals.

The warm oak-panelled halls were never filled with the promised art, only with echoes and accusations. By the beginning of the Solar War, the Museum had been abandoned and forgotten.

But one piece had been installed, and here it remains, perfect and bright, even after all these centuries. The title of the exhibit, *The Sound of Us*, is carved into a brass plaque in Spanish, English, Portuguese and French, the four languages most prominent in the Americas. It is on display in a space inspired by – and larger than – something called the Turbine Hall at the Tate Modern Museum in London. It is a room for enormous installations, to support the expression of limitless imagination.

Ilimitada imaginación.
Imaginação ilimitada.

Imagination illimitée.

The first and only installation, as seen from the side, looks to be a massively tangled jumble of red tubes that begins at a single point near the floor on one side, rises to the ceiling, where the entanglement fills most of the hall, and then, at the far end, descends again to another single point.

As the spectator stands at the southern tip, however, the perspective changes and it becomes clear that the tangled tubes are an impressionistic but still discernible map of the entirety of the Americas, from Islote Águila in Chile all the way to Cape Columbia on Ellesmere Island in Canada at over 83 degrees north – a point even further north than the destination where Alessandra has argued that a D&R must be sent: Svalbard, Norway.

The long red tube that meets the viewer is a mouthpiece.

'Speak,' says the plaque in four languages, 'and become *The Sound of Us.*'

And so the child – it's so often a child – says something into the open end, something simple, even trite.

'¡Hola!'

The enthusiasm of that greeting enters the tubes made of aluminium and carbon fibre and travels to the far end – but not in a straight line, and nor does it travel only once. Instead, the message splits thirty-five times, staggering and cutting, colliding and harmonising so that the sound, symbolically passing through all thirty-five states, becomes a kind of music.

When Lilly was young and opened the Harrington Box and shocked the people of the Stadium into action by announcing that never again would the world be darkened by ignorance and superstition, she was driven – she knows now – by fear. The death of her mother had been the prime mover and she was the turbine that turned that experience into a new energy.

Here, among the Mexicans of Oaxaca and high up on a hill that was once inland and overlooking the plains of Veracruz (which have long-since vanished under the water, making the Sierra Madres a coastal mountain range now), no one is driven by fear any more.

They had been rent from their homes and set out on a journey – an Exodus – that should have broken their spirit and made them bitter, but instead they walked the devastated lands and found them empty: a world bereft and in need of husbandry and hope and possibility.

And when they arrived, they met a people who believed in that already, and in their hearts, without ever having had to make that same arduous trek.

So when Lilly sat with Graham and Henry and Gabriela deSoto and a lovely man named Don Carlo (who sported a stylish, close-ly-cropped grey beard and had almost black eyes), she pitched her plan and they heard it with new ears, for by then, they too had spent days on the Quantum Drive, following their own curiosities into stories and pictures, emotions and recriminations about how foolish – how *damned* foolish – mankind was.

When Lilly explains the plan, it comes out more ... *technical* ... than she had planned. But she is far too excited to filter her thoughts. She feels forty years younger, with the energy of a stallion.

They sit at the table Lilly has had hauled into the gift shop – which she has renamed the Communications Room, leaving out any reference to weapons. This, she explains, is going to be the hub for a new global network of communications. This is where the Commonwealth will steer the fate of humanity.

Gabriela and Don Carlo both speak English. The kind of English Lilly is now speaking – having spent weeks in dialogue with the Librarian – makes no sense to anyone. Her enthusiasm, however, speaks volumes:

'Understanding challenges of propagation for the HAM radios is going to be a major problem if we want to start getting positive reception at serious distances on a stable basis,' Lilly sort-of explains. 'What we need, but don't have access to, is solar flare activity and information on background x-ray flux. The thing is, the green skies that we are all accustomed to, especially in Northern Command, are caused by charged particles in the Earth's upper atmosphere interacting with the Earth's natural magnetic field lines. What happens is, HAM radio signals scatter off these particles, greatly enhancing propagation on the VHF and UHF radio bands – the truth is, it was sheer dumb luck that I had tuned the Stadium's radio to an F-layer frequency, which is what allowed long-distance signals to better refract off the ionosphere, especially at night. That's how we first managed to hear those distant voices. Dumb luck, though,' she concedes, assuming anyone is understanding her, 'isn't a strategy. So what I'm proposing is that we fill this room with radios using the information that the Librarian has given us on where we might find them using our new D&R teams, and then I suggest we train up our Explorers into a new class of traveller we'll call Engineers. They'll need to have the skills of Runners and the minds of Scribes. I want these people to position and build and maintain as needed a set of relay-stations at various intervals all across the Americas – and beyond the Americas, if we can get there. Those radio signals I caught over the last fifty years? Now I know how the radio works, we're going to look for them. And we're going to learn their languages. It turns out that "*Sayonara*" is Japanese – it actually means goodbye. No more messing around: I want the song of us to be heard *everywhere*.

'And once that's done, I want to talk about boats, because Alessandra Wayworth – now Commander Wayworth, because apparently we need three of those – has plans that involve a small island in the heart of the Arctic Circle.'

SVALBARD

Seven months later, Lilly sits in her wheelchair in front of Workstation Three in the Communications Room, having displaced Maria Consuela Lopez (despite Maria being their best Radio Operator). The tumour in her spine is growing larger and there is constant discomfort, which gets worse when she's immobile too long. The Southerners – with a more caustic wit than their northern compatriots – have dubbed her wiggling and adjusting movements as *baile del Diablo*, or the Devil's dance, but there's little she can do about it. There might be only one Commonwealth connecting two continents now, but there's definitely more than one sense of humour.

Lilly doesn't care about any of this at the moment for she is growing extremely impatient. 'Would it kill your daughter to send us a message?'

'She's busy, Lilly,' Graham says, trying to calm her down as one might a child.

Alessandra is on an ice-breaker in the Greenland Sea, latitude seventy-eight degrees north and approaching their final destination. She is leading the first intercontinental Discover &

Recover in the Commonwealth's history. It will also be among the most important, if she's successful.

Everyone is waiting to find out the results and Lilly's anxiety is palpable. Those gathered know she doesn't have time for these long pauses any more and Lilly's heart – say those who knew Verena well and loved her and drank with her and cried with her and have heard a thousand stories about Lilly long before the woman herself arrived – has done too much waiting.

Su corazon. Everything is about the heart with these people. Lilly rather likes it.

This gathering and the interminable quiet are the results of Alessandra and Elimisha's experience in the bunker where they discovered that baby polar bears are cute and followed that sentiment to the discovery of the vault – a discovery which set the Wayworths in motion again. Henry and Graham took to the land, and Alessandra made preparations for the sea.

The Quantum Drive possessed a detailed roster of all the markets, stores and warehouses that once sold or repaired VHF and HF radios in Mexico City, which was northwest of the Museum, and Guatemala City, to the southeast, which meant the expeditions would know where to look within a few metres – or at least, they would once they'd all learned to read maps.

Guatemala City was, at the time of the Librarian's last update, 1,500 metres above sea level, and Mexico City was over 2,200. Each, they hoped, a fantastic sprawling metropolis in some state of disrepair with treasure waiting to be claimed.

Henry and Graham led separate and parallel D&R teams of twenty: Graham went to Mexico City; Henry to Guatemala City.

The expeditions both took three months.

Each city was a jungle now, with towers rising out of the green the way the Gone World rose from the sands.

The teams each established two tower-top signal relays and returned with nineteen radios between them.

That left Alessandra's project by sea.

As her parents ventured out into the unknown jungles, Alessandra's team made for the waters to the east, coming from the Sierra Madres and into the state of Veracruz, where the Atlantic Ocean had long since inundated the city of Heroica Veracruz, scattering its memories across the western world on the North Atlantic gyre, the currents of the Gulf Stream.

Lilly and Alessandra were both counting on the Mexican government's long-term preparations for climate change at the Veracruz Shipyard, which had been built in 1982, then considerably updated and expanded in 2051 by a Dutch architectural firm specialising in industrial off-shore projects for facilities that had once been coastal or inland. As it was Mexico's first heavy naval construction centre, the D&R teams considered the Floating Veracruz Shipyard the most likely place to still possess open-water craft able to take them north – that's as long as they'd not otherwise been sunk, stolen, vandalised or wrecked.

Alessandra's first dictate as a D&R commander was that everyone on her team learn how to swim. No one from the Stadium could and only a few from the Museum knew how. Alessandra had had to get video instructions from the Quantum Drive. The transition from classroom to open water had not been smooth.

They found the shipyard one and a half kilometres out at sea. The inland waters lapped against vegetation rather than sand and beyond was nothing but flotsam; most of it plastic bottles that had still not broken down and sunk below the surface. Sea Glass Lake was a glittering and serendipitous jewel forged in the unwitting fires of a catastrophe. This was the opposite: a floating mass of colorless filth caused by the apathy of inhumanity.

There would be no swimming through it, even if they could have managed the distance in the open ocean, which none of them could. After two weeks of searching, the team unearthed an 'unsinkable' Boston Whaler with a Unibond hull construction (according to the Librarian), sitting on a pile of rust that must once have been a carrier. The building housing it was now so covered in vines and hemmed in by trees that it took four days of chopping and hauling before they could extract the boat and pull it onto the main path that was once a road. After that they were able to lift it on steel wheels and a trellis.

It took another week for it to touch water.

And a day of rowing back and forth to move them with all their gear to the flotilla.

Their efforts, however, were not wasted, for there, dry-docked on the shipyard, was the very thing they'd been seeking: a Littoral Combat Ship, a near-shore vessel with open-water capabilities. It was the most sophisticated piece of engineering anyone had ever seen: built late in the twenty-first century for the Mexican Navy, it had survived not just the war, but also the rising acidity levels of the Gulf, because it had been stored in a wrapper the Librarian called 'Time Capsule Technology' designed to keep unused ships in pristine condition prior to deployment.

Alessandra named the ship the *Saavni* after the first Master of the Order of Silence.

The inexperienced crew focused their attention on learning the basics, especially propulsion and piloting, and tried their best to touch nothing else. Many of the systems were dependent on satellites and connectivity, none of which functioned, but the ship's electrical generators were powered by wave motion, each wave striking the hull turned into the electricity that turned the engines and propelled them forwards.

Below decks, they found ten pulse rifles similar to those at the Stadium.

Alessandra assigned one of the older men to be pilot. He was about the same age as her parents, with the scars and lines on his face to prove it. When he asked why he was being given that assignment, Alessandra told him she liked his name.

Everyone called him *Suerte*: Lucky.

He considered that an excellent reason.

They installed one of Lilly's radios and stocked up with provisions and finally, after months of preparation, they set sail for the north.

They followed the coast of Yucatan to the Cuban archipelago and from there, turned northwards to Florida, enjoying a lively debate on whether to retain the classical names or to respect the new ones they learned from the locals watching in awe and wonder as the Corvette glided past their simple dwellings.

In South Carolina, they met natives who fired at them as they sailed past. Alessandra ordered them into deeper waters.

Lucky piloted their ship successfully to the Norfolk Navy Yard, where they expected to find armaments and a possible settlement. They found nothing but destruction.

*

They docked the *Saavni* in Canada, because they now needed a craft that could handle more than the coast and more than mere cold.

They needed an icebreaker.

Despite the unimaginable levels of detail provided by the Librarian, no one really knew what awaited them. The Knowledge they had was four hundred years old, and as everyone agreed: *things change*.

Alessandra knew it was a gamble travelling to St John's in Newfoundland in search of the new boat, but Canada had maintained superb public records of the Coast Guard's actions and responses to climate change and war right up until the end. When the waters started rising in Labrador, the Canadian Coast Guard had, at considerable expense, started a new programme they called *Longevity*, futureproofing ships and facilities as best they could and dry-docking its fleet in newly built berths. The result was that her D&R team soon found her a new ship – an electrically powered Arctic 8 Icebreaker – in excellent condition.

Knowing that a single error – a single unnecessary risk – could doom the mission, it took them twelve days to figure out how to get it down from its perch and into the water.

The crossing from St John's to Ikerasassuaq at the southern tip of Greenland forced them into the Labrador Sea, the first stretch of open water they had ever faced – which made them the first humans to be surrounded by nothing but water since the Solar War.

They had to fight the southeasterly Baffin Currents dropping down the Canadian coast, then the East Greenland currents pushing them westwards as they tried to make for land.

It wasn't just the ocean causing problems. Even though they grew accustomed to the twenty-four-hour sun, the eternal light during the night-time confused them, filling them all with a restless energy that sapped them by day. Their skin darkened and their faces grew weathered. Their constantly squinting eyes were wrinkling on even the youngest crew members.

When they saw the coast of Svalbard they stood on the deck and cried.

Their approach to the island was the last Lilly heard of their location. Their lack of contact may have been due to the radio's signal being hard to maintain. Or maybe they sank. Or perhaps Alessandra was busy as a Captain and Commander of a mission.

Her theory, which she shared with Graham and Henry in the Comms room with dozens of others gathered around, was that Alessandra was a twenty-one-year-old former Urban Explorer and all-around pain-in-the-ass who couldn't be bothered to share what she was seeing at the moment.

In the Communications room, the windows are open and everyone is silent. The wind through the palm trees sounds like rain.

It is too much for Lilly, who starts barking orders to the operators. 'Give me a global radio check.'

Japanese, French, Mandarin, Spanish, English and German are spoken simultaneously into the radios, and each uplink transmission is followed by a brief pause before the foreign operators respond – and when those voices reassemble, they become a global *Song of Us*, filling the oval room with a cacophony of sound the likes of which the world has not heard since the fall of the Tower of Babel.

Each Radio Operator, trained to hear ambient noise as the enemy, wants to use headphones to avoid this din, but on this day Lilly has forbidden their use. She wants to hear the answers, even if she can't understand them; she wants to hear the world talk and answer back, to feel their voices in her chest.

'Maybe,' Lilly hears Graham say to her, 'we should play that song she wanted to hear? We come up on the hour in two minutes. Maybe it'll get her attention. What do you say?'

Lilly sniffs.

Commander Alessandra Wayworth, Captain of the Commonwealth Icebreaker *Elimisha*, stands at the prow in her red parka and stares ahead over the waters to the snow-capped mountains. Her glacier glasses are tight around her eyes. It is bright, but there is less ice than expected. The *Elimisha*'s electrical propulsion system offers maximum torque from one knot, which proved a blessing when they encountered an expanse of deep ice that had broken free of Greenland's glaciers and they'd had no way to avoid it, so had had no choice but to barrel through it. Now the *Elimisha* is cruising at ten knots through thin plates of floating ice that are no threat to the boat or her now-experienced team.

There are fair skies and visibility is excellent. The air smells like the colour of the sky.

Approaching the inlet that should take them to the vault, Alessandra turns backwards and uses her walkie-talkie to speak with the command deck above. 'Why am I not hearing anything?'

Lucky's voice crackles over the intercom. 'I think Southern Command is expecting you to call in.'

Abril has joined her at the prow. She is ten years older, and

Museum-born. Alessandra chose her as much for her glowing and optimistic personality as for her engineering prowess and problem-solving skills. She is taller than Alessandra and her black hair is long and tied at the back. Her smile is expansive, her enthusiasm contagious. She smiles out over the sea.

Lucky says, 'I lost the signal, Commander. I'm switching to the secondary band.'

'Pipe it through the speakers if you get it. It's coming up on thirteen hundred hours and they promised me a song. I don't want to miss it.'

Moments before the hour Lucky announces he has made contact again, and through the loudspeakers mounted to the deck, Alessandra hears Lucky's intercom being dragged across the table to the HAM radio's small speaker.

A woman's voice – more beautiful than any voice that has sung out over the waters of the Northern Hemisphere since *El Cambio* – starts her song with a simple hum before telling a story of defeat and love and loyalty as a man returns to Georgia on a midnight train.

The ten men and four women under Alessandra's command join Gladys Knight and the Pips sing 'He's leavin' . . .' as the ice-breaker glides east-northeast into the Isfjorden on the western coast of Svalbard, Norway.

The black rock to the south welcomes them like an out-stretched hand. The land is utterly bare, like it was at home when she was young, but this is a new, treeless tundra and not a desert.

'Two hundred years of recorded music before the Change,' says Abril, 'and the nineteen seventies are still the best.'

'Is that true for Spanish music too?' Alessandra asks.

'Oh, yes. I still have so much to listen to, but that is what moves me the most. That and the twenty fifties, because there was a roots revival then as the world tried to turn back the clocks and recover their national souls. It might have been a bad time for politics but it was wonderful for music.'

Abril has two younger sisters and a younger brother. She talks about them constantly. She tells Alessandra that she reminds her of her youngest sister in disposition but her brother in the heaviness behind her eyes. He fought against the Hidalgos fifteen years ago, experiencing terrible things, but he doesn't talk about it. Alessandra should meet him – *Do you like boys? You do? This could be good, then.*

Abril stops talking and squints ahead as the boat slows. Lucky is keeping them in the centre of the inlet. The sonar is working, but their maps are dated and they have learned that flotsam tends to collect in natural harbours like the one they're approaching, so they slow to two knots.

'Lucky,' Alessandra says, once the song ends, 'tell Lilly where we are. I suspect she's driving everyone crazy back there. I can't make that joke last for ever.'

Their electric engine is silent. They have the waves, and the birds and the wind for accompaniment when the song ends. Abril points to the right and those on deck turn to see, floating in the water near shore, the sterns of seven boats bobbing like dabbling gadwalls. The crew has come across this before, in Maine and Halifax: boats chained to piers now submerged, their hulls floating ever-upwards towards freedom. They are perches for seabirds, and serve as rough measures of rising sea-levels.

The hulls clap together as the *Elimisha* approaches: a waiting audience for their arrival.

'From the position of the boats, I suspect the water here has risen by two or three metres at the most,' Abril says, analytically. 'That's nothing. They say the vault's one hundred and thirty metres up the mountain. It should still be okay.'

When Lilly's voice bellows out of the *Elimisha*'s speakers, it is somehow lower, deeper and louder than in person, despite being nine thousand kilometres away.

'So have you found it yet or what? Over.'

Alessandra waves off the question and Lucky knows he's to take such calls himself, and privately, until there's something to report, which is much like being instructed to throw his body on a grenade.

'She's become more formal,' Abril murmurs to Alessandra as the boat rounds another twenty degrees to the northeast.

'Yeah,' Alessandra says. '" Over" was a nice touch—'

Lucky blows the horn. Condensed air is sent screaming out across the waters as an announcement, a declaration, a warning: *We are here.*

One of the D&R team, a young man in a purple knit hat, shouts as he sees the vault and its distinctive crystalline sculpture facing them like a signal mirror. It is halfway up the sloping crest of the mountain, bright and vibrant against the black volcanic shale that surrounds it.

As they draw closer to their destination, the rest of the vault entrance rises out of the ground, exposing the horizontal striations of the venting below and – when they are close enough to make out details – the twin doors themselves. The structure is as much a sculpture as it is the entrance to a facility. It was built as a beacon to travellers; now it is a clarion call for rebirth.

'When I lived in the desert at the Stadium,' Alessandra says to Abril over the sound of the wind, 'we could see the Gone World from the tops of the walls. At sunset the light would—'

But she stops suddenly, because there, on the black shale, drawn by Lucky's horn rather than repulsed by it, is a powder-white bear cub with eyes as big and black as rare pearls.

Everyone on board points and – for reasons Alessandra cannot understand – all the Museum-born wave at it.

'What is that?' Abril asks, her voice filled with excitement.

'An *is bjørn*,' Alessandra says. 'A polar bear cub.'

'It's so . . .'

'Cute.'

'You have seen one before?'

'Don't pet it.'

Abril raises binoculars to look more closely at the bear, but Alessandra gently nudges her back to the Vault.

'*Si, claro*,' Abril says.

'The doors?' Alessandra asks.

'They are closed.'

'Check again.'

'They are closed.'

'That could be the angle. They might be—'

'*Están cerrados. Absolutamente.*'

'We've come a long way,' Alessandra says, 'and someone could have looted it since then.'

Abril lowers the binoculars and gives Alessandra a hard look.

'Fine,' Alessandra says. 'If you're positive, I'll be positive.'

Everyone except for Lucky, who has volunteered to remain on board and man the radio, proceeds to the shore in two heavy rubber dinghies. On landfall, their boots crunch on the shale; they climb up to a road and follow it as it winds up the hill.

471

They walk in the grooves of tyre tracks that have hardened in the mud like the footprints of dinosaurs.

Seen from the side, the entrance to the vault is not a rectangular monolith but slopes downwards at the back, descending into the earth as though it were the top of a sunken building like those of the Gone World. The face is only four metres tall but, alone against the black rock and against the blue sky like this, it towers in their imagination.

They have talked about it for so long: to see it in person is nothing short of a miracle.

There is a sign on the right side of the building. What they notice first is four words next to an abstract symbol – a black crescent encircling or maybe protecting a blue orb of sky. Beneath it is a single green leaf. Perhaps the black is the darkness and seclusion of the island – which sits 78 degrees north inside the Arctic Circle – and the daylight is a future hope; the leaf the promise? Alessandra is no Evaluator; this is not her concern. Only the words matter:

Svalbard Global Seed Vault

Together, and stationing no guard outside, they cross a small footbridge to the heavy steel doors.

The polar bear cub has been met by a parent. They sit together, two hundred metres to the north, watching these creatures that walk on two legs and travel in packs.

It is Abril who steps to the front, past her Captain and her mates, to place her two palms against the door before turning and smiling at everyone.

'*Ahora*,' she says, all business now. 'Who has the key?'

*

At the Museum, the radio comes to life with a crackle and Lucky's voice, a resonant baritone that could sing duets with thunderclouds, fills the Comms room.

'We've found the vault,' he says in his heavily accented English.

He's speaking English for Lilly's benefit, only it isn't beneficial because Lilly knows he would have said more if he'd been speaking in his native Spanish. She has come to find the Museum-born loquacious and she'd been counting on getting more information.

But apparently that isn't how it works.

She has come to the grudging conclusion that people are harder to reverse-engineer than objects.

'I'm going to hang that guy by his feet like a . . . a . . . what the hell are they called?'

'A piñata,' comes a woman's voice from the back of the room.

'Right. One of those.' She's ranting, she knows that. She's old and – on balance – she's possibly saved more lives than she's taken (although the numbers are big on both sides), so no one interrupts. 'Of course they found it,' she says. 'I want to know if it's intact and full. There should be millions of seeds there, matched to their originating countries all over the world. It was once the largest gene bank on the planet and I need to know if it still is. If this works, the potential for ecosystem restoration, food cultivation, medicinal research—'

'Lilly,' says Henry, gently, 'in your condition, you can either yell and drop dead immediately or wait quietly for the answer and die later. Your heart can't take it. You can't do both.'

'It's always *el corazon* around here, isn't it? Fine. I'll quiet down.'

But she doesn't. Lilly has no idea how to shut up and the learning curve looks too steep.

'They said,' she continues, 'that the vault was designed to be fail-safe – but nothing's fail-safe. *Everything* fails – our imaginations fail; our memories; our patience. You can't separate out the human condition from engineering. That's why the term "futureproof" is preposterous.'

'Alessandra's not answering,' Graham tells her, 'because she knows you're probably acting this way and she's enjoying every moment of it even if she can't hear it.'

'You're probably right,' Lilly says, realising she's been played.

'Chief?' says Maria Consuela Lopez, who has resumed her position at the radio now that Graham has physically rolled Lilly away from it. 'General Anoushka at Northern Command is requesting an update.'

'Tell her she'll know when everyone else knows.'

'Yes, Chief, she figured you'd say that. But I've been asked to remind you that today is her wedding day with Moishe and she would consider this a special gift.'

'They're in,' says Lucky through the radio.

'Tell the General that they're in and to stand by and shut up, I don't care what day it is.'

No one speaks. Birds are calling to one another and the wind blows through the palms outside the windows. The light flickering through their enormous fronds makes the room feel overgrown with life. It is impossible to stop thinking of seeds.

'They're passing through a kind of tunnel,' Lucky reports. 'They're on a walkie-talkie so I'm losing reception as they get further into the mountain. I'm moving the *Elimisha* closer for better line-of-sight. Stand by.'

Despite now having access to the exact time of day, Lilly continues to watch Mickey Mouse instead. She has discovered that digital clocks are better for knowing the exact time, but analogue clocks are better for understanding the relative passage of time. Waiting is not a digital activity.

Mickey's hand moves three excruciating minutes before there is another human sound.

It is Lucky again. 'They say the storage room is filled with plastic boxes, just like in the pictures. We're opening them.

'There are . . . seeds. Many, many, *many* seeds, We will have some inventory to take, but Abril is giving me the thumbs-up from the entrance to the Vault. It all looks intact, Chief.'

A roar of clapping begins spontaneously. Lilly waits for the emotions to settle and for all eyes and ears to return to her, ready for the command they have all been waiting for her to issue.

A dozen lands are waiting for the results of the expedition; partners who will meet the Commonwealth Global Explorers in harbours along the European and African coasts first, and then, after Alessandra and her crew return and a new team takes their place, they will try and make the trip to Asia, where other colonies will invite them to port. There are seventeen in all: the entirety of the known world. Maybe fifty thousand souls.

Out there, in the darkness and the silence, there are more.

Their stories are all different – but their hunger is all the same, because the Roamers back in the desert were right: there is a sickness living in the soil, which is transmitted to people through contaminated water and foods. This sickness once decimated cultivated crops, forcing people back to hunting or migrating.

It is Lilly's theory that returning uncontaminated seeds with the capacity to germinate to their original lands will help revitalise their native soils, allowing people to repossess the land again and take root.

Time will tell.

A stretch of time that will, unfortunately, be measured in years and possibly decades; far more time than Lilly has. When the answer is revealed and the first grains are milled, the first bread baked and then broken in a *fiesta*, she'll be in the ground beside Verena.

And yet, for Lilly, it is enough to have made it this far in only one lifetime. It is a journey that began with her mother's murder and has resulted in the unification of the world.

There's still work to do. General Anoushka says the Keepers remain, but they know nothing about Southern Command. Just as the Commonwealth was blind to the build-up of the Keepers forces and the depth of their philosophy and conviction, so too are the Keepers ignorant about the Commonwealth as an intercontinental learning machine and a hub for the dissemination and accumulation of Knowledge and rebirth.

In this way, they have already won, because now it is the Keepers who are contained behind their walls of ignorance and the Commonwealth which is free to move and grow. In time, the Commonwealth will encircle them.

And if they can find another direct connection to the internet itself?

That is only a matter of time.

Lilly and Gabriela deSoto, Henry and Graham – they all know that there is now a chance to rebuild what was lost. Doing it the right way will require someone better than her: someone who can rise above her own fears and not be driven by them. Someone like the girl she used to be.

After opening the Harrington Box, Lilly found a card inside the Thucydides book. Somehow – in a story now lost to time – the book had travelled west from the Boston Public Library on the East Coast. Maybe Colonel Harrington had expected to return it some day – or maybe he knew he never could. Either way, written on the card was the sentence Lilly had used to name the Commonwealth and craft the foundations of their culture: one she has since learned was once etched in stone across the frieze of the Boston Public Library, a building long-since submerged under the cold waters of the Atlantic:

The Commonwealth requires the education of the people as the safe-guard of order and liberty, said the card, *free to all*.

So young, Lilly had thought it meant the education to build walls, build weapons, build power. She hadn't then understood that what the Commonwealth really required was the wisdom to govern itself that could only come from universal education.

That was why it was 'free to all' – because only the educated can work wisely together.

She had helped build the Commonwealth on a misinterpretation of an ancient text, and in doing so had had to watch it fall. Now, however, she is going to get it right.

Lilly snaps her fingers to command the attention of the radio operators. All eyes turn to her, ready to begin a spirited journey into a better future.

'Begin The Crossing,' she says.

ACKNOWLEDGEMENTS AND DENIALS

Not enough people helped me in the writing of this book.

Oh, sure. I know the convention. I'm supposed to wax on about the vast number of people without whom none of this would be possible, but the simple fact is that a little more help would have been great. From whom, you ask? Well, off the top of my head: urban planners, environmental-change modellers, metallurgists, stadium designers, horse wranglers, pole-vaulters, technology futurists, spelunkers, musicologists, bunker designers, and would it have killed someone to bring me a cup of coffee with some of Lilly's lizard poison in it once in a while? I mean, honestly, sometimes I wonder why I bother.

Despite having been abandoned by academia and the entire engineering community, I will admit that the people at Janklow and Nesbit – especially Rebecca Carter – once again set the standards for excellence by connecting me with the world's greatest publisher of science fiction, Jo Fletcher (who should also be able to snap her fingers for coffee, but I digress). JFB at Quercus and Hachette has been a God-send as I ventured forth from literary fiction and into science fiction. Thanks for believing in me and helping make this possible.

Meanwhile: thank you Dr Jennifer Milliken, Dr Una McCormack and Dr Bernard Finel, who provided wonderful ideas and insights on early drafts. Obviously, any gross errors in the manuscript are theirs and folks should contact them directly. Cut out the middle-man, that's what I say.

Thanks to Nicola Howell Hawley for creating the map of the Commonwealth and the Territory.

I listened to many versions of the *Goldberg Variations* while writing this. The one that moved me most for the chapter on Moishe was the interpretation by Simone Dinnerstein.

The graffiti in Elimisha's bunker – 'Without power . . . it is just a cave' – is taken from a stencil inside NORAD at the Cheyenne Mountain Facility.

The line: 'If it's very very beautiful, or very very ugly, don't touch it' was uttered by Dive Master A. Sami E. Samaco when I earned my PADI Open Water Diver certification in Bahrain in 1999. Is that great or what?

The conversation between Birch and Lilly in the Hollows was inspired by – and one sentence taken directly from – Daniel J. Boorstin's introduction to Edward Gibbon's *The Decline and Fall of the Roman Empire* ('The daily habits of remote and unfamiliar peoples help us understand their life-and-death commitments'). I have a Ph.D. in international relations and spent more than a decade with the UN working on issues of local knowledge and designing cooperative solutions to complex problems and security challenges with communities. Needless to say, I agree with Boorstin. Also worth reading in this regard are Jerome Bruner's *Jerusalem Lectures*; Clifford Geertz's *Local Knowledge*; and Adda B. Bozeman's *Political Culture in International History*.

Graham's interpretation of the Melian Dialogue is my own. The Neo-realists really screwed that one up, in my opinion, but I'm too busy to write the peer-reviewed article debunking them. I am available for lectures, however.

The chicken joke was adapted from Garrison Keillor's *Pretty Good Joke Book*. I'm not going to say that I improved upon it because . . . that's unnecessary. I will, however, mention that I'm not mentioning it.

This book owes a debt to Walter Miller Jr.'s *A Canticle for Leibowitz* (1959). The abbey is an homage to Miller's own, and my Francis is a second chance for Miller's hapless one who met such a poor fate ('eat, eat!'). I consider *Radio Life* (and what I hope to be the subsequent series) to be in *direct* conversation with that 1959 novel on whether or not we are doomed to repeat our own mistakes. I also hope to contribute something of value to that conversation.

This book also owes a distant but real debt to the song *Telegraph Road* by Dire Straits. If this story had an origin, it might have been that song, which I first heard when I was sixteen.

Radio Life is dedicated to my daughter Clara who inspired, one way or another, every brilliant, bold, wilful, adventurous, thoughtful, curious, ass-kicking warrior-poet in this story; you inspired those women, Clara, because you inspire me. I am so lucky to be your Dad.

Derek B. Miller,
Oslo, Norway,
August, 2020

Derek Miller was born in Boston, Massachusetts and grew up in New England. He did his Master's in National Security at Washington DC's Georgetown University, then studied at The Hebrew University in Israel and St Catherine's, Oxford before completing his Ph.D. in International Relations at the Graduate Institute in Geneva. Before becoming a full-time novelist, he worked all over the world for a variety of organisations, including the United Nations. His first novel, *Norwegian by Night*, won the CWA John Creasey Dagger and was an *Economist* best novel of the year; subsequent crime novels *The Girl in Green* and *American by Day* were both shortlisted for the CWA Gold Dagger. *How to Find Your Way in the Dark*, an American mid-century epic, is due out in 2021. *Radio Life*, his first science fiction novel, inspired by his love for the classic *A Canticle for Liebowitz* by Walter M. Miller (no relation!), shares a grand if troubled vision about the role of knowledge and wisdom at the heart of any of our possible futures. He lives in Oslo, Norway, with his wife and children.